BRIDGET BRANNIGAN

Also by Sheila Jansen

Mary Maddison
Della Dolan

BRIDGET BRANNIGAN

Sheila Jansen

HEADLINE

First published in 1995
by HEADLINE BOOK PUBLISHING

10 9 8 7 6 5 4 3 2 1

British Library Cataloguing in Publication Data

Jansen, Sheila
Bridget Brannigan
I. Title
823.914 [F]

ISBN 0-7472-1421-2

Typeset by
CBS, Felixstowe, Suffolk

Printed and bound in Great Britain by
Mackays of Chatham PLC, Chatham, Kent

HEADLINE BOOK PUBLISHING
A division of Hodder Headline PLC
338 Euston Road
London NW1 3BH

To my husband, Henricus,
and my sister, Shirley

PART I

Chapter One

1880

Bridget moaned and opened her eyes. 'No . . . no . . . dear Lord, no.' Through a haze, like breath on a mirror, she saw a bulky shadow in the foreground. She groaned and blinked until the shadow evolved into a solid grey mass looming over her. She was lying in a bed.

'You're all right, girl.' A calloused hand stroked her forehead.

'Where am I?' Her lips were stiff. She blinked again and the misty background became a whitewashed room, the grey mass an old woman sitting beside her on the bed. The woman's face was worn and deeply spotted like a seagull's egg. Strands of white hair escaped from a blue scarf bound round her head. But her faded grey eyes brimmed with kindness as she smiled at Bridget.

'You're safe, girl,' she said. 'Me man and his mates picked you up two days ago. Your ship went down. God only knows how you managed to hang on to that flimsy piece of wood. I'm Mrs McNamara. I've been looking after you.'

The nightmare of the shipwreck surged back to Bridget. She tried to raise herself but felt too weak to move. 'Me da? And me brothers and sisters? Where are they?'

Mrs McNamara dipped the corner of a towel into a jug on a wooden chair by the bed, dabbed at Bridget's mouth and squeezed drops between her cracked lips. Bridget stared up at her, her wisp of a face contorted in horror, her chestnut curls tangled on the pillow like a snarled fishing net.

'Where are they?' she repeated, trying to rise again, but Mrs McNamara eased her back and squeezed more drops from the towel.

'They went down, girl. There was only one lifeboat made it, and there was none of your kin in it.'

The cool water ran down Bridget's tongue and she choked as she swallowed. 'No, they're not gone! They can't be!' Her hazel eyes grew wide in disbelief.

3

'Aye, girl, they're all gone. Nobody's claimed you. We've been trying to find out who you are. By God! You're a miracle, and that's the truth!' She felt Bridget's forehead again. 'Thanks be to God! The fever's gone down.'

Bridget screwed her eyes shut and sobbed. The memory surged back: the wild, pounding sea, her father helping her to get the little ones into a lifeboat, people pushing and shoving and screaming all around them. He was handing down the last, little Maureen, into Bridget's grasping hands when the ship shuddered one final time. Again, she saw her father plunge into the icy depths, still clutching Maureen. She covered her face with her hands and sobbed.

'There now, have a good cry, girl. It'll make you feel better. I'm going to get you some hot broth. I've had it ready for nigh on two days but there's never been a peep out of you.' Mrs McNamara rose, but Bridget grabbed the rough grey dress.

'The rest! Where are they? They were with me in the boat when it capsized. I was holding on to them. They can't be gone! I wouldn't ever have let them go.'

Mrs McNamara sat again on the bed. 'Nay, girl, you couldn't possibly have held on to anybody in that sea. Don't fret yourself.'

Bridget screamed and pounded her fists against her forehead. 'No! Dear Lord, no! Me little ones, all gone, and me still alive and breathing. God forgive me.'

'Don't blame yourself now. 'Twas the devil's work. And God must've saved you for a purpose. Aye, 'twas a terrible thing . . . a terrible thing. There was too many people in that ship and in them lifeboats – a right scandal to be sure.' She sighed and her huge chest heaved.

Bridget buried her face in the pillow and moaned, a low, animal moan. She wanted to scream again, to give full rein to her anguish, but she could only moan, and the sound went on and on.

Mrs McNamara stroked Bridget's curls. 'That's right, girl. Grieve all you need. The broth'll have to wait.'

Bridget felt herself slipping away. She thanked God for His mercy. She was going to join her father and her brothers and sisters.

Three hours later, she cried out as she emerged from the deep sleep of despair that had overcome her and returned to the reality of the whitewashed room. Mrs McNamara rose from her chair by the stove and stirred a large black pot. ''Tis all right, girl, don't fret. You'll feel

4

better with something hot in you.' She ladled steaming broth into a bowl and placed it on the bedside chair. Too exhausted to resist, Bridget allowed herself to be raised and fed. Tears washed down her cheeks as the hot liquid stung her lips and seared her throat.

'There, there, now, just a bit more.' Mrs McNamara persevered, but Bridget averted her head and the broth spilt on the pillow. 'All right then, that's enough for now.' She set the bowl on the floor and again dipped the corner of the towel in the jug and squeezed water between Bridget's lips. 'I've been doing this since they brought you in,' she said. 'Otherwise you'd have dried up like a kipper.'

Bridget tried to will herself to sink into that blackness again. But she couldn't. Despite her efforts to clamp her eyes shut they kept opening. 'Where am I?' she asked, and wondered why she'd bothered. She didn't care where she was.

'You're near Formby, and that's near Liverpool.' Mrs McNamara covered the jug with the towel and eased her bulk on to the wooden chair by the bed. 'Thanks be to God it wasn't but a couple of miles offshore. We're naught but a little fishing village, but it was a safe harbour for you.'

'Liverpool,' Bridget whispered. 'We were going to land at Liverpool and then go on to Newcastle, to a new life. We have an auntie and uncle there. They were going to take us in till Da got a job. I'll have to tell them.' She attempted to sit but Mrs McNamara held her down.

'Aye, well, there's time enough for that. You're not strong enough to go anywhere yet. What are you called and how old are you?'

'Bridget Brannigan and I'm fifteen. Me brothers and sisters were all little.' Her eyes filled again. 'I was their ma to them. And they're all gone. All of them . . . and Da. Oh, I wish God had taken meself as well!' Her face crumpled as despair gripped her like a pain in her heart.

Mrs McNamara clasped Bridget's hands and sighed. 'Don't talk like that. God saved you for a purpose, just as He took *them* for a purpose. There's no understanding His ways sometimes.'

Her passion spent, Bridget stilled, and Mrs McNamara laid the damp towel on her forehead. 'There now, if you're bent on going to Newcastle to your kin, me man and me'll set you up for the journey when you're well enough. You'll need the fare and some clothes.'

Bridget looked down at herself for the first time. She was enveloped in a white flannel nightgown several sizes too large. 'What happened to me clothes, ma'am?'

'I'm Mrs McNamara, Bridget – no need to be calling me ma'am.

And your clothes were only fit for the ragbag when they fished you out. The neighbours brought some things over and I've washed and ironed them for you, but you won't be needing no clothes today.'

The door opened and a burly figure clad in dripping oilskins and Wellington boots stepped over the threshold. He had to stoop under the low doorway.

Mrs McNamara jumped up from the bed and made the sign of the cross. 'Thanks be to God! You're home!'

'And haven't I always got home so far, woman?' The man removed his sou'wester and revealed a leathery, weather-beaten face. It was a strange face, like a linear drawing, without depth, as if flattened by the blows of life. Yet the eyes were the blue of the sea on a sunny day. His gaze fell on the bunk in the corner where Bridget lay staring at the ceiling. Then he turned to his wife. 'How is she?'

'She's awake, praise God. But she's taking it hard about her kin.'

Mr McNamara shrugged off his wet cape and hung it on the door, then sat on one of the wooden chairs by the scrubbed table. Bridget's eyes opened and, as she watched him listlessly, she noticed the table and chairs for the first time, and the two wooden armchairs by the stove. Mrs McNamara knelt to pull off her husband's Wellingtons. He heaved a sigh of relief, then stood and dropped his braces and oilskin trousers to the floor. Underneath he wore a moth-eaten jersey and ragged corduroy breeches.

Mrs McNamara set the Wellingtons near the stove and hung the oilskins on the line strung across the mantelpiece. Her husband took a paper spill from the hearth and lit a clay pipe. ''Tis good to be home,' he said, sitting again at the table and puffing blue smoke.

'How was the catch?' She placed another pot on the stove, then set the table with bowls, cutlery and a loaf from the dresser.

He shook his head. 'Bad! 'Tis still too rough to go but a mile or two out.'

'After the meal I'll go and help the women with the gutting. I've missed two days already. You can keep an eye on her now she's awake.' She inclined her head towards the bed.

Bridget was staring again at the ceiling, once more unaware of her surroundings, silently trying to come to grips with reality. She'd lost everyone she loved. She was alone in a strange place. Oh, why hadn't God taken her with them? They'd be together now, up there. She shuddered. But they were down there, lying at the bottom of the cold, grey sea. An anguished cry escaped her.

6

Mrs McNamara hastened to her. 'What is it, Bridget?'

'They're all at the bottom of the sea . . . little Paddy and Mick and Peggy . . . and—'

'There, there! Stop your fretting,' she said. 'Their souls are in heaven. 'Tis naught but their bodies down there, and no use for them they have now. Maybe they're the lucky ones, Bridget. Look on it that way. Come and take a drop more broth. And I'm boiling some haddie for me man and me, try a few bites of that.'

Bridget shook her head. 'Just water, please.'

'You can have water after you've had a drop of broth.'

'No, no broth, please. Just water.'

'Well, I'm not going to force you.' She took a tin mug from the dresser and filled it from the jug. This time Bridget swallowed eagerly. Mrs McNamara grunted with satisfaction as she placed the empty mug on the bedside chair. 'There, now, that's better.'

'I . . . I have to go to the privy,' Bridget whispered, embarrassed to voice her private needs in front of the man.

'Well, you can't go out this weather in your state. It's bucketing down.' She bent to retrieve a large enamelled chamber pot from under the bunk. Bridget flushed and her eyes travelled to the man.

'I can't go here.'

'It's all right, Bridget, I'll take you to the other room.' She disappeared through a door with the chamber pot and returned for Bridget, easing back the blankets and helping her to rise. 'Jesus, Mary and Joseph!' she cried, as she helped her. 'There's naught but a pound of flesh on your bones. We haven't got much, but I'm bent on fattening you up before you go anywhere.' She lowered her on to the pot and waited a few moments. 'Tell me when you're done.'

'I'm done now.' Bridget felt like a child but was glad of the strong arms that raised her and led her back to bed. For the first time since she'd heard the news, she made the sign of the cross and prayed silently for the souls of her loved ones. Then with imaginary beads, she recited the rosary in her head: *Hail Mary, full of grace, the Lord is with Thee . . .*' The repetition lulled her and she drifted into an uneasy sleep. She dreamt she was walking on the bottom of the sea and Da and all the little ones stood in the distance beckoning her. She tried to run to them, but seaweed coiled about her legs and anchored her. She cried out and woke up in a sweat. But she felt the cool towel being placed on her forehead and drifted off again.

* * *

7

Mrs McNamara was kneading bread on the table when Bridget opened her eyes the following day. As her situation flashed back, she cried out and jerked up.

Mrs McNamara wiped her hands on her apron and sat on the bunk. 'How you feeling, Bridget?'

Tears trickled down Bridget's face at the sound of the kindly voice. 'Bad,' she said, whimpering. 'I don't ever want to wake up again.'

'That's enough of that nonsense now.' Mrs McNamara's voice was brisk. She turned to the stove and poured water from the kettle into a brown teapot. 'You're going to have a hot drink and a bite of bread and you'll feel better. I mashed the tea for me man this morning but there's still a bit of life in it.' She poured the tea and added milk and sugar before handing it to Bridget. 'And now I'll be getting you a piece of bread,' she said, taking half a loaf from the dresser and cutting a wedge. She sat on the bunk and offered the bread. ''Tisn't fresh. I'm just baking now. But you can soak it in your tea.'

Bridget nodded her thanks. She sipped the weak tea and soaked the bread. Her stomach felt empty but she had no desire for food. After a few bites she gave up, but continued to sip the tea. 'What time of day is it?' she asked.

''Tis morning and the rain's let up for a bit.' Mrs McNamara had resumed her baking. 'Where do you hail from, Bridget?'

'County Cork. Me da was a farmhand. Me ma died five years ago giving birth to little Maureen.'

'How many kin did you have, then?'

'Five not counting me. I was the oldest by five years. Me ma lost three after me and then they started coming every year.' Her knuckles turned white as she gripped the empty mug. A sob escaped her and she bit on her lip. 'I was the little ones' ma.'

Mrs McNamara continued her kneading but nodded in sympathy. 'Aye, you've had a hard time. But so have we all. Me and me man hail from Dublin. Thirty-two years ago now. I had a new life growing in me that we'd prayed for for ten years. 'Twas after the rebellion in 'forty-eight. We'd had no taties for two years and me man decided 'twas time to get out. We went to Liverpool for work, but so did everybody else. That's why we came here. Me man reckoned that fish can't get the blight, so we'd always have something in our bellies. And 'tis true enough, though it's been a hard life to be sure.' She punched the dough into a loaf tin as if wreaking vengeance on it. 'Aye, the sea gives life and it takes life. It took our only son from us nigh on ten years ago, and

8

I pray every minute me man's out there that it won't take him.'

'The sea took all mine, missus,' Bridget said. 'Oh, I wish we'd stayed where we were. Me da saved for five years for the fare, ever since me ma died. Every week he'd put a penny or two in the jug, and he was so pleased when he'd scraped enough together. Hardly a drop of porter he touched in all that time.' Bridget's voice became a whimper and her face crumpled.

Mrs McNamara set the dough on the hearth to rise. 'Aye, you've just got your own life to get on with now, and you must make the most of it seeing that your da got you over here. How could you get in touch with your auntie and uncle?'

'I . . . I could write them a letter.' She wiped her eyes on the sheet and took a deep breath to compose herself.

'You know reading and writing?' Mrs McNamara's voice showed her surprise.

'A bit. Me ma taught me till I was ten, and her ma taught her before that. I kept practising after she died by reading the catechism and the hymn books at mass. I learned a lot more words.'

'And do you know where your auntie and uncle live?' She dusted the flour off the table with a rag and shook it over the flames.

Bridget nodded. 'I always wrote to them 'cause me da didn't know much writing.'

'Then when you're feeling better I'll get you pen and paper and you can write and tell them what's happened, and that you'll be going as soon as you're able.'

At the thought of telling her aunt and uncle the news, Bridget's thin face twisted in pain. She began to say the rosary silently. It was the only thing that soothed her and took her mind off the horror.

A week later she sat in the trap beside Mr McNamara on their way to Liverpool station. She clutched the bundle Mrs McNamara had made up for her long journey. The white rag contained a loaf of bread, a large piece of cheese and a smoked halibut. And deep in her skirt pocket lay the two shiny sixpences Mr McNamara had given her.

The wooden wheels rattled and skidded on the rutted cart track. The mud created by the recent storm had turned to ice during the following cold spell. Bridget pulled her black cape more closely about her and gripped the wool shawl draped round her head and shoulders. She shivered, more with apprehension than the cold. She hadn't told the old couple of her worry. Her aunt hadn't replied to her letter. And she

9

always replied promptly. Bridget prayed nothing was wrong, that it was only a delay in the post.

'No but another hour, Bridget,' Mr McNamara said.

She nodded. She was grateful that this part of her journey was nearing its end but nervous about taking the trains. She would have to change at Preston and Carlisle, and there would be many stops and waiting in between.

Soon the muddy cart tracks gave way to cobbled streets, adding the problem of dealing with the increased traffic. Traps, hackneys, landaus and, as they neared the city centre, horse-drawn trams, all jostled for their place on the road.

At last they waited in the station, Bridget clutching the ticket Mr McNamara had bought for her. After half an hour the giant iron horse trundled up to the platform hissing clouds of steam. She trembled with apprehension as Mr McNamara helped her up the high step. Shyly, she held out her hand and he took it roughly. 'Thank you, Mr McNamara, for everything,' she said.

''Twas all we could do, Bridget. No need for thanks. God speed you on your journey.' He left abruptly. She watched his bent back disappear into the crowd and bit her lower lip. She was truly alone now. She made her way through the jostling passengers to find a seat in a third-class carriage. All the wooden benches were taken, but from where she stood she could see through the dirty windows. She strained for a final glimpse of the big city, though the view of the backs of grimy red-brick buildings didn't cheer her. She wondered what Newcastle would be like and hoped it would be nicer than Liverpool.

10

Chapter Two

A day and a half later Bridget trudged from the train at Central Station. The journey had been long and arduous. Due to a two-hour delay she'd missed the Preston train and spent the night sleeping on a wooden bench in the waiting room. Tired and sore, she ploughed through the crowd to the exit. Outside, she gazed in awe at the grand grey-stone buildings. Even on this bleak day her first sight of Newcastle impressed her. She approached one of the cab drivers waiting outside the station. 'Excuse me, sir. Where can I get a tram to Byker?'

'What part of Byker, hinny?' The old man rubbed his bony hands together to keep warm.

'Norfolk Road. It's near the Stag's Head Inn.'

'Why, lass, you're lucky. There's one goes all the way. You won't have to change.' He pointed to a queue of people across the road. 'It stops over there. Just ask the conductor to put you off at Norfolk Road.'

Bridget thanked him and dodged across the busy street. Wooden wheels clattered on the cobbles as carriages and carts seemed to aim at her from all directions. When she'd reached the safety of the tram stop she noticed that the waiting passengers were no better dressed than she. They all looked cold and shrivelled in their shabby coats and shawls. The woman next to her looked up at the threatening January sky then grinned a toothless greeting: 'Eey, 'tis cold enough for snow,' she said, stamping her feet to keep warm. Several blue toes poked out from large holes in her boots.

''Tis freezing indeed,' Bridget replied, while silently thanking Mrs McNamara for the stout boots she'd given her.

After ten minutes the tram approached. The horses' nostrils puffed clouds of steam in the frigid air as they laboured to pull the heavy vehicle. Bridget dug into her skirt pocket to pull out a penny for the fare, though she hoped it would be only a ha'penny. She still had one sixpence intact and two pennies, having spent the rest the previous day on tea and bread when her food had run out. Grateful to get off her shaking legs, she sat on a wooden bench near the tram exit. 'To Norfolk Road,' she said to the conductor and handed him her penny. 'And would you mind telling me when we get there?'

'Why, aye, lass.' He nodded and gave her a ha'penny change and a small blue ticket. She was glad of the change, and the fact that it must be a short journey.

After passing through more elegant city streets and, later, a high bridge, they came to rows of red-brick terraced flats. They looked mean and dismal in the grey sleet that had begun to fall. Bridget's spirits slumped. She must be nearing Byker. She hoped it wasn't like this. But at the next stop the conductor shouted, 'Your stop, lass.' She jumped up in agitation. 'It's the first street on the right,' he told her as she alighted. She thanked him and bent her head against the onslaught of sleet and wind.

She found number twenty-seven without trouble and knocked on the door, praying aloud: 'Please God let someone be home, and please God let them have got my letter.' It seemed to take for ever before she heard shuffling footsteps and the blistered brown door creaked open. 'Auntie Annie?' She peered at the gaunt, grey-haired figure in the doorway.

'You're Bridget! God be praised you're here!' Annie flung her thin arms round Bridget and burst into tears. 'Oh, me poor bairn! Such a terrible thing! Losing your da and the little ones. God save their souls!'

Bridget's face puckered at the mention of her family and her grief again overflowed. They clung together and wept until Annie pulled herself away and rubbed her sackcloth apron over her eyes. 'And what am I doing keeping you standing out here in the cold and wet, lass? Come on in and let's have a look at you.'

She led Bridget down a narrow passage to a tiny room where a fire burned in a black stove. 'My, but you're a bonnie little thing,' she said, again wiping her eyes. 'Let's get these wet things off you. You look half-starved.' She removed the soaked shawl and cloak, and Bridget's grief merged with relief that her ordeal was over. 'Come on now,' Annie said, ushering her to one of the wooden armchairs flanking the stove. 'Stop them tears and sit down here.'

Still sniffing, Bridget wiped her eyes on her dress sleeve. She was grateful for the small fire. 'Thank you, Auntie. 'Tis cold out indeed.'

Annie bustled around her. 'I'll mash a cup of tea and make you something to eat, though 'tis only bread and dripping. But the morrow's Friday so we'll be having a bit of fish.'

'Let me help you.' Bridget rose but Annie eased her down by the shoulders.

'No, hinny, you sit and rest, after all you've been through.'

Bridget sighed. ''Twas a terrible time – losing Da and them all. If those kind folks hadn't taken me in, sure I wouldn't be here now. I must write to thank them and tell them I arrived safe.'

'Aye, pet, I wept buckets when I got your letter. It only came late yesterday afternoon. I was just about to go to the post office to answer it. I didn't expect you so soon.' Annie rested her skinny hands on her protruding hip bones and surveyed Bridget. 'Eey, but I'm that glad to see you. Though I only knew you from afar, you're the nearest to kin I've got.' She swallowed hard and her stringy neck constricted, but she composed herself and emptied the teapot into the slop pail. 'Eey, it was grand getting your letters. I thoroughly enjoyed Mrs Foster at the post office reading them to me and writing down what I wanted to say to you.' She spooned tea into the pot. 'And, dear Lord, I was that looking forward to having bairns around the place. 'Tis a lonely life I lead with your uncle out most of the time.' Her drooping eyelids partly obscured the pain in her watery green eyes, and her skin, like a wrung-out dishcloth, sagged in folds under her cheekbones and jaws. As she bent to fill the teapot from the sooty kettle, wisps of white hair straggled around her face. It was a face that had suffered, but the jut of the chin showed determination. She shook her head as she set the teapot on the table. ''Twas God's will He took them and we must accept that. Though 'tis hard to know sometimes what He has in mind.'

Bridget nodded. 'Aye, me da always said we could never know what the Lord had up His sleeve.'

Annie finished setting the wooden table with mugs, a loaf, and a jar of dripping from the dresser in the corner. 'Come on and eat, hen. You'll feel better.'

Bridget joined her at the table and devoured the meal, the first she'd had that day.

Annie gave her a worried look and cut more bread. 'By God, you poor bairn, you look as if you haven't had a bite for weeks.'

'I bought a cup of tea and bread at the station yesterday after me food ran out. I'm a day late 'cause one of the trains was delayed.' Suddenly she remembered the money in her pocket and placed it on the table. 'Those people gave me two sixpences but I tried to save as much as I could for you – for me keep till I get work.'

Annie poured more tea. 'Work! Aye, that's not going to be easy. I'm still scrubbing houses, but I'm down to three days a week. I lost three of me day customers so I make it up three nights, scrubbing offices. It's back-breaking, but if I didn't earn something we could either eat or pay the rent, but not both – not on what I get from your uncle after he takes out his beer and baccy and gambling money. Five shillings a week for these two rooms! A right scandal. And six shillings upstairs 'cause there's a roof space. I hope we can find a better life for you, luv.'

Bridget sipped the last of her tea and put down her mug. 'I'm used to hard work, Auntie. I don't mind what I do.'

Annie nodded. 'Aye, more's the pity, hen. I started asking around when I got your letter and me neighbour's daughter's leaving her post to get married in a few days. She's a scullery maid for a landed family yon side of Morpeth.' Bridget froze with fear at the thought of being sent away, but relief welled over her like a warm bath as Annie went on, 'It wouldn't be no good for you though. You need to find something close to be with your kin.'

'Yes, indeed, I'd rather stay with you and Uncle Frank. Sure, 'tis a terrible feeling to be alone. I'll find something. I'll start looking tomorrow.' Bridget leaned back in her chair. It was wonderful to be with her own kin at last.

'Mind you, Bridget . . .' Annie paused and gave her a wary look. 'I have to warn you, your uncle's not an easy man to live with. *You* just stand up for yourself and don't let him upset you.'

The back door to the kitchen creaked and Annie's hand flew to her face. 'Heavens above! That's him home now. And I haven't got his tea ready. I clean forgot about the time.'

As she scurried to refill the kettle from the tin jug on the hearth, a large podgy-faced man wearing a black overcoat and cloth cap filled the small doorway. His bleary eyes fixed on Bridget. She stared back in surprise. He didn't look a bit like her father's brother.

'Well, she's arrived I see.' His voice was slurred. He banged the door shut behind him and belched loudly. Then he hung his soaked clothes on a door-nail, revealing dirty blue overalls.

Annie threw up her hands. 'Glory be, Frank Brannigan! You've been boozing again even afore you get home. And no doubt you'll be going out for more after.'

'I only had a couple on the way, woman. Stop your nagging.' He slumped into one of the fireside chairs and bent to remove his soaked boots. Bridget stared at the streaks of pink scalp showing through his sandy hair. When he straightened, his gaze returned to her. His moon face was mottled with tiny purple veins. She glanced away, embarrassed that he'd caught her looking at him.

'So you're Bridget, eh? You're a fine-looking lass. How old are you then?'

'Fifteen,' Bridget said, feeling uncomfortable under his stare.

Annie looked warily at Frank, then at Bridget. She set more bread on the table. 'Your food's ready,' she said to Frank through tight lips. 'And it's bread and dripping you're having, same as us.'

He grunted and sat at the table facing Bridget. 'I was sorry to hear about me brother and the rest,' he muttered with his mouth full. 'I told him he should've stowed away and come over long ago when I did, instead of marrying your ma and getting bogged down with all them bairns.'

Bridget bowed her head. How could her uncle be so different from her father? Now she understood her aunt's warning, and she determined that whatever he said she wouldn't get upset.

Annie shuffled to the door, threw on a coarse black cloak and tied a black wool shawl about her head and shoulders. 'I've got to go to work now, luv,' she said to Bridget. 'Let me show you where you'll be sleeping.'

Bridget followed her down the front passage into a small room crammed with a high double bed and a large mattress on the floor. There was barely space to walk.

'I got this ready for you all,' Annie said with a catch in her voice.

'Thank you.' Bridget felt near to tears again. 'I haven't never slept alone on a mattress afore. We all slept on the mattress and me da had blankets on the floor.'

Annie put her hand on Bridget's trembling shoulder. 'Aye, well them days is over now, hinny.' She made the sign of the cross and added, 'God rest their souls.'

Bridget also made the sign of the cross and blinked away her tears. But her voice shook: 'I'll just wash the dishes, and then I'll be going to bed early.'

'That's right, hen. You could do with an early night. It'll be late when I get home and your uncle won't be back from the boozer till midnight, I'll be bound. You have a good rest now. I'll try to keep him quiet when he comes in.' She glanced over her shoulders as she left. 'I forgot to tell you, hinny. You might get a few visiting bugs. I hope they don't bother you none. I done all I could by whitewashing the rooms, but the little beggars gets in through the cracks from upstairs and next door. And don't be frightened if you hear any rats. I always keep traps set. And it's the food they're after, not you.' She managed a forced smile and Bridget smiled back to reassure her.

'That's all right, Auntie. Sure, I'm well used to both.' She returned to the kitchen, where Frank was seated by the fire, his fat lips sucking on a clay pipe and his feet resting on the brass fender. He followed her movements as she filled the kettle and cleared the table. Again she felt uncomfortable under his gaze. She kept her eyes down at her tasks. She was drying the dishes at the table when he passed behind her to the back door.

'I'm out for a bit,' he said, throwing on his wet outdoor clothes.

Bridget remembered her manners. 'Thank you for having me here.'

''Twas her wanted it, not me.' When he opened the door grey sleet blustered in. Bridget shivered. She would stoke up the fire for Annie coming home, then go to bed.

A touch on her shoulder awakened her. Startled, she opened her eyes but could see nothing in the dark. She froze. A rat on the bed? No! She smelled the pungent odour of ale. 'Uncle Frank?'

'Aye, lass.' His voice was more slurred than earlier.

She cringed as his weight flopped on the mattress beside her. 'What is it you want?'

'Just a little kiss, Bridget, that's all. You don't mind giving your uncle a little kiss, do you?'

Her nerves tied in knots. 'No . . . yes!' Confused, she rolled herself into a ball, as if her smallness would protect her. The smell of his body and the ale and tobacco on his breath made her feel sick.

He leaned closer and pressed his flabby lips to her cheek. She shuddered and wriggled towards the wall out of his reach. But he found her mouth. She pushed him away with all the force she could muster. 'No, no, please, Uncle Frank.' She clambered over him to the other side of the mattress, over the high bed, and out into the passage. As she felt her way along the dark wall, she thought she heard his boots behind her on the bare wooden floor. She panicked. Where could she go? Heedless of her bare feet and thin underwear, she ran to the kitchen where the oil lamp still burned. She tried to open the back door. It was swollen with the damp. She pulled with all her might and welcome sleet slapped her face. She stumbled over the threshold and collided with a dark figure outside.

Annie's voice was shrill: 'Good God, Bridget! What are you doing out here with no clothes on? You'll catch your death of cold.'

Bridget whimpered with relief. 'Oh, Auntie.'

Annie took her by the elbow. 'Come on in, for heaven's sake. If you want to go to the privy put something on first. You should have more sense.' She ushered Bridget towards the fire and peered at her in the lamplight. 'By God! You're as white as a sheet!' Her hand flew to her mouth and her face contorted with pain. 'He's been at you, hasn't he?'

Bridget lowered her head.

'Dear God! I thought he'd at least have the decency to lay off his own kin.' Annie put her arms round Bridget's shaking shoulders and took a deep breath before she asked, 'What did he do to you?'

'Don't get upset, Auntie. 'Twasn't much he did. But I was scared.' Bridget tried to sound reassuring.

'Where is the swine?'

'I don't know. I thought he came out of the bedroom.'

Annie picked up the oil lamp and marched down the passage. A few minutes later she returned and set the lamp on the table with a thud. 'He's passed out on your mattress – too bloody drunk to find his own bed. You go and sit by the fire and I'll make you a hot drink. 'Tis only water, but it'll warm you from the inside. I have to save the tea for the morrow.' She removed her wet clothing and threw it over a chair before wrapping her undershawl round Bridget. 'Now you just try to relax, luv. I'll stoke up the fire and get the kettle going.'

Though chilled, Bridget felt warmed by Annie's presence. The knots in her nerves began to untwine. 'Don't fret, Auntie,' she said. ''Tis thankful I am you're home.'

But Annie's face remained grim as she set the kettle on the hob and sat opposite Bridget. 'I suppose I should've warned you, pet. But I really never thought he'd touch his own family. It wouldn't have happened if your da was here.' She ran a work-roughened hand over her brow. 'He's a beast when he's full of ale. And nowadays that's every minute he's not at the docks.' She sighed and the bones in her chest rose like springs through a worn-out mattress. 'I must've been out of me mind to think that you being family would make a jot of difference to him.'

Bridget felt a pang of sorrow for her aunt and reached forward to take her hand. ''Tis sorry I am to cause you trouble, Auntie.'

Annie shook her head. 'Nah, none of your doing, hinny. He doesn't touch me any more, thanks be to God, but he gets it wherever he can.

Lord knows, I don't want you to leave, though now I think you'd best take that Morpeth post if you can get it.'

Bridget gasped in disbelief. She'd be alone again, like a bobbing piece of driftwood. Annie, the only person she had in the world, was sending her away. 'But I'll keep meself out of his way. I promise I won't cause any more trouble.' Her voice begged.

Annie gave her a hopeless look. 'You don't know the man like I do, Bridget. How can you keep out of his way in a little flat like this? And I've got to go to work. I can't be around all the time to keep an eye on you. 'Tis better you get out of his reach, hen. If he's tried it once, he'll try it again.' The kettle hissed and she rose wearily. 'You'll be sleeping in my bed the night. He'll be as good as dead till morning anyway.'

Bridget gripped the wooden chair-arms and closed her eyes. She prayed in a whisper: 'Holy virgin, mother of God! Please, please, let something go right for me soon!'

Chapter Three

Frank appeared at breakfast unshaven and dishevelled. He slumped at the table still wearing his clothes from the night before. Bridget lowered her head over her bowl.

'You oughta be ashamed of yourself, Frank Brannigan!' Annie flashed at him. 'Can't you even keep your filthy hands off your own kin?' She rose to get his porridge and slapped it on the table before standing over him, hands on hips.

Frank glowered at her. 'What are you talking about, woman? I never touched her.'

'Now don't try to tell me you don't remember, Frank Brannigan. God knows you were drunk enough! But how do you explain waking up in her bed?'

Frank bent his matted head over his porridge. 'I must've lost me way in the dark, that's all. Stop your nagging, won't you?'

Annie still stood over him, her face tight. 'And how is it you never lost your way afore, even though that mattress has been down three weeks waiting for them? 'Tis a born liar you are, man. All me life I prayed for bairns, but now I'm glad they didn't come, not if they'd turned out like their da – a lying, drunken, dirty swine.'

'Shut your trap, woman!' Frank threw down his spoon and stormed to the back door. He flung on his outdoor clothes and left, slamming the door behind him.

Annie wrung her hands and hunched into a chair at the table. 'Now he's going to sulk on the privy for half an hour before he goes to work, and without his bait and all.' She took a deep breath and raised her chin. 'Lord knows why I should care if he goes hungry. He gets a belly full of ale at dinner time anyway. Those blasted bars have the pints lined up on the counter even afore the siren goes. I like an odd sip meself, but why men put it afore feeding their wives and bairns I'll never know.'

Bridget pushed back her chair and put her arms round Annie's shoulders. 'Oh, Auntie, I'm feeling so bad about your troubles. And 'tis my fault this time. I'm so sorry to cause you pain, and the first day I'm here and all.'

'Don't blame yourself, lass. And anyway, if it's not one kind of bother he's bringing on me it's another.' Annie patted Bridget's hand and rose to stoke the fire.

'Will he really stay in the privy for half an hour? I've got to go.' Bridget's tone was urgent.

'Aye, well, you've got to learn to hold it here anyway, especially in the mornings. There's but one privy for four families, and one water tap and all. I can't say we're much better off than *you* were at home. Maybe life'll be better for you in service after all. I'll pop down to Bella's and get that address for you.' She peered through the tiny window. 'Thank the Lord the sleet's stopped. But 'tis still cold enough for snow.' She prised herself out of her chair, put on her outdoor clothes and left through the back door.

Though Bridget knew Annie didn't want her to leave, she felt as abandoned as a leper. She longed to go back to bed and escape in tears and sleep, but the dishes needed washing and the coal pail filling. She wrapped herself in her shawl and, shivering, filled the pail from the nearest of the four coal sheds in the yard. She hoped it was the right one. Back inside, she threw some coal on the fire. Clouds of smoke and coal dust belched back at her. She coughed and wiped her face with her skirt. Why, she wondered, didn't English people burn peat? She almost liked the smell of peat; it smelled more like the earth.

She'd just finished scrubbing the kitchen floor when Annie returned. She looked with approval around the spotless kitchen but shook her head. 'Thank you, luv, but you didn't have to do that. I'm not working the day. 'Tis better you write for this job afore it gets taken, if it isn't already. Thanks be that your ma saw to it you learned your letters. 'Twill surely be a help to you in life.'

'Aye, I learned more from me ma than I did from the schoolteacher.' Bridget threw the pail of dirty water into the yard and returned with chattering teeth.

Annie was warming her hands before the fire. 'I borrowed two pieces of paper and two envelopes for you, so you can write to thank them kind folk in Liverpool and all. And don't be making no big mistakes 'cause that was all the paper I could get.'

Laboriously, Bridget spelled out her letters, afterwards reading them

20

over several times. She frowned and shook her head. 'Sure, that doesn't look right.' She sounded out the words. 'Aplying for the sculery maid posision.'

'It sounds fine to me, luv,' Annie said. 'Don't be worrying your head too much about it. I bet they don't get many written applications from scullery maids anyway.'

After some thought, Bridget crossed out 'posision' and wrote above it 'position'. 'And I don't know if scullery has one "l" or two, Auntie. What shall I do?'

'Leave it be, hen. I'm sure it's a grand letter just as it is.'

Bridget folded the letters and tucked them in their envelopes. ''Tis ready they are. I'm going to post them now. Where's the post office, Auntie? And can I be getting you anything while I'm out?'

'Aye, you could get three penn'orth of cod, and a penn'orth of carrots and some tea. I've got enough flour for bread. The shops are all at the top of the road.'

'Is that the money tin?' Bridget pointed to an old tea caddy on the mantelpiece.

Annie shook her head and fumbled under her apron in her skirt pocket. 'Nah, lass, there's nowt in there. I have to keep me money on me body all the time. If I don't, the old goat helps himself for beer and baccy money when he runs out.'

Waiting for the reply to the job application was an anxious time. Relations between Annie and Frank remained strained. In order to keep an eye on Bridget, Annie sent a message to her evening employers to say she was too ill to work.

A few days later, Bella's daughter, Nellie, hurtled through the back door. Annie looked up in surprise from the trousers she was mending. 'Why Nellie, don't tell me you've left the job already? Sure, me and Bridget's been sitting on hot pins waiting to see if she gets it.'

'Nah, I haven't left yet. The housekeeper gave me two extra days off instead of a leaving bonus, so I could get ready for me wedding.' Breathless with excitement, Nellie nodded a greeting to Bridget, who was ironing Frank's Sunday shirt on the table. 'I just ran over to tell you,' Nellie went on, 'that if your Bridget wants the job she'd better go to see Mrs Kennedy, the housekeeper. I put in a good word for her on your account, and she seemed right pleased when she got Bridget's letter and heard she just hailed from Ireland. She came over herself thirty-odd years ago, so she seemed sympathetic like.'

Annie beamed. 'Eey, that's grand news, hinny! We're right grateful to you for putting a good word in.'

Nellie paused long enough to return Annie's smile, her bright green eyes dancing with excitement. 'Aw, that's nowt,' she said. 'The new girl'll be getting one and ninepence a week, on top of room and board. I get two bob now since I was promoted to first scullery maid. Of course, the scullery maids don't get no uniform like the rest, only a cap and apron. You've got to buy your own frocks and they get worn out quick doing all the mucky jobs.'

Bridget stood at the table, iron poised, task forgotten. One and ninepence a week and all found seemed a fortune after feeding and clothing a large family on her father's nineteen shillings a week and paying four and sixpence rent. She'd always been out of money well before pay day. She gave Nellie a shy smile. ''Tis right grateful I am to you, Nellie.' Plump, pretty and red-headed, Nellie was everything Bridget wished she were. Though about her own age, Nellie was outgoing – even boisterous – and bathed in a glow of happiness.

'Aw, I told you 'tis nowt,' Nellie repeated, backing towards the door in her haste. 'Mrs Kennedy said to be sure to get there the morrow, 'cause she's making her decision then. You were right lucky. You were just in time. There's been hordes after it. You can come back with me. The cart leaves at five in the morning. I'll come and get you afore then. And if you miss the cart back you can sleep with me and get the next one. Mrs Kennedy won't say nothing. She's a canny soul. We're dead lucky to have her as housekeeper.' She opened the door and flung over her shoulder: 'And I'll be living nearby when I'm wed. You can come and see me. Now I've got to run. Ta ta, then.'

'Thanks be to you, lass,' Annie said and smiled as Nellie charged out of the door as fast as she'd charged in.

Bridget felt as if she'd been reprieved from a prison sentence. Nellie was nice. If she got the job, she'd at least have one friend there. She forgot her ironing and ran to hug Annie. 'I've got an interview tomorrow! And Nellie asked me to visit her!'

Annie smiled at her. 'It seems your prayers might be answered this time, hinny. Maybe something's going to go right for you after all. One and ninepence a week's a good start.'

Bridget returned to her ironing. 'I pray to God I get the job. But how much will it be costing to get to Morpeth?'

'Never you mind about that now. I'll see to it. Mr Jones is a right old skinflint. See that he doesn't charge you no more than fourpence each way, that's what he charges Nellie. But you being a stranger and all he might try to sting you for more. It's not but twenty-five miles, but it takes nigh on six hours. Old Jones picks up anybody and everything he can on the way.'

'Fourpence! That's not too bad.'

Annie stood and threw the mending on to the chair. 'And now we've got to get you cleaned up, lass. There's no time to wash your frock but we can sponge down the stains and iron it. And we're going to fill the tub for a bath for you. Your spirits'll be better if you feel fresh and clean. And you have to look your best for an interview. Now leave that ironing and help me fill the pots.'

An hour later, two large pots and the kettle bubbled on the stove. Annie and Bridget had hauled in the zinc tub that hung on the outside wall and set it before the fire.

Annie started emptying the pots into the tub. 'Get your things off, hen. A real treat you'll be having. Just fancy – a bath with the water all to yourself and 'tis not even Friday night.'

By the time Bridget was undressed, Annie had filled the tub and placed the kettle back on the fire to boil to top up the water when it got cold.

Bridget lay back in the tub and the tension flowed out of her body into the six inches of clean, warm water. 'Ooh, it feels lovely! At home I always was second last and the water was long cold by then and none too clean after the little ones. And me da's turn was after me.' Her eyes filled. 'Oh, Auntie, if only God hadn't taken them, it would be so lovely being here.'

'Aye, 'tis hard on you, luv. You'll be grieving for a long time.' Annie puffed as she knelt by the tub with a clean rag and a bar of carbolic soap. 'Eey, you're that thin, lass! But you'll be a right picture when we get some flesh on those bones. You're the spitting image of your ma – and she was a beauty when your da married her. I'll wash your hair and scrub your back now, and you do the rest while I clean up your frock and iron it. You'd best be wearing me Sunday frock till the morrow or you'll be all mucked up again.'

Washed, dried, her hair brushed and hanging in damp ringlets down her back, Bridget put on Annie's best black Sunday dress.

'Eey, hinny, watch out when you're walking,' Annie warned. 'It's hanging in puddles around your feet. Such a tiny thing you are!'

Bridget raised her chin as if to make herself taller. 'I'm strong though. Me da always said I could do the work of two women.'

'Aye, well let's hope they'll not be expecting that.' Annie took a fork from the dresser and advanced on Bridget.

'And what would you be doing with that?' Bridget asked.

''Tis for cleaning your nails. Sit your self down and I'll see to them.'

'Me nails!' Bridget's mouth fell open but she sat obediently by the fire. 'And what's wrong with me nails? Haven't I just had a bath?'

'That's not enough, hinny, at least not when you're going for an interview.' Annie knelt and, holding Bridget's thumb steady, poked a fork prong under the black rim.

'Ouch!' Bridget pulled her hand away. 'I haven't ever done that before, so why would I be needing it now?'

'I told you. Because you're going for an interview. It's called a manicure. It's what ladies have.'

'And what sort of impression would I be making looking like a lady when I'm applying for a scullery maid's post? Sure, 'twould be better to look as though I'm used to hard work.'

Annie knelt back on her haunches. 'Aye, you've got a head on your shoulders, Bridget. I never thought of that. Just bite them down a bit more then and tidy them up.' She stood with difficulty, rubbing her back. 'I wish it *was* a lady's post you were going for though.' She looked wistful for a moment, then smiled. 'But with your brains and hard work there's always a chance you could end up a lady's maid.'

At five minutes to five the next morning Bridget and Nellie stood shivering at the cart stop. Underneath her cloak and shawl, Bridget's freshly sponged and ironed dress looked clean and tidy. With Annie's help she'd plaited her chestnut curls into a thick rope and coiled and secured it with hairpins after Annie's fashion. She clutched the bundle of food Annie had given her – two slices of bread and two pieces of cheese, half to be kept for the return journey.

Above Nellie's chatter, Bridget heard a clip-clop from around the corner and grabbed Nellie's elbow. 'Listen! 'Tis the cart I hear.'

'Nah, luv. The cart comes from the other way. That'll be the miners coming off the night shift.' As she spoke, a group of black-faced men wearing wooden clogs clattered into view. Bridget was used to seeing dirty, weary farmhands after a ten-hour shift in the fields, but she'd never seen such black faces and hands. They passed, nodding a greeting, and the smell of coal dust from their grimy clothes stung her nose.

Nellie sighed. 'Eey, I'm glad Jack's not down the pits. He smells like a slaughterhouse, even after he's had a bath. He's a butcher's boy, you see. But he never gets dirty like them lot. I don't know how I'd keep him clean.' Nellie hadn't stopped talking since they'd left home and gave no sign of stopping. 'You know, I never thought any lad would look at me with me carrot top and all. They used to tease me about it when I was little, but now they seem to like it, especially Jack. Oh, he's lovely, Bridget. I met him at Morpeth in the market when I was buying meat for Cook, and he said they were just closing up and could he carry me basket for me. From that minute I knew he was the one.' Despite Nellie's red nose, and cheeks pinched from the cold, she seemed to glow from inside and her eyes sparkled with excitement.

'You're lucky to be marrying a butcher's boy,' Bridget said. 'At least you'll not be going short of meat.'

'Aye, well, I do right well for grub now anyway. Mrs Kennedy fiddles the books a bit to get extras for the staff. She says she doesn't see why them lot upstairs should sit around all day doing nothing but feeding their faces while we work our fingers to the bone and eat their scraps.' She pushed back a gleaming red curl from her forehead and gabbled on. 'She's a religious woman but the rumour is she says God wouldn't count changing the figures a sin – more like He'd count *them* the sinners for keeping their workers hungry. The mistress is too bone lazy to keep an eye on the kitchen accounts anyway, so it serves her right.'

Bridget was glad the conversation had finally steered towards work. Interested as she'd been to hear Nellie's wedding plans, she was longing to learn more about the job and the Hayward family. But before she could embark on the barrage of questions she'd prepared, a heavily pregnant woman who looked too old to be bearing children puffed up the street.

'Eey, I just made it,' she said as she joined them. 'I seen him coming round the corner.'

'So you did! And about time.' Nellie nodded as the clatter of a horse's hooves on the cobbles heralded the carter's approach.

Mr Jones rumbled the rickety cart to a halt. The ancient carthorse, head down, plodded wearily and stopped willingly as Mr Jones pulled on the reins and yelled, 'Whoa, me lad!' The animal looked more as though it were finishing its journey than starting it. Bridget was shocked by the sight of its ribs poking through its scant flesh. At home no farm horse would ever be treated like that. She disliked Mr Jones instantly.

25

He grinned a black-toothed greeting and doffed his cloth cap. 'Morning, lasses! Up you get.'

Nellie turned to the woman: 'You sit in the front, missus. Your belly'll be more comfortable sitting straight.'

'Thank you, hinny,' the woman said, and Nellie and Bridget hoisted her up to the wooden bench beside Mr Jones. They clambered over the side on to the back and Bridget squatted in a corner on the dirty planks. Nellie nudged her with her boot.

'We've got to move further up. There's more passengers'll be getting on and off and they'll be climbing all over us.' They shuffled up towards Mr Jones' cargo for the journey thus far – a half-dozen barrels of ale. Wedging themselves close to the side of the cart, they entwined arms behind them on the rail for support and huddled together for warmth.

Bridget's nose twitched. 'Does he always carry ale? I hate the smell of it.'

'Nah!' Nellie grinned and gripped the rail tighter as the cart bumped on its way. 'He carries whatever he can get asides people. You're lucky! He lugged a pig on the way down – pigs, hens, rabbits, sacks of flour and taties, even an old rusty bedstead one time. It took up the whole bloody cart and we all had to sit on it and hang on for our lives. It was raining and all. You're lucky the day. If you get the job and visit your auntie you'll have a lot worse journeys than this.'

As Annie had predicted, the journey to Morpeth took six hours. Nellie jostled Bridget's arm. 'We get off here,' she said, as passengers began alighting.

The cart had stopped by a row of pretty cottages built from the local grey stone. Bridget looked around and saw some grander buildings on a wide street further on, which she guessed to be the town centre. She was puzzled. 'But isn't it two miles beyond Morpeth we're bound?'

'Aye, it is and all.' Nellie rolled her eyes towards Mr Jones, busy collecting fares. 'But do you think that old devil would go out of his way for us? He'd charge us through the nose for taking but two passengers to the back of beyond. It's shanks's pony from here. Watch out you don't catch your skirt on the way down.'

Bridget approached Mr Jones first and handed him four pennies.

'That'll be fivepence, lass,' he said, still holding out his hand. His sly brown eyes glinted as he smiled at her.

Nellie pushed her aside. 'The devil it will, you old skinflint. 'Tis fourpence to Morpeth and she knows it.'

The smile slid from his face under Nellie's angry stare. 'Aye, well, seeing she's a bonnie lass we'll say fourpence then.'

Though it was hard work plodding down the muddy track and trying to keep her boots and skirt clean, Bridget was glad to be walking after the bone-rattling journey – at least until her new boots blistered her toes and heels.

'We're almost there,' Nellie said as they turned a corner.

Bridget stared at the sight. In the distance was a high wall with ornate wrought-iron gates and a gatehouse like a tower. Behind stood a majestic mansion made of the same stone as the town buildings. 'Jesus be!' she said. 'Isn't it grand? 'Tis a palace!'

Nellie pulled a sour face. 'Aye, they live like they was kings and queens. They don't care that some folks has to scrimp and scrape and live in hovels. Me da used to say all men were equal in the eyes of God, but he never saw nothing like this place.'

Bridget took a hesitant step towards the gate and Nellie laughed. 'Nah, luv, you've got a lot to learn about working for the gentry. We go in the servants' entrance.' She took Bridget's arm and led her along a mud cart track to the back of the house. 'Them's the stables.' She pointed to a large courtyard with rows of stables on three sides. 'And them's the kitchen gardens.' She waved over an area covered with brown earth, except for a few unidentifiable frostbitten leaves here and there. 'The stuff's mostly stored in the cellars now,' she explained, 'but in the spring it's full of everything you can imagine.'

They entered the basement through a heavy doorway. The windows, below ground level, were protected by iron bars. 'It's like a prison,' Bridget said, disappointed. In the stone-flagged hall, barely a peep of light wormed its way through the windows, and it was almost as cold inside as out.

Nellie chuckled. 'Aye, it's a bit like a prison in more ways than one. But you don't need to worry about the cold, you'll be too busy to notice it. And at meals and before bed we always sit in the kitchen. That's a lovely warm place to be.' She ushered Bridget down a long passage to a heavy door. 'This is the housekeeper's sitting room. There's always a fire on in here,' she whispered before knocking. A muffled voice bade them enter.

Mrs Kennedy sat at a wooden table, her pepper-and-salt head bent over what were presumably the housekeeping accounts. She looked up as they entered. Her face was round and plain as a pie dish. Deep lines

27

etched round her mouth and puckered it as if she were sucking through her teeth. The effect could have given her a prim appearance, except that her grey eyes were soft and regarded Bridget kindly.

'So you're Bridget,' she said. 'I'm making me mind up today. You just made it in time. Come and sit down.' She indicated the chair opposite her and waved Nellie away. 'Cook's been screaming her head off for you all day, Nellie. You'd better get there quickstick.'

Bridget perched on the edge of the wooden chair as if her body were bound by a tourniquet. She took in the woman's neat black dress, starched white apron and lace-trimmed cap. At least thirty keys dangled from a chatelaine round her waist, attesting to her high status. Bridget felt the tourniquet round her body tighten.

Mrs Kennedy stretched her puckered lips into a smile, revealing a missing front tooth. 'There's no need to be nervous, hinny. I'm not going to eat you. I hear you just hailed from Ireland.'

'Yes, ma'am.' Her voice sounded like a squeaky door hinge.

'I hear you had a terrible time and lost all your kin and all.'

'Yes, ma'am.' Bridget bowed her head and swallowed hard. Tears always started at the mention of her family, and she mustn't feel sorry for herself at an interview. She must make a good impression.

Mrs Kennedy sighed and leaned back in the wooden chair, her podgy hands clasped over the rise of her belly. Bridget noticed the white fingernails. Maybe she should have cleaned her own after all.

'I know what you've been through, lass,' Mrs Kennedy said. 'I came over meself when I was your age. I lost me kin and all before I left – the cholera it was. To be sure, if they could've got a doctor and hadn't been so half-starved they might've survived. I came over hoping to find a new life. I got work here as a scullery maid and fell in love with one of the farm hands. He was Irish and all. We got married and lived in one of the cottages.' Her huge bosom, which seemed to start at her neck and finish at her waist, heaved as she reminisced. 'But he was killed four months later.'

'Sure, I'm sorry to hear that, ma'am,' Bridget burst out. Then, remembering she shouldn't have interrupted, she sealed her lips.

But, carried away with her memories, Mrs Kennedy went on as if she hadn't heard, 'It was hunting season and he was taking a short cut to the farm through the woods. He always warned me never to do that during their hunting parties, but he must've forgotten that day. He got a bullet through his belly. But he died instantly, thanks be to God. Nobody knew who did it, but it would've made no difference anyway.

'Twas an accident. Sure, some of them drink that many stirrup cups before the hunt they can't tell a deer from a house.'

''Tis a sad story indeed, ma'am,' Bridget said, forgetting herself again.

'Aye, 'twas hard at first. But I came back to the house and gradually worked me way up and, 'cause I had no man, they finally gave me this job. I always wanted bairns, but the good Lord didn't want it to be.' Her eyes, which had stared past Bridget while she talked, suddenly focused on her. 'Eey, take no notice of me, girl. Sometimes I lose meself when I start thinking. I didn't mean to be jabbering on about meself when I want to hear about you.' She leaned over the table as if to inspect Bridget more thoroughly. 'How old are you, and what experience have you had?'

'Fifteen, and I was after keeping house and bringing up me little brothers and sisters since me ma died when I was ten. And before that I helped her a lot. Sure, I know all about hard work, ma'am, and I'm not afraid of it.'

Mrs Kennedy smiled. 'Eey, 'tis good to hear an Irish voice again. I miss the old country, even though it never did any good for me.'

'You still sound quite a lot Irish yourself, ma'am.' Bridget smiled back, now feeling more comfortable with this kindly woman. She'd expected to be treated like a servant, and here she was chatting freely with the housekeeper.

Mrs Kennedy shook her head. 'Nah, hinny, I sound as much Geordie as Irish now. 'Tisn't possible to live here for thirty-five years without picking some of it up.' She sat straight and cleared her throat, her manner suddenly more businesslike. 'And now, did Nellie tell you about the work and the pay?'

'Yes, ma'am. Scrubbing the floors and benches and pots and pans and doing fires and running messages and things. And cleaning out the closets upstairs. I'm used to those jobs. I'm not afraid of mucky work.' Though she didn't know whether or not it would be in her favour, she added as an afterthought, 'And me reading and writing are quite good, ma'am.'

Mrs Kennedy nodded. 'Aye, I was surprised to get your letter. Did you learn it at school, lass?'

'I went to school half time for two years, ma'am, till me ma died, but I didn't learn that much there. 'Twas me ma taught me to read before that really, and some sums and all. Her family had some education and they weren't happy when she married me da.' She paused, wondering if

29

she'd said too much, but Mrs Kennedy remained silent. Encouraged, Bridget went on, 'After Ma died I learnt a lot more words by reading the catechism over and over and the hymn books at mass. And when I had to leave school to look after me family the teacher gave me a fairytale book to keep 'cause the cover was torn. I used to read it to me little brothers and sisters every night before I tucked them in.' She stopped abruptly, and lowered her eyes. She *must* have prattled on too much now. 'I'm sorry, ma'am. Sure I didn't mean to gabble so,' she said.

'I like to know all about me staff, Bridget. That's why I ask questions.' Mrs Kennedy leaned back in the chair, and her eyes again looked beyond Bridget. 'There were no schools when I was a lass. I used to clean the priest's house and afterwards he'd give me an hour's lesson free. I thank God for it now or I wouldn't be where I am.' Her gaze returned to Bridget. 'If I was you I wouldn't let on to the staff you know reading and writing – at least for the time being. You don't need to tell any lies. Just say nowt.'

Excitement warmed Bridget inside like a cup of hot cocoa. Did this mean she'd got the job?

'If you were a man 'twould be all right to let on you're lettered,' Mrs Kennedy continued. 'But 'tis not the same for a woman. Most here can't even write their names, even them that went to school. Sure, 'tis mostly religion them teachers force down the bairns' throats, and handy things like sewing or woodwork. They don't really want the working class to be lettered, just taught the Bible. They want to keep them where they are. Somebody has to do the mucky jobs.'

'Aye, me ma used to say that and all.' Bridget checked herself again. Surely it wasn't seemly to be talking like an equal at an interview with the housekeeper. But she must agree to do as she was told. 'I promise I won't be after telling anybody,' she said, and sealed her lips.

Mrs Kennedy looked well pleased. ''Tis only for your own good, Bridget, for the time being at least. The others might think you're putting on airs and graces above your station.' She took a sheet of paper from her desk drawer and wrote on it. 'I can't say I'm not favouring you a bit because you're one of me own kind, but I think you'll be right for the job anyway. When can you start?'

Bridget had to swallow before she could speak. 'Oh, any time, ma'am. Today if you want.'

Mrs Kennedy put the paper in a green cardboard file on her desk. ''Tis May's day off tomorrow – that's the second scullery maid – and Mrs Brown'll be coming in from Morpeth. I'll send one of the girls to tell her to take the day off with pay. The poor old thing could do with it. You could help Nellie and she could show you around.'

'Oh, yes, ma'am. I'd truly like that.'

'Good. You'll get one and ninepence a week to start. Nellie's not leaving till the end of the week, but you can either go back to your auntie's or stay on and help out till then. There won't be any pay till you start officially, but you'll get fed, and you can share Nellie's bed when May comes back.'

Bridget decided immediately. If she went back, her aunt would lose more time at her evening jobs. 'I'd like to stay, ma'am. But I'd have to be letting me auntie know.'

'I'll see to that, Bridget,' Mrs Kennedy said. 'I'll tell Molly, the vegetable maid. She's going to Newcastle tomorrow. She can tell your aunt. 'Twas she who got me Nellie, so I know she lives nearby, and 'twill save the postage.' She placed the green file in a drawer and stood to indicate the interview was over.

'Thank you again, ma'am.' Bridget rose and tried to walk towards the door as if her blisters didn't hurt. Halfway, she turned, feeling stupid. 'Where do I go, ma'am?'

But Mrs Kennedy was already on her way. 'I'm going to the kitchen. I'll take you. I've no doubt you'll be wanting a cup of tea after your long journey.'

'Oh, indeed I would, ma'am.' As she followed Mrs Kennedy she said a silent prayer: Thank You, Lord, for answering me prayers, and thank You for making Mrs Kennedy so nice.

31

Chapter Four

Nellie poked Bridget in the ribs. 'Come on, we've got to get up. It's five o'clock.'

Bridget grunted and turned over. 'How do you know?'

'I've been doing it that long I've got a clock inside me head,' Nellie said, yawning. 'And keep your voice down or the others'll start squawking.'

Nellie lit a candle and Bridget opened her eyes. She sat in her underwear on the narrow bed. Icy draughts blew through the tiny skylight and under the door. She jumped up and threw on her dress and the grey apron and white mobcap Mrs Kennedy had given her. A glance at the other two bunks in the small attic confirmed she hadn't awakened the laundry maids.

Wearing only her thin petticoat and camisole, Nellie cupped her hands in the frigid water in the bowl on the dresser. She took a sip, swished it around her mouth and spat into the slop bucket. Her teeth chattered as she splashed her face and dried it on one of the strips of torn sheets that served as towels for the maids. She threw the towel at Bridget.

Bridget laced her boots and stood. She winced. Her feet felt as if they'd been pumped with bellows. 'Ouch! Me blisters've burst. I don't know how it is I'm going to walk.'

Nellie buttoned her dress bodice and came to her aid. 'Sit down and get them boots off.' She tore a dry rag into strips and bound Bridget's feet.

'Oh, that feels better!' Bridget sighed with relief as she laced the boots again. The soft padding felt like balm on her broken skin.

'Aye, if you wore stockings your feet wouldn't hurt so much.'

Bridget looked as surprised as if Nellie had suggested she wear a fur coat. 'Stockings! I've never had stockings in me life. To be sure, I was

32

lucky I had boots, at least in the winter.'

'Shhh!' Nellie warned her again and glanced at the sleeping figures. 'Them lucky beggars doesn't have to get up till six.'

Nellie lit the wall lamps from the candle as they crept down the back stairs to the privy. Bridget looked at the empty hallway in surprise. 'Are we the only ones up?'

'Aye, except for the midden men. They do the servants' privies. We've got to get the fires on afore the finer staff gets their lazy carcasses out of bed. We start in the kitchen so Cook can make breakfast, then we do Mrs Kennedy's sitting room. Next comes the breakfast room. It's got to be nice and cosy afore the family eats. And after that we do the big drawing room, Madam's private drawing room, library, hall and dining room, in that order.'

'Holy Moses! What a lot of fires!'

Nellie laughed. 'That's not all. After they're up and downstairs, we clean out the grates in their chambers and set the fires, so the chambermaids can put a light to them if their majesties want to take a little snooze, or afore they go to bed – just in case their tiny tootsies get frostbite and drop off.' She giggled and her pupils reflected like emeralds in the candlelight. 'But afore they're up,' she went on, lighting the final lamp in the hallway, 'we fill the log baskets for the butler and valet and the upstairs maids to keep the fires going. They don't want to see our mucky faces, so we can only do them jobs when they're abed.'

At the back door, Nellie lit two hand lanterns. 'Here, take this so you can find the hole,' she said, and giggled again.

As they crossed the courtyard to the servants' outhouses, the icy morning air slapped their cheeks. Nellie emerged from her cubicle holding her nose. 'The midden men haven't been yet, the lazy buggers! There'd be a fine to-do upstairs if we were late emptying *their* closets. And I'll let you into a little secret. Theirs smell just as bad as ours.' She tittered and poked Bridget in the ribs. 'In some things God made us all the same, eh?'

At the house, they started with the kitchen fires. Bridget surveyed the white walls, the shining copper pots and pans hanging everywhere, the huge scrubbed table where Cook worked and the long trestle table where the staff ate. She thought of the supper she'd shared with them the previous evening – mutton stew, green peas and potatoes, followed by plum tart and custard. Such a feast she'd never known except on Christmas Day. It was only then that her father had dipped into the jar of precious savings for their fares to England. She sighed with gratitude. Her luck had turned at last.

'For the Lord's sake, stop mooning!' Nellie said. 'I'll go and get the things.' She disappeared to the scullery and returned with two buckets and shovels.

Bridget attacked the mountain of ash in the grate, careful not to let dust rise over the monster ovens that flanked it and the hotplate above. 'To be sure, this kitchen's ten times the size of our old house. I've never seen such a grand place,' she said.

Nellie, on her way out to empty a pail, shouted over her shoulder, 'Just wait till you see the rest. You won't hardly believe your eyes.'

Nellie was right. Awestruck, Bridget followed her as they worked their way through rooms many times larger than the kitchen, each more splendid than the last: gilt and velvet-covered furniture, wood-panelled walls relieved by brocade and satin hangings or decorated with huge paintings and banners, the family crest in gold above the enormous fireplaces with alcoves on either side big enough for people to sit in – except that in most stood suits of armour or large statues. Everywhere, crystal chandeliers sparkled and gold or silver ornaments shimmered.

'Mother of God! Have you ever seen a table the likes of that?' Bridget said when they reached their last call, the dining room. She gazed down the length of the mahogany table. 'It's as long as me auntie's street. Sure, this place is just like the pictures in me fairy-tale book.'

Nellie laughed. 'Aye, except it's not fairies that live here. *She's* more like a witch and *he's* more like a devil – at least he's a devil with the ladies. He's got more than one of the servants into trouble so they say. But *we* needn't be afeared of him, he's only interested in the upstairs servants. Scullery maids are too low-class for him. And besides, he never claps eyes on us anyway.'

Bridget looked puzzled. 'Why does he get them into trouble? I mean, if they're doing their job right and everything . . .'

Nellie guffawed. 'How they do their job's got nowt to do with it, you daft thing. It's how they look that matters. It's only the pretty ones he bothers with.'

'Oh.' Bridget wasn't about to admit she still didn't understand why the master would want to cause trouble among his servants, pretty or not. She shrugged. Anyway, if he didn't bother the scullery maids, it was none of her business. 'What do they do to have all this money?' she asked as they made their way down the back stairs with their ash pails.

It was now light enough to see without lanterns, and a few downstairs servants went about their tasks.

Nellie shook her red curls. 'Don't ask *me* how they got their money! They don't never do nothing but sit around, eat and entertain and go out to be entertained.' They emptied the last of the ash into the outside bins and Nellie pushed back her hair from her forehead. 'Come on, now it's time to play midden maidens.'

'What's that?'

'We empty the gentry's closets, you nitwit.'

As Bridget followed her towards the stairway, they passed various uniformed servants. Some nodded a greeting and eyed Bridget, some joked with Nellie, while others simply passed them with their noses in the air. 'Stuck-up snobs,' Nellie muttered as two such maids stalked by.

Bridget ignored the snubs.

When they entered the first closet she couldn't believe her eyes. The walls were papered with a red and gold flower design and, instead of a wooden bench, a leather seat stretched across the back wall. Extra padding surrounded the single hole, which was covered by a lid, all upholstered in black leather. It looked more like a luxury carriage seat than a privy. A row of brass jugs and bowls adorned the mahogany shelf to the side, beside them a neat stack of white linen hand towels.

After collecting two pails each, they trudged half a mile to a derelict spot in an empty field behind the stables. Here Nellie set down her pails and lifted an old door lying on the ground.

Bridget held her nose and took a step backwards.

Nellie snickered. 'What d'you expect? 'Course it stinks! That's why they make the hole so far from the house. And when this one's nearly full they fill it in with soil and start another one. Sometimes guests walk over the old holes and fall in. Eey, it's always good for a laugh downstairs when that happens.' She tipped the pails into the hole and pulled a face.

Bridget held her breath as she emptied her loads, and together they eased the door back in place. 'Pheeoow! That's a relief!' When they turned to go she gulped in the fresh air. But the smell stayed in her nose. Though undismayed, she looked forward to the more pleasant tasks of the day.

'Plenty more journeys like this,' Nellie said. 'They've got more closets upstairs than privies for the servants. Thank your lucky stars

35

we don't have to lug them big things all this way like the midden men.'

'Do they empty ours here and all?'

'Why aye, man. You might say it's the only way we ever mingle with the gentry.' Nellie doubled up at her joke. 'Now don't tell me you're squeamish.'

Bridget coloured. 'Of course I'm not. Indeed, I'm well used to emptying privies. But I thought a scullery maid worked mostly in the scullery, and here we've spent all this time just doing fires and closets.'

Nellie swung her empty pails as they walked. 'Eey, you've got a lot to learn, hinny. We're the skivvies. We do all the dirty work. The only jobs you might call clean are scrubbing the floors and scouring the pots and pans.'

'Aye, I don't mind those jobs at all, and I like peeling vegetables and washing dishes and things.'

'Nah, not here, luv. Maybe in littler houses, but here they've got a dishwasher and a vegetable maid for them jobs. They wouldn't trust us with their precious china and crystal, and they wouldn't want us doing vegetables with our mucky hands. The vegetable maid's Cook's lackey.'

'Well then, one of these days I'm going to become dishwasher or vegetable maid,' Bridget said with determination, then felt contrite. ''Tisn't that I'm not grateful for you getting me the job, Nellie. I truly am, and it's a wonderful start. But I want to work me way up in life.'

'Aye, well, it's either that or get wed, like me. I'll bet you sixpence some fella'll sweep you off your feet afore you ever make it to dishwasher or anything.' She flicked Bridget a curious look. 'Have you ever had a lad?'

'Sure, now why would I be after having a lad? I was always too busy for things like that.' Bridget sounded flustered and Nellie gave her another sidelong glance.

'Too busy, my foot! You'd have made time for lads if they were after you. But I bet they start chasing you soon – at least when you fill out a bit with Cook's grub.' She grinned and quickened her steps. 'Let's get a move on afore we freeze to death.'

At the house, the basement bustled with life and the smell of frying bacon pervaded the hallway. Bridget's nostrils twitched. 'Bacon! I can't remember the last time I smelled bacon.'

At Bridget's tone the corners of Nellie's mouth turned up. 'Don't get too excited, luv. We only get it on Sundays, and sausages on Wednesdays. The rest of the time we get eggs though, and butter on the bread and porridge with milk. We do all right. I wish me ma and da did half as well. Afore I go home I slip a few things off the table into me pocket. Last time I sneaked half a jar of jam and bread and butter, and the blasted jam oozed all over me frock. Just be careful what you pinch. And watch out for Cook, and all. She copped one of the lasses at it and there was hell to pay. In fact, watch out for Cook anyway. She's a stingy bugger. She'd have us eating the slops if she had her way. We only get good grub 'cause she has to do what Mrs Kennedy tells her.'

After the last of their chores, placing eight buckets of water on the servants' landing beside the log baskets, Nellie groaned with relief. 'Now we've got to go to the scullery and wash our hands quickstick. The staff gong'll be going any minute and Cook won't allow us in the kitchen till we've washed our hands. She's dead set on that.'

Bridget gazed at the green baize door separating the basement from the rest of the house. 'One of these days I'm going to go through that door wearing a clean white apron and starched bonnet,' she said with resolve.

Nellie grinned. 'Get off it, I told you, you'll be married with a horde of bairns long afore that.'

After washing their hands at the scullery pump they sat on the scrubbed bench and waited for the gong. Bridget's stomach felt as hollow as a trumpet. 'What time would it be, do you think?' she asked Nellie. 'I've never been up this long without at least a hot drink inside me.'

'Aye, me belly thinks me throat's been cut and all. It's probably about nine o'clock.'

The gong echoed throughout the basement. They jumped up and scurried to the kitchen in a most unladylike fashion. The place suddenly teemed with servants: some liveried, some in black dresses with white caps and aprons, and some – the stable and garden staff – in leather or sackcloth aprons over dirty breeches and shabby shirts. As nervous as on the previous evening, Bridget kept her head low and followed Nellie to the far end of the table where the lower-class servants sat. The butler, valet, and Cook took their meals in Mrs Kennedy's sitting room. Though Cook was never seen upstairs, she'd been at the house for twenty-five years and had great status as the best cook in Northumberland.

Bridget's eyes scoured the table. Boiled eggs sat in proper egg cups on each plate, and in the centre were plates heaped with chunks of bread, butter, jugs of milk and – she could hardly believe her eyes – pots of what looked like strawberry jam. As before, they sat next to the two laundry maids, but this time a blond, curly-headed youth joined them. He wore patched corduroy breeches and a grey jersey, and, from his leather apron, Bridget guessed he must be a stableboy.

He lowered his tall, broad frame on to the chair opposite Bridget and surveyed her. 'I haven't seen you here afore.' His rough voice contradicted his face, which was long and fine-featured except for his wide nose. But his mouth had a gentle upward curve and his smile revealed a set of neat white teeth. Bridget couldn't take her eyes off his. They were a fathomless blue and twinkled as they looked back at her. 'When did you start then?' he asked.

Embarrassed, she lowered her gaze. 'Just yesterday,' she said with difficulty. She'd seen plenty of boys before. Why did this one make her feel funny?

'Oh, aye. It was me day off yesterday.' He placed his elbows on the table, laced his work-calloused fingers and rested his chin on his hands. He kept his eyes on her face. 'I'm Tom. What are you called?'

'Bridget,' she whispered, while Nellie kicked her foot and gave her an 'I told you so' look.

Ignoring the rest of the company, Tom probed further. 'Where you from, Bridget? Not around here?'

Bridget swallowed hard before replying, but her voice sounded as if she had a bird whistle stuck in her throat. 'No, I hail from Ireland.'

'Aye, I thought so, a little Irish colleen! *Tooral ooral ooral*,' he sang out of tune, then grinned. 'Me granny was Irish. She used to sing that to me. She was the only kin I had. But I'm a Geordie, born and bred.'

All the chairs at the table were now occupied, the signal to start. Bridget was grateful both to eat and to end the conversation. But Tom continued. 'What do you do then, Bridget?' He spoke with his mouth full of bread and butter.

'I'm second scullery maid.' She buttered her bread with shaking hands and wished he would stop talking and let her eat.

'I've been here four years – worked me way up to second head stableboy.'

'Why, that sounds a grand title.' She managed to remove the top of her egg without mishap.

'Nah, it's only a title. I'm still doing the same job – mucking out. But one of these days I'm going to be head groom.'

At last Nellie came to Bridget's rescue. 'Why don't you shut up and let the poor lass eat her breakfast, Tom Banks. 'Tis not everybody talks with their gobs full like you.'

He clapped his hands to his mouth in mock apology. 'Oh, sorry I spoke. Pardon me for being friendly.'

'Aye, and everybody knows what you're after when you're "being friendly" to a lass,' Betty, the head laundress, cut in. She was fat, fortyish and homely. A set of pink gums showed where her teeth should have been and her lips had disappeared into the cavity. Nevertheless, she turned pink when Tom playfully pinched her cheek.

'Aw, I'm sorry, Betty. Am I neglecting *you* the day? And how's me bonny lass doing this fine morning?'

'Enough of your nonsense, Tom.' Her pink flush turned crimson.

Tom continued to banter with the other women but his eyes kept straying back to Bridget. She was thankful when the meal was over.

He winked at her when he left the table. 'I'll be seeing you then, Bridget. Welcome to the manor.'

'Thank you.' She retreated to the scullery at Nellie's heels and pressed her hands to her hot cheeks.

Nellie closed the door behind them and positively gloated. 'What did I tell you? And on your first day and all, afore you're even fattened up. You'd better watch out for Tom though. I should've warned you about him . . . but I wouldn't never have thought you'd be his type.'

Bridget leaned against the sink to steady herself. 'So what *would* be his type then? And what would be wrong with him?' Despite its tremor, her voice was indignant.

Nellie grinned and eased herself on to the draining board beside Bridget. 'Don't get your hackles up! I only meant that he usually goes for more, well, you know what I mean, more rounded lasses. And he's a terrible flirt – never stays with one lass long. There's been a lot of broken hearts mooning about this place. He didn't never tackle me, though. He mustn't like redheads.' She snickered and added, 'But I admit I wouldn't have minded if he had. He's a fine-looking fella and loaded with what *you* would call the blarney.'

'Aye, that's true, to be sure.' Bridget smiled, a slow, uncertain smile. 'I'll tell you the God's honest truth, Nellie, me heart fluttered like a butterfly and me belly did somersaults the whole time. I've never felt like that before.'

Nellie's eyebrows arched like question marks. 'God forbid! You've fallen for the lad! Dear oh dear! Another heart's about to be broken to smithereens.' She shook her head in dismay.

'Well I don't know about "fallen" but 'tis sure I liked him and . . . and I liked him paying me attention like that. It made me feel funny but nice. And I was near starving to death yet I could hardly touch a bite.'

Nellie heaved an exaggerated sigh of despair. 'Oh, Lord! You *have* fallen for him. Just you look out for yourself, luv. It was plain as a pikestaff he was after you, and I know he'll be laying on the charm some more. If it's just a little fling you're after and a bit of kissing and cuddling – or even a bit more – then Tom's all right for that. But if you've got anything more serious in mind, forget it now. He'll drop you like a hot brick as soon as another pretty face comes along.' She gave her an anxious look. 'Don't fall for him, Bridget.'

'Saints in Glory! I'm not looking for anything serious.' Bridget's tone was adamant. ''Tis too young I am to be thinking of things like that. And anyway, I'm going to work me way up in the world. Indeed, why would I be wanting to spend the rest of me life with a man that smells of horse dung?'

'Oh, getting hoity-toity now, are we?' Nellie sounded hurt and Bridget felt penitent.

'I was only joking, Nellie. But 'tis true I want to make something of meself. When I think of me poor ma, God rest her soul, and me auntie and other married women I know, 'tis a hard life they have indeed. And just look at the grand life Mrs Kennedy has, and she worked her way up to it.'

'Aye, but she's got no man and no bairns and nobody to love her,' Nellie reminded her.

'That's true,' Bridget conceded. 'But then she's got no troubles either, and people respect her.'

Nellie jumped off the draining board. 'Come on. We've got to do the pots and pans. You'll change your mind about getting wed when the right lad comes along. But *mind* me, it's not that Tom lad.'

Bridget nodded. 'Now don't you be worrying about me, Nellie. As me auntie says, I've got me head screwed on. I'll mind you.'

Chapter Five

Bridget splashed her face then pinned back her hair at the dresser mirror. Having saved up her first three days off, she was on her way to visit her aunt. She smoothed down her black dress, newly sponged and ironed, and threw on her cloak and shawl. She must hurry to catch Mr Jones' cart before he left on his return journey.

'Good day to you, Bridget. You're in a rush.' Tom Banks' voice startled her as she passed the stables on her way to the cart track.

She lowered her head to hide her flushed cheeks. 'I'm off to Newcastle to see me auntie.'

'Why then, I'll walk with you. I'm on me way to Morpeth. It's me day off and all.' He wore a cloth cap and a worn black overcoat over his work clothes, making him look larger than ever.

She kept her head down. 'Well, if you want to then.'

'Nice day for February.' He fell into step beside her.

Suddenly tongue-tied, she nodded her agreement.

'I've been trying for weeks to talk to you alone,' Tom said, 'but there's always too many folk about at the house.'

She cleared her throat and found her voice. But it sounded like a bird chirping. 'And what would you be wanting to talk to me about?'

He grinned. 'Now there's a daft question for you! You know full well, Bridget Brannigan, that I've a fancy for you. I'd like to ask you to walk out with me.'

Though excitement vibrated through her body like plucked harp strings, she heeded Nellie's warning. 'Walk out with you! And when would I be having the time to do that?'

'Well, you get days off same as all of us. Don't tell me you're going to save them all up to go to Newcastle. And we could walk out after supper at night and all.'

'Why 'tis cold and dark at night. Only an idiot would want to go out

41

in it.' Nellie would be proud of her, but she wished she could swallow her words and accept his invitation.

Tom looked at her sideways, a glint of humour in his eyes. 'Why then, I'm an idiot. I love to go out when it's cold and dark – but it's even nicer with company. I often walk down to the stream at night and just sit and listen to it. And it's extra romantic if the moon's out. You can count the stars. And I could hold your hand in the moonlight – if you'd let me.'

'Tom Banks! Chance would be a fine thing!' She could have cut out her tongue. Nellie didn't know everything. He seemed like a very nice person. She paused, then went on, 'But I might just walk out with you when the weather gets a bit warmer. Though I don't know about letting you hold me hand. The nuns at school said 'twas dangerous and a sin to hold a lad's hand.' As if for protection, she clasped her hands in front of her as she'd seen the nuns do when they walked.

Tom threw back his head and laughed. 'Eey, you're a funny one, Bridget Brannigan.' Still laughing, he took her hand and held it at his side.

She felt his big fingers envelop hers and was powerless to pull away. His touch was warm and comforting, and strangely exciting.

He gave her a triumphant look. 'There you are, you see. Holding hands is nice, and there's nowt sinful about it. You'd best forget all that stuff and nonsense them nuns told you.'

'Nuns are good women and they know a lot.'

'Aye, maybe, but they don't know nowt about holding lads' hands, do they? That's why they're nuns, 'cause no lad'll have them.'

Bridget flushed with indignation. 'Tom Banks, how could you say that? They don't want lads 'cause they're married to God.'

Tom chuckled. 'Poor God! Having that lot for wives! I've got better taste in women meself.'

She failed in her effort to suppress a smile. 'Was that meant to be a compliment then?'

'Why, aye! You're a bonny lass, Bridget, and don't tell me you don't know it.'

She cast her eyes down. 'I . . . I've never thought about it. Vanity is a sin. And it leads to all sorts of evil.'

He chuckled again. 'Aye, I suppose them nuns taught you that and all. Don't be daft, Bridget. I don't believe in all that religious stuff. But, say there was a God, then didn't He make you?'

'Indeed there *is*, and He surely did make me and every living thing.'

'So, He made all this, eh?' Tom made an expansive gesture encompassing the velvet bank of cloud in the winter sky, the chessboard fields flanking the hedgerows, the browsing sheep and cows. 'Well, if He *did* make you, shouldn't you be grateful for all His blessings?' He bent to pluck a snowdrop that peeked out from the grass verge and stuck it in her hair.

'Yes, and I truly am grateful.' She touched the snowdrop with her free hand.

'Why then, being pretty's a blessing. It means the lads'll like you and want to marry you, and you won't have to become no nun,' he finished with a chuckle.

Despite herself, Bridget laughed. 'You're a heathen, Tom Banks. Sure, a good Catholic girl like me has no business walking out with a sinner like you.'

'But you could try to convert me.' He grinned down at her and mimicked her Irish accent, 'Sure now, wouldn't that be another blessing, if God put you on this earth to convert a poor sinner like me?'

She laughed again. ''Tis plain your grandmother was Irish. Indeed, you've got the gift of the blarney all right.' She was enjoying his company and suddenly realized that today was the first time she'd laughed since she'd set foot in England. Surely God never said it was a sin to enjoy yourself. She considered for a moment. 'Well now, when the weather gets a bit warmer or when I take a day off in Morpeth, I might just think about it.' A thrill tingled through her at the thought of walking in the moonlight with her hand in Tom's.

'Why not make it your next day off then? Don't tell me you're going to save them all up so you can see your auntie. You spend most of the time sitting in that bumpy cart anyway.'

She smiled up at him. 'Now didn't I just tell you, Tom Banks? I'll think about it.'

The cart ride proved as uncomfortable and crowded as on the previous journey. Bridget was glad when they reached Byker. She let herself into the flat and ran down the passage to the kitchen. It hadn't struck her before how gloomy and meagre the flat was. Even the servants' quarters where she lived were more spacious and cheerful, and the attic windows looked out over rolling farmland, not brick walls. 'Auntie Annie! I'm home!' She was happy to see her aunt again, though she shuddered at the thought of her uncle.

'Eey, me little cherub!' Annie got up from her chair and threw her arms round Bridget. 'I'm that glad to see you. I was so excited when I got your letter I nearly wet meself.'

Bridget laughed as she hugged her. ''Tis good to see you, Auntie.'

'Aye, you and all, luv. You were here such a little while, I never thought I'd miss you that much.' Annie's eyes misted as she took Bridget by the shoulders and scrutinized her. 'Eey, you look that bonny and healthy, lass!'

''Tis all the good food, Auntie. You wouldn't believe your eyes.' She threw her cape and shawl on a chair and delved into her dress pocket. 'I brought these for you. Just look you now.'

Annie opened the bundle wrapped in a white rag. Her eyes widened. 'Well, I'll be! Sausage rolls, and . . . meat!'

''Tis roast mutton. We had it yesterday. I took an extra large helping and saved it, and May, that's the first scullery maid, took some extra for me as well.' But Bridget's excitement evaporated as Annie stared at her in horror.

'Surely to God, lass, that's stealing!'

'Indeed, 'tis no such thing. Everybody gets plenty to eat anyway, and what's left goes to the pigs. Can you believe that, Auntie? The pigs eat better than most people. You haven't ever seen such luxury and such waste in your life.'

Annie softened and gazed again at the food. 'Aye, well, if you put it like that, I see what you mean, hinny. Better us has it than the pigs. Now sit yourself down and I'll mash the tea. I waited to have mine till you got here. If we're lucky we'll have it in peace and quiet afore your uncle gets home. He's getting later and later every night.' She placed the kettle over the fire and rubbed her hands together with pleasure. 'I just baked a fresh batch of bread and I've got some pickled onions to go with the meat. We'll save the sausage rolls for a treat afore bed.'

While Annie bustled about, Bridget sat by the fire. ''Twas a cold ride,' she said, lifting her skirt to feel the warmth on her legs.

Annie gazed at her in wonder. 'Eey, your legs has filled out. And the rest of you and all! You're getting quite a chest on you. I bet the lads'll be after you soon. You just watch out for yourself, luv.'

Bridget turned pink. 'A lad's already asked me to walk out with him, Auntie.'

Annie gave her a delighted grin. 'Now wasn't I right then? Did you say yes?'

'Well, sort of.' Bridget looked at the floor. 'But nothing could ever come of it. I like him a lot, but he's not Catholic. He doesn't even

44

believe in God. And what would I be doing walking out with a heathen?'

'If he's a good lad, I don't see why not. Look at your uncle. I married him because he was Catholic and you see where it got me.' Annie shook her head as she sliced the bread. 'There's good men and bad men and it doesn't make no difference if they believe in God or not. It's what they do when they're not at church that matters. If you ask me, it's the ones that confess their sins of a Saturday and take communion of a Sunday that think they've got a clean slate to start sinning afresh the next week. I should know.'

Bridget's face lit up with relief. 'Oh, Auntie, do you really think so? He said I could try to convert him and that would make it all right. But I think the priest might still say it's a sin.'

'I'm sure Father Donlan would say 'tis better he's a heathen than a Protestant. You see, the lad just hasn't found the right path yet, it's not like he's already taken the wrong one.' Annie stifled a chuckle but Bridget swallowed her aunt's words whole.

'Do you honestly think he'd be after saying that, Auntie?'

Still keeping a straight face, Annie nodded. 'Aye, I'm sure, luv. Why don't you walk out with the lad on your next day off? You don't want to be saving up all your free time to spend with an old crow like me. I'd be happy to know you had a nice fella.'

'He *is* nice, Auntie. And he's very handsome.' Bridget looked at the floor again. 'But Nellie told me he's got a bit of a reputation with the lasses.'

'Oh, aye? What sort of reputation?' Annie clattered mugs and plates on to the table.

'Sure, 'tis nothing bad. He just takes a lot of girls out and goes from one to another, and he leaves lots of broken hearts behind – so Nellie says.'

'Why then, you be careful, hinny,' Annie said, laying the sliced meat on a platter. 'Make sure you keep him at arm's length. Men are only after one thing, and you don't want to get yourself into trouble. But I'm sure I don't need to tell you that. You're a sensible lass.'

Bridget wanted to ask what that thing was exactly. She'd heard the girls at the house joking about men only being interested in getting between girls' legs, and Tom had never touched her legs. But Annie gave her no time to enquire further.

'How old is he then, and what does he do?' She opened the pickled onion jar with a flourish.

Bridget pondered on Tom's age. 'I've never asked him. But I'd say he's about seventeen, and he's a stableboy, and very ambitious.'

Annie smiled. 'Seventeen and handsome! Well, I'm sure he's just being a lad and sowing his wild oats while he's young. Me brother was like that, but he got married at twenty and settled down like a saint. God rest his soul!' She picked up the poker and pushed the simmering kettle further over the flames. 'Just don't allow the lad no liberties now.'

This time Bridget plucked up the courage to ask the question. 'What sort of liberties, Auntie? Do you mean like holding me hand?'

Annie shook her head. 'No, lass, holding your hand's all right, and maybe if you get really serious, a little kiss. But nothing more, mind you. One thing leads to another.'

'But what more is there than that, Auntie? Do you mean no cuddling, and not letting him touch me legs?'

Annie paused in the act of lifting the kettle from the fire and looked at Bridget with surprise. 'You mean you don't know, hinny? And you didn't know what it was your uncle tried to do to you?'

Bridget's eyes found the floor again. 'Not exactly.'

'It's high time you did then.' Annie replaced the kettle and sat opposite Bridget. She cleared her throat. 'Surely you know that men are made different from women?'

'Well, yes, but—'

'And you must have seen animals on the farm . . . er . . . mounting each other. Well it's the same with people. You mustn't let no man do that till you're married, do you hear?' Annie poked the fire and Bridget didn't notice her pink face.

'No, Auntie, I swear I wouldn't ever let anyone . . . mount me.' Bridget was still puzzled. She'd seen animals playing and riding one another, but what did that have to do with people? She opened her mouth to ask the question. But Annie, seeming satisfied that she'd done her duty, stood and took the pot holder from the line under the mantelpiece.

'Don't look so scared, hinny. It's nowt when the right man comes along.' She lowered her head to pour the water into the pot. 'Come on now. I'm making the tea extra strong for a treat. And I got some sugar and milk special for you coming. Let's hurry up and have ours afore the old goat gets home. Me mouth's fair watering at the thought of that mutton.'

Bridget sat at the table. It was obvious her aunt didn't wish to discuss the subject any more. She didn't want to appear too curious, but the question lurked in her mind.

Halfway through the meal Frank arrived. He glanced at Bridget and grunted a greeting as he hung up his coat.

'Good day to you, Uncle Frank,' Bridget said in a polite but cold voice, while Annie got up to fetch him a plate and mug.

'You'll be having a treat the night,' she said to him.

'Oh, aye?' He sat at the table and stared at the plate of cold meat. 'And where would you be getting the money for that? You'd think the bloody queen was coming to tea.'

'The "bloody queen", as you call her, fetched it for *us*,' Annie snapped back. 'She went without her own food yesterday to give us a treat. Though God only knows why she bothered for *you*.'

Frank grunted again and stabbed a slice of meat with his fork. 'She must be living like royalty then.'

'I work hard for me living,' Bridget cut in, trying to quell her rising anger. She mustn't cause a scene in front of her aunt.

Annie returned to the table and glowered her disapproval at Frank. 'And 'tis but two slices each, Frank Brannigan, so watch your manners.'

The meal continued in silence, until Frank scraped back his chair. 'Aye, a nice bit of mutton,' he said, pulling on his outdoor clothes again. When the door banged behind him Annie sighed with relief.

'Thanks be! He's not even having his usual pipe the night. We'll have a nice quiet time together, luv.'

Bridget bit on her lip as she got up to wash the dishes. 'I'm so sad for you, Auntie. I wish he was nicer to you.'

Annie's face creased with pain as she eased herself off her chair. 'Aye, there was a time when he treated me right, but that was afore we were married and afore he started drinking so heavy. 'Tis the devil's brew that ruins many a man.'

As Bridget set the enamelled bowl on the table and filled it with water from the kettle, she wondered if Tom drank.

On her next day off, Tom took Bridget to Morpeth. They wandered hand in hand along the clean cobbled streets and she'd never felt so happy. The pretty stone houses and impressive tall buildings in town enchanted her.

Tom laughed at her 'oohs' and 'ahs' and said, 'It's nowt but a little market town, you daft thing.'

'But so pretty and clean it is. I wish me auntie lived here.' She paused as a thought struck her. 'But Nellie does! And isn't that handy now? We could go calling on her. I haven't seen her since she got wed.'

Tom pulled a face. 'Don't be daft. Why would I want to see Nellie? I asked you out 'cause I wanted to be with *you*. You can see Nellie on your own. Maybe when the nights get lighter you could call on her after supper, but not on your day off with me.'

Bridget smiled. 'And that reminds me, Tom. It's wondering I've been how you get the same day off as me twice in a row.'

Tom chuckled. 'Now that's a secret. I've got ways of working things.'

'You must've had to swap with somebody.'

'And what if I did?'

They were passing a tea room and Tom stopped. 'Let's have a cup of tea and some grub now. Me belly's been complaining for the last hour.'

Bridget raised her eyebrows in surprise. 'Honest to God, Tom Banks! 'Tis extravagant you are. We can wait till supper at the house. Sure, I'm quite used to me belly complaining.'

Tom pulled her by the hand. 'I'm not going to let it complain when you're out with me. And anyway, I like spending me money on bonny lasses.'

Bridget allowed herself to be led into a pretty room dotted with small tables with white cloths. Several pairs of eyes turned on them: fashionable women with dainty hats on their coiffured curls perched on the ends of their chairs, their tea gowns with extravagant bustles and skirt frills taking up most of their seats. The bustles and frills alone would afford enough material for a frock. The men, in stylish worsted suits with matching waistcoats, fancy shirts and starched wing collars, looked like the dummies in tailors' windows.

Tom pulled out a chair for Bridget and she sat, clutching her cloak about her. 'I'll take that,' he said, seemingly unperturbed by the stares. 'You'll feel the cold when you go out.' He helped her off with her cloak and, head high, marched to the hall stand near the entrance. He hung up the cloak and took off his overcoat, returning in his patched corduroy breeches and sackcloth waistcoat. Bridget thought he looked more handsome than any man in the room.

A young waitress approached carrying two menus. She wore a starched white apron over her black dress and a disapproving expression on her pretty face. She dumped the menus on the table and left.

Bridget fixed her eyes on the shiny menu and kicked Tom's foot under the table. 'Holy saints, Tom, let's be going,' she whispered. 'This place is too grand for me. Sure, I've never been waited on in me life. And it's too nervous I am to eat with all them fancy folk staring at us.'

'Aw Bridget!' Tom didn't bother to lower his voice. 'Stop being so scared about everything. We're as good as anybody here and it's high time you started telling yourself that. You're the prettiest woman here by far.'

''Tisn't so, Tom. And please keep your voice down. Look how grand they're dressed and how they glare at us. And that waitress looking down her nose at us and all.'

'We're staying. Now what would you like to eat?' Tom shook out the white napkin and tucked it under his chin.

Bridget gave in and picked up the menu. 'All right, if we're staying, would you be needing any help with this?' She eyed the menu discreetly.

'Nah, I can manage this much.' He ran his finger slowly down the list.

Bridget scanned the menu for the cheapest item. 'I'll have tea and bread and butter.'

'No you won't, lass. I know why you're saying that. I'm having a toasted teacake and strawberry jam. And you have whatever you like.'

'The same then.' She put down the menu and folded her hands on her lap as the waitress approached, her chin set at a haughty tilt.

'What do you want?'

'Two teas, luv, and two toasted teacakes with strawberry jam.' Tom grinned disarmingly at the girl and she flushed before she flounced off. He gave Bridget a satisfied look. 'There you are, you see. There's nowt to it. I can't stand snobs, and I can't stand folks that's afraid of them. You've got to be proud of yourself, Bridget – especially with all those blessings you got from the Lord.'

Despite her embarrassment Bridget smiled. 'And talking of the Lord, Tom Banks, when are you going to let me start converting you? So far you haven't let up talking long enough for me to get a word in on the subject.'

He raised his eyes to heaven. 'Aye, well, there's time enough for that. You'll have to break me in slowly like. The Lord wouldn't want you pushing me into it afore I'm good and ready.'

She cast a furtive glance around the room and was relieved that most people had resumed their chatter and were ignoring them. 'And when will you be good and ready, pray? Conversion takes a long time.'

A wicked grin stretched like an elastic band across his face. 'I'll have to get acquainted with you a lot better first, to find out if it's worth changing me beliefs for you.'

In her earnestness she clasped her hands on the table and leaned towards him. 'But you haven't got any beliefs, so how can you change them?'

'Aye, I've got plenty of beliefs all right. One of these days I'll tell you some of them.' He took her hands on the table. She flushed and pulled them away as the waitress arrived. Surly-faced and silent, she set their food before them.

'Ta, hinny,' Tom said to her, grinning at Bridget as the girl turned an arrogant back. 'I think she expected me to call her ma'am.'

They both giggled and embarked on their teacakes, Tom's conversion forgotten for the moment.

It was growing dark when they walked home. Though tired and footsore, Bridget felt exhilarated. It had been a wonderful day. And she marvelled that Tom seemed to like her so much. Hand in hand, they neared the cart track to the servants' entrance. But he led her aside towards the wooded area at the foot of the lawns fronting the house. It remained unfarmed. The Haywards didn't wish to mar their splendid view with fields of crops.

Bridget panicked. Slight though her knowledge of men was, her instinct told her that the woods at night were a dangerous place to be. She held back. 'Tom, where are you going?'

Tom laughed at her frightened tone. 'Where do you think? I just want to spend a couple of minutes alone with me lass afore we go in.'

'But isn't it alone we've been all day?'

'Aye, but not like this.'

He drew her close and tilted her chin. She felt his lips touch hers and her head reeled. Holding hands was nothing compared to this. She found herself reaching up to him, but pulled away, breathless.

He grabbed her back. 'What did you do that for? Didn't you like it?'

'Yes, yes, Tom,' she said, agitated. 'But 'tis not right. Me auntie says I should be knowing you proper before I let you kiss me.'

He chuckled. 'And what's knowing me proper then?'

She flushed and was glad it was dark. 'Well, to be sure, it means knowing you better than I do at this minute. Let's be getting home now.'

'As you wish, m'lady.' He let her go with reluctance and led her into the open. 'I can see you're not one that can be rushed. But just how long is it going to take you to know me better?'

Bridget laughed. 'Indeed, about as long as it'll be taking me to convert you.'

Chapter Six

Bridget made her way down to breakfast. She'd never felt so happy. The cloudy winter skies had finally relented and it was a beautiful April day. A gentle spring sun peeked through little pillows of white clouds. It was her day off. She and Tom planned to spend it walking by the river and lazing in the sunshine. They would save some of their breakfast for a picnic at lunchtime.

'Hello, luv.' Tom took her hand as she joined him at the table. In order to have a few minutes alone they always arrived early for breakfast.

As always when he held her hand, Bridget glowed with pleasure. But she searched his face and frowned. 'Good morning to you, Tom. And why is your face on the floor this beautiful day? You look as though you've lost a shilling and found a penny. Sure, isn't it our day off and all?'

'Aye, it *was* me day off, but not any more.' His voice was like a petulant schoolboy's and Bridget's happiness vanished like a puff of steam.

'Oh, no, what's happened?'

'The groom's ma's took ill sudden and he's got to go home. He's leaving in an hour. He said I could have half an hour off after breakfast, but that's not like a whole day. And I was that looking forward to you singing and dancing for me again.'

She squeezed his hand and gave him an encouraging smile. 'Oh, 'tis a crying shame! And such a wonderful day it was going to be! But cheer up. There's still time for me to give you a little song or dance maybe.'

After breakfast, Bridget's arm tucked in Tom's, they strolled to their favourite spot by the stream. Shielded by a grove of elm trees, it was

52

private and peaceful. The willows on the bank trailed their branches in the water, curving like green snakes as they yielded to the flow.

Bridget sighed. 'How I love this place. I could spend a whole day just walking along the bank and listening to the water, and the birds, and the trees.'

Tom sat on the grass and pulled her down beside him. 'Aye, well you'll *have* the whole day to do that. At this minute I've got other things in mind.'

'Tom! 'Tis broad daylight.' She wriggled away. 'Indeed, we can't be kissing and cuddling now. Someone might see us.'

Tom pulled her back and held her round her waist. 'Nah, nobody ever comes down here, and anyway, it's sheltered against nosy parkers. Give a poor lad who's got to work all day a kiss then.' Bending, he kissed her mouth gently and, as usual, she melted at the touch of his lips. His fingers ran through her hair. On her days off she always left it loose to please him. He held her in his arms, his hands tracing the curve of her back. She trembled with delight. But when the pressure of his mouth increased and his hands strayed to her bodice, she pushed him away, breathless.

'Is it a million more times I'm having to tell you not to do that, Tom Banks?'

He pulled a face. 'Aw, Bridget, there's nowt wrong in it. I only want to touch you, that's all. Why would God make kissing and cuddling so nice if it was a sin?'

She smothered a smile. 'Now, stop your blarney, Tom. The only time you ever mention God is when you're after making me do something sinful. To be sure, I don't think you're ever going to be converted.'

'You might manage it easier if you were nice to me.' He tickled her nose with a blade of grass and grinned.

Bridget's laugh tinkled. 'Save your breath to cool your porridge now. And hadn't you better be getting back to the house?'

Tom groaned. 'Aye, I'll see you at dinner then.' He kissed her forehead and rose, turning to wave before he disappeared behind the trees.

Bridget lay on the grass with a sigh. She'd been so excited about this day. But she would make the best of it. She would walk into Morpeth to see Nellie, whom she still hadn't seen since her marriage. For the moment, though, it was bliss just lying on the soft grass listening to the stream and the birds.

On impulse she took off her boots and shuffled a few inches further down the bank to dip her feet in the water. Oh! It was cold – but nice. Invigorated by the sharp sting on her ankles, she hoisted her skirt higher and stood, crying out with discomfort and pleasure. As she paddled and splashed like a child she found herself singing:

> *If I could spend my time on a bright hillside*
> *With nobody near but an Irish colleen*
> *I would be courting her with fond embraces*
> *And wouldn't that be a fine way to be*

Carried away, she didn't hear the sound of horse's hooves.

'Good day to you,' a male voice boomed down at her from the bank. 'And what might you be doing on my land?'

She froze with fright, then raised her eyes to see a middle-aged man in riding habit mounted on a fine black stallion. Good Lord! It must be the master. Perplexed, she dropped her skirt in the water, but not before Richard Hayward had eyed her finely shaped bare calves and ankles.

'Oh, sir! I'm sorry, sir. Sure, I didn't know we weren't allowed here.' Dear Lord! She hoped she wouldn't lose her job. 'I'm one of the servants – a scullery maid,' she added, remembering that Nellie had said he didn't usually make trouble for scullery maids. She scrambled up the bank and pulled on her boots.

His gaze rested on her pink cheeks, her curtain of shining curls, and he smiled. His face was ordinary, ruddy and square; his eyes, despite his smile, a dull brown; and his teeth slightly crooked – not half so nice as Tom's. He was not at all what Bridget had expected the gentry to look like. Except for his fine array and magnificent mount he could have been one of the servants.

'What's your name, girl?' His voice sounded like gentry all right, refined and haughty.

'Bridget Brannigan, sir. And it's me day off. I'm not skipping off work, sir.'

He dismounted, tethered his horse to a tree, and strode towards her. Of medium height, he was thickset, with a paunch almost as big as her uncle's.

She jumped to her feet, her boots still unlaced.

'You have a sweet voice, Bridget,' he said, his eyes scouring her. 'And what was that pretty song?'

She blushed. 'Thank you, sir. 'Tis called "The Irish Girl".' She curtsied and turned to leave but he beckoned with his hand.

'It's all right, Bridget, you don't need to go. Sit down a while. I like to get to know my staff. You must be new. Come and talk to me.' He sat on the bank and patted the grass beside him.

He wanted to talk to her! A scullery maid! She couldn't believe her ears. It must mean he wasn't going to cause any trouble about her trespassing. Yet a vague feeling of anxiety snuffled about her like a cold-nosed rat as she sat by him. She kept a respectful distance.

'How long have you worked here?'

'Just since February, sir.'

He inched closer. 'So that's why I haven't seen you before. You're too pretty to keep hidden below stairs, Bridget.'

She flushed and bent her head. 'Thank you, sir. Indeed, I hope one day to get a promotion.'

'I'm sure you will, Bridget.' He moved even closer and pulled a small silver flask from his pocket. After taking a sip, he offered it to her. 'Have some, it'll warm you up after that cold water.'

She smelled whisky and tried not to grimace. 'No thank you, sir.' Though still longing to escape, she couldn't leave without his permission.

'How old are you, Bridget?'

'I'll be sixteen next month, sir.'

'Sweet sixteen, eh? That's a good age to be. It's a time to have fun before you get married and settle down.' His eyes slid over her, taking her in from head to toe. 'I'm surprised a pretty girl like you spends her day off alone.'

'I was supposed to be seeing me lad, sir, but he had to work.' Feeling increasingly uncomfortable, she looked down at her clenched hands in her lap. Did all masters talk to their servants this way?

'So you've got a lad, eh? One of the staff?'

'Yes, sir. He's a stableboy.'

'Then you're not so innocent as you look.' He stared at her in the same strange way her uncle did.

Bridget inched away. 'To be sure, I . . . I don't know what you mean.'

'Of course you do, Bridget. You've got a boyfriend. You're bound to know.' His face was flushed and his thin-lipped smile spread to a leer. She tried to get up but he pulled her down, pushed her back on the grass and leaned his heavy body over her just as her uncle had done. Fear compressed her like a vice.

'Please, sir . . . please, sir, no—'

But his mouth was hard on hers, his weight pinning her down. She

55

tried to struggle, to no avail. She was trapped in his grip. Tears ran down her cheeks and her eyes pleaded, but he was carried away. He eased his body up for a second, his hand frantically pulling at his riding breeches. Bridget took the opportunity to scream. But his other hand clamped over her mouth. She felt him fumbling with her skirt and wriggled helplessly. This excited him even more. His breathing became laboured and, forcing her knees apart with his legs, he thrust his body wildly between her thighs. She hammered on his chest with her fists, but he pressed down on her, burying her beneath his bulk. Suddenly, she felt pain, like a hot knife slashing at her insides. She tried to bite the iron hand over her mouth, but she was powerless. She couldn't even scream, only muffled moans came from deep in her throat. Her eyes screwed shut in agony as she braced herself against the excruciating invasion of her body – over and over again. Dear Lord! Was this what she'd seen animals do – and she'd thought it was play. The musky, sweaty smell of his body sickened her, but the repeated scorching pain in her loins overwhelmed her nausea.

It seemed like a lifetime before he groaned and fell over her, panting like a dog. She struggled for breath under his dead weight. His hand fell off her mouth, but still she couldn't scream, only her moans went on and on. After a few minutes, he recovered himself and knelt to fasten his clothing. He seemed to hear her moans for the first time and glanced at her paper-white face. 'Are you all right, girl?' His voice was anxious. He shook her shoulder and pulled down her skirt. 'Are you all right?'

She opened her eyes slowly and stared up at the sky. Her moaning stopped.

He grunted with relief. 'Thank God! You had me frightened for a moment, Bridget. Now this is our secret, do you hear? If one word leaks out about it, you're dismissed.' He stood and dusted off his clothing. 'I like you, Bridget. If you could grow to like me, we could become good friends . . . and I'd see that you got that promotion you want. How would you like to be an upstairs maid, eh?'

Bridget closed her eyes in despair.

'Well, you think about it. I'm sorry I hurt you. I didn't know it was your first time. The second time it won't hurt, and you'll like it, Bridget.'

Suddenly she found her voice and wailed, 'No . . . no . . . never!'

'Hush, hush,' he said. 'Not a word to anyone, do you hear – or both you and your boyfriend will be looking for new jobs.'

She bit her lip and nodded before turning her head into the grass and sobbing. She didn't even hear the horse gallop off.

When her sobs abated she didn't know how long she'd lain there. She must take hold of herself. She must get clean. It took every ounce of her strength to drag herself up. She took off her boots and lay in the stream, gasping as the icy water engulfed her. She spread her thighs and cried out as the water stung her scorched, defiled body. Closing her eyes, she held back her head to let the water lap over her face and scalp, the lips he'd kissed, the hair he'd touched. Would she ever feel clean again? Such shame! Would God ever forgive her?

Shivering, she climbed out and, barefoot, walked blindly along the bank. Her wet clothes clung to her. She couldn't go back to the house like this. Maybe if she waited till after midday she could sneak up the back stairs while the staff ate. She trudged on until the sun told her it was past noon. Like a furtive criminal, she made her way to the house. Her timing was right. She heard chatter from the kitchen. Tom would be in there waiting for her. Dear God! She could never see him again. Head down, she hurtled up the stairs, fresh tears flowing at the thought of Tom.

'Good Lord, Bridget! What in the world's happened to you?' Mrs Kennedy almost collided with her at the top of the stairs.

Hanging her head, Bridget whispered, ''Tis nothing. I fell into the stream.'

'And is that why you're crying, lass?' She gave her a suspicious look.

Bridget nodded, but Mrs Kennedy was not to be put off. 'Is it that Tom lad made you cry?'

'Oh, no, ma'am! 'Twas not Tom.'

'Well, who was it then, and what's happened to you?'

'Nothing, ma'am, I told you.'

'I don't believe you, Bridget. Just look at you – soaked to the skin and crying! And where are your boots?'

'Oh, I forgot them. I left them on the bank.'

Mrs Kennedy's lips disappeared into a tight line. 'Bridget! You're not telling me the truth. Come with me. I'll dry your clothes and get you a hot cup of tea, then you can tell me all about it. If one of the staff's been up to mischief I need to know.'

'No, ma'am, I swear 'twas none of the staff.' Bridget allowed herself to be led down the stairs and into Mrs Kennedy's bedroom.

'None of the staff, eh?' Mrs Kennedy's eyes narrowed as she seated Bridget by the fire. ''Twas *him* then, wasn't it?'

Bridget swallowed hard and feigned innocence. 'Who, ma'am?'

'Come on, girl, you can't fool me. I've been here long enough to know what he gets up to. How much did he do to you?'

Bridget put her hands over her face and moaned. But Mrs Kennedy's kindly tone forced her to speak of the horror she'd decided to hide from the world. 'Oh, I'm so ashamed!' she wailed. ''Tis a mortal sin he did to me. Will God ever forgive me?'

'Lord in heaven!' Mrs Kennedy clapped her hands to her face, then bustled out to the kitchen and shouted to no one in particular, 'Bring me a cup of tea. I'm too busy to eat just yet.' In the few seconds before a tap on the door announced the tea's arrival, she'd whipped a blanket off the bed. 'Get those wet things off and I'll get the tea.' Mutely, Bridget obeyed. Mrs Kennedy opened the door just wide enough to take the teacup, muttered a gruff thanks and slammed it shut. 'Here, get this down you and you'll feel better, hinny.'

With shaking hands Bridget took the cup, spilling most of the tea in the saucer. Mrs Kennedy knelt beside her and helped her. 'Jesus be! Such a state you're in!'

Bridget managed to take a few sips before pushing the cup away. 'Thanks be to you. That's all I want,' she said through chattering teeth.

Mrs Kennedy sat in the chair opposite and sighed. ''Twas the master, wasn't it? You've no need to defend him. It's by no means the first time he's had his way with the servants, though there's some as do it willingly for promotion – or money. I know you're not that kind, Bridget. Just tell me, now – did he go all the way?'

At the memory, Bridget's face contorted with pain. 'He forced himself into me. Dear God, I didn't ever think such a thing was possible. And how it hurt!'

Mrs Kennedy clamped her eyes shut in horror. 'Dear Lord! You poor bairn! As if you haven't been through troubles enough.'

At the sympathy in the woman's voice Bridget's eyes again filled. 'I don't know what I'll be doing with meself now. I can't stay here and I can't go back to me auntie's, excepting for visits. She can't go out to work when I'm there. She has to stay in to look after me.'

'And why does she have to do that?'

Bridget lowered her eyes. 'Me uncle tried to do the same thing. Only I didn't know what it was he was after then.'

Mrs Kennedy's mouth fell open. 'Saints in Glory! You're going to stay here, Bridget. There's ways of making sure it won't happen again.

Just never go outside on your own. He doesn't come below stairs. You're walking out with Tom Banks, aren't you?'

'Yes, ma'am.'

'Well, Tom's a bit of a lad with the lasses himself, but I take it he hasn't been a trouble to you. Just you make sure when you go out that you walk with Tom or one of the girls.'

'Oh, ma'am!' Bridget clapped her hand to her mouth. 'I couldn't ever walk out with Tom again. I'm too ashamed.'

'*You* ashamed! You've got no cause for that, Bridget. 'Tis that bugger should feel the shame. He forced you! You did nothing wrong, do you hear?'

'But I was paddling in the stream with me feet and legs bare and singing. I shouldn't have done that. It wasn't ladylike. And he must've thought—'

Mrs Kennedy broke in: 'Stuff and nonsense, Bridget! As if a young lass can't enjoy an innocent plodge without men lusting after her. You don't carry any sin on your soul – just you remember that. And there's no reason why you shouldn't see Tom.'

Bridget shook her head. 'Never! I'd feel bad, ma'am. To be sure, I could never bring meself to tell him and that would be the same as a lie – a sin of omission.'

'Bridget! How many times do I have to tell you? 'Twas not your fault it happened. You must learn to put it behind you. There's no guilt you should be feeling.' She raised her eyes to heaven. 'The Lord knows what happened, and to Him you're still as innocent as the day you were born. That's all that matters now.'

Bridget sighed. 'Indeed, I'd like to believe that.'

Mrs Kennedy rose and turned back the wool bed cover. ''Tis true, Bridget. I'd say you needed a bath, but it seems you've flushed yourself out already. Now I want you to lie down here for a while and rest. You'll feel better if you can sleep.'

'But I can't sleep in your bed, ma'am.'

'And why not, lass? Do as I say.'

Bridget obeyed and Mrs Kennedy covered her with the bedspread. Before leaving, she hung the wet heap of clothes over the line across the mantelpiece. 'These should dry while you rest, hinny. And I'll pop in later with some food for you.'

Bridget's face crumpled. ''Tis so kind you are to me, ma'am. I don't know how to thank you.'

'By pulling yourself together, Bridget, that's how. You must try to put this out of your mind and start again. You've got a long life ahead of you, lass.'

When the door closed, Bridget shut her eyes, made the sign of the cross and prayed aloud: 'Thank you, Lord, for making Mrs Kennedy so good to me, and I promise I won't ever let anything bad like this happen to me again. Amen.'

Chapter Seven

Richard Hayward sat in the library after lunch and looked out disconsolately at the early May sunshine. He felt tempted to go riding and postpone telling Mildred his plans. But no! He'd put this off long enough. He stood and poured himself a port. It wasn't going to be easy. But he must do it. And now. He pulled the bell by the fireplace and a liveried butler entered.

'Henry, would you please tell your mistress to join me.'

The butler bowed and retreated. Richard sat by the fire with his port, lit a cigar and puffed heavily.

Angry at having her afternoon nap disturbed – and by a summons, no less – Mildred Hayward made her way to the library. In her late thirties, she had the look of a woman worn out before her time. Her large powdered face sat like an egg in a cup in the frilly high collar of her gown. Barely a hint of her earlier comeliness remained, her idle life and indulgences having taken their toll. Her heavy eyelids hooded her pale blue eyes as if from too much sleep, and her mouth, though still full, already drooped slightly. Her single remaining claim to beauty was her hair. Blonde and elegantly coiffured into a mound of ringlets on top of her head, it bounced as she strode across the room. She panted slightly from the restraint of her corset, though her bearing was that of a woman accustomed to giving orders rather than taking them. She sat opposite her husband, carefully rearranging her velvet skirts. 'What's so important that it can't wait till teatime? You disturbed my afternoon nap.' Her voice contradicted her lacklustre appearance. It rang with force and, at that moment, betrayed her annoyance.

Richard rose to refill his glass. 'I wish to talk to you alone. I'm sorry to have to do this, Mildred, but I've been thinking about it for a long time, and now I know I must do it before it's too late.' He sat again and looked straight at her. 'I want a divorce.'

'A divorce!' Mildred couldn't have looked more horrified if he'd said he was about to behead her. 'Richard! You can't be serious! How could you even think about such a thing after all these years?'

He sipped his port. 'Yes, Mildred, it's been fifteen years – and ten since you bore me a daughter. That's my point. You know I need a son, and it's obviously not going to happen now. I owe it to my family to keep the line going.'

Mildred couldn't argue against this. She must use guile to win him back. 'But I'm not too old to bear another child. We can try harder. We could start today, Richard.' She spoke in a soft, seductive voice and looked at him from under her pale eyelashes. But Richard shook his head.

'I've no more time to wait and hope, Mildred. You've been a good partner, I don't deny that. You're an excellent hostess and you know your place as a wife. You've never interfered in my private life and we've grown used to each other. But you've failed to give me the main thing I've wanted all these years. I must face reality. I'm not getting any younger, and I want to live to see my son grow up and take over the estate. I need a young, fertile wife.'

At the finality of his tone, Mildred blanched. But outrage overtook her reason. 'You couldn't do such a thing! You'd have to prove I'd committed adultery. You could never do that. My reputation is impeccable.'

'There are ways and means, Mildred.' Richard's voice was calm. 'With money anything is possible. Of course, I'll see to it that you're well provided for. You could have a house in London if you like.'

'And Margery? What about her?' Mildred's bosom rose and fell with indignation.

'She's ten years old. She can decide which of us she wants to stay with.'

Mildred put her hand to her head and lay back in the chair in a semi-swoon. Life without Richard! Though he wouldn't believe her if she told him, she couldn't tolerate it. Despite their lifeless marriage, she'd never quite lost those first feelings she'd had for him. He was a necessary part of her life. But he was capable of anything. And the disgrace of it! A divorced woman – ostracized by society for the rest of her life. No! She wouldn't let him get away with this. She collected herself and sat up. 'I'm absolutely not going to let this happen, Richard. I'll do everything in my power to stop you.'

Richard flicked his cigar ash into the fire. 'Stop me? Since when have you the right to stop me, even if you could?' He rose and placed his hands on the marble mantelpiece, his back to her, a gesture that told her he considered the matter settled. But *she* did not.

'I'll slander you. Don't think I've been blind to all your affairs over the years. I simply ignored them to keep life smooth and—'

'Yes, yes, Mildred.' Richard took another sip of port. 'I grant you that. But my affairs are already well known, my dear. Nobody blames a man for having the odd fling, especially when his wife is frigid – and barren.'

Mildred flinched as if she'd been struck a blow. She'd thought she'd managed to conceal her distaste for the marital bed. She swallowed deeply and spoke more calmly. She mustn't let him get the better of her. 'If I'm frigid, as you say, Richard, why would I want an affair with another man? You contradict yourself. Everyone knows who the unfaithful one is.'

He turned to face her coolly. 'We've covered that, Mildred. It poses no problem, I assure you.'

'I suppose you've already got some little hussy lined up to take my place,' she hissed.

'Not exactly, though I have thought of a likely candidate.'

'And what if she doesn't want you? If she's young and pretty, why would she want to marry a fat, ageing philanderer like you? And as you get older she'll start having affairs herself and causing you trouble.' She paused, regretting her outburst. Insults would get her nowhere. Her voice turned pleading. 'I've never created any scandal. I've been faithful to you all these years.'

Richard nodded. 'I agree your conduct has been exemplary, and I know a young girl will be harder to control. But there's many a little maid I've pleased in my time beyond their wildest expectations, my dear. They tell me I have the knack. Although, of course, you wouldn't know anything about that.' She winced, but he relit his cigar and went on. 'And there's always the money. No woman can resist that. If you remember, you were attracted by it.'

She shot up her chin. 'I'll see to it that you're ruined first.' Yes, she would. If she couldn't keep him.

'My dear,' he said as if talking to a child, 'you'd better get it into your head that the Hayward name has been established for centuries. There've been blackguards in it from time to time but that only makes it more interesting. Nobody would accept your word against mine.

63

Your family can barely afford to run their London town house, let alone their paltry estate.'

She winced again. He was right. She must go to her chamber and think. 'I refuse to listen to any more of this, Richard,' she said, rising. 'You won't get away with it. My family may not be as wealthy as yours but they hold clout in high places.'

'Your family?' Richard dismissed the threat with a look of derision. 'I'd hoped you wouldn't take it so badly, Mildred. But you *will* see sense. I assure you, though your house will be smaller, your life will be no less comfortable. I'm truly sorry to have to do this but I have no choice.'

'Spare me your sympathy, Richard.' She held her head high as she strode to the door. But when she reached her chamber she flung herself on the bed and wept.

How could he do this to her? Since their first meeting she'd wanted him. Her fiancé had been killed in a riding accident and, at twenty-four, she'd done too many seasons to be considered a catch. She'd been flattered by his attentions. It was, of course, in his favour that he was rich, but he'd also been handsome then, and charming and considerate. Until their wedding night. And what a revelation that had been! Though nervous, she'd been excited at the prospect of the conjugal bed and all its mysteries. But after his hasty and painful assault on her body he'd returned to his chamber, leaving her devastated in her discomfort and disappointment.

Since then she'd endured his attentions and had been relieved when they'd become less frequent. Some time later she'd discovered he was gaining his satisfactions from other women. Even so, she still loved him, though she'd never been able to show it. She even had trouble showing affection for her daughter. She'd settled for the luxurious life Richard provided and the status of being his wife, immersing herself in her social activities and becoming the most fashionable hostess in the county. And now he was planning to take even that from her! There had to be a way to stop him. She wiped her eyes on her lace handkerchief. Yes, she would think of something.

Three weeks later Bridget met Tom early at breakfast. She looked pale and drawn.

He took her hand as she sat down. 'You're looking a bit peaky, Bridget. Are you poorly? You haven't been yourself for a while.'

''Tis a stomach upset I've got, that's all.'

'Well, I've got something to cheer you up.' Tom's eyes twinkled as he delved into his pocket and placed a small box before her. 'Happy birthday, Bridget Brannigan!'

She smiled, unable to bring herself to tell him that her birthday wasn't until the following day. 'Oh, Tom!' she said with genuine delight. 'How did you remember it was me birthday? And chocolates! Indeed, you shouldn't be squandering your money on luxuries for me. I've never had such a grand present in all me life.'

He puffed out his chest with pride. 'I've been counting up the dates the whole month. Look!' He fumbled in his pocket and thrust a crumpled sheet of paper at her.

She glanced at the clumsy figures – many crossed out and altered – and stifled a smile. ''Course you did,' she said, crossing her fingers under the table so that God would understand it was only a white lie. 'Today's the twenty-sixth.'

Tom looked very pleased with himself. 'Go on, have one afore breakfast.'

But as she opened the box of rich milk chocolates her stomach turned over. She gritted her teeth, but the rising tide of nausea overwhelmed her and she ran outside with her hand over her mouth.

Bewildered, Tom followed her. 'What on earth's the matter with you?'

Still with her hand over her mouth, she waved him away and dived into one of the privies, just in time.

When she came out he still stood open-mouthed. 'Good God, lass! Don't try to tell me there's nowt wrong with you.'

'I've just been sick again. I told you, 'tis only an upset stomach.' Her voice was thin.

He took her arm and they walked back to the house. 'You look really poorly, Bridget. You shouldn't be working the day.'

'Sure, a little sickness doesn't stop me working. It'll wear off as the day goes on.' But she gripped his arm for support as they walked back to the kitchen, where breakfast was in progress.

May, the first scullery maid, grinned as they approached. 'Don't tell me you two's been hanky-pankying afore breakfast.' But her grin vanished when she noticed Bridget's white face. 'Eey, you look poorly, luv. Are you all right?'

'Sure I'll be fine. 'Tis just a little sickness. It wore off yesterday.' Bridget looked at her bowl of now cold porridge and grimaced. 'But it's no breakfast I'll be having today – just a cup of tea, I think.'

May's blue eyes searched Bridget's, her thin face anxious and her wide mouth open in dismay. 'You didn't tell me you was sick yesterday.'

'Oh, it was nothing much.' Bridget waved her hand to dismiss her friend's concern and sipped her tea.

'Well, if you say so, but you look terrible poorly. I hope you're right.' May bit on her bread and pointed a skinny finger at the chocolates. 'What's them doing there? It was all I could do not to scoff the lot, but nobody knew whose they were.'

Tom gave her a warning look. 'You keep your mucky hands off them. That's her birthday present from me.'

May turned to Bridget in surprise. 'But I thought you said your birthday's—'

''Tis today, sure enough.' She silenced May with a kick on the shins.

Bridget excused herself before supper and went upstairs to lie down. An hour later May bounded in. 'You've hardly touched a bite all day. I'm going to ask Mrs Kennedy for something for your stomach. You'll never be fit for work the morrow at this rate.'

'Please don't be bothering Mrs Kennedy,' Bridget begged. 'I'll be fine after a good rest. And anyway, 'tis me day off tomorrow.'

May pulled herself up to her full five feet and glared at Bridget in defiance. 'Aye, and the way you look, you'll be spending it in bed. I don't care a bugger what you say. I'm getting you something for that stomach whether you like it or not.' She neatened her blonde hair, straightened her mobcap and marched off to approach the housekeeper.

When May knocked on the door Mrs Kennedy was knitting by the fire in her sitting room. 'Who is it?'

'It's May, ma'am.'

'Come in, lass. What is it?'

May closed the door behind her and stood to attention. 'I haven't come for meself, ma'am. It's Bridget. She's been bad the last two days and she's hardly eaten nothing. She keeps being sick. I thought you might have something to settle her stomach like. She's right poorly, ma'am.'

Mrs Kennedy put down her knitting with a frown. 'Bridget?'

'Yes, ma'am.'

'Is she too bad to come herself?'

'Well, no, ma'am. She's worked all day, but she's just having a lie-down now. She wouldn't come herself. That's why I come.'

'I'm glad you did, May. Ask her to come this minute. I don't want to give her anything till I know better what ails her.'

'Yes, ma'am.' May bobbed and retreated. She almost ran up the steep three flights and panted to Bridget, 'She says you've got to go down to see her. You'd better tidy yourself.'

Bridget sat up in her bunk. 'Glory be! Why is it you couldn't leave well alone, May? I'm just tired now. To be sure, I don't want you doing any more interfering.'

May's pretty face looked crestfallen. 'It was for your own good I done it.'

Bridget relented. 'I know that. I'm sorry I got cross.' She trailed to the dresser, splashed her face and pushed her hair under her mobcap.

Mrs Kennedy's sitting room door was open. She looked up from her knitting when Bridget tapped on the doorpost. 'Come in, Bridget, and close the door.' She beckoned her to the opposite armchair. 'What's this I hear about you being sick?'

Bridget perched on the edge of the chair. 'Indeed, I've only got a little stomach upset, ma'am. 'Tis May making a big fuss about it, not meself.'

Mrs Kennedy looked closely at her. 'How many days have you felt sick?'

'Only three, ma'am. But it wears off after the mornings. I just feel a bit tired now. I'll be fine tomorrow.'

A dark shadow of dismay spread over Mrs Kennedy's face. 'And when was your last bleeding?'

Bridget flushed. 'Why, I don't know what that's got to do with it, ma'am.'

'It could have a lot to do with it, Bridget. When was it?' Mrs Kennedy's tone was firm but gentle.

'I can't remember exactly, ma'am. I never count up. Me . . . er, monthlies often go queer when I get upset.' She pondered for a moment. 'It must be six or seven, maybe eight weeks now. I haven't thought about it.'

'Have you had one since that . . . that day the master touched you?'

Bridget stiffened at the mention of that terrible day. 'No, I surely haven't, ma'am.'

'And when you've got upset and missed your bleeding afore, did you ever feel sick?'

'No, ma'am. I've always had a strong stomach. 'Tis a funny thing for me to be sick, especially when I've never had such fine food in me life.'

Mrs Kennedy took a deep breath and let it out slowly. 'Bridget, do you know anything about how babies are made?'

Bridget bowed her head. 'No, ma'am. But I know it happens mostly to married women, and when it happens to one who isn't married 'tis called a bastard child.'

Mrs Kennedy clasped her hands on her lap and leaned forward, her voice low. 'I don't want to scare you, Bridget, but you should know. It's the same thing the master did to you that makes babies.'

Fear, like a rat gnawing at her insides, gripped Bridget. 'You mean? Jesus, Mary and Joseph!' She clapped her hand to her mouth.

'Now then, don't fret.' Mrs Kennedy rose and put a comforting hand on Bridget's shoulder. 'Lift up your skirt and let me feel your belly.'

Trembling, Bridget obeyed, and Mrs Kennedy stroked and prodded her gently. 'Nah,' she said, 'you feel a little bit bloated but that's probably just being late and having an upset belly. I want to keep an eye on you just the same, though. Let me know how you're feeling every day, and tell me immediately if the bleeding starts. In the meantime, I'll give you something to help the sickness.'

'So, is it that I could be having a baby that's making me feel queer?' Bridget's voice was hushed.

'I can't deny it's possible, but don't start worrying about it just yet. It'll be another week or two afore we can know for sure, but I don't think so.'

Despite Mrs Kennedy's soothing words, panic overtook Bridget's fear, sweeping through her being like gusts of fire. 'But ma'am! What if it's true there's a baby growing in me belly? What is it I'm going to do? And it'll be *his* – the master's. Indeed, 'tis better dead I'd be than having that monster's child.' She clutched herself and rocked back and forth, moaning. But Mrs Kennedy calmed her.

'There, there, now, Bridget. I told you not to trouble yourself about it just yet. I'll see that you're all right – if the worst is true. Now you go and get some rest.' She took a bottle of green liquid from the mantelpiece. 'I got this for you. It's only peppermint, but it'll settle your belly.'

Bridget nodded her thanks and trailed up the stairs in a stupor.

That night she dreamt she held a tiny baby in her arms and placed it in a drawer before going to work. When she returned, the drawer was empty. Riddled with guilt and shame at her neglect, she searched frantically in other drawers, under the bed, on top of the wardrobe. But the baby was gone.

Three weeks later she again sat in Mrs Kennedy's sitting room, having submitted to more probing of her belly.

Mrs Kennedy lowered herself into her chair, her forehead creased like a washboard. ''Tis a fact, luv, and you'll just have to accept it. It's three months now, and you *have* got a rise. I'm not very experienced in these matters but I know that much.' She spoke softly, then clenched her fists in anger. 'God Almighty! That it should happen to you of all people! And that heathen bastard up there getting off scot free.'

Bridget felt the walls close in on her like the sides of a coffin. 'Are you certain?' she whispered, tears trembling on her eyelashes.

Mrs Kennedy nodded. 'Aye, luv. I wish I wasn't. But I've been thinking how I could help you if the worst happened. Sure, it could've been me when I was your age, except that the master's poor dead father was a better man than him upstairs'll ever be.'

As usual, Bridget stiffened at the mention of the master. 'Dear God, dear God,' she said, her eyes filling with tears.

'You're not the first he's got into trouble, I'm sure,' Mrs Kennedy went on. 'There's been a few in me time as left of their own accord and went back to their families – better that than get fired with no references. They never said, of course, but I had me suspicions.' She paused, looking uncomfortable. 'You understand I'm telling you this in confidence. 'Tis not me place to talk about the master's doings. But in your case it's different – you already know what he's like and you need to know the situation.'

Bridget nodded and wiped her eyes on her apron. 'And why would I be telling anyone about him? 'Tis the devil's grip I'm in. I must've done something terrible for God to heap such troubles on me. Sure, I don't want to go on living.'

'Now don't talk like that, Bridget. I've been preparing for the worst and I've got a plan for you. It's the rule that if an unwed servant begets a bairn, she's sacked. But I'll see to it that you're not. I'm going to talk to the mistress.'

Bridget's mouth gaped. 'You're not going to tell her 'twas the master?'

Mrs Kennedy shook her head. 'No, Bridget, though the Lord knows I wish I could. But I can say you're me kin, that just afore me sister died she sent you to me to look after you, and that I can't send you out

69

in the streets when you're in a condition. I'm a good housekeeper and I've got another twenty years' work in me. She'll not be wanting the bother of finding a replacement – that lazy she is. I think she'll agree.'

'But 'twould be a terrible lie to tell her I'm your kin. I couldn't be letting you do that for me, ma'am.'

'A white lie indeed, Bridget!' She made the sign of the cross. 'The good Lord will forgive me that one. And the rest's mainly the truth. I'll tell her I found you afterwards, all crying and upset, and saw the proof on your clothing that you'd been . . . attacked. We'll just say it was a man you never seen afore, so you couldn't tell me who it was. It's not like the mistress is one of us, but she's a woman. She must have some compassion in her. I'll tell her if she'll let you stay on and have the bairn I'll cover your food out of me own pocket. And it would be no skin off *her* nose to let you have a room to yourself downstairs. There's plenty lying empty just collecting dust.'

Bridget's mouth felt dry, as though it were stuffed with cotton wool. 'If you say so, ma'am. But I don't know why you'd be going to all this trouble for me.'

Mrs Kennedy managed a smile. 'You're a good girl, Bridget. I knew that from the minute I clapped eyes on you. You remind me so much of meself at your age. And now, wouldn't it be a grand thing for me to have a niece and a grandbairn I could call me own!'

''Tis that kind you are to me, ma'am. Indeed, I don't know that I deserve it.' Bridget's torment mingled with gratitude, until she suddenly remembered her nightmare about the baby stored in a drawer. She shook her head. 'But I can't see how it could happen, ma'am. I'd have to go on working for me living and I couldn't work and look after a little one at the same time. I couldn't leave it by itself.'

Mrs Kennedy nodded. 'Aye, I know that. But when you're well enough to work again you could take off in shifts to feed it. Though I'm sure the mistress would insist you give up your days off in return for the favour. And while you're working there's always plenty about could keep an eye on it, especially me. There's nowt I'd like better.' She managed a smile of encouragement. But Bridget remained unconvinced.

'And what about the disgrace?' she said, her voice rising. 'Me being an unwed mother! Surely to goodness the mistress wouldn't want a bastard child about the place.'

'Now, don't you be calling it that! And I've told you, I'll deal with the mistress.'

70

Bridget's lower lip quivered. ''Tis for certain I don't deserve all your kindness, ma'am. I could save you all this trouble and go back to me auntie's.'

'Does your auntie know what happened?'

Bridget lowered her head and knotted her hands in her lap. 'I couldn't let on to her, ma'am. I was too ashamed to tell her. And I haven't seen her since you told me I might be with child. I didn't want to worry her till I knew for a fact.'

'You could never go back to live there, Bridget!' Mrs Kennedy's voice rang with determination. 'What about that uncle of yours? You'd be jumping from the frying pan into the fire. Do you want it to happen again?'

Once more Bridget felt the walls closing in on her. 'Lord knows I don't, ma'am. 'Tis just that I don't want to be putting on you.'

Mrs Kennedy rose and placed her arms round Bridget's shoulders. 'You're not putting on me, lass. Haven't I just told you I want to help you? And you've got to think of the bairn. It'll get fine food and fresh country air. What sort of life would it have if you went back to your auntie's?'

Bridget savoured the comfort of the arms round her and, for the first time, thought of the living creature in her womb. 'You're right, ma'am, even if it *is* that man's child growing in me, I should treat it right.'

'*And* yourself! Tomorrow's your day off, so have a good rest. Will you be seeing Tom?'

At the mention of Tom, a new pain, like a giant hand wrenching out her heart, overwhelmed Bridget. She bit on her lip to quell her tears. 'I can't be seeing Tom again, ma'am, not now that I know for sure. 'Twas guilty enough I felt seeing him and keeping what happened a secret. I've lied to him all this time, letting him think I was still pure.' She paused, her hands plucking at her apron. 'And anyway, he surely won't want any more to do with me when he finds out, and he's bound to if I stay here.'

Mrs Kennedy sighed and returned to her chair. 'Aye, Bridget, you're right. I can't see Tom, or any lad his age, wanting to get stuck with another man's bairn. Do you love him, lass?'

'Love?' Bridget stared into the fire. 'I'm not sure I know what loving a lad means. But I know I feel a deep fondness for Tom – different from the way I loved me brothers and sisters. And he seems to feel something for me. He's very affectionate. 'Tis broken-hearted I am not to see him again.'

71

'What will you tell him then?'

Bridget's mouth suddenly tasted as if she were sucking a penny. She'd thought and thought about what she'd say if the worst happened. But now it was real. 'I plan to say I don't want to be walking out with him again because he won't be converted. And if that's not enough, I'll have to tell him I don't feel for him any more, though that will be hard indeed. But when he sees me with a belly on me he'll be glad not to be courting me.' She swallowed again but the iron taste persisted. 'It's me day off tomorrow. We were going to Morpeth. But I'll just say what I have to say after breakfast and get it over with and then stay in me room.'

'Oh, your poor bairn!' Mrs Kennedy raised her eyes to the ceiling. 'It's more than one trouble that bugger up there's heaped on you.'

Bridget rubbed her forehead to clear her mind. 'Do you think I should write and tell me auntie now, or should I wait till you've talked to the mistress so I can say whether I'll be leaving or staying?'

'You'll know something by tonight, luv. I'm going straight up there after they've had their dinners.'

Mrs Kennedy knocked on the mistress's sitting-room door. She usually retired here after dinner while the master took his port in the library.

'Who is it?'

'Mrs Kennedy, ma'am.'

There was a pause before Mildred spoke. 'I'd rather not be disturbed. Is it urgent?'

'Yes, ma'am.'

'All right, you may come in.' Her voice was peevish.

Mrs Kennedy squared her shoulders before entering. The mistress languished on the *chaise-longue* by the window. She must have overindulged at dinner again, Mrs Kennedy thought. A glass of peppermint linctus stood on the table beside her and she looked listless and miserable. Mrs Kennedy was aware that the master was travelling to Newcastle on some legal business the following day but surely that couldn't be the reason for Mildred's ill humour. The master often went to Newcastle.

She stood at her usual respectful distance and cleared her throat. 'I'm sorry to bother you, ma'am, but I need a word with you.'

'About what?' Mildred asked without interest.

'It's about me niece, ma'am.'

'Your niece? I didn't know you had one.'

'Well, she only came over from Ireland a few months ago. She's been working here as a scullery maid. Something bad's happened to her, ma'am. And if I may be so bold, I'd like to ask a special favour, her being me kin and all.'

'What sort of favour?' Mildred gazed out of the window.

'Well, it's like this, ma'am . . .' Mrs Kennedy embarked on her story, her rehearsed words tumbling out. When she'd finished, Mildred stared intently at her.

'Is this niece of yours walking out with anyone?'

'Yes, ma'am, Tom Banks, one of the stableboys. But it wasn't him,' she added quickly. 'Bridget swears he's done no more than kiss her. She's a good girl, ma'am, I know she's telling the truth. And Tom was working when it happened. That's a fact.'

'I see,' Mildred said slowly, staring past Mrs Kennedy now. 'And she swears it was none of the staff?'

'Yes, ma'am. 'Twas a stranger for sure.'

Mildred sat up, her face suddenly alive with interest. 'A stranger? On our land, you say?'

'Yes, ma'am. It must have been a trespasser.' Mrs Kennedy lowered her eyes.

'You're not telling me the whole truth, are you?'

'Oh, yes, ma'am, to be sure I am,' she insisted, raising her eyes slowly.

A look of triumph lit up Mildred's pallid face. 'It was the master, wasn't it? You've no need to cover up for him. I well know what he gets up to.'

'I . . . I—'

'And don't tell me you don't know what I mean. I want the truth. Be assured there will be no trouble in it for you or your niece.' Mildred's coaxing tone perplexed Mrs Kennedy still further. Fancy the mistress admitting the master's behaviour to *her*! And she even seemed pleased at the news.

'I . . . I didn't mean to tell you a lie, ma'am, but I thought it wrong to tell you the truth.'

'Don't worry. I promise this is our secret. I may have another solution for your niece. Let me think on it. I will let you know tomorrow. You may go now.'

'Yes, ma'am.'

Outside the door Mrs Kennedy paused and let out a deep breath. The interview certainly hadn't gone as expected. The mistress had taken the news very strangely, and she hadn't spoken to her like staff. Puzzled, she made her way back to the basement. What 'other' solution could Madam have in mind? But at least she hadn't refused the request. That was hopeful.

Chapter Eight

On Richard's return from Newcastle the next day, Mildred followed him into the library. 'I need to talk to you, Richard.' He sat at his desk and she took the chair opposite, in her excitement poised like a bird ready for flight.

Richard began sorting through his post. 'If it's about the divorce, you know I've got no more to say on the matter.'

'You will when you hear this.'

'Hear what?' He slit open an envelope with a silver paperknife.

'Mrs Kennedy's niece is with child.'

He looked up and shrugged. 'What's that got to do with me?'

'It's *your* child, Richard.' Her eyes challenged him to deny it.

'What the devil are you talking about? I didn't even know the woman had a niece.'

'She's Bridget Brannigan. The scullery maid you forced your favours on by the stream. Does that stir your memory?' From her tone it was evident she was enjoying herself.

'You're talking rubbish, woman.' He slit open another envelope. But she was gratified to see that his hands shook.

'I know every detail. Mrs Kennedy found the girl in distress just after you'd left her, and there's proof she was pure before you took your pleasure of her.'

'And you take this . . . this scullery maid's word before mine?' He stared coolly at her and drummed his fingers on the desk, his composure regained.

Mildred met his gaze. 'You know I wouldn't normally take a scullery maid's word, but I'd take Mrs Kennedy's word before yours any day. She came to me herself and tried to cover up for you, but I got the truth out of her.'

'So what, if it's true?' He waved his hand in dismissal. 'The girl asked for it, prancing about half-naked.'

Mildred smiled with satisfaction. 'So you admit it's your child.'

'What if it is? I doubt it's the first I've fathered.'

'It could be the son you want, Richard. I've got a proposition to put to you. You say you don't want the trouble of a divorce and a frivolous young wife. If it's a boy we could adopt it and pass it off as mine. That way you'll carry on your line. It will be *your* son.'

'Acknowledge a byblow as my son!'

Mildred curled her lips in distaste. 'Whatever you wish to call it, the girl is carrying your child. It would only mean postponing the divorce a few months to find out if it's a boy. Then you could adopt your own son, you wouldn't have to keep two wives, and we'd continue our lives as usual. You said yourself you find our marital . . . arrangement . . . satisfactory.'

Richard thought for a moment then shook his head. 'Are you out of your mind, Mildred? A scullery maid's child?'

'Mrs Kennedy's a fine woman. And it's *her* niece. I also take it that the girl's pretty or you wouldn't have wanted her. And remember, it's *your* child inside her, *your* flesh and blood. I would feign a pregnancy. No one would know.'

'And what if it's a girl? Have you thought of a way out of that?'

'Absolutely! Then my child would die in childbirth as far as the world knows, and you could go ahead with the divorce. Don't you see?' Mildred tried to quell the pleading tone that had crept into her voice; she mustn't lose ground now. 'No one would know. You would have your own son in just a few months. And I wouldn't have to go through the shame of a divorce. The girl would leave immediately "of her own accord" and after she's gone I'll see that her young man is fired. The servants will draw their own conclusions. I shall make no mention of the stableboy yet, of course. The girl may be fond of him and it could sway her decision.'

Richard stroked his chin, deep in thought. 'You're a scheming witch, Mildred, but you've got a point. It's a fifty-fifty chance but, if it *is* a boy, it would be an easy solution. I suppose a few more months wouldn't make much difference.'

'Then you agree?' Mildred looked triumphant.

'Not exactly, I'm simply saying it may be worth considering. But we'd have to cover it up. Have you thought how to go about it? And what if the girl doesn't agree? Sometimes they want to keep them – or they change their minds later.' Despite his doubt, Richard began to sound interested.

'There will be no problems, Richard. As you so often say yourself, money talks. And yes, I've thought of ways and means. I'll talk to Mrs Kennedy. We'll pay her niece fifty guineas to keep her condition secret, and we'll send the girl away to the midwife in Morpeth. They can all be silenced with money. If it's a boy, we'll pay the girl another fifty guineas on signing the adoption papers. If not, she still keeps the fifty guineas.'

'Hmm.' Richard twisted the paperknife still in his hands. 'So, you think she'll agree?'

'She's sixteen and penniless, Richard. Talk sense! What unwed girl in her right mind would want to go through the disgrace and hardship of bringing up a bastard child – particularly the child of a rape – when she has an offer like that? Either way, it's a fortune to her. If the child is a girl the niece can afford to go away somewhere and start a new life.' She stood up, her expression like that of a fox that had just caught its prey. Now she would go for the kill. 'I will go to my room and summon Mrs Kennedy. After I've put forward my proposition she can talk to her niece. I have no wish to see the girl – ever.'

Five minutes later Mrs Kennedy appeared at the open drawing room door. Mildred, seated in a wing chair by the window, beckoned her enter. 'Come in and close the door.'

'Yes, ma'am.' Mrs Kennedy stood before her, wondering again why the mistress looked so pleased about this affair.

'I have a proposition to put to you,' Mildred began, rearranging her skirts and sitting back in her chair as far as her bustle would allow. 'My husband and I will adopt the child.'

'Adopt it?' Mrs Kennedy squeaked in surprise.

'Let me lay the offer before you. As you must know, my husband needs a son to carry on the family line – and this is his child.'

'But . . . what if it's a lass, ma'am?' Mrs Kennedy interrupted, forgetting her place in her amazement.

'Let me finish,' Mildred said curtly. She continued to lay out her plan while Mrs Kennedy listened, stunned.

'The arrangement will be kept secret, you understand. The child will be passed off as my own.'

'I . . . I see, ma'am,' Mrs Kennedy said when Mildred had finished. 'I don't know what to say. I'll have to talk to Bridget first.'

Mildred gave her a confident smile. 'I'm sure she'll agree. What girl in her position could refuse such an offer? She must leave immediately, on whatever pretext you wish. I shall make arrangements for the midwife in Morpeth to take care of her. The girl must be kept out of sight. Of course, you may visit her,' she finished, adding icing to the cake.

'Yes, ma'am. I'll tell her, ma'am.'

'See that you do, and return immediately.' She stood to end the interview.

Dazed, Mrs Kennedy retreated and hurried upstairs to the servants' quarters. Bridget lay on her bunk staring at the ceiling. She pulled herself up as the housekeeper entered.

'I've got some news for you, lass. Surely to God things never go as we expect them to.' She sat on the bunk to regain her breath, her hand rising and falling on her chest.

Bridget looked alarmed. 'Jesus, Mary and Joseph! Is it more bad news you have, ma'am?'

'Sure, 'tis not bad . . . but strange . . . a far cry from what we expected.'

Bridget listened to the tale, astonished. 'Glory be! Should I agree, ma'am? Indeed, 'tis too surprised I am to think at this minute.'

Mrs Kennedy sighed. 'Well, Bridget, it *is* an unusual offer, but you've got to do what'd be best for you and the bairn. I think you'd be well advised to take it.' She looked crestfallen for a moment. 'There goes me dream of having a grandbairn about the place! But I'm just being a selfish old woman. Don't you see, hinny? If it's a boy, he'd be one of the gentry and have the sort of life you could never give him, and nobody would know your disgrace. And if it's a girl, fifty guineas would be a blessing to help feed and clothe it. Not many unwed mothers have that sort of luxury.'

But Bridget looked doubtful. ''Tis right enough you are, ma'am. A generous offer it is, but I feel queer about it. Those upstairs are heathens. The boy wouldn't be brought up Catholic, and that would be a sin on me conscience for the rest of me life.'

'Bridget Brannigan!' Mrs Kennedy's voice rose in exasperation. 'I know well what you were brought up to believe, but life's not all black and white like you were taught, and you'll learn that as you get older. I married a "heathen" as you would call him, and he was the best man I ever came across – a right saint. I know for certain he's up there now.' She pointed her finger to the ceiling. 'And he'll be looking down on you and smiling at your youthful ignorance. You've got to forget that silly nonsense that only Catholics go to heaven. You'll find out when you get up there that you'll meet all sorts – even *me*. If only the Lord forgives me for fiddling with the food bills.' An attempt at a smile creased her face like tissue paper. But Bridget couldn't smile back.

'I'm that sorry if I upset you, ma'am,' she said. 'I know I'm just a silly young lass. Me auntie said the same as you about Tom. And you're both a lot wiser than me. But 'tis hard for me to put everything I was taught at school and at church out of me mind all of a sudden.'

Mrs Kennedy patted Bridget's knee. 'That's all right, lass. It's fine for you to hold those notions for yourself if you want to, but it's wrong to place judgement on others just 'cause they don't believe all the same things you do.'

'Sure, I promise I'll remember that from now on.'

'That's good, hen. I know 'tis not my place to make decisions for you, but what do you think now about the bairn?'

Bridget lifted her chin with determination. 'You're right, ma'am. At least the little one would never know the pangs of an empty belly like me little brothers and sisters.' As she spoke a deep sadness overwhelmed her. ''Tis queer, me dead little ones are more alive and real to me than this living thing *he* put inside me. But I must do what's best for it.'

Mrs Kennedy nodded. 'Aye, 'twould be folly to refuse such a chance, especially as me other plan for you wouldn't work any more, now that the mistress knows the truth.'

Bridget bit her lip and thought for a moment. 'Indeed, the money would be a godsend to me auntie and all. I could go back there afterwards and she wouldn't have to work at night, and we could eat good food. 'Twould solve a lot of problems.'

'Aye, it would, hinny. I'm glad you see the sense of it. But I'd be right sorry to see you go back there. It wouldn't solve the problem of your uncle. You'd have to stay out of his way. And always keep a pepper pot in your pocket to throw in his eyes if he lays a hand on you. That'll stop him long enough for you to get away.'

Bridget shuddered. 'But me auntie would be home at nights. I'd never be left alone with him.'

'Aye, but just in case, it doesn't hurt to be sure.'

Suddenly, sadness at the thought of leaving Mrs Kennedy overwhelmed Bridget. 'You've been that kind to me, ma'am. I'll never forget you.' She struggled to hold back her tears.

'It's not goodbye yet, lass. I'll be visiting you while you're with the midwife. And if it's a girl child we could visit each other. I'd love to see the bairn grow up.'

79

'Thank you, ma'am. I'd like that . . . but 'tis ashamed I'd be to come back here with a little one. All the servants – and Tom – would know my disgrace.'

'You've got to learn to hold your head up, Bridget. What does it matter what the servants think? And Tom . . . well, time will have passed by then, and time heals.' She took a deep breath and her bosom rose almost to her chin. 'I'd better tell the mistress you've agreed, and I'll be asking her if you can have three days to go to Newcastle afore you go to the midwife. She can't refuse such a small request.'

'Oh, thank you, ma'am. I'd love to see me auntie, but I'll have to tell her the truth. I couldn't lie to her. And she'll find out anyway if it's a little girl.'

'That's all right, Bridget. You can't hide it from your kin. Her upstairs won't know nowt about that.'

Before breakfast the following morning, Bridget sat alone, waiting for Tom. Now she was glad she hadn't told him about her situation, for she was able to soften the blow. Deep in thought, she jumped when she felt a hand on her shoulder. 'Oh, you startled me, Tom.'

He grinned down at her. 'Daydreaming, are you?'

She silently asked God's forgiveness for the lies she was about to tell. 'Tom, I just got word this morning, I've found a better position in Newcastle. I'm leaving today.'

His mouth fell open as he slumped beside her. 'Newcastle! But that means I'll hardly never see you.'

Bridget could barely speak for the lump that blocked her throat. ''Tis for the best we never see each other again, Tom.'

He stared at her in disbelief. 'But *why*, Bridget? And why didn't you tell me this afore?'

'Haven't I just told you, Tom? I only heard this morning. 'Tis sorry I am, but it has to be God's will.' Her lower lip trembled and she was close to tears. God's will! Was it God's will that one burden wasn't enough for her to bear – she also had to suffer losing Tom?

'Aw, you and your God!' He thumped his fist on the table and glared at her. 'Everything bad that happens you blame on Him, yet you still worship Him and think everything He does is for the best. It just doesn't make sense to me.' Then he looked suddenly wretched, like a condemned man. 'I've grown right fond of you, Bridget, and I know you were growing fond of me. It's not right that you go away.'

'That's why 'tis better I go away, seeing as you're never going to be

80

converted.' Bridget hoped God would forgive this one lie, or at least be pleased she'd tried to convert a heathen.

'But . . . but you could keep on trying,' Tom insisted.

She shook her head. 'Me mind's made up, Tom.'

'You're going to end up like one of them nuns.' Tom's voice was angry again. 'No man's going to want a woman that thinks going to church is the most important thing in life. What about loving somebody – and them loving you?' He lowered his eyes. 'I had a fond hope that you were growing to feel something for me.'

'Oh, I . . . I was. I mean . . . I do.' Her stomach churned as she groped for words. He was trying to tell her he loved her and she was casting him out of her life. She wanted to fling herself into his arms and tell him the truth – maybe he would understand and forgive her and they could be together forever. But no, she could never tell him her shame. He couldn't possibly love her if he knew she carried another man's child inside her. She heard her voice saying quietly, 'I feel a deep fondness for you, Tom, and I'll never forget you. But, we're too . . . too different. I've given me notice and me new life is planned. You must understand.' Her voice begged.

He looked at her with hurt in his eyes and shook his head. 'I swear I'll never understand you, Bridget. But I'll miss you. I never thought I'd get this struck by a lass.' The rest of the staff began arriving, and his teeth etched a white line on his lower lip. 'And now I won't even have a chance to say goodbye to you alone.'

''Tis better not, in any case. Sure, I'd probably cry.' She imitated a smile. 'Now the others are here I can say goodbye to you all at once.'

Later that day, still nauseated from the bumpy cart ride, Bridget let herself into her aunt's flat and left her small bundle of possessions in the passage. She wanted to break the news to her aunt gently. The gold coins in her pocket jingled as she made her way down the passage to the kitchen.

'Heavens above!' Annie started with such surprise the potato she was peeling dropped with a plop into the bowl.

'Hello, Auntie, I'm sorry if I startled you.'

'Eey, it's a grand startle indeed.' Annie wiped her hands on her apron and returned Bridget's embrace. 'I'm that pleased to see you, luv.'

'And me you, Auntie.'

Suddenly Annie pushed Bridget away, her welcoming smile fading.

'But nowt's wrong, is it? I mean, why aren't you at work? Are you all right, lass? You look like a washed-out dish rag.'

'I'm fine, Auntie. Mrs Kennedy got me some special time off. 'Twas just the cart ride made me queasy.'

'Aye, you look sickly right enough. Come and sit by the fire. I wish you'd let me know you was coming. I've got hardly nothing in the house.'

'I didn't know till today. I've come 'cause I've got something to tell you.' Bridget sat and embarked on her story, hoping to get it over before Frank came home.

Annie listened in shocked silence, punctuated by moans of despair. Only when Bridget had finished did Annie explode in outrage. 'Them rats!' She shook her fists in anger at the ceiling. 'Just because they was born rich they think they can do what they like with other folk's lives. God help you, me poor bairn. But you know you've always got a home here, whatever happens.'

'I know that, Auntie, and I thank you.' Bridget pulled the bag of coins from her pocket and held it out. 'And this'll pay for me keep . . . and for the little one.' She swallowed hard. 'I mean, if it's a girl. And it'll help you out and all.'

Annie waved the bag away. 'No, hinny, never! That's for you to keep. You'll be needing it more than me in any event.'

Despite Bridget's entreaties, Annie remained adamant. But Bridget had the last word: 'Well, if you won't take the money, I'll just have to buy things for you.'

'And where am I going to tell your uncle they came from? Put that bag away afore he comes home and sees it. Do you want him swilling it away in ale? He's not going to know nothing about that money, ever, and nothing about this whole business – unless it's a little lass and he has to know.'

Bridget stuffed the bag back in her pocket. 'Never! Never will he be getting a farthing out of me! But I'll find a way to look after you, Auntie.'

Chapter Nine

Bridget stared out of the window in the midwife's small cottage, where the mistress had sent her to live since the agreement had been drawn up. It was a sunny late October day and the kitchen felt like a prison cell. Its low, oak-beamed ceiling and dirty whitewashed walls were relieved only by a small square of light filtering through the single window. She longed to go into the garden to enjoy the fresh air and sunshine. But she was only allowed there after dark. Her belly jumped as the baby kicked and, as usual, sadness suffused her. Even before she'd felt the baby's first movement, she'd begun to love the living child within her. However often she told herself she must not – not until she knew for sure it would be hers – she failed. Every night she prayed for a girl.

'I'm off now,' Mrs Sharp, the midwife, said. 'I've got a couple of calls to make in Morpeth.' True to her name, everything about the woman was sharp: the knife-like nose, the pointed chin, the angular cheekbones, the pinpoint brown eyes piercing Bridget as she spoke. 'Is there anything you want?' she asked, tying her bonnet over her grey hair.

Bridget shook her head. 'No, thank you, I've got more than I need.'

'I don't know how long I'll be. Why don't you have a lie-down?' Even the woman's voice was sharp. It rasped like a hacksaw cutting metal.

Bridget straightened in her chair and rubbed her back. 'Sure, I'd rather *do* something. And the floor needs scrubbing. I wish you'd let me do it.'

'You know the mistress's orders, Bridget. You're not to do nowt but rest. Though you could sit down and peel the potatoes if you like.' She turned to leave and Bridget watched the narrow black back retreating.

Sit down! Peel the potatoes! When she wanted to move and breathe! She trudged to the dresser – only two potatoes left. Then she would *have* to go into the garden. But she knew she was making an excuse. The potatoes could wait until Mrs Sharp returned.

Half an hour later temptation outweighed Bridget's caution and she made her way into the sunshine. The back garden was surrounded by a low stone wall. Beyond lay rolling fields, a patchwork of autumn gold, green and rust. Few people passed this way but Mrs Sharp was adamant about carrying out the mistress's instructions. Bridget sucked in the fresh air and held up her face to the fragile autumn sun. She took the garden fork from the shed and tiptoed between the neat rows of vegetables Mr Sharp tended in his free time. The soft black earth gave easily and she dug until she'd collected a small mound of potatoes. She stood and rubbed her back, surveying her handiwork with satisfaction.

'Bridget? Bridget Brannigan?' a surprised female voice cried.

Bridget turned, her face a picture of guilt and fear. 'Nellie!'

'God almighty! Bridget?' Nellie looked in amazement at Bridget's belly. 'You're . . . you're—'

Bridget rescued Nellie from her embarrassment. 'Yes I am. But 'tis through no doing of me own.' She still wished she could believe that completely, though Mrs Kennedy insisted it was so.

'Oh, Bridget!' Nellie's green eyes filled with compassion. 'What happened? And what are you doing here?'

''Tis a long story, Nellie, and a secret. All I can tell you is that a strange man forced his favours on me, and I know someone who wants to adopt the child if it's a boy.'

Nellie gave her a strange look. 'You're giving it away?'

'I've got no choice,' Bridget said, lowering her eyes. 'And 'tis all a secret. You mustn't tell anybody or there'll be a heap more trouble on me to be sure.'

'I . . . I won't. I promise. But why didn't you go home to your auntie's? Does she not know?'

'Yes, she knows. But I can't talk any more about it, and I can't stay out here. I'm supposed to stay inside. But it was lovely seeing you, Nellie.' With difficulty, Bridget bent to place the potatoes in her apron and made for the door before clapping her hand to her forehead. 'Oh, 'tis terrible I am! I haven't even asked you how you are.'

'Oh, I'm wonderful!' Nellie flung her arms wide as if to embrace life, then dropped them, seeming awkward at showing her own happiness when Bridget was in such a plight. 'But I wish you was better, and I wish it was me with a belly on me and not you. Nothing's happened yet, but I keep hoping every month. I'm working on the farm, just over there.' She pointed towards two stone buildings in the distance, surrounded by fields of wheat stubble. 'I often walk this way home. I live but half a mile beyond. Can I see you again, Bridget?'

'Surely, I'd love that, Nellie. But I'm not allowed to see anyone. And I'd better be getting in before Mrs Sharp comes back. When this is all over I'll visit you, I promise. I've kept the address you gave me. Do you still go home to see your ma?'

'Aye, I'm going in a few days.'

'Then would you be minding telling me auntie you saw me and that I'm doing fine. I write to her but 'tis not the same as word of mouth. Though mind you, don't ask her any questions. She can't say more than me.'

''Course I'll go, luv.'

'Thank you, Nellie. It was grand to see you again.'

Bridget lumbered into the house and stood at the window watching Nellie disappear round the garden wall. She sighed. Would life ever be normal for her again?

That evening Mrs Kennedy paid one of her visits. At the sound of a horse and trap outside, Mrs Sharp gave Bridget a warning look that told her to disappear into her bedroom. Bridget groaned inwardly as she rose. Little though she enjoyed Mrs Sharp's company, being confined to her bedroom was worse. It was more like a cupboard than a room, with barely enough space for the single iron bedstead and only a grimy skylight for a window. She was relieved and delighted to hear Mrs Kennedy's hearty voice, and a few minutes later, her bulky presence filled the doorway.

'Hello, Bridget. How're you feeling?' Her crinkled lips stretched into a warm smile.

'Better now that you're here.' Bridget rose from the bed and hugged her. They'd long since dispensed with formalities and Bridget felt as though Mrs Kennedy were indeed her aunt.

'I brought you some more wool. Pink again!' Mrs Kennedy sat on the bed and smiled again. Like Bridget, she also prayed the child would be a girl.

'Oh, thank you. I've almost finished the last one.' Bridget pulled out a basket from under the bed and proudly showed her latest creation – a tiny pink wool bonnet. She leaned forward, her eyes begging comfort. 'It's going to be a girl child, isn't it? I daren't even think any more about it being a boy. It'd be like losing all me little ones all over again. I . . . I don't believe I could—'

'Hush, now.' Mrs Kennedy stroked Bridget's hand, her voice comforting but her eyes pained. 'You mustn't think on it. Only the Lord knows, and He knows best.' She sighed as if a mountain lay on her chest. 'But I feel that bad. If only I'd had one of me own, I might have known you'd come to love the child, no matter how it was begotten.'

'No, you mustn't feel bad. Neither of us knew then.'

Mrs Kennedy nodded. 'Aye, we did what we thought was best for the bairn, and we mustn't forget that. I'm sure it'll turn out right in the end, hinny. You want to have a healthy bairn, whatever happens, and fretting won't do it any good. Don't look on the black side. And anyway, with both of us praying, the Lord's bound to hear one of us.' She changed the subject. 'Eey, I swear you won't believe what's been going on up there.' She always entertained Bridget with the latest events at the house.

'And what would that be?' She forced a smile.

'Well, Cook burnt the joint to a cinder on Sunday. She had to scrape off the burnt and make it into a hash. You should've heard the rumpus upstairs – especially from Madam – when they were served hash of a Sunday.'

'And how is Madam?'

Mrs Kennedy grimaced. 'Well, that creature's taking things a bit too far if you ask me. She's got her corsets padded enough for twins and hardly leaves her bedroom except at mealtimes. And now she's even started having some meals taken up. She's thoroughly enjoying her "condition".'

Bridget bit her lip. 'I wish *I* was.'

'It won't be much longer now, hen.' Mrs Kennedy patted Bridget's belly. 'You're getting a right size. Looks like it'll come afore Christmas at this rate.'

'I wish it would come tomorrow.' Bridget's upper lip trembled and she burst into tears.

A look of sorrow shadowed Mrs Kennedy's face as she handed Bridget a white handkerchief. 'Now didn't I just tell you that fretting'll harm the bairn?'

Bridget dried her eyes on the handkerchief. 'I try not to, but 'tis hard. And I still can't stop thinking about Tom either. How's he doing?' she asked, still happily unaware that the mistress had fired him the day after she'd left.

'As far as I know, he's fine.' Mrs Kennedy rearranged herself on the bed and avoided Bridget's eyes.

'Does he have another lass yet?'

'Now how many times do I have to tell you? I can't possibly know all the staff's private affairs . . . but I still haven't seen him with a lass,' she added gently.

Bridget suddenly remembered her encounter with Nellie and wrung her hands. She would have to tell Mrs Kennedy. 'I . . . I saw Nellie today.'

'You what?'

'I'm sorry. I know I shouldn't have. But I went into the back garden for some potatoes and she was passing by.'

'Eey, by God! What did you tell her?'

'Just that I didn't know who the man was and that the child was being adopted – and that she must keep it secret.'

Mrs Kennedy let out her breath. 'Well, I'm sure she will, hinny. Nellie's a good girl. But never go out there again.'

As her confinement grew nearer Bridget spent more and more time in her room. She lay on the bed staring up at the skylight, her mind racing in circles. What a terrible thing she'd done! What if it was a boy? If only she'd known she would love the child like this. She prayed to God to show her a way out. At night she would fall into an exhausted sleep and dream she was running for her life, a fox-like animal at her heels. She clasped a bundle to her and ran, faster, faster, until finally, exhausted, she fell to her knees. And when she looked back, she saw the animal crouched and howling in the distance.

After eight excruciating hours in labour, at five minutes to midnight on Christmas Eve Bridget gave birth.

'It's a boy!' Mrs Sharp cried triumphantly.

Bridget's face contorted, anguish overcoming her exhaustion.

'Here, look!' Wiping the baby's face, the woman thrust him in front of her. 'It's a beautiful boy! Oh, the mistress will be pleased. What a grand Christmas present! It's too late to disturb her now. I'll take him over first thing in the morning.'

Bridget looked at the puckered little face and felt overwhelmed with love and despair. 'Let me hold him,' she begged.

'In a minute, lass. I'll just clean him up first.' Mrs Sharp left and within minutes returned with a tight white bundle. 'Here you are. Let's see how he suckles.'

Bridget grasped the little parcel of life and gazed at the face before unwrapping him to see him completely. 'Oh, how beautiful he is!' Her hopeless tears fell on the baby's cheeks.

'Now, put him to you and do as I tell you,' Mrs Sharp ordered.

With shaking arms Bridget held him to her, and when she felt the little mouth against her nipple she cried out, 'He's mine! He's mine! I won't ever let him go!'

'Hush, lass! What rubbish you're talking! You've given him away already. You knew what to expect.' Mrs Sharp's razor voice sliced through Bridget's soul.

'No! No! I didn't! Indeed, I didn't know it would be like this.' Bridget sobbed as the baby began to suckle. 'She can't have him. I won't ever give him up, *ever*. He's mine and I love him.'

Mrs Sharp poked her pointed face at Bridget. 'You're out of your mind, lass. You've made a legal arrangement and accepted money. You haven't got no choice. You'll see the sense of it when you're not so tired.'

'I've still got the money. I'll give it back. And I haven't signed the final adoption papers yet. I can't and I won't!' As she spoke the words, the seemingly impossible dream of escape that had plagued her these past months, suddenly became real. She rocked her body gently, her eyes devouring the baby. 'He's *my* son.' Her voice was adamant.

'We'll see about that! I'll give you a sedative and you'll see sense when you feel calmer.'

'No! Never! Never! I'll never change me mind. All the money in the world couldn't make me give up me own flesh and blood.' Though her eyes were still clouded with tears, Bridget gave Mrs Sharp a defiant look. 'And not you or her or anybody else can stop me!'

'Oh, no?' Mrs Sharp sneered and left the room, returning a few seconds later with a wooden cradle. She squeezed it in the narrow space between Bridget's bed and the wall. 'You'll have him till morning. When the wet-nurse comes he won't need you no more. Put him in there when he's finished suckling.'

But Bridget held him all night, giving him up with reluctance only when Mrs Sharp came to change him. Exhausted as she was, she couldn't sleep, she was too busy thinking how she could possibly keep her son. Suddenly her mind was no longer imprisoned by thoughts of lawyers and legal documents. By morning she had a plan.

Mrs Sharp plunked a tray at the foot of the bed and advanced with outstretched arms towards the infant. 'I've brought you some breakfast. I'll take him now.'

'You can't have him,' Bridget said quietly, clutching the baby tighter.

'Now stop acting yourself, you little bitch. I've got to change his nappy. Then you can feed him one last time. Me man's gone for the wet-nurse and then we're going to the house.'

'No, never!' Bridget pulled herself up to a sitting position. 'As God is my witness, you're not taking him,' she said, surprised by the strength in her voice. It didn't seem to come from her throat, but from some deep, unknown place within her. 'If you take him there the whole of Morpeth and Newcastle and everywhere around is surely going to know about the respectable Hayward family's little scheme. I've saved up enough money of me own to put an announcement in the newspaper. They can have their dirty money back. But if they try to fight, 'tis certain I'll use every farthing of it to pay a solicitor. I'll pay it back somehow. And there's other people knows the truth that'll back me up. Even one of your own neighbours saw me in the garden with a belly on me. Now the mistress wouldn't want a scandal like that, would she?'

Mrs Sharp looked as if she'd been kicked in the face by a wild horse. 'You scheming little bitch,' she hissed. 'You went out to the garden deliberately.'

'No I didn't. I went to get some potatoes. I wasn't out but five minutes, but 'twas lucky for me.' Bridget spoke with an air of victory, enraging Mrs Sharp further.

'You . . . you couldn't never do such a thing! Who would take the word of a slut like you against the mistress's?'

Bridget looked Mrs Sharp calmly in the eye. 'I've got proof. I've got the fifty guineas. And now where would a girl like me be getting that sort of money?'

'She'd say you stole it.'

'She can't say that.' Bridget almost smiled in satisfaction. 'I've got more than that – a signed paper from the mistress, a promissory note she called it, for the rest of the money when the adoption papers were signed – if the child was a boy. She was that eager to do it all proper and legal like so that I couldn't change me mind. But now I *have* changed me mind! And I don't give a tinker's farthing about lawyers. I can use the paper against her.'

Mrs Sharp's pinpoint eyes seemed to pop out of her face. 'You wouldn't dare!'

'Oh, indeed I would.'

The woman's voice rose in fury. 'I'll talk to the mistress. She won't let you get away with this.'

'Let her try. She can't stop me.' Calmly, Bridget put the baby to her breast, just as the sound of the horse and trap announced Mr Sharp's return with the wet-nurse. Mrs Sharp looked immeasurably relieved.

'That's them back now. I'm going straight to the mistress to tell her about your . . . your treachery. She'll get the better of you, you little trollop.'

Bridget searched her new son's face as he suckled. Yes, she thought happily, he looked like a Brannigan.

Still agitated, Mrs Sharp drove the trap at a gallop to the main gates, her delivery bag beside her. This must look like an official visit. When the butler answered her knock, she assumed a voice of authority. 'Please announce to the mistress that I'm here.'

It seemed like an eternity before Mildred's chambermaid appeared in the hall and announced that Madam would see Mrs Sharp. She jumped up from the settle where she sat and scurried after the maid. She wondered if the girl knew the truth. Surely she would have to, being the mistress's personal maid. No doubt she was another one being paid for her silence.

'Mrs Sharp, madam,' the maid announced, then withdrew unobtrusively.

Mildred was sitting up in bed, her breakfast tray on her lap. She greeted Mrs Sharp eagerly. 'Is it good news?'

'Well, yes, and . . . no, ma'am.' Mrs Sharp felt stumped for words. She would certainly be in trouble for delivering such a message.

'Well, what is it, woman? Get on with it,' Mildred snapped.

Mrs Sharp took a deep breath before relating her story.

Mildred's face grew pink, then purple with fury. 'The conniving little slut!' she screamed when the woman had finished. 'She won't get away with this!'

'I'm sure she won't, ma'am. I knowed you'd have a way around it.'

'There must be many ways.' Mildred's voice was filled with venom. 'Leave me to think on it. How dare that brazen little harlot think she can outdo me! I will send for you when I'm ready. But in the meantime, it looks good that you paid me a visit. And one thing is sure, whatever happens, that scheming little brat will regret this till the day she dies.'

* * *

90

After Mrs Sharp's departure Mildred rang for the maid and had Richard summoned to her bedside.

He stood by the bed, listening in stunned silence. Then he paced the room. 'I should have known your plan wouldn't work, woman. I warned you that sometimes women change their minds about these things.'

Mildred's features knotted and her manicured fingernails dug into the satin eiderdown. 'Oh, how could we have been so stupid! We should have had her sign the adoption papers at the time of the agreement. We shouldn't have waited until we knew it was a boy.'

'Afterthought! Afterthought! What good does that do now? And anyway, she could still have changed her mind and caused a scandal.' Richard stopped pacing and turned to her. 'Perhaps if we increase the offer she'll see sense.'

Mildred considered for a moment. 'First I intend to send Mrs Kennedy to talk to her. We'll double the final payment to a hundred guineas. The slut would be crazy to refuse that. But if she *is*, we'll go up to a hundred and fifty. I think it better I talk to Mrs Kennedy alone, Richard. Please go now.'

Five minutes later Mrs Kennedy stood at the foot of the bed and listened in dismay to Mildred's news. 'Dear God, ma'am! I don't know what to say. It sounds to me as if she's made up her mind, and if I know Bridget, more money won't make a bit of difference to her. But I'll go and talk to her, of course.'

'Do anything you can, do you hear?' Mildred's voice rang with the force of a hammer striking an anvil. 'Whatever she wants – within reason of course – she can have. Go now and hurry back.'

'Yes, ma'am.' Mrs Kennedy retreated in a daze, the mistress's words 'whatever she wants' imprinted on her mind. She took the trap she was allowed for her personal use and drove, deep in thought, to the cottage.

Mrs Sharp answered her knock and ushered her into the bedroom, placing herself in the doorway. 'I pray to God you can talk some sense into the little harlot,' she said in a voice shrill with anger.

'I must talk to her alone.' Mrs Kennedy dismissed the woman with a look and closed the door in her face.

Bridget's eyes filled at the sight of her friend. 'Oh, I'm so glad to see you. Come and look. Isn't he beautiful?' She unwrapped the bundle and Mrs Kennedy bent to look, cooing with delight.

'Oooh, now isn't he a bonny little lad! I swear he's going to be like you, Bridget.'

Bridget beamed with pride. 'I think he is already. Would you like to hold him?'

'Eey, I would that, hinny.' Mrs Kennedy rewrapped the sleeping baby and held it gently, rocking it to and fro with tears in her eyes.

'I suppose the mistress has sent you to get me to change me mind.' Bridget set her mouth in a tight line.

'Aye, that she has,' Mrs Kennedy whispered. 'And keep your voice down. I'll bet that old crow's got her ear to the door.'

'I couldn't do it, Mrs Kennedy. I . . . I was awake all night thinking on it. I just couldn't be giving him away. I suppose 'tis a sin to break me word, but I know now 'twould be a bigger sin to give away me own flesh and blood. God'll forgive me, I'm sure.'

Mrs Kennedy sat on the bed, still searching the sleeping baby's face. 'Aye, I know how you feel, luv. Just looking at him, I know I couldn't do it either. But I've got to tell you the mistress's offer. That's what she sent me for.'

'More money?' Bridget set her mouth even tighter and shook her head. 'All the money in the world couldn't buy him, not now that I know what it's like to have a son.'

'Aye, she offered more money, but she also said you could have anything else you wanted, within reason, that is.'

'There's nothing I want except me son.'

Mrs Kennedy sighed. 'Well, let's just talk sensible for a minute, hinny. I've been thinking all the way here what's best for the bairn and you, and I think we can work something out. I don't need to remind you what a hard life for both of you it would be if you keep him, and what a grand life he'd have as the gentry.'

Bridget bowed her head. 'Is it selfish you think I'm being, wanting to keep him for meself and bring him up poor and fatherless?'

'No, luv, it's natural. But hear me out. The mistress said you could have what you want within reason. It's a scheming old witch I'm turning into, but I don't think she's in a position to refuse if you said you would let her have him so long as she employs you as his nursemaid.'

'His nursemaid!' Bridget's eyes grew wide in amazement.

'Don't you see? That way you would bring him up and be with him all the time. Indeed, the gentry never bring up their own bairns anyway. And just think – he'd have the best life in the world.'

'But I couldn't bring him up Catholic.'

'Now haven't we been through all that before, Bridget? What a lot of baloney those nuns taught you! I've lived long enough to know that good people go to heaven and bad people go to hell, no matter what their religion. And you could still teach him about God. Think sensible! Would you rather have your son grow up a half-starved Catholic bastard – and you well know how Catholics feel about bastards – or a respected member of society, with a full belly to boot.'

Bridget winced. 'Oh, I can't bear to hear him called that.'

Mrs Kennedy looked penitent. 'I'm sorry, luv. But it's the truth. I'm only trying to make you see sense. I've had to do a lot of quick thinking since I saw the mistress.'

'Yes, yes, 'tis the truth you speak. But at first, when I still thought of him as *that man's* son, it didn't seem so bad that he wouldn't be Catholic. Now that he's mine 'tis a harder thought to bear.' She sniffled and wiped her eyes with the back of her hand. 'But I'll just have to bear anything that's best for him.'

'Aye, it's hard on you, luv. But you'd be with him all the time and that would make up for a lot.'

Bridget couldn't quite take in the new plan. 'But . . . what about when he grows up and doesn't need a nursemaid?'

Mrs Kennedy gave her a sad smile. 'When they grow up they get married and leave you anyway, hinny. But he would stay on as master of the estate. And you could still see him. You're in a position to insist that afterwards they keep you on as an upstairs maid, perhaps a serving maid in the dining room. You'd see him at mealtimes. And as his old nanny, he'll always love you.'

Bridget looked doubtful. 'And what would happen when I'm too old to work? To be sure they'd throw me out then.'

'No, they couldn't do that, hinny. We'd have it all written down legal like, that you'd have your own quarters in the house when you retire. And if I know you, Bridget, that lad'll be visiting you a lot, I'll be bound.'

'I feel that upset at the minute I don't know what to think. But you're much wiser than me. I surely know what you say would be best for me son.' She lay back on the pillows and closed her eyes. ''Twould be selfish of me indeed to deny him such a life, especially as he'd still be mine in a way. And I'd suckle him and all. I couldn't let anybody else do that.'

'Eey, I don't know how we could manage that, luv.' At Mrs Kennedy's doubtful tone Bridget sat up abruptly.

'It could be kept a secret – everything else would be. She could still employ that wet-nurse to pretend.'

'But the woman would lose her milk, hinny, and it's her livelihood.'

Bridget thrust out her chin. 'If she can be bought to do it, she can be bought not to do it.'

'Aye, maybe! The mistress wants this bairn that bad, she doesn't seem to care what she has to do to get it.' She shook her head, frowning. 'I know the master needs a son right enough, but I've a funny feeling there's more to this business than meets the eye. She's the one fighting for it most, yet she never cared for motherhood with Margery. I don't understand it.'

'The master!' Bridget's mouth fell open in dismay. 'And now, what if the mistress did agree and I was taken on as nursemaid, how would I be keeping out of the master's way? What if he . . .?' Her face turned white at the unspeakable idea.

Mrs Kennedy scratched her forehead. 'Aye, I didn't think about that. But, no, I don't think he'd dare lay a hand on you again. She'd see to that and all. She wouldn't want any more trouble. You've already given her a big enough dose of that.' She stifled a chuckle and went on, 'You've got the upper hand there now, luv. If he ever laid a finger on you, you could threaten to tell the mistress. You've got more power over him now than you had the last time.'

'Yes, that's true. I never thought of that.'

A slow smile spread over Mrs Kennedy's face. 'If they want this bairn as much as they seem to, if you ask me, you've got their hands tied behind their backs and their legs around their necks and all.' She clapped her hand over her mouth to smother her mirth lest Mrs Sharp hear her.

Though partly reassured, Bridget's mind still couldn't take in the complicated and drastic step of giving up her son. 'But me own son would never call me "ma". And he'd never know he's me own flesh and blood.' At the thought, her lips quivered.

'Aye, that's true,' Mrs Kennedy conceded. 'But I'll bet you a pound to a penny he'll love you a lot more than he'll ever love that one.'

'Do you really think so?'

'I know so, hinny.'

A new thought occurred to Bridget. She sat up. 'And the staff? What about them? There'd be trouble there for sure. An ex-scullery maid brought back as nursemaid!'

'Aye, you're right there! But there's ways and means around everything. You were nursemaid to your five brothers and sisters since you were ten years old. If that doesn't make you qualified I don't know what does. And we can let the word out that you're me niece and I got you the position. There'll be a lot of jealousy, of course, but I think you can cope with that.'

Bridget nodded. 'Why, I could cope with anything just to bring up me son, healthy and happy, and be with him all the time.'

'And he'd be rich! A landowner and a gentleman! And *you'd* be set for the rest of your life. And just think – I know it's a selfish old woman I'm being – but I'd see a lot of him and all, and of *you*. You know I've grown right fond of you, Bridget. And I could eat this little bairn alive already.' Her eyes misted as she looked down on the sleeping child in her arms. 'It would be almost like what we first hoped for, but better in the end for the little lad. And the easiest and best way for you and all.'

'I know you're right.' Bridget sounded convinced, but suddenly another thought struck her like a blast of cold air. She clapped her hand to her mouth. 'And Tom? What would I be doing about Tom? I couldn't be walking out with him again, and I couldn't ever marry him. I'd have to stay at the house with me son.'

Mrs Kennedy braced her shoulders before she confessed. 'You don't need to worry about Tom, lass. I didn't tell you afore 'cause I didn't want to upset you more than you were already, but Tom's left.'

Bridget's jaw dropped in surprise. 'Left! Why? He liked his job. And he was ambitious.'

'Them buggers sacked him, luv. The day after you left. I don't know rightly what monkey business she was up to, but I suspect it was to lay suspicion on Tom in case anybody guessed or found out why you left. All I know is he went back to Newcastle.'

'Jesus, Mary and Joseph! Poor Tom! And 'twas none of his doing.' Bridget closed her eyes to take in the terrible news. It was several moments before she found her voice. 'Well, in a way 'tis just as well. Not for him, I mean, but for me. I don't think I could bear being near him and not able to see him or touch him again like before. I pray he's found a good job – and even another lass.'

The baby whimpered and Mrs Kennedy stood to rock him. 'Aye, you're a sensible lass. So do you want me to go and put forward your conditions to the mistress? I have a right funny feeling she'll agree to just about anything, she's that desperate.'

Bridget nodded. 'Yes, as you say, 'twould be best for him, and so long as I can be with him all the time just like his own ma, I'll have to be satisfied with that.'

Mrs Kennedy placed the still whimpering child in Bridget's arms. 'You take him then. I'll be off now and come back as soon as I can with the news.'

'Indeed, I don't know how to thank you for all your kindness.' Bridget's eyes again filled as she put the baby to her breast.

Mrs Kennedy pressed her forefinger to her lips, and tiptoeing towards the door, flung it open. 'Aye, I thought you'd be snooping,' she said to a startled Mrs Sharp. 'But I know you couldn't hear anything. It was private business between the mistress and her.'

'And how do you know I couldn't hear nothing? I heard it all,' Mrs Sharp said with a sneer.

'Oh, aye? And that's why you were still standing there with your nose to the door after you heard me say I was going? Just waiting to get your conker bashed in, were you?' Mrs Kennedy grinned with satisfaction as she left.

In a most unladylike tone, Mildred interrupted Mrs Kennedy's speech throughout. 'How dare she! I can't believe the nerve of the little hussy. What she's asking is preposterous!' She fell back on to her pillow after Mrs Kennedy had finished.

Richard stood at the foot of the bed, silent, grim.

Mrs Kennedy cleared her throat. 'That's her conditions, ma'am. She's a strong-minded lass. I know she won't budge an inch.'

'You may go now.' Richard dismissed her with an impatient wave and sat on the bed. 'We shall summon you if we need you further.'

Mrs Kennedy leaned against the door after she'd closed it. She'd witnessed many of the mistress's tantrums in her time but never anything like this.

'Take hold of yourself!' Richard spoke sternly to Mildred, who still sniffled and dabbed at her eyes. 'I know you're upset, but it's disgraceful to put on a show like that in front of the servants. Let's just think calmly about this whole unfortunate business. Maybe we can get around it.'

'Get around it!' Mildred sat up and glared at him. 'Didn't you hear what the woman said? How can we get around that? The girl's made up her mind and that's that! That damned scullery maid's got her head screwed on all right. She knows she's got us cornered.' She clasped her hands till her rings dug into her flesh, but Richard appeared cool.

96

'Yes, we're in a spot. That's why we must be sensible. Now think clearly. As you yourself were so quick to point out in the first place, the child *is* my own flesh and blood. Would you rather have the girl in the house as a nursemaid, *I* have my son, and *you* your position here or . . . well . . . the alternative?'

Mildred looked as if she were about to swoon. He was threatening divorce again! And now it could be worse than that! If the girl didn't get her own way she might talk. Disgrace! And scandal! She was trapped like a snared rabbit. She had no choice but to accept the slut's conditions. The girl was using *his* son to buy herself a secure position in this house for life. 'All right,' she said at last. 'She shall have her way. But I'll see to it that she knows her place with me. She'll get her keep and the same as she earned as a scullery maid – not a penny more. And needless to say she must return the fifty guineas.'

Richard pulled a cigar from his pocket and lit it thoughtfully. 'Yes . . . yes, you know she doesn't care about the money. And I'm quite sure you *will* keep her in her place, but I suggest you calm down now.'

'Calm down, you say! When a scullery maid is laying down *her* conditions to *us*, forcing us to accept her under *our* roof!' A new thought occurred to Mildred and she looked closely at Richard. 'Surely to God you wouldn't dream of going near the girl again, would you? After all this?'

'Do you take me for an utter fool, woman? I've got better fish to fry than that little troublemaker.' Richard jumped up and marched to the door. 'I'm going to the library to draft the agreement and then I shall summon the lawyer. Christmas Day or not, that boy will be legally mine by tomorrow.'

Chapter Ten

Bridget rocked Anthony Richard Charles Hayward's cot and cooed, *Tooral ooral oral, tooral ooral ay.* As always when she sang to him, his round hazel eyes looked up at her with delight. At five months, he was a chubby, cheerful baby. And Bridget was happy. Despite having to deal with the mistress's rancour, which showed no signs of abating, looking after Anthony was a constant joy. She set him in his cradle and stroked his chestnut curls. 'Now you go to sleep, little one. 'Tis well past your nap time. And after that I'll be taking you for your outing. Go bye-byes now, there's a good lad.'

His mouth spread into a gummy grin, revealing the first signs of his two front teeth, like tiny seed pearls set in coral. His dimpled legs kicked off his blankets. Bridget shook her head in mock despair and tucked him in again. 'All right then – one more song. How about "The Irish Girl"? You like that one, don't you?' He chortled as if in affirmation, and she began:

> *If I could spend my time on a bright hillside*
> *With nobody near but an Irish colleen*
> *I would be courting her with fond embraces*
> *And wouldn't that be a fine way to be*

His transparent eyelids fluttered, the dark lashes like silk fringes against his cheeks. Bridget devoured his sleeping face and smiled, then tiptoed out to the nursery playroom. Mrs Kennedy would be coming to take tea with her any minute – one of Bridget's favourite times of the day.

A few minutes later a knock on the door heralded the tea's arrival. 'Come in, Nancy,' she called to the wet-nurse. Nancy acted as assistant nurserymaid instead of in her official capacity. And so far, none of the

98

servants had discovered the conspiracy.

'Teatime,' Nancy said as she set the tray on the table between the two rocking chairs by the fire.

'Thank you, Nancy, but Mrs Kennedy isn't here yet. I hope she's coming.'

'Aye, I just seen her and she said she'll be up in a minute.' Nancy brushed back a lock of fair hair from her broad forehead with the back of her hand. A stout woman in her late thirties, she looked exactly as Bridget had imagined a wet-nurse. Constant suckling had taken its toll on her body and her large bosom hung almost to her waist. She'd confided to Bridget that she was delighted to have a change from her usual occupation. This job would last several years and after that she'd be too old to give milk anyway. She peered into the cot. 'Ah, sleeping like an angel!'

'Aye, but I fear not for long. You might manage a short nap before he wakes up.' On the rare occasions when Bridget left Anthony's side, Nancy took over.

After the first outrage at the ex-scullery maid being hired as nursemaid, most of the staff had gradually accepted Bridget in her new position. After all, she *was* Mrs Kennedy's niece, and Mrs Kennedy ran the house. Nobody could really blame her for looking after her own kin. Even the most resentful had to admit that without Mrs Kennedy their own lives would be much less comfortable.

'Hello, luv.' Mrs Kennedy's breath came in short gasps after climbing the three flights. 'How's me bonny lad the day?'

'Livelier than ever. I had a job to get him off.'

Mrs Kennedy peeked into the cradle before sitting heavily in one of the rocking chairs. 'Has she seen him yet?'

Bridget pulled a face. 'Indeed, she hasn't set eyes on him for almost a week. But she's asked to see him before his walk this afternoon. The master came up yesterday though.'

Mrs Kennedy pursed her lips in disapproval. 'She'd better start taking more interest in the bairn soon. You'd think she'd at least have sense enough to put on a better show. If she's not careful he's going to grow up without even knowing she's supposed to be his mother.' She clasped her hands on her round stomach, rested her feet on the brass fender and rocked in her chair.

Bridget rose to pour the tea and grimaced. 'It would be fine by me if she never saw him. But I can't be that selfish. At least his father pays him some attention.'

'Aye, but still not enough! And where's Margery?'

'In the schoolroom with the governess, and then she's got a piano lesson. She hardly ever sees Anthony either.' Bridget shook her head, puzzled. 'When I think how I loved me little brothers and sisters when I was her age I just don't understand why she's jealous.'

'Aye, that one's a right chip off her mother's block all right – selfish as they come. Ta, luv.' Mrs Kennedy took the cup Bridget handed her. 'And I think I'll have one of those currant scones.'

Bridget passed her the scone plate and sat opposite, nursing her cup. 'And would you by chance have any fine downstairs gossip for me today?' She smiled in anticipation of one of Mrs Kennedy's entertaining tales.

'Eey, well, not from downstairs! But I've got some good news.' In her excitement she almost choked on her scone crumbs. 'I seen Nellie in Morpeth yesterday and she's finally done it. At long last she's got a bun in the oven and she's tickled pink about it.'

Bridget's eyes lit up with pleasure. 'Why, that's grand news! Oh, how I wish I could see her.'

'Well, hinny, you knew there'd be no days off for you till you can stop nursing the bairn. But I'd better tell you now that Nellie's guessed about Anthony.'

'How?' Bridget was stunned.

'She heard from one of the staff about you being promoted to nursemaid because you were me niece and all, and of course she knows that's a load of old hay. But she swears she won't breathe a word to a soul.'

Bridget let out a deep breath of relief. 'So long as 'tis only Nellie. She's not stupid. I might have known she'd put two and two together. I'm ashamed I had to be telling her lies. When I can get out to go to confession again 'tis a long list indeed I have for the priest.'

'Nellie understands why you couldn't tell her the truth, Bridget. Don't worry your head about that. And the Lord knows that what you've done was with good intentions. Don't look so downhearted. Why, now that Nellie knows I don't see why you couldn't write to her, and maybe she could meet you one day when you take the bairn for his walk.'

Bridget's eyes sparkled with excitement. 'What a grand idea! Lord knows I'd rather be feeding Anthony than having days off, but I do miss getting out now and then . . . and I miss seeing me auntie.'

'Aye, all in good time, hen.'

'What else did Nellie say? Has she seen me auntie lately?'

100

Mrs Kennedy nodded. 'Aye, a couple of weeks back. Your auntie told her she's that grateful for the money you send her. Her joints is getting worse and she's only got two days' work a week. She tried taking in a bit of mending to help make ends meet but her eyes were too bad. And, need I tell you, the old man's still drinking himself to death. If you ask me, it'll be a blessing for her when he kicks the bucket.' She rose to pour herself more tea.

'Oh, me poor auntie!' Bridget said with a sigh. 'Sure, I wish I could send her more money. I feel that bad that I'm living in such fine style and—'

But Mrs Kennedy cut her off. 'You've no need to feel bad, hen. You do your best by your auntie out of the pittance they pay you, and that's all you can do.'

Bridget stared into the empty fire grate and gave no reply.

'Nellie saw Tom in Newcastle, hinny,' Mrs Kennedy said, eyeing Bridget closely.

She clattered her cup on to the saucer. 'Tom! And what is it she said? How is he faring?'

'He's doing all right for himself, so Nellie said. He tried to get a job as a drayman 'cause he wanted to stay with horses. But he got a better-paying job with a company in Bewick Street. He says he earns more than he'd get going down the pits.'

Bridget's face saddened. Hearing news of Tom intensified her terrible feeling of loss, the wound as fresh as on the day she'd left him. But she was glad he was doing well. 'Thirty shillings a week! And what does he do for that?'

'He's a packer and loader,' Mrs Kennedy said cryptically and sipped her tea.

'But that sounds a fine, clean job! Why would it be paying better than the pits? What is it he's packing and loading?'

Mrs Kennedy looked innocent. 'Don't ask me, luv. That's all Nellie said.'

'Did . . . did she say if he's got a lass?'

'Now, that's not a proper question for her to ask the lad.'

Bridget persevered, but she couldn't keep the tremor out of her voice. 'Well . . . did he ask about me then?'

'He asked if she'd seen you but she thought she'd best say she hadn't, in view of your situation like.'

'Aye, she did the right thing.' Bridget gazed into her cup to hide her disappointment.

101

After tea Bridget returned to the nursery to feed Anthony before his walk.

Nancy was sitting on Bridget's bed holding him. 'I was about to come and get you, Bridget. He just woke up and he's whimpering. He woke me up and all, but I had a nice forty winks.'

Bridget took Anthony and sat on the bed to put him to her breast. 'Are you hungry then, my precious? Oh, and you're wet and all. I'll make you comfortable soon, my little one.'

Fed, changed, and dressed for his outing in a white silk suit, Anthony babbled contentedly as Bridget carried him down to Mildred's ground-floor drawing room. She held him tightly and braced herself before knocking on the door.

'Who is it?'

''Tis Bridget, ma'am. You wished to see Anthony before his walk.'

'Oh, yes, bring him in.'

Mildred's tone was irritable. She was seated at her dainty kneehole desk writing invitations for the grand ball she planned the following month. She continued to write and stuffed a gilt-edged card into its envelope before turning a frosty face. 'Well, how is he doing? Let me see him.'

Bridget approached from the doorway where she'd stood waiting and held out Anthony for Mildred's inspection. She'd never touched him.

'Well, he's growing. That's gratifying.' Mildred scrutinized his face as if searching for a blemish.

Bridget shivered inside. She knew the mistress's concern. At times it worried her too that Anthony looked so much like herself and bore no resemblance to his father.

'All right, you may go now,' Mildred snapped, 'and see that he gets some more colour into his cheeks.' She turned her back and resumed her writing.

Bridget retreated, clutching Anthony. Dear Lord! Had she done the right thing after all? she asked herself for the hundredth time. Anthony would certainly have a comfortable life, but he would never know a real mother's love.

As usual, Nancy had prepared the perambulator with fresh white satin sheets and pillows and left it at the front entrance. The footman opened the door for Bridget and she loaded her precious cargo into the elegant carriage. He whimpered as he left her arms but soon gurgled with pleasure when she rocked the carriage and walked him towards her favourite retreat by the stream.

Since that fateful day, she'd avoided the spot where she and Tom used to go; it held too many painful memories. Instead, she walked along a narrow gravel path that led to a small copse near the stream. Here the ground was level enough to push the carriage, and the trees, uncut for many years, provided a delightful canopy of privacy yet allowed the sun to shine through the clearings. No one ever came here, not even the master on his daily rides. In fact, her only contact with him was on his occasional visits to the nursery. He treated her curtly and with distance, as he did all the servants. For this she was grateful. His interest in Anthony was that of a father impatient for his son to grow up. He would always comment on the child's growth and progress, but took little pleasure in playing with him. Bridget knew it would be different when he could teach him to share his own pleasure in riding and hunting and later, perhaps, gambling. She shook the thought away. She had her son entirely to herself for the present.

The May weather was warm enough to sit on the grass with Anthony in her lap. These were some of her happiest moments. Soon he would be toddling and playing in the stream. She sighed with mixed pleasure and sadness – pleasure at watching him grow into a strong little boy and sadness at the thought of his growing up and needing her less. Time flew so fast.

She lifted him from the carriage and sat on the grass, then bounced him gently on her lap. He grinned with delight and, her momentary sadness melting, she sang softly to him:

> *The summer will come and the grass turn to hay*
> *Green leaves will come on the tops of each spray*
> *My true love will come at the dawn of the day*
> *And he'll strike up a tune to drive sorrow away*

She clutched him to her bosom and rocked him. How silly that she always regretted her decision after meetings with the mistress. Of course he had a real mother's love! And she could give him more than that cold-hearted creature ever could.

103

Chapter Eleven

Bridget hummed as she pushed the perambulator towards town. Though Anthony was now four, she'd removed the mid-section of the bed to form a seat for him when he got tired of walking. He was too heavy for her to carry far. Her face dimpled with pleasure as she looked down at him. 'Now, aren't you in for a fine time today, Anthony?'

'We're going to see Nellie.' His muffled voice came from behind the thick wool scarf wound about his neck and covering his face up to his nose. Between his wool bonnet and the scarf all Bridget could see were two bright hazel eyes and two pink cheeks. 'That's right! We're going to see Nellie. And you're going to have tea.'

Bridget and Nellie had been meeting secretly almost weekly for three and a half years. When the weather allowed they met at the copse. When it did not, Bridget daringly walked halfway to town and cut through the old unused cart track leading to Nellie's cottage. Nellie's Jack had given up his job at the butcher's shop when she was pregnant and now worked on Hardy's farm. It paid less and the work was harder, but the two-roomed cottage came with the job. Nellie was thrilled to bring up Lizzie in a proper house with a real bedroom. The roof space at Jack's parents', which had been their home, was cramped and dangerous for a child.

'It's *me*, Nellie,' Bridget shouted through the door. She lifted Anthony from the perambulator and set him down. 'My, but I swear you weigh as much as a millstone, Anthony. Such a big lad you're getting.'

'Nellie! Nellie!' Anthony ran to the door as it opened and Nellie bounced out.

'Why, hello, me bonny lad!' She swung him up in the air as if he were the weight of a newborn. Since her daughter's birth she'd grown buxom, her face round and ruddy, her red hair straggling down carelessly from her mobcap. Never naturally prone to neatness, after her release from service she'd lapsed into her old ways. Her grey sackcloth apron was spotted with signs of the various meals she'd cooked that week, her black serge frock torn at the hem. But her green eyes glowed in her boisterous face, so full of life and passion. She set Anthony down and he ran inside shouting for Lizzie.

Bridget turned back the perambulator cover and unloaded a bundle wrapped in a white tea towel. Nellie watched eagerly. 'Well, well! What's our thieving Mrs Kennedy sent for us the day?'

'She said not to open it till we got here. 'Tis a special surprise for Anthony's birthday.' Bridget's eyes misted. 'For his *real* birthday, I mean, not tomorrow, like Madam says.'

Nellie took Bridget's free hand. 'Now come on in and don't fret about that no more. You're letting the cold into the house, and here I've been struggling all day to get it warm.' Once inside the tiny whitewashed room Nellie kicked the door shut behind them with a bang.

Bridget set her bundle on the grubby wooden table and hung her bonnet and cloak on the nail in the door. 'Sure, I'm glad to be indoors. 'Tis cold enough for snow,' she said, holding out her hands to the fire.

Despite her hardships, she'd changed little over the years. Her wide hazel eyes looked out at the world with the same innocence, her smile revealed the same gentleness, and her slim neatness in her blue uniform frock and starched white apron contrasted with Nellie's careless disarray.

Anthony already sat on the clippy mat by the fire, Lizzie by his side. A replica of her mother, the fire flamed her red curls and flecked her green eyes with yellow as she grabbed the toy soldier Anthony thrust at her. Although a year younger than Anthony, she was a bright child and they played well together.

Bridget knelt to remove Anthony's bonnet and overcoat. Playfully she tousled his unruly chestnut curls, now grown almost to his shoulders. For formal occasions she was obliged to train the curls into ringlets but whenever possible she preferred to see his hair natural and free.

Nellie almost tore open the bundle. 'Well, would you believe it! She's sent a birthday cake. And look, she's written "Happy Birthday Anthony" on it in icing.'

Anthony looked puzzled. He wriggled out of Bridget's grasp and ran to examine the cake. 'But my birthday's not till Christmas Day and that's tomorrow.'

Bridget's smile couldn't hide a tinge of sadness. 'This is an extra birthday cake, before your big one tomorrow, so that you can share it with Nellie and Lizzie. Now wasn't it nice of Mrs Kennedy to think of that? But remember, 'tis a secret! And so is our visit today, just like all the other times.'

'I like secrets,' Anthony said. 'I like playing with Lizzie and Nellie.'

Bridget felt guilty about teaching the child to conceal the truth, but innocent though her visits to Nellie were, she knew that if the mistress found out there would be trouble. And, she reassured herself, she had a right to some free time. She hadn't had one day off since Anthony was born. In fact, but for occasional meetings at Nellie's, she wouldn't even have seen Annie. Bridget wished her aunt could have been with them today but the cold weather aggravated her rheumatics.

'Me see! Me see!' Lizzie rose, and grasping the table with sticky hands, pulled herself up to admire the cake. Still not satisfied, she climbed on to a chair. 'Oooh! Icing!' She dipped her finger into the sticky sugar and sucked it. Nellie laughed.

'Our Lizzie, now I'm sick of telling you, you mustn't do things like that when Anthony's here. He'll learn your bad habits. Now you both sit down and be quiet while I mash the tea. And then you can have some cake.'

Nellie filled the kettle from the bucket and placed it over the flames. 'I should've remembered to put the kettle on afore you came,' she said with an apologetic grin. 'Our Jack says I'd forget me head if it was loose.' She surveyed Bridget for the first time. 'And look how nice and tidy you are! He's always grumbling that I look like a bundle of dirty washing.'

Bridget smiled as she took a soiled tea towel from the line above the mantelpiece and wiped Lizzie's hands. 'You wouldn't be *you* if you were organised, Nellie. I like you just the way you are. But I do have to be back by four today. Madam wishes to see Anthony after his nap, so we'll be having to make it a quick tea party.' She replaced the towel, collected dishes from the rough wooden shelves Jack had fixed to the wall, and set the table.

Nellie sat in one of the two chairs flanking the stove and pulled a face. 'What does she want to see him for then? Don't tell me she's going to do her motherly duty for a change.'

'Sure, I don't know what it's about.' Bridget frowned and sat opposite Nellie. 'I expected her to see him tomorrow, it being Christmas Day and his official birthday. But not today and all. And dressed in his best, Madam said. She'll have something up her sleeve, I'll be bound.'

'Well, don't fret yourself about it, luv – and shut up, you two, and

106

sit still.' Bored with admiring the cake, the children were fighting over the toy soldier.

Bridget got up and took the toy. 'Toys are for playing with, not fighting over. Anthony, why don't you sing your new song for Nellie and Lizzie while we're waiting for the kettle?' She sat again and hid the toy in her apron pocket. 'Sure, he's picking up songs faster than ever,' she said to Nellie. 'He has but to hear me sing them only a few times now and he remembers all the words and gets the tune right.'

Anthony joined her and pulled her apron over his head.

'Come on, now,' Nellie coaxed. 'I know you're not shy, and Lizzie would love to hear your new song.'

'I know lots of songs.' He emerged from under the apron, and first making sure he had everyone's attention, stood tall and piped in his thin, sweet voice:

It's down beside the sea I'd be, where all my people dwell
My mother and my father too and all my friends as well
When you're going into your bed at night a prayer for me do say
That home I'll be amongst my friends for the cutting of the hay

Nellie clapped. 'Whey, now, that was lovely, Anthony. Wasn't it, Lizzie?'

Lizzie kicked the table leg and puckered her face. 'I want cake.'

'In a minute! The kettle's just boiling.' Nellie grinned at Bridget. 'She's like her ma – only interested in her belly.' She rose to take the kettle off the hob and patted Anthony's head. 'Thank you, hinny. One of these days you're going to be an opera singer.'

'Indeed, I wouldn't be surprised,' Bridget said. 'I didn't even know he knew that latest one till he came out with it yesterday. I swear, I don't teach them to him like I do nursery rhymes. I just sing when I'm about me tasks or doing me knitting. I know I learned them from me ma the same way, but not at his age.'

Nellie gave Bridget a knowing wink over Anthony's head. 'Aye, he's intelligent and talented like his ma. He takes after you all right. Now let's have some of that cake.'

In the nursery, Anthony stood mutely while Bridget knelt to brush his curls and twist them into the tight ringlets Madam favoured. He now wore a new blue silk sailor suit with two wool vests underneath. Away from the fires, the house was cold and draughty. She surveyed him with pride. His bright eyes, so full of love and trust, gazed up at her as she put the finishing touches to his hair. To think that she'd brought such a beautiful child into the world! Not simply pretty – beautiful – and everyone said so. 'There now! You look a right picture. Your mama *will* be proud of you.' As always, when an interview with the mistress was imminent, Bridget felt as if someone had taken a suet-grater to her nerves. She took Anthony's hand and started for the door. But he pulled back.

'I don't want to see Mama. I want to play trains in the nursery.'

'Later, when you come back.' Bridget marched him out and along the landing. She was worried. Lately he'd become more and more reluctant to visit the mistress. She squeezed his hand in encouragement. 'But you love Mama and you like to visit her.'

'I don't love her. And I don't like to visit her. I love you and Mrs Kennedy and Nellie and Lizzie.' He hesitated and his lips quivered. 'And I loved Nancy, but she went away.'

'Nancy had to go away, sweetheart. Her job was finished. But that doesn't mean she's stopped loving you. And your mama loves you and all. It's just a different kind of love. She doesn't have time to play with you like I do.'

Anthony thought for a moment. 'Papa plays with me sometimes. But he shouts loud, and Margery shouts. And she nips me when I don't do what she says.'

Bridget attempted a stern voice but failed. 'They all love you, Anthony. I won't be having you say they don't. And I want you to behave yourself like a good little lad when you're with them, do you hear?'

'Yes . . . but—'

'No "buts", Anthony.'

They neared Mildred's drawing room door and Bridget put a finger to her lips to quieten him. The suet-grater had done its work. Her nerves were now completely shredded. She knocked.

'Come in.'

She raised her chin as she entered the pink velvet room, dragging Anthony in her wake. Mildred was entertaining her lady friends to tea. Half a dozen immaculately coiffured heads and powdered faces turned towards them. Immediately, Bridget understood. So that was why Madam wanted Anthony today – to show him off to her friends. She never spent time alone with him. He clasped Bridget's hand tighter as she stepped forward, still keeping a respectful distance from the group.

'Well, Anthony, come over here and let us see you.' Mildred assumed a motherly tone and patted her knee in encouragement.

Anthony stood, still and silent.

'Bring him here, girl.'

'Say good afternoon to Mama, Anthony.' Bridget groaned inwardly as she put both hands on his shoulders and propelled him forward. She dreaded another bad scene – and in front of visitors. Madam would be furious. 'Say good afternoon to your mama,' she repeated in an urgent whisper.

'Good afternoon, Mama.' Bridget stopped pushing him and he stood still again, looking from under his eyelashes at the array of lips arranged in forced smiles.

'Go to Mama,' Bridget urged.

Slowly, he advanced and stopped in front of Mildred's chair.

'And now say good afternoon to the ladies, Anthony.' Mildred spoke through her teeth.

Anthony looked at the floor and mumbled, 'Good afternoon.'

'Have you been a good boy today?' She grasped his hand in a grip that forbade him to move a muscle and parted her lips in what passed for a smile. She pulled him to her and lifted him on to her lap. But he wriggled free and stood to attention before her.

'Yes, Mama, I've been a good boy. Can I go and play trains with Bridget now?'

'Indeed not!' This time Mildred didn't bother to control her voice and Anthony ran back to the doorway and buried his face in Bridget's skirts.

'I want to play trains, Bridget,' he whimpered.

Her face coloured as all eyes turned on her. 'No, Anthony, no trains. Do as you're told and go to Mama.' She tried to push him forward again but he clasped his arms round her legs.

'No! No!'

Mildred appeared to have regained her composure and gave her friends a sugary smile. 'Well, it seems Anthony isn't feeling like himself today. He's normally such a good child. He must need a nap.' She stood and addressed Bridget in the same sweet tone: 'Please give him his nap now. And in future make sure he has it *before* you bring him downstairs.'

Bridget bowed her head. 'Yes, ma'am. I'm sorry, ma'am.' She forced out the words calmly while seething inside. The mistress knew Anthony always had his nap after lunch. She untwined Anthony's arms from her legs and led him out by the hand. 'Don't cry, sweetheart,' she soothed as soon as they reached the hall. 'But you were a bad boy not to do what Mama said. Whatever got into you?'

Anthony stopped crying and stuck out his lower lip. 'I don't want to do what she says. She shouts. And she hurts when she holds my hand. And I don't want a nap.'

Bridget bit her lip. There would be trouble now. Anthony was definitely getting a mind of his own. She'd never said a bad word to him about the mistress, but he was wise enough now to feel her rancour. What could she do?

At dinner that night Mildred waited until after dessert, when the servants had left, before she stormed at Richard. 'We've got to do something about that girl, Richard. The boy is getting out of control and she's to blame. She's deliberately turning him against me. He showed me up in front of my friends this afternoon. I will not tolerate such a public display of bad behaviour.'

'What did he do?' Richard asked without much interest. He'd eaten too well and wanted nothing more than to retire to the library and smoke a cigar with his port.

'He disobeyed me. He wouldn't come when I bade him. And in front of all my friends! He ran back to that . . . that bitch!' Mildred's voice was squeaky with indignation.

Richard stretched back in his chair, placed his hands on his portly belly, and burped loudly. 'Well, you hardly ever see the boy. Perhaps if you took a bit more interest—'

'Interest? How do you expect me to show interest in a child who is rude to me? I expect him to behave as a dutiful and obedient son. Is that too much to ask?'

Richard picked a piece of meat from between his teeth with his fingernail before answering. 'He's growing up, Mildred, and he's not stupid – after all, he *is* my son. Children sense things. If you behaved a bit more like a mother, perhaps he'd start treating you as such.'

'You're taking that monster child's part against me!' Fury rose inside Mildred like foam in a rabid dog. 'And that girl! She'll have to go, Richard. It's all her doing.'

Richard was now apparently engrossed in cleaning his left thumbnail with his right. He was too tired to get into an argument with Mildred and spoke calmly. 'You're talking nonsense, woman. You were the one who made the bargain and now you'll have to learn to live with it.'

'Bargains can be broken. She broke *her* side of the first contract, and now she's doing it again – turning the boy against me. *That* is not written in her contract. I intend to get rid of her tomorrow.'

At the determination in her voice, Richard looked up. 'Are you out of your mind? Have you forgotten the stink the girl made about the adoption? What do you think she'll do if you turn her out?'

Mildred leaned forward, her eyes filled with resolve. 'Don't worry, I will think of some way round it.'

'Careful, m'dear. She couldn't be bought before, so don't think you can buy her off now. And don't forget, she provided me with an heir.' Wearying of the discussion, he pushed himself out of his chair. 'I'm adjourning to the library. And I suggest you forget all about your silly idea. Were it not for the girl and the child, you wouldn't be sitting here now.'

Mildred looked as if she'd just sucked a lemon. She held her tongue. She would work out a scheme alone and then present him with a *fait accompli*. There had to be a way. She was still the mistress here. She could employ and dismiss staff as she wished. That was no part of Richard's duty anyway. Filled with determination, she rose and stalked to her drawing room.

Half an hour later, reclining on the pink *chaise-longue* by the fire, she let out a long breath of satisfaction. Yes, that was it! And so simple! Why hadn't she thought of it before? But what about the damned housekeeper? She would have to get rid of her too. No, that would look strange. What reason could she have to dismiss her because of her niece's conduct? The woman had an exemplary record and, besides, it would be bothersome to have to find a replacement. Satisfied with her plan, she pulled the silk tassel by the fireplace. Almost immediately the butler entered and bowed.

'Please summon that nursemaid at once.'

'Yes, madam.' The butler bowed again and retreated.

Mildred smoothed her velvet gown over her stomach. She'd felt heavy after dinner, but now she felt elated, as if she had but to flutter her wings and she could fly. For the moment, she would simply deal with the girl about the boy's disgraceful behaviour. He would be allowed no birthday or Christmas presents. But tomorrow . . . tomorrow – she savoured the thought – she would settle that trollop once and for all.

Bridget bundled a disgruntled Anthony into his outdoor clothes. True to

111

her word, Mildred had denied him his Christmas and birthday presents. Though Bridget had tried all day without success to cheer him up, she persevered. ''Tis cold but dry out. We can have a good long walk. Won't that be nice, sweetheart?' As an idea occurred to her she gave him a wide smile. 'We could go to see Nellie and Lizzie again. Would you like that?'

Anthony gave her a half-hearted nod and Bridget sighed as she put on her cloak and bonnet. It was criminal to treat a child so. She took his wool-mittened hand and said in a light voice, 'Come on then, off we go.' But as they left by the main entrance, she didn't see Mildred watching from the dining room window.

Bridget knocked before opening the cottage door. There was no fire on and no one there. Of course! How stupid of her. They would be at Jack's parents' on Christmas Day. Anthony looked around, puzzled, then whimpered, 'Nobody's here.' She bent and hugged him, hating herself for disappointing him further.

'Oh, me love, I'm so sorry. But we'll go home and have a nice early tea in the nursery. And we'll see if Mrs Kennedy can come today. I bet she'll bring Christmas cake and birthday cake and all.'

He didn't protest as they turned back towards the house, but she felt sad for him. He seemed to be getting used to disappointments.

When Bridget reached the portico the footman wordlessly lifted Anthony from the perambulator and carried him up the steps as usual. But when he reached the massive hall he handed him over to Mary, the top-floor maid, who stood at the foot of the stairway. As she led Anthony upstairs she turned and threw Bridget a helpless glance. Baffled, Bridget began to follow, but the footman stepped in her way. 'Madam wishes to see you in her drawing room,' he said in a stiff voice.

Bridget quailed. What was the mistress up to now? But as she started nervously down the corridor towards the large oak door, she stopped dead. Her bag stood against the wall. Dear God! Was the mistress sending her away? She gulped in air and grasped the doorpost for support. No! She couldn't! That was all settled legally. But whatever the woman was up to, it couldn't be good. Despite her trembling as she knocked on the door, when Mildred's voice bade her enter she took a deep breath, straightened her shoulders and raised her chin. Whatever this was about, she held the final card. 'You wished to see me, madam?'

Mildred, festively dressed in a scarlet velvet gown trimmed with gold thread, stood with her back to the fire, her hands behind her back. She lifted a gloating face towards Bridget and held the look for some time, obviously savouring her frightened expression. 'Yes,' she eventually said in a cool, level voice. 'As from this moment you are dismissed from your post in this house.'

Bridget stared at her in disbelief. 'Dismissed! But you can't! I've kept *my* side of the bargain. I've done nothing wrong.'

'You have taken that child out of the grounds without permission.'

Bridget's mouth gaped.

'Oh, yes, I had someone follow you. I knew you couldn't be trusted. And what is worse, you have subjected him to only the Lord knows what on your . . . disgusting . . . visits to your lover – if one can use that word.'

'Me lover! But I haven't got a lover.' Bridget strove to keep her voice steady. She would not be browbeaten by this woman. She had her legal rights. 'I confess I've taken him to visit me girlfriend and her little daughter, but he enjoys it. He has no playmates in this house. And I've not had one single day off in four years. I'm by his side the whole time, taking good care of him. Surely I'm due a few free moments now and then to visit me friend? There was nothing written in me contract to say that I couldn't be doing that.'

'Contract? What contract, girl?' A look of pure pleasure crossed Mildred's face. She withdrew her hand from behind her back and waved a sheet of paper in the air. 'You mean this?'

Bridget's stomach turned over. Her legal contract! And her belongings were out in the hall! The mistress had been through her room. Dear God! And she'd thought the contract would be safe sewn into her pillow. The woman must have torn apart the room to find it. Stunned, she watched as Mildred waved the letter daintily by the corner.

'No, it's mine!' She ran towards her, her hand outstretched to grab the contract. But hardly had she taken two steps, than with a look of triumph, Mildred opened her fingers and let the paper flutter into the flames. Bridget stopped dead, hypnotized by the sight. In seconds the flames licked around the sides of the paper, then devoured it, leaving only a twisted lacework of ash that disintegrated into nothing.

'There never was a contract.' Mildred licked her lips like a cat who'd caught a mouse and was unable to decide which was more enjoyable – the catch or the pleasure of playing with the prey.

Suddenly Bridget came out of her trance. She looked squarely at Mildred. 'Don't think you're going to get away with this. There are others as knows the truth will back me up.'

Mildred stood with her back to the fire, her eyes mocking. 'Oh, yes! Mrs Kennedy? I doubt you would wish your aunt to be dismissed as well, for lying to save her niece's skin. And that wet-nurse creature? She was paid for the job, and paid off, and can be paid off again. I've no doubt she would be glad of it, since she's lost her livelihood. But there will be no need for that. You would have trouble finding her. I am informed that she returned to Newcastle when the job finished. And as for the midwife, whose side do you think she would be on? That is, if you had the money to go to court out of a scullery maid's wages.'

As Bridget listened to the venomous voice, tears drained down the sides of her face, into the locks of hair the wind had tugged from under her bonnet. She thought wildly. She couldn't let Mrs Kennedy be fired. And the mistress was right. She had no idea where Nancy was, even if she could talk her into telling the truth. And money always had the last word. Nellie! Yes, Nellie would stand up for her. She found her voice. 'Me friend I visit saw me when I was with child and knows the whole truth. She'll back me up, even if it comes to court.'

'Your "friend"?' Mildred sauntered around the room as if to prolong her pleasure, before resting a scornful gaze on Bridget. 'Your "friend"?' she repeated, and laughed. 'Who would take the word of two little sluts against mine? In addition, I have my lady friends as witnesses that you are quite, quite unsuitable as a nursemaid. Turning a child against its own mother, indeed! In truth, you're not suited to take care of *any* child.' She lowered herself slowly on to the couch and leaned back against one arm, giving Bridget a look of pure malice from under her pale lashes. 'Of course, I shall see to it that you get no references.'

Bridget felt as though an invisible hand had grasped at her stomach and pulled out her insides. She clutched herself and closed her eyes. The room was moving. Mildred's scarlet figure faded into the distance, then loomed towards her. She backed to the door and leaned against it for several moments until her head began to clear. She should have known she could never win with this woman. 'I'll find a way,' she heard her voice saying. 'I won't let you get away with this.'

'Oh, yes?' Mildred daintily put her hand to her lips to suppress a feigned yawn. 'One last thing. If you ever got it into your head to steal the boy, without a doubt it would be prison for you. The staff have been informed to take . . . er, certain precautions, should you ever show yourself in the vicinity of this house again.' She waved her arm languidly. 'You are dismissed now.'

Numb, Bridget turned to open the door. As she stumbled out, the floor sloped away from her, then up towards her. She must get to the fresh air. She must sit down. She felt as if she was walking on a ship in a storm, and Anthony was calling her from the dark, lashing sea below, his voice chorusing with her brothers' and sisters'.

When she came back to life she was huddled against the wall on the portico steps, her bag beside her. It was some moments before her memory returned. Dear God! What would she do now? She pushed back the tear-stained locks from her cheeks as if to make way for the new flow. She would go to Nellie's and wait for her return. Nellie would help her. She pulled herself up by the wall, though her frozen hands couldn't feel the cold stone. Slowly, stiffly, she inched her way down the steps, her numb feet seeming not to touch them. She forgot her bag.

When Mrs Kennedy flung open Nellie's cottage door she found Bridget sitting rigid in one of the chairs by the fireless grate, her eyes wide and staring into the ashes.

'Bridget! Oh, Bridget, me bairn!' She knelt and took her in her arms. 'Are you all right? Dear God! You're freezing to death.' She took off her wool gloves and rubbed Bridget's frigid hands.

Her mouth moved. 'She . . . she . . .'

'Aye, hinny, I know. I came straight away after she told me. I knew you'd come here. But where's Nellie?'

'At Jack's ma's,' Bridget said through chattering teeth.

'Oh, me poor lamb, on your own at a time like this.' She raised her hands in despair. 'I'll swear the devil's in that woman. Who'd have thought anything like this could happen? But what's the good of lamenting now? First I've got to get you thawed out and then you can talk. God's truth, you're blue, girl.' She picked up her gloves from the floor and pulled them over Bridget's stiff hands, then strode to the bedroom and returned with two thin wool blankets, shaking her head. 'These are all they've got, poor things, but they'll help.' She covered Bridget with the blankets and placed her own cloak on top before kneeling to start the fire.

Listlessly, Bridget watched her. She bit hard on her stiff lips, yet felt no pain. But by the time the fire flared weakly the warmth of her coverings had begun to seep through her. She moved her fingers inside the gloves and felt the blood begin to flow once more. 'What . . . what am I going to do?' Her voice came out as a thin wail.

Mrs Kennedy finished filling the kettle and set it over the flames before answering. 'Don't you worry. Me mind's been working fifty to the dozen since I heard, hinny. I've got a plan.' She sat in the opposite chair and held out her plump hands to the fire. The years had wrought no noticeable change on the woman. Still the same stocky body, the strong, round face, the soft grey eyes, the underlying decency and compassion. 'I've got me life savings,' she went on. 'I'll spend every penny I've got to get you out of this – I'm the one as got you into it.'

'No, no, you can't.' Bridget shook her head. 'I've thought and thought while I've sat here. You'll be fired. And what would happen to you then? 'Tis me own fault for being so stupid and keeping the letter with me where she could get it.'

Mrs Kennedy stared at the flames flickering around the kettle and sighed. 'Aye, I never thought of that either. I suppose we should've known she'd stoop that far.' She leaned forward and gazed earnestly at Bridget. 'Look, hinny, I've been through hard times before, and I've had it soft for a long while now. There's not many years left for me anyway. I'll get by. But *you've* got your whole life ahead of you. You must be sensible – and think about Anthony. Fight for him, lass.'

Bridget's face creased. 'Oh, me darling little lad! Sure, I'll never see him again.'

'Now don't talk like that. I've worked for that family for most of me life and I'm respected around here. Maybe not as much as her ladyship, but if I was to back you up that you were telling the truth – and Nellie – and your own auntie? And the boy looks the spitting image of you, nobody could deny that.'

Bridget groaned in despair. 'Don't you see? We'd have to lie in court that you were me auntie, and to tell a lie in court is worse than just a sin – 'tis a crime. And how could I suddenly have two aunties and you have another relation? Everybody knows you have no kin here, except for the lie we told about me. Me ma always said that your sins will find you out in the end. The court would know that we lied then, so why would they believe we were telling the truth now?' She slid further down into the chair and sank her chin into her chest. 'Oh, 'tis all a terrible mess.'

'Aye, that it is. But if we just think it out slowly like, we'll find a way. Don't give up, lass.'

'But don't you see?' Bridget's voice was shrill with anguish. 'You've got to stay on at the house. I've been racking me brains all the time I've been here. We could never win such a case. You're the only one who

116

loves Anthony and can keep an eye on him and let me know how he is. Indeed, without *you* there I'd lose him completely.'

Mrs Kennedy wrung the corner of her apron. 'Aye, hinny, I have to admit you're talking more sense than I am. All I can think about is fighting to get the bairn back. I'm that upset, I never thought of all the ins and outs.' The kettle puffed steam and she stood to get the teapot. She moved wearily, like an old woman. Her usual attitude of strength and authority had suddenly deserted her. She carried the teapot from the littered table to the stove and reached for the tea caddy on the mantelpiece. She shook it and sighed. ''Tis empty. Them poor bairns! I didn't know they were that hard up. I'll have to see what I can do.' She replaced the caddy and lifted the teapot lid. 'There's still some leaves in here. Looks as though they've been used more than once, but a hot drink'll warm you up anyway.' She poured water into the pot and set it on the hearth to stew.

Bridget was suddenly ashamed of her thoughtlessness. 'Warm *me* up indeed! You look frozen yourself and here am I all wrapped up.' She threw off her coverings and placed Mrs Kennedy's cloak and one of the blankets round her shoulders. 'Now you sit down and I'll pour the tea.'

Both seated again by the fire, cups of a hot pale liquid that passed for tea in their hands, they fell into a hopeless silence. Eventually Mrs Kennedy spoke. 'Aye, thinking on it, you're right, Bridget. 'Tis best I stay on and you go back to your auntie's, even with your uncle there. Just keep well clear of him. I'll keep a wary eye on the bairn, don't you fret. And I'll write to you regular to say how he's faring. Maybe something'll turn up. But God only knows.'

'There's nothing left for me but to go back to me auntie's,' Bridget said, then raised her chin, her eyes firm with resolve. 'But I'll come back. I'll come to see you and Nellie whenever I can and maybe sometimes . . . maybe I could see Anthony. Not at the house, of course!' she added quickly, seeing Mrs Kennedy's look of alarm. 'But you could let me know where the new nurse takes him for his walks, and I could at least have a peek at him. I wouldn't let meself be seen, I swear.'

'Of course, luv, I'll do everything I can.' Unwillingly Mrs Kennedy rose and fastened her cloak. 'God knows I hate to leave you like this but I'd better get back now afore somebody notices I'm gone.' She pulled a small cloth bag from under her cloak and handed it to Bridget. 'Even in me panic I had the sense to know you'd need money. 'Tis not much but it should keep you going till you find work.'

Bridget rose to hug her, her eyes brimming. 'Indeed, I'll be missing you that much.'

Mrs Kennedy pulled herself away. 'It won't be long, take my word. I'll be visiting you at Newcastle and all. Now you just stay warm till Nellie gets back.'

Bridget nodded, but the broad, black-cloaked back was already out of the door.

Chapter Twelve

Cramped and stiff from the cold, Bridget climbed down from the cart. The journey to Byker had been as uncomfortable as usual. To avoid joining in the general conversation, she'd huddled between two crates of hens and feigned sleep. But whenever she closed her eyes she saw Anthony's face, and the emptiness in her heart was like a physical pain.

A leaden sky threatened snow as she stood in the queue to pay Mr Jones. She watched the dozen or so men, women and children in front of her. The adults looked as hopeless and weary as she, but the children chatted happily. It was Boxing Day, and most people carried parcels or bundles for friends and relatives. Bridget wondered if Anthony would be allowed to open his presents today. She closed her eyes and clenched her teeth to stop her tears. How sad and frightened he must be without her!

When her turn arrived she gave Mr Jones one of the thirty shillings Mrs Kennedy had given her and held out her hand for the change. The old man dug in his pockets, laboriously counted six pennies and placed them on her hand. 'Happy Christmas, lass,' he said in his cracked voice.

Bridget remembered his tricks of old. ''Tis short,' she snapped.

'Nah, hinny, it's gone up a few times since you were here last. A man's got to make a living.' He gave her his black-toothed grin and slapped the reins on the old nag's emaciated flanks. A bone-spavin stuck out grotesquely from its hind leg.

Bridget had to look away. Her own pain was too much to deal with, she couldn't bear to witness the suffering of another living creature. She dropped the coins into her pocket and stood for a moment looking about her. After more than four years in the countryside the narrow cobbled street seemed even meaner than she'd remembered, the tightly packed terraced flats even more soulless. Their grimy brick faces reflected their occupants – worn and weary of striving to hold themselves up year after year. A few watery snowflakes fell and she pulled her cloak tightly about her. But the air was too damp and raw for the snow to last. She forced one numb foot in front of the other, praying her uncle wouldn't be at home.

As she opened the door and trudged down the gloomy passage an unfamiliar musty smell assailed her. She felt a sense of foreboding.

In the kitchen, Annie sat huddled over the puny fire. She screwed up her failing eyes and peered at the small figure in the doorway. 'Bridget? It is! Dear Lord! What's wrong?' She raised herself slowly by the chair-arms.

'Oh, Auntie!' Bridget rushed to her and clung to her.

'What's happened? Tell me, hinny.' But Bridget couldn't speak. Annie led her to the fire and lowered her into a chair, clucking over her all the while. 'It's all right. Just take your time and tell me when you can. I'll heat up some broth to thaw you out.' She wiped her watery eyes on a corner of her apron.

While Annie set the heavy pan over the flames and eased herself into the opposite chair, Bridget regained her voice. Slowly, she told her story. 'I . . . I still can't believe it, Auntie,' she finished with a wail.

Annie rocked back and forth in anguish. She wiped her eyes on her apron again, but this time they were real tears. 'Eey, by God! That witch! As if you haven't been through enough already.'

'Sure, God must be punishing me for me sins.'

'Rubbish! You're too trusting of folk, that's all, and that's no sin. But you need to learn to look out for yourself. There's lots more like her in the world. You've got to pull yourself together and start over. A woman who carries the weight of her past can either collapse under it, hinny, or make her shoulders stronger. And I know you'll be strong. You're a brave lass. I thank God you at least had me to come to.'

'Aye, that's a blessing, Auntie,' Bridget said, but she suddenly felt as if a snake slithered down her spine. In the emotion of the moment she'd forgotten her uncle. 'Where's Uncle Frank? And what is it we're going to tell him?'

'He's out swilling ale, as ever, and we'll just tell him you gave up your job to be near me. God knows I'm glad to see you, but not like this. Now get some of this broth into you and you'll feel better. It'll fill you up and all, it's got barley in it.' She began to raise herself but Bridget jumped up and flung her cloak back over her shoulders. It was too cold in the room to take it off.

120

'Sure, I'm not letting you wait on me, Auntie. You're the one that needs looking after.' She took a rag from the line under the mantelpiece to lift the sooty pot and placed it on the hearth. It felt strange being back in the dingy little kitchen after so long. As she collected two bowls from the dresser and a mug to use as a ladle she noticed that the floor looked as if it hadn't been scrubbed for months. She searched her aunt's face and for the first time realized how thin and pinched it looked, and how red and watery her eyes. She knelt by her. 'Are you feeling all right, Auntie?'

'Aye, just muddling along, hen.' Annie shook her head when she saw the two bowls Bridget held. 'None for me. I'm not hungry. Have yourself a bowl and the rest's for Frank's tea.'

Bridget gave her a suspicious look. 'Have you had something today, Auntie?'

'Aye, luv, I had some tea at breakfast. That's all I want. I'm losing me appetite in me old age.'

'Dear Lord!' Bridget set the dishes on the hearth and took Annie's hands. 'I feel that guilty. Here I am going on about me own troubles and you're not well. How are your joints? And your eyes?'

'Well, I can't say they're getting any better. And me stomach's shrivelling up with the rest of me, that's all.' Annie managed a smile but Bridget was not reassured.

'Is it starving yourself you are to feed that man, Auntie?'

Annie averted her eyes. 'Nah, hinny, I swear—'

'You've been spending what little I could give you on *him*! And now haven't I told you not to do that?' Bridget's voice rose in a mixture of concern and anger, but her heart was filled with sorrow. 'Now that I'm here I'll make sure you get enough to eat. Mrs Kennedy gave me thirty shillings to help out till I find work, and she said if ever I'm short to let her know. But I wouldn't dream of taking any more of her savings. I'm going to look for a job first thing in the morning.'

Annie nodded. 'That was kind of her. She's a right good soul. Now you have that soup afore it gets cold just sitting on the hearth.'

Still on her knees, Bridget served herself some soup. 'Turnips and barley!' She sat on her chair and stared into her bowl. 'And this is Christmas! You never told me you were this bad off.'

Again, Annie looked away. 'Why, what's the use of complaining, hinny? Times has been hard since I had to give up working. But without what you've been sending things would have been a lot worse. I get by.'

121

They both started as the door burst open. Frank swayed on the threshold, his mouth falling open at the sight of Bridget. 'You're back, then, are you?' As usual, his voice was slurred, his eyes bleary.

Annie gave him a look that dared him to complain. 'Yes, she's come back to help out, and you should thank your lucky stars for that.'

'Hello, Uncle Frank,' Bridget said stiffly. She bent her head and took refuge in her soup.

'So, you've decided to slum it with us again. What happened to your fancy job? Got the boot, eh?' Frank removed his cap and muffler but kept on his coat and sat at the table. 'Well, if you've come back to help out, what about me dinner then?'

Seething inside, Bridget put down her bowl and filled the other. She set it in front of him with such force that the broth splashed over the sides.

Frank thumped his fist on the table and glared at her. 'Temper, temper! If you want to stay in *my* house, you'd better learn to behave yourself.'

Nauseated by the smell of ale that pervaded the air around him, Bridget curled her lips in distaste and retreated to her chair. She mustn't cause a scene on her first day back. She cringed inside. It was only mid-afternoon. How could she get through a day with him in the same room?

Annie seemed to read her thoughts. 'Well,' she said, 'you can't look for work on Boxing Day and it's freezing out there anyway. We'll just have a quiet time together, *you and me*.' Bridget felt immeasurably relieved that Annie had stressed the last words. He must be going out again.

Frank plunked his spoon down in his bowl and belched loudly. 'Any more soup?'

Annie shook her head at Bridget to warn her to sit still, and slowly raised herself. 'Aye, there's a bit more. You can have it now, but that means there's nowt for your supper.'

'I'll have it now then. It's about time you did some work again for your keep, woman. Do you want a working man to starve to death?'

Enraged, Bridget opened her mouth to speak but Annie shot her a look. Bridget snatched up Frank's bowl and tipped the remains from the pan into it. She sat again, rigid hands clenched in her lap, uttering a silent prayer for help to keep her mouth shut till he went out again.

'Why don't you get your things and put them away in the bedroom, luv?' Annie suggested in an obvious attempt to get her out of Frank's way.

'Yes, I'll do that.' Now was not the time to let her aunt know that she'd left her bag back on the steps of the big house, and that it was probably in the dustbin by now. But she could make up her bed. She went through the hall to the bedroom and again the musty smell hit her. The bare mattress still lay on the floor by the window but the whitewashed wall above it was stained dark. Bridget knelt and felt it. It was wet. So that was the smell! She pulled the mattress away. The skirting board had rotted along the entire length of the wall and the mattress was soaked. She ran her hand across the surface of the rest of the wall. It was all damp.

Outraged, she marched back to the kitchen and stood in the doorway, as far from Frank as possible. 'The bedroom wall's all wet,' she said to Annie, as if accusing her. 'How long has it been like that?'

Annie shrugged in resignation. 'Aye, quite a while now. I've been at the landlord a dozen times but he won't do nowt about it. The bricks need repointing but he says it costs too much.'

'Costs too much, indeed! 'Tis a right disgrace! He charges you a fortune in rent to live in a damp house and sleep in a damp bed! The mattress is dripping wet.'

Annie clapped her hands to her mouth. 'Oh, I should have moved it. I wasn't expecting you back. I'll help you bring it in and we can dry it out a bit by the fire.'

'No, it would take up all the heat. And it'll take days to dry anyway. I'll sleep on the floor in here tonight. But I'm going to see that landlord tomorrow and give him a piece of me tongue. A disgrace it is that he charges five shillings a week for a place that's not fit for pigs to live in. No wonder your joints are bad.'

Annie sighed wearily. 'It won't do no good, luv. And it's six and six now. He's put it up twice since you left.'

'I won't let him get away with it.' Bridget's voice was shrill with anger.

'Will you stop your shouting and let a man get some peace and quiet in his own house?' Frank shot up from his chair and glowered at her. 'If it's not swanky enough for you here, you know what you can do. Nobody invited you anyway. I'm going to bed now.' He loomed towards her in the doorway. She stepped quickly aside and flattened herself against the doorpost till he'd passed. The door slammed shut.

'Oh, Auntie!' she cried. 'Why do you put up with him? Couldn't you leave him?' As the words came out, she wondered why she hadn't thought of it before. She sat again by the fire and begged Annie with her eyes. 'I'll find another place for us – just the two of us. If he wants to live like this, let him.'

Annie's eyebrows shot up in astonishment. 'Eey, I couldn't leave him on his own, luv. Whatever he is, he's me man. And anyway, he doesn't know how to look after himself. He'd die of starvation. His money covers the rent and coal and his beer and baccy, and that's about it. If it wasn't for what you've been sending we'd have had nowt to eat at all.'

'Then he'll just have to do without his beer and baccy. I *mean* it, Auntie. I'm taking you away from here.' Bridget's voice was like granite.

'Why, it's nice of you to think of me, hinny,' Annie said, her faded eyes imploring Bridget to understand. 'But I couldn't let you do it. And I just couldn't leave him.'

'Do you mean you still love him?' Bridget was incredulous. Surely to God she couldn't?

Annie shook her head sadly. 'Nah, hinny, that died in me a long time ago. He killed it himself. But I still remember with fondness what he was like afore we got married . . . and I still feel me duty towards him.'

'Duty indeed! And what sort of duty does he feel towards you? To him you're just a lackey to see to his needs.' Bridget paused and softened her voice. 'Just look at you, Auntie. You can hardly move with pain and yet you run around after him. Does he ever get a bucket of coal or water for you? Does he ever do anything to help you? 'Tis plain you're not well. And just look at this place. I've never seen it dirty like this . . . and I know you wouldn't let it go if you could help it.'

'Aye, you're right there.' Annie stared hopelessly into the fire. 'It drives me mad to look at it. Just doing the shopping and cooking and getting the coal and water's too much for me. Nellie's ma's been taking me washing to the wash house. I can't manage it no more.'

At this news, Bridget bit her lip. She supposed Nellie hadn't told her so as not to worry her. But she wished she hadn't found out like this. 'Oh, if only you'd let me know, Auntie,' she began softly, then her voice took on a determined note. ''Tis not too late. I'm going to get us both out of here. He'll just have to learn to go without his beer and baccy if he wants to eat.' But at the look of concern on her aunt's face, she melted. 'Don't worry. I promise I'll keep an eye on the place and see that he's fed. And he's hardly likely to miss you, Auntie. Whenever he's at home he's in his bed anyway.' But her conscience smote her as she thought of the damp bedroom. 'I'll write to the landlord to try to get the damp put right. Though Uncle Frank deserves no better, I couldn't leave him here to die of pneumonia.'

Annie gave her a frightened look and plucked at her apron. 'Eey, but I'm scared to think what he'd do to me if I left him. And I couldn't go far . . . not leave all me friends and neighbours and all. He'd be bound to find me sooner or later, and God knows what he might do.'

'You can tell your friends and neighbours where you're going, but warn them they mustn't breathe a word to him. He'll never dare harm you, Auntie. I'll make sure of that.'

After a moment's silence, Annie spoke. 'It does sound lovely. Just the two of us in a cosy little place. And no shouting and bickering. I could have a hot meal ready for you when you got home from work and do little bits to help. And if I left him, I might get a bit each week from the parish to help out.' She leaned forward, obviously warming to the idea, then paused and looked far away for a moment. 'But he's still me man. God knows, after all these years I'd feel funny running away from him.'

'Such nonsense you're talking! You should have done it years ago.' Bridget was surprised by the force in her voice. He was *her* kin, too – her own father's brother – yet she felt no guilt or compassion at the thought of leaving him to fend for himself.

Annie gazed into space for a long time, then shook her head. 'No . . . I couldn't do it, luv. I'm an old, sickly woman. What about when I can't get around at all no more? I don't want to force meself on you. You've got enough on your plate.'

Bridget used her last defence. 'But don't you see, Auntie? I want to look after you anyway, and it would be much easier for me if I didn't have to deal with him and all. I was that afraid when he pushed past me in the doorway. What if he tries something again? I can't be keeping meself out of his way all the time.'

Annie sat up abruptly, then winced and rubbed her back. 'Eey, I'm getting stupid as well as sickly in me old age. I never thought about that. You're right, hinny. If it's the last thing I do, I'll make sure he never lays a finger on you again.' She leaned back again with a sigh of relief. 'Aye, if I have to choose between the two of you it'll be you for sure.'

'Oh, that's wonderful, Auntie!' Bridget's voice was triumphant. 'I'll find us a place tomorrow and then I'll get a job. I have a need to keep busy. Whenever I stop to think I cry about me little Anthony.' As she spoke his name, the tears started. She brushed them away with her fists and lifted her chin. 'But *whatever* that woman says, I'm going to see him . . . even if I can never hold him and kiss him again . . . or sing to him.'

After an uncomfortable night on the kitchen floor, pillow-less and wrapped only in a moth-eaten blanket, Bridget opened her eyes at five thirty. Cold and miserable though her awakening was, she was glad to be free of the hideous dreams that had plagued her fitful sleep. She'd had her old nightmare that, filled with guilt, she was placing a child into a dresser drawer. But whereas in the past the child had always been small and unknown to her, this time it was Anthony. He cried as she closed the drawer on him but she put her fingers in her ears and left to go to work. When she returned, instead of the drawer being empty as in her earlier dreams, the entire dresser had disappeared. Childish voices called her. She ran outside to what seemed to be a sandy beach. The dresser bobbed on the grey water, and Anthony's voice mingled with her brothers' and sisters', crying out her name. She ran into the sea to retrieve the dresser, but her feet sank in the sand.

She shook her head to dispel the nightmare, stretched and rubbed her sore bones. But the voices still rang in her ears. She got up. She would put the fire on and make some hot tea. By then it would be light enough to go out on her errands. She had no wish to encounter her uncle this morning. And today she would go to church, and confession. She must unburden herself of her sins before she could make a new start.

Within a fortnight, after trudging around the neighbourhood day after day in search of a place to rent, Bridget had moved her aunt into a new, though identical, flat a few streets away at 40 Conyers Road. She'd bought a double bed from the second-hand shop and a few items of kitchen furniture and pots and pans, leaving sufficient for Frank's needs at the old flat. The move was planned with care. After Frank had left for work, they packed the few belongings they were taking and slipped out in the grey morning light, leaving a note to say they would not be back, and instructing him how to order the coal and where to pay the rent. Even Annie had shed no tears. Closing the flat door for the last time, she'd said quietly, 'Funny, after all these years I don't feel nothing but compassion for him, the same as I would a dog.' She'd looked up to heaven and asked the Lord to keep a caring eye on him, then walked to the waiting cart without glancing back.

The landlord of the new flat, reluctant to let it to Bridget as she had no man to support her, had given in when she'd thrust her bag of money under his nose and paid two weeks' rent in advance. Again, four houses shared one tap and one privy in the yard. The flat was dirty and the walls needed whitewashing. But before taking it Bridget had made a thorough inspection for signs of damp, rats or bugs, and had been happy to find only a few mouse droppings.

After cleaning, whitewashing, settling in and making Annie comfortable, she devoted herself full time to looking for a job. It took three tiring and fruitless weeks before she found work at William Nunn's, Fishmongers, in the Grainger Market, and another week of waiting before she could start. She was down to her last shilling of Mrs Kennedy's money. The job paid thirteen and six a week, which would have to cover the rent, tram fares and food. She calculated that if she was careful she could manage, especially as she would receive a portion of fish at the end of each day as a bonus. She was to start at seven a.m. when the fish was delivered from North Shields, her first duty to stock the front shop ready for the early customers at eight, and to store the remaining fish in the back. After closing time at half past five she had to scrub the marble counters and chopping blocks, sweep up the sawdust and lay fresh for the following day.

She would have to do the washing on Sunday evenings and leave it for her aunt to hang in the lane on Mondays, weather permitting. She'd asked Father O'Malley if this would be a sin, but after some thought he'd confirmed that God wouldn't object, as it *was* necessary work and she couldn't do it on Mondays.

'How was it, luv?' Annie asked when Bridget returned on Monday from her first day.

'All right.' She placed a newspaper-wrapped parcel on the table and, still wearing her cloak, sat by the fire and held her swollen red hands to the flames. 'But 'tis the coldest job I've ever done in me life. I don't see why they need to keep the fish on ice this weather.' She sniffed at herself in distaste. 'And I smell like a glue works. I'll have a hot wash by the fire after supper. And do you think I could wear your Sunday dress after? I'll have to be keeping this one for work now and get another one to change, and some more aprons.'

Annie nodded. 'Aye, of course, you can have the dress, luv. You can take the hem up and keep it. You've got more need of it than me. I wish you could've found a better job.'

'Indeed, I was lucky to find anything, and I'm not going to start grumbling about it on me first day. I'll get used to it.' Bridget nodded towards the table. 'And Mr Nunn gave me that parcel of fish.'

Annie unwrapped the paper and peered at the contents. 'By God! Two cod's heads and a handful of roe. Is that the best the old goat could do for you after the day you've put in for him?'

Bridget's shoulders slumped with disappointment. 'Well, Monday's a busy day after the weekend. Maybe when there's more left over I'll get more.' She didn't tell her aunt that there had been several salmon and a whole cod and haddock left over, which Mr Nunn had ordered her to store for sale the following day.

'Never mind, pet,' Annie said, rewrapping the parcel. 'The heads'll make a tasty soup for the morrow, and the roe can do for your sandwiches. I've made a nice hotpot with that left-over mutton, and I baked some fresh bread this morning.' She grinned. 'Eey, I swear I'm getting a new lease of life since I got away from that man. Get your things off and have it now.' She took a simmering pie dish from the oven.

Bridget removed her cloak and sat at the table. 'It smells nice, Auntie.'

'I've got to confess,' Annie began in a guilty tone, 'I took a bowl to Frank's for him to heat up. I . . . I just couldn't bear to think of him coming home to no supper.'

Bridget smiled at her as she cut herself a slice of bread. ''Tis no sin to confess, Auntie. I know you took him things last week and all. I saw them when I went there meself with food. But I hope you're being careful what time you go.'

'I'm not daft, hinny. I only go when he's at work, and I peek through the window first just to make sure.'

'Well, that's fine. But mind you, we can't afford to be feeding him forever. When his belly starts to hurt he'll soon learn he's got to fill it himself.'

Annie looked relieved, then guilty again. 'Eey, and I forgot this!' She pulled an envelope from her pocket and handed it to Bridget. 'This came for you today, hen.'

'Oh, it'll be from Mrs Kennedy. Thank God! I've been that worried that she hasn't written.' Forgetting her food, Bridget tore open the envelope. Annie sat next to her and eagerly watched her face as she read:

Dear Bridget
    I was that pleased to get your letter and to know that you have moved into a nice flat with your auntie. I pray that you find a job

128

soon and that everything turns out for the best. Please forgive me, hen, for not answering your letter earlier, but I've been flat on me back with a bad bout of the influenza, half the staff has had it and all. Since I got up a few days ago I have been keeping an eye on Anthony again and he is doing all right. He cried a lot the first few days when you left and he is still a bit quiet, but he seems to be taking well enough to the new nurse. She is not soft on him like you, mind you, keeps him in his place, but she has got him eating again, it was a job to get anything down him the first few days when he was grieving for you. Mind you, that doesn't mean he isn't grieving still, but bairns is hardier than we give them credit for. It seems the old witch told him you left him because he was a big boy now and you only liked looking after babies. I tried to soften it a bit and told him you didn't want to leave him but you had to go to another job. I couldn't tell the bairn his mother was a downright liar, could I? He hung on to me words though, I mean that you didn't want to leave him. The new nursemaid's called Mabel, so far she has not taken him out much, the weather's been that bad. She has just had him in the grounds around the house and you know you can't go near there. I will keep up me spying and maybe when the weather gets better she will take him somewhere you can get a peep at him. I miss you terrible and I am going to give meself a day off and come and see you. I can't come this Sunday or next because Madam is having two weekend house parties in a row, but I will come the next Sunday. I hope that's all right. I'll take me trap and leave early, so expect me late morning.
Yours
    Kate Kennedy

P.S. I forgot to say earlier but I have been doing a bit of thinking, and now that you're free again and back in Newcastle I don't see as why you couldn't get in touch with Tom if you want to. I know he is working at a dynamite company in Newcastle and there can't be many right in the town. Why not try to find out where he is and go and see him or write to him, hinny.

Tears sparkled on Bridget's eyelashes as she read the letter twice, then placed it in her pocket.

Annie's face was anxious, her hands clenched. 'Eey, hen, not more bad news?'

'No.' Bridget shook her head. ''Tis not bad. She's been poorly and that's why she didn't write, but she's better now. I just feel so sad hearing about me little lad being looked after by a stranger. She says he misses me, and she's coming to pay us a visit in a couple of weeks.' She picked up her knife and fork, then put them down again. 'And she says Tom's working at a dynamite company in Newcastle.' She shuddered. 'It sounds dangerous. She says maybe I should try to find him.'

Annie's faded eyes brightened. 'Eey, pet, I don't see as why you shouldn't. You're a free woman now, and if you still feel for the lad and him for you—'

'I most certainly do still feel for him, Auntie,' Bridget cut in, then paused and stared into space. 'But sure I don't know as he still feels for me after all this time . . . especially seeing as how I treated him.'

'You didn't do it on purpose, hinny.'

'But he doesn't know that. And wouldn't it be forward of me to get in touch with him again? I mean, 'tis not a woman's place to chase a man. But anyway, he's bound to have another lass by now . . . or even be married.' At the last words, her voice sank to a hopeless whisper.

But Annie was excited. 'Well, you'll never know if you don't try, hinny. You could just write a friendly letter, and if he hasn't got another lass and wants to see you *he'll* do the chasing.'

Bridget propped her elbows on the table and rested her chin in her hands. 'And how in the name of all the saints would I explain meself?' she said after a few moments. 'And what I've been doing all these years and why I suddenly decide to write to him? I'd have to lie through me teeth again. And haven't I just been back to confession for the first time in years and purified me soul? Indeed, I'm not going to start sinning all over again.'

'What rubbish you're talking!' Annie rose with determination and emptied the two plates back into the pie dish. 'I'm going to heat these up again. And after we've eaten why don't you go out and get a paper. There'll maybe be something in the advertisements about dynamite companies. You can write to them all. I don't see why you need to tell him nothing.'

Bridget was still doubtful. 'But I'd have to tell him something.'

'Just drop him a friendly line and say you only today heard from Mrs Kennedy where he works and you hope he's faring well, that you've left your position in Newcastle and you're back in Byker with your auntie.'

130

'Aw, Auntie, I can't just say that.'

'Yes you can. Leave it up to him if he wants to see you again. And all depending on how things go, you can decide later on if you want to tell him the truth or not.' Annie's voice sounded as if she were coaxing a child to eat its porridge.

'Do you really think so, Auntie?' Bridget's eyes looked misty and far away. 'Sure, I'd dearly love to see him again. But not just now. I need a little more time to settle meself and get over me pining for Anthony. I wouldn't want Tom to see me the sorry misery I am now.'

'Well, you could start writing to some dynamite firms and at least find out where he works,' Annie persisted.

'Maybe. But I need to think on it a bit more.' Bridget chewed on her thumbnail.

Chapter Thirteen

Two weeks later, as Bridget pulled down the shutters of the open shop-front, Tom poked his head underneath. 'Bridget?'

Her heart almost came through her ribcage. 'Tom! Why, how you startled me!'

He leaned over the counter, his eyes never leaving her face. 'Hello, Bridget. I got your letter when I went home last night, so I came straight over after work. You know I'm not much good with letters.'

She felt giddy with excitement. Was she really once again listening to Tom's voice and looking at his handsome face? ''Tis nice to see you, Tom,' she said almost calmly. 'But I'm not off work yet. I've still got to scrub out the shop.' She tried to keep her voice low, aware of Mr Nunn chinking coins from the till as he counted the day's takings.

'I'll wait here then.' Tom withdrew his head from the narrow opening like a turtle retreating into its shell.

Bridget closed the shutters and leaned against the cold marble counter to collect herself. She hadn't expected such a quick response. And in person. He must be eager to see her – and she was all messy and smelly.

In record time she cleaned the shop, sprinkled fresh sawdust, then scrubbed her red, sore hands with carbolic under the cold tap. They stung even worse than before. Undaunted, she soaped her face and neck. But the smell still clung. She picked up the towel and put it down again. It stank of fish and would do more harm than good. She would let the air dry her. She removed her bloodstained apron and the cotton scarf she wore around her head. What to do with them? She stuffed them under the counter before retrieving her cloak from the back shop. She sniffed it. It was only slightly tainted. On her way to the door she put her hands to her hair and anchored the straggling ends under their hairpins. She took two deep breaths. She'd lain awake at night mentally composing her reply to his letter should he write. Now she tried to recall her rehearsed words. Though it would be more difficult saying them to him, she was glad she'd prepared her lines. 'Goodnight, Mr Nunn,' she said as she braced her shoulders and let herself out.

Tom was leaning against the shutters, arms folded. He stood to attention when she emerged. 'How are you, Bridget?' His voice sounded older, deeper.

'I'm doing fine, thank you.' She soaked up the details of his face. His blond hair, unruly as ever, tumbled out from under his cap. His face had lost its boyish look, yet he was subtly more handsome in his maturity – his jaw squarer, his blue eyes deeper. He looked like a man who'd learned to master life.

Suddenly aware that she was staring at him, she went on: 'So you got me letter.' But he was staring at her too. She prayed she didn't look too grubby.'

'Aye, I was right surprised to hear from you, Bridget . . . but pleased and all.' He smiled, a hesitant, guarded smile, unlike his easy grin of old. He moved towards her and took her arm. 'Let's go somewhere we can talk.'

Bridget absorbed the feel of his arm through her clothes, through her pores. 'All right, but I can't stay out long. Me auntie's expecting me home.'

'We can go somewhere close by.' He steered her along the tiled floor to the end of the market, past the closed shutters of the window fronts.

Bridget was glad of Tom's arm for support. Her feet couldn't feel the ground. She floated beside him around a corner, down a street, another corner, and into a dingy pub. Her feet hit the ground again. The bar was quiet, only a few people sitting at the high counter, feet resting on the brass rail, but the smell of ale nauseated her and reminded her of her uncle.

'Can't we go somewhere else, Tom? You know I don't like pubs.' She hoped she didn't sound complaining. But his voice was even.

'There's nowt else open where we can sit and be warm . . . unless you want to come to me room. I've got a cosy little place above the stables.' He twitched his mouth in amusement, obviously expecting her to refuse. Bridget flushed. It wouldn't be seemly to go to a man's room.

'No, this is fine.' She slipped on to one of the hard wooden benches against the wall. She didn't want to seem prudish. And the Lord knew she had no right to be any more. 'No, it's nice here,' she lied. 'I'd love a lemonade.'

Again his lips twitched. He took off his cap and placed it on the stained wooden table. Bridget's eyes followed him as he went to the bar. His brown wool overcoat looked new and expensive. He must be doing all right as Mrs Kennedy had said. Before going to the barman he went over to an old woman who sat hunched over the counter studiously sipping clear liquid from a small glass, a clay pipe clutched in her other hand. He bent and shouted in her ear, 'Hello, Fanny, like another one?'

'Wehey, Tom, God bless you, me bonny lad.' She raised her wrinkled face and opened her mouth in a toothless grin.

Tom patted her shoulder and nodded to the barman. 'Evening, George. I'll have a lemonade, a beer, and,' he indicated the old woman with his head, 'another gin for me best girlfriend over there.'

George shrugged. 'God knows, she's had that much, one more won't make no difference.'

'Aw, she needs the cheer, George. Let the old girl enjoy herself.' Tom placed some coins on the counter and picked up the lemonade and beer.

'God bless you, lad.' Fanny waved her pipe at Tom as the barman planted another glass in front of her.

Tom waved back and made for the table.

He was as generous as ever, Bridget thought fondly, lowering her eyes as he drew near. It wouldn't do for him to catch her staring again.

'Here you are then.' He set down the glasses and sat in the wooden chair opposite her. 'Cheers!' He sipped his beer then put the glass down and searched her face, his eyes puzzled, even wary. 'I thought I'd never see you again, Bridget. I was that surprised to hear from you.'

She tried to make her voice casual. 'Oh, I just thought it would be nice to see you and say hello again, and to see how you're faring. I didn't know where you worked till Mrs Kennedy told me in her letter.'

'How is the old girl?'

'As kind as ever.' Bridget spoke slowly now, she must weigh her words lest she give herself away. She would speak as she'd planned to write, telling him no actual lies, but guarding the truth. It wouldn't really be a sin of omission. He had no right to know her past anyway.

He looked closely at her again. 'I don't understand you, Bridget. But then I never did. Why did you leave your post to work in a fish shop and live back with your auntie? It seems like a step down. And you were always that ambitious.'

'Me auntie's right poorly. I've taken her away from me uncle and that awful damp flat. He's getting worse in his old age and was treating her bad. I'm looking after her now. Sure, I can't be doing that and be a live-in nursemaid.'

Tom arched his brows in surprise. 'A nursemaid! I knew you moved to better yourself but that's a big step up from the scullery.' He took a tin of tobacco and a polished wood pipe from his pocket. His eyes never left her face as he shredded tobacco and pressed it into the pipe.

'I didn't know you smoked a pipe.' This gave her time to prepare her story.

'Oh, aye. I couldn't afford baccy afore.' He lit the pipe and sucked on it, continuing to study her.

Now for it. 'I was promoted quickly,' she said. 'He was a lovely little lad. I'm right sorry I had to leave him.' She cast her eyes down in case they give away her anguish and went on lightly, 'But that's enough about me. What's been happening to you, Tom? You're looking grand.'

He took a long draught from his glass, set it down and wiped his mouth with the back of his hand. 'Aye, I can't complain. I've got a good job at Graham's Dynamite.'

'And what would you be doing with dynamite, Tom? It sounds like dangerous work.'

He laughed. 'I'm not blowing things up, you daft thing. I'm a carrier. I just load and deliver the stuff – dynamite, gunpowder, fuses and detonators. I deliver to the pits and the railways. But the best part of the job is that I'm in charge of the horses. I've got a room above the stables. It's rent free 'cause I look after them and save a stableboy's wages. You know I could never live without horses.' He sipped his beer again, then puffed out his chest. 'And I get thirty-six bob a week. I'd get four bob a seven-hour shift down the pits, but if you add that up, for a ten-hour day above ground I get six bob, not counting the time I put in on the horses of course. But I get the room for that – and no night shift. Aye, when that old cow at the house sacked me she did me a favour. I fell on me feet all right.'

His words reverberated through Bridget's head. 'Why, that's a lot of money, Tom. But they're not paying it for nothing. I don't like the sound of it – rattling over the cobbles with a load like that, and all the carriages and trams and things when you're in the town, and bumpy cart tracks when you go to the mines.'

Tom waved his hand to dismiss her fears. 'Nah, I know as how to look after meself, Bridget. I haven't had a single accident in over four years.'

135

'Have others?'

He made little circles on the table with his glass. 'Aye, a couple. But one was drunk and the other was too old for the job – he lost control of the horses. Now can you imagine me ever doing that? You know me with horses. Come on,' he said with a grin. 'You haven't touched your lemonade.'

She picked up her glass and sipped slowly. Her stomach felt wobbly. It suddenly hit her that her feelings for Tom were even deeper than she'd thought. She couldn't bear the idea of his risking his life every day. 'I . . . I just don't like the sound of it, Tom – money or no money.'

He gave her a quizzical look. 'I don't know why you're worrying your head about me, Bridget. It's not like you care about me any more. You made that plain a long time ago.'

'Oh, Tom—' She was stuck for words. How could she tell him that she'd never stopped caring? It would be forward of her. And besides, it would entail some explanation. She compromised. 'I cared enough to want to see how you were getting on, after I found out where you were, that is.'

'Oh, aye? You mean if you'd known earlier you'd have wanted to see me?' The question was casual but his gaze was not.

She picked up her glass and concentrated on the bubbles. 'Maybe.' Was that vague enough? Obviously not. His voice took on an eager and more intimate note.

'You mean you haven't got a lad? I used to think you'd probably be married by now with a tribe of bairns at your heels, either that or you'd be a nun.' He gave her a mischievous look.

'No, I'm not cut out to be a nun.' Outwardly Bridget smiled, but her head reeled. So he *had* thought about her! Encouraged, she said boldly, 'And I thought you'd be bound to have a wife – or at least a serious lass.' As the words came out, she realized her foolishness. For all she knew he *could* be married, or walking out with someone. 'I take it you're not wed then?' she added.

He guffawed and slapped the table. 'Me! Wed! Nah, there's time enough for that.' Then his eyes twinkled the way they used to. 'I can't say as there hasn't been a few lasses, though.'

She smiled again, directly at him this time. 'You haven't changed in some ways, Tom Banks.' Eager to know if there was a special girl in his life, she struggled to phrase the question without sounding too interested. 'And who's the lucky lass at the minute?' she asked at length.

'There's a few,' he said with a chuckle.

She felt elated. So there was no special one! 'Tom Banks,' she chided. 'I don't believe you'll ever grow up and get married like other lads.'

He took another long draught of ale, set down the glass, and when he spoke his voice had lost its chuckle. 'You know I'd have married *you* if you would've had me, Bridget.'

An uncomfortable silence fell as her rehearsed words deserted her. She hadn't banked on his being so frank. 'Yes, I know, Tom,' she managed. 'But I was young and silly and didn't know me own mind. A poor wife I would've made you.'

'Do you know your own mind now then, Bridget?' His voice was light again but his eyes regarded her seriously.

'Sure, a bit better than I used to.' She fidgeted with her shawl under her cloak. This was going so fast. In her wildest dreams about meeting Tom again, she'd never imagined having such a conversation with him – and so soon.

'I'd like to see you again, Bridget.'

'Why, that would be very nice, Tom,' she heard herself saying calmly, while little bubbles popped in her head like those in her glass.

He laid his pipe in the ashtray and leaned over the table, hands clenched. 'I'd like to take you somewhere nice where we could have some fun.'

She came back to earth. 'I'd like that, Tom. But I told you me auntie's expecting me. She'll be worried already and me supper'll be burnt to a cinder.'

'Tomorrow night, then?' His voice was urgent.

She nodded. 'But not straight from work. I can't go anywhere nice in these clothes. I smell like a fishwife.' She looked apologetic and he gave her his old grin again.

'I didn't want to say nothing, but you don't exactly smell like a rose the way you used to. Couldn't you get a better job?'

'Indeed, I was lucky to find anything. I was out of work for three weeks and couldn't afford any more time off. I'm keeping me eye open for something better, though.'

'Aye, I can't see you sticking it long after a posh position.' He looked at her the way he used to, with fondness in his eyes. 'All right, tomorrow then. But if you go home first the night'll be half over. I don't bloody well care if you stink of cow dung, Bridget. You still *look* like a rose to me.'

137

She felt tears starting. 'Sure, you've still got the gift of the blarney, Tom Banks. But I truly couldn't go anywhere nice like this.'

'Why then, bring a clean dress to work with you and you can wash yourself and change at *my* house . . . I mean room. It's in Ridley Court, yon side of the Groat Market, only a step from here.' His eyes twinkled as he saw her look of horror. 'You needn't worry. I'll wait outside.'

'Well, indeed I'll do that.' A rising excitement brought colour to her cheeks, and for the first time since she'd lost Anthony, a spark of happiness kindled within her. She rose unwillingly. 'But now I'd better be off. I can't keep me poor auntie worrying any longer.'

Tom stood and put on his cap. 'I'll walk you to the tram then.'

He took her by the elbow as they ventured into the cold night air and, with his big arm supporting hers again, she felt a forgotten sense of security. With Tom she'd always felt protected. With her family, Anthony, and her aunt, she'd always been the protector.

He guided her sure-footedly through the eerie night, helped her step down from the pavements by the shrouded light of the gas lamps, crossed the black roads confidently, directed only by the faint white glow of distant lamps. When he helped her on to a waiting tram and let her arm go, she felt almost bereaved. But she waved to him as the horses took up a trot and the tram trundled off.

Throughout the journey she recalled every detail of their meeting and anticipated every detail of the next. She'd never dreamt God would give Tom back to her after the way she'd treated him. But as she stepped down from the tram and felt the hard cobbles under her feet, stark reality hit her. If she continued to see him she must tell him of her past. Would he still want her if he knew?

The next evening Bridget poked out her head before closing the shop shutters. He was there, leaning in the tobacconist's doorway opposite. She waved and he nodded a greeting.

'I'll be off now then, sir,' she said to Mr Nunn when she'd finished cleaning.

He looked up from the till at the clock on the wall, then his eyes, like boiled cod's eyes in his pink face, swivelled to survey the spotless counters and fresh sawdust on the floor. 'Have you done the back and all?'

'Yes, sir.' She could feel her cheeks hot from the exertion and anticipation and hoped she didn't look flushed.

'All right, you can go. I'm quite pleased with your work, Bridget.'

138

'Thank you, sir.' She picked up the shopping basket that held Annie's Sunday dress, now taken in and the hem turned up.

'Don't you want your fish then?' Mr Nunn came after her with a parcel. 'You forgot it last night and all.'

'Oh, yes, thank you.' She took the fish and with reluctance placed it in the basket. She could leave it in Tom's room when they went out.

'Hello, Bridget.' Tom took her hand almost shyly. It was out of character. He was obviously still unsure of her.

'Hello, Tom,' she returned as they fell into step.

'What would you like to do then?'

'I don't know – whatever you think. I've never had a night out in Newcastle before.'

He flashed her a strange look. 'And you've been working here all these years. What did you do on your time off?'

Bridget realized she must guard her tongue. 'Well, being a nursemaid, most nights I had to look after the bairn, and then I had to see me auntie.'

'Oh, aye. Well, after you've changed your dress, I'll take you for something to eat and then we could go to the pantomime if you like. *Aladdin and His Wonderful Lamp*'s still on at the Palace. It's been running since afore Christmas so it must be good.'

Christmas! Was it only two short months since she'd last dressed Anthony for his walk, held his hand? In a false, cheerful voice, she said, 'Go to the pantomime *and* eat out. That's a terrible extravagance, Tom Banks. Why, I've never been to a pantomime in me life and I'd love to go, but I can wait to eat till I get home.'

They'd reached the end of the market. Tom stopped to face her and put both hands on her shoulders. 'Bridget Brannigan, do you still not know that when you walk out with me you do things in style? It's nigh on five years since I took you anywhere, and we're not stinting ourselves the night. It's a celebration.'

'Well, seeing as you put it like that . . .' Bridget walked on and gripped his hand tighter. Despite herself, excitement rose within her. She'd read about Aladdin and his magical lamp. She felt as if she were living a fairy tale herself – the magic of the feel of Tom's big hand, his body so close as they walked, the sound of his voice. If only Anthony could be with them . . .

He turned into a small courtyard. 'Here we are. I'll take you up and light the lamp, then I'll go down to feed the horses.'

By the light of a small lantern fixed to one wall, Bridget saw that wooden packing crates and boxes littered the yard. Several carts were parked against a side wall. From the rear she heard the whinny of horses. Tom steered her around the carts and packing crates and up a steep flight of stone stairs by the side of the stables. 'Wait here,' he said as he opened a small door.

She heard the clump of his boots over bare floorboards, the sound of a match being struck. The small room lit up. A round black stove stood in the centre, a pan of water on top. On a marble washstand near the window sat an enamel bowl, a bar of green soap and a folded white towel.

'I heated some water afore I came for you,' Tom said. He picked up the pan and half filled the bowl. 'There's cold in the bucket if it's too hot.'

'Thank you.' Bridget was touched.

'I'll see to the horses now and wait outside till you're ready.' He backed out, again seeming awkward, not at all like his self-confident appearance.

Before undressing, she studied the room. A patchwork quilt covered a narrow bed in one corner, two dining chairs stood at each side of a small scrubbed wooden table, and two stuffed wooden-armed chairs flanked the round black stove in the centre. Two of everything, she thought. He obviously entertained visitors here. She scanned the shelves of the green-painted dresser in the far corner – two bowls, two plates, two mugs. The room was immaculate, and warm.

She set the parcel of fish on the dresser with a grimace. Thank goodness she wouldn't have to take it to the theatre. Quickly, she washed, changed and tidied her hair at the shaving mirror on the wall above the washstand.

When she opened the door, Tom was standing outside. Suddenly she felt shy. 'I'm ready, and thank you for the hot water,' she said.

He walked past her. 'I'll just turn off the lamp and close down the stove then.' A few seconds later he returned and guided her down the stairs and across the yard again.

'Such a nice room you have, Tom, and so clean.'

He chuckled and tightened his grip on her arm. 'I mucked it out last night for you coming, and I mucked the stables out this morning. I like the smell of horses but I know *you* don't.'

Again Bridget felt that delicious sense of security. 'Why, you shouldn't have done that special for me, Tom. I'm a fine one to complain about smells. But I do appreciate that you thought about me.' They'd reached the bottom step and he steadied her as she almost missed her footing.

'Think about you, Bridget . . . aye . . . I've done a fair bit of that in me time.'

Hearing the hurt in his voice, she fell silent. She'd treated him badly. If they were truly to start walking out again she had a lot to make up to him. He steered her through the gate and down the street. The gas lamps hissed as they struggled to shed their eerie white light through the fog. Bridget felt unreal. Was this truly happening to her? Walking arm in arm again with Tom, and he seeming to feel the same about her as he'd felt all those years ago? But she must keep a grip on reality. He didn't know her past.

He broke her long silence. 'Penny for them.'

'I was just wondering where you're taking me to eat.'

'How about here?' They were passing a cheerfully lit café and he ushered her in. 'I come here a lot 'cause it's near and the food's tasty.'

'It looks fine.' She peered around the small room, dotted with oilcloth-covered tables. The main dinner hour being over, only a few late diners remained.

Tom led her to a table near the back. 'It's warmer here near the kitchen,' he explained as he took her cloak.

Bridget sat, remembering the time he'd taken her to the tea room in Morpeth. This place wasn't so fancy, but the smell from the kitchen was enticing. He hung up their damp clothes while she studied the menu, scrawled untidily on a blackboard on the wall. She surveyed him as he joined her and sat down. He looked handsome and immaculate in his brown corduroy suit and matching waistcoat, and his union striped shirt looked fresh from the laundry. She felt shabby in her aunt's old black Sunday dress and nervously smoothed her skirts.

Tom, sitting opposite, looked into her eyes. 'You look right pretty tonight, Bridget.'

'Why, thank you, but 'tis just me auntie's old black dress.' She fidgeted with the collar.

'I don't mean the dress, you ninny.'

Bridget's hand flew to her face. Excitement had flushed her cheeks and the fog had curled her hair into damp ringlets on her forehead. She looked at the blackboard to escape his gaze. 'Well, now . . .' She pretended to deliberate. 'There's one thing I'll not be having, and that's the fish, but anything else would be fine.'

'The steak and kidney pudding's always tasty.' He stretched his long legs under the table and Bridget moved her knees to make room, but not before his calves had brushed against hers. She tingled with pleasure. With difficulty she kept her voice level.

'Steak and kidney! That sounds like a feast.'

'Two steak and kidney puddings, Millie,' he called to the owner's wife. She waddled out from the kitchen, easing the weight of her fifteen stones from side to side. The floorboards groaned.

'Why, Tom, nice to see you.' She gave Bridget a nod and Tom a flirtatious grin. 'I swear, you know how to pick the pretty ones.'

Tom returned the grin. 'Second choice, Millie, as usual, seeing as you're already taken.'

'Get away with you, lad, or me old man'll be after you.' She poked him playfully in the shoulder before plodding back to the kitchen.

They ate quickly in order to catch the beginning of the pantomime at eight, and Bridget was careful to keep the conversation light. Millie helped, as she sat with them and bantered with Tom most of the time.

'That was the best steak and kidney pudding I ever had, Millie,' Bridget told her when they rose to leave.

'Aye, lass,' Millie said without modesty. 'I've got a light hand for pastry.' She saw them to the door and wagged a fat finger at Bridget. 'Now you watch out for that lad, d'you hear? He's got an evil streak in him with the lasses.'

'Get off it, Millie, you're just jealous.' Tom took Bridget's arm in a proprietorial manner that made her feel proud.

The foyer at the theatre thronged with people rushing to get their tickets in time for the performance. While Tom stood in the queue at the box office, Bridget peeked behind a red velvet curtain into the auditorium. It was larger even than the ballroom at the big house, and just as grand – the walls panelled in red and gold, the rows of seats covered in red velvet. She squinted high into the gallery. There, steep wooden steps served as both seats and stairs. It was already packed with bodies. They would have to stand at the back, and it would be difficult to see from such a height and distance. But nothing could spoil her first pantomime. She waited by the door marked 'Gallery'. But when Tom returned he ushered her to the red-curtained entrance to the stalls.

'Tom! We can't go in there.'

He flourished two tickets. 'Why not? You don't think I want to mix with the riffraff, do you?'

'Tom, you're a terror!' Bridget tried to look disapproving but her face creased into a delighted smile. She felt like a princess as he guided

142

her down the plush carpeted stairs to the front row.

People settled into their seats and the tinny band tuned up. Bridget was filled with wonderment. Tom slid something on to her lap. She drew in her breath. A box of chocolates! 'Oh, Tom, you shouldn't have,' she chided him weakly. She opened them – the same assortment he'd bought her when . . . She suppressed a shudder.

He looked at her closely. 'I remembered you like those ones.'

'Indeed, I do. Thank you.' She bit her lip to hold back her tears and took his hand.

A roll of drums indicated that the band was about to strike up and the hubbub in the audience stopped at its command. Bridget sat entranced throughout the performance, especially when with a puff of smoke the two genii miraculously appeared as if from the lamp.

As they walked back to Tom's room, she clung to him and babbled like a child. 'I haven't ever seen anything so wonderful in all me life. Thank you for taking me, Tom. I always wanted to go to a theatre, but I never dreamed I'd ever see a real pantomime.' He remained silent but gripped her arm tighter. 'How I wish I had a magical lantern like that,' she went on. 'Just think! If all you had to do was rub it and your every wish would be granted!'

'What would you wish for then?' His voice was serious.

She sighed. 'Oh, such a lot of things. I'd wish for a nice house for me auntie and me, and enough money so I could just stay at home and look after her.' She hesitated as she thought of the wishes she couldn't tell him. 'And lots of other things.'

'Oh, aye, what sort of things?'

She turned the question around. 'What would *you* wish for, Tom?'

They were nearing the yard. 'Well, at this minute I'd wish that if I put some water on the stove while you get your workdress, you'd stay and have a cup of coffee with me.'

'Coffee! Getting stylish, are you?'

He chuckled. 'Well, it always impresses the ladies.'

'Indeed, that's a modest wish, Tom. But I have to be getting home.' She couldn't tell him that she longed, but was afraid, to be alone with him.

'Just one cup.'

She gave in. 'All right. But just one, mind you.' She mustn't let her aunt know that she'd spent time alone with Tom in his room – she was starting to sin again already.

143

They neared the stables and he helped her up the slippery steps. At the door he hesitated. 'I've just changed me wish, Bridget.'

'Indeed, and what would you be wishing now?'

His teeth flashed white in the gloom. 'That you'd wait to change your dress till after.'

She laughed and all her nervousness vanished. 'Would you be trying to tell me something, Tom Banks?'

'Well, nothing as you don't know already. I like it better when you smell like a rose. Come on.' He jerked her hand and pulled her behind him into the room. After lighting the lamp he opened the stove door. The ashes still glowed red and he threw more coal on top from the scuttle. 'Sit down and warm yourself,' he said. 'It'll be blazing in a minute or two.' He took her damp cloak, threw it over the iron bed rails and pulled off the patchwork quilt. 'You'll need this till the heat gets going, though.' He draped it round her shoulders and pressed her down into one of the stuffed chairs.

She dissolved into the quilt's soft warmth and watched as he filled a metal jug from the water bucket, added coffee from a brown paper bag and set the jug on the stove. No man had made anything for her before. Feeling awkward, she stood. 'Let me do it, Tom. It just doesn't seem right, you running around after me.'

He pushed her gently back in the chair. 'I'm quite used to looking after meself now, Bridget. You'll see what a good cup of coffee I can make. And I've got some digestive biscuits.'

Bridget grimaced and placed her hands on her stomach. 'Glory be! I'm that stuffed after that lovely dinner and those chocolates. Just coffee, please.'

He took off his overcoat and sat in the opposite chair.

Again she couldn't help staring at him. Even the thick corduroy trousers couldn't disguise his muscular thighs, nor the tight waistcoat his powerful chest. His eyes met hers and she stammered, 'That's . . . that's a fine suit you're wearing, Tom. 'Tis plain you're doing well for yourself.'

He nodded. 'Aye, I'm faring well.'

She held out her hands to the stove. 'But I hope you don't always spend that much money on taking a girl out or it's the workhouse you'll be bound for.'

'You know I've always liked to spend me money on pretty lasses, but especially you, Bridget.'

'Thank you.' She lowered her eyes under his scrutiny. 'You

always *were* a one for compliments, Tom.'

'Only when I mean them.' The coffee puffed steam and he rose.

She watched his supple movements as he walked to the dresser and set two enamelled mugs, a milk jug and a sugar bowl on an old tin tray. He knelt by the fire and put the tray on the floor, waiting for the pot to boil.

'I feel that strange being looked after by a man,' she said again with a note of awe in her voice.

The pot bubbled. He poured the black liquid, added milk and sugar and handed her a mug before he spoke. 'Don't you like being looked after then?'

'I surely do. But I'd have to get used to it.'

He set his mug on the floor and knelt beside her. 'I could help you get used to it.'

At his serious tone she slopped coffee over the sides of her mug. 'I'd like that well.' She smiled to hide her nervousness, but he continued to regard her seriously.

'Look, Bridget, I'm not going to play the waiting game any more. If you married me you could have your wish. Your auntie could stay with us and you wouldn't have to work. I'd look after both of you.' He flung the idea at her like a challenge.

She opened her mouth but no words came out.

'Well, what do you say?' He leaned closer, his eyes level with hers.

'But . . . 'tis so sudden, Tom.'

'Sudden!' He jumped up and paced the room. 'I know it's not romantic me saying it like that. But by God, *sudden*! I wanted to ask you four and a half years ago, Bridget, and ever since I've thought of little else but having another chance with you. I used to walk all around Byker, knowing your auntie lived there, just in the hopes of seeing hair or hide of you. I even wrote to Mrs Kennedy to try to find out where you were, but I tore up the letter.'

Bridget closed her eyes. If only he'd sent the letter, things might have been different. 'Why did you tear it up?'

'Because I was too proud. I couldn't go crawling back and begging you again, even if I knew where to go. God knows I did me share of begging at the time. But I used to dream that you would somehow come back into me life and that I could ask you in a manly fashion to be me wife.'

He sat in the chair again and stared at her almost angrily. 'And here you are, and here I am – *practically* begging.'

Stunned, Bridget fumbled for words. 'But you don't understand. I

145

had to go away. I couldn't get in touch with you. Even though you've been in me thoughts all this time as well.'

His fist thumped on the chair-arm. 'Then why in God's name did you run away from me?' He checked himself. 'Oh, aye, that's a laugh! It *was* in God's name that you didn't want no more to do with me.' He scowled and his voice became harsh. 'And do you want to know something else, Bridget. I even decided I would be converted, go to church, do whatever you wanted, just to get you back again.'

She stared at him in surprise. She hadn't expected such an outburst. But she understood. She'd made him suffer, and lied to him. Now, whatever happened, she must tell him the truth. Her hand trembled as she set her mug on the floor. How to begin? There was no time to prepare her speech, to make it soft on him, less damning on her. She kept her eyes on him. 'I lied to you. I didn't want to leave you . . . and it wasn't for the reason I told you.'

'Then *why*, Bridget? Why on earth—'

'I was with child, Tom. I . . . I couldn't bear to let you know the truth about meself.' As soon as it was out, she wished she could take back the words.

He stared at her, uncomprehending. 'You? With child?'

'Yes, Tom.' She could hold her gaze no longer, unable to bear the puzzlement and hurt in his eyes. She spoke to the floor. 'A man . . . took advantage of me.'

'A man! You were seeing another man when you were with me?' Anger took him over again. His eyes, like red embers from the fire's glow, burned through her.

Bridget twisted her hands in her lap. Here she was, hurting him again. 'No, Tom! I was seeing nobody but you.' She dared to look him in the eye once more. 'He was a stranger. He . . . he raped me.'

'Raped you!' He jumped up, clumped across the room and back, then towered over her.

Bridget froze inside. She shouldn't have told him. She should have known. He was ashamed of her. Tom was proud. He could never take a fallen woman for his wife. Why had she even dared to hope? 'Tom, I'm sorry—' she began. But he cut her off.

'Sorry! By God you should be sorry!' He stormed back and forth across the room again.

'I'll be going now.' Bridget stood, tears trickling down her cheeks. It was painful enough reliving that memory without having to bear Tom's disgust.

146

He came at her and pushed her roughly back in the chair. 'Who?' he yelled.

'Tom, there's no point. Let me go now, please.' She longed to escape, to escape into the dark from her guilt and shame, to escape from Tom's fury and disgust. How stupid she'd been! Now she'd humiliated him even more – and herself. She pressed her hands to her temples and tried to gather her thoughts. Shame! She chastised herself. How could she be ashamed of her beautiful son? Of her love for him? She felt as if she'd been split in two by a cleaver. No! If Tom couldn't accept her past, then she must put her love for him aside. She tried again to get up but he loomed over her.

'Tell me who!'

'Tom, please, there's no point—'

'No point? I'll tell you the point. I'll break his bloody neck. That's the point!'

Shocked, Bridget looked up at him. 'Break his neck?'

'Aye, and worse. A man that does that to any lass deserves the worst. But *you*, Bridget, *you* of all lasses! I'll bash his blasted face through to the back of his skull.'

'You mean you're . . . you're angry with *him*?' The lamp flickered and his face looked dark, then light again. She blinked. 'You're not angry with me?'

'Of course I'm bloody angry with you.' His eyes tunnelled into her for a moment, then with an impatient shrug he turned his back. Once more his heavy boots thumped on the bare boards, away from her, then back. 'Hell's bells! What a stupid woman you are! Why didn't you tell me then? You lied to me and ran away, when all you had to do was tell me and I would've put matters right for you.'

Bridget lowered her head and folded her hands in her lap like a schoolgirl reprimanded for not knowing her catechism. Dear Lord! Put matters right? That could only mean he would have married her then – even in her disgrace.

When she raised her head he was standing over her again. Her voice quivered. 'Oh, Tom, how stupid I've been! I thought you wouldn't want any more to do with me in me shame.'

He bent and shook her by the shoulders. 'Shame! He's the one to feel the shame. For the last time – who did that to you?'

She had to steel herself to speak the truth. There must be no more lies between them. ''Twas the master.'

He fell to his knees beside her and grasped her hands, his voice a

147

cracked whisper. 'The master . . . For God's sake, Bridget, why didn't you tell me afore?'

His touch released an emotion she'd buried deep inside all these years. She sobbed for a long time before she could speak. All the while, he remained on his knees, gripping her hands.

'It's all right, now, take your time.' His tone was soft, as if soothing a child.

'He found me that day at the stream, Tom. That day you had to work. I tried to fight him off, I swear. I felt bad enough seeing you at all after that, but when I found out I was carrying his child . . . I just couldn't. I didn't want to burden you with me shame.'

'*Your shame!* God in heaven, girl, stop using that word. I've told you, it's his shame. I swear I'll go up there and knock him to kingdom come.'

Bridget darted him a frightened glance. There must be no more trouble at the house. 'Indeed, there's no purpose to be served by that, Tom.' His face became a blurred blob as more tears started. She blinked furiously. 'And anyway, it's all over now . . .'

'All over? But what happened to the bairn?'

'*They've* got him. Oh, Tom, they took me little Anthony away from me. At first I prayed for that monster's child to die in me belly. But I grew to love him so much.'

When he drew her to him she buried her head in his chest, felt the rough corduroy of his waistcoat against her cheek, his big hands stroking her hair in long slow strokes, and she found comfort in his strength. Then he eased her down beside him on the floor and cradled her in his arms.

It was a long time before he spoke. 'Tell me all about it, Bridget.'

She let out a deep breath, but it sounded like a groan. 'Yes, I owe you that.' Her story came out. Slowly, haltingly. She shuddered when she'd finished.

'Oh, Bridget, me little Bridget.' Tom gripped her tighter and rocked her. 'If only you'd told me. I don't deny I'd have been upset, but I would've wed you, didn't you know that? There's never been a lass in me whole life I was so sweet on as you. I'd have done anything to keep you and to make you happy. And I'd probably have grown to love the bairn the same as you. He's part of you, isn't he?' He held her at arm's length and gripped her shoulders almost roughly. 'Look, I'll get him back for you, Bridget, if I have to spend every penny I earn.'

She shook her head to silence him. 'No, no . . . 'tis hopeless, Tom.

I've told you, I've been through all that. He's legally theirs.'

'God's truth!' He dropped his arms from her shoulders and clenched his fists. 'I know what I'd like to do with the pair of them. I just can't pretend it never happened.'

'No, and neither can I, but it's all in the past. I've had to settle for seeing me little lad from a distance when I can. Mrs Kennedy's going to arrange it.' Washed by a wave of relief at sharing her secret with Tom, she snuggled closer into him. 'But I'm so happy that you know and that you still care for me. Sure, I was a stupid young thing then to think . . . But I know now, it was mostly me pride. I couldn't bear the shame of telling you.'

'Shhh.' He put his finger to her lips. 'There you go using that word again. You've got nowt to be ashamed of.' He tipped her chin and pressed his lips lightly against hers, still damp with tears. She savoured the tenderness of his touch and felt overwhelmed with love.

When he gently pulled away she flung her arms round his neck and clung to him. The warm smell of his skin, so familiar, so comforting, took her back all those years and she cried for what they'd lost for so long. He untwined her grasp and tilted her chin. 'I'd like you to stay here with me forever, Bridget. But you'd better go now. If it takes all the strength I've got, I'm not going to lay a finger on you till you're me bride.'

'Bride,' she repeated, crestfallen. 'Sure, I could never be a true bride to you now, Tom. I'm so sorry—'

'Yes you will.' He rose to his feet and pulled her up. 'I'll still be the first man to make love to you. What that man did to you wasn't love, Bridget, and don't ever think it's like that. I know I was young and . . . well . . . sometimes a bit hasty with you. But I've waited this long, I can hold meself till we're wed.'

Bridget marvelled at the gentleness in his big voice. She knew it would cost him a lot to keep his manliness under control. The sadness left her eyes and she smiled up at him. 'Aye, you were a right rascal in your time, Tom Banks. Many's the time I felt the need to slap your face.'

He chuckled. 'Why didn't you then?'

'Because me hands were always too busy keeping *yours* in check.' She laughed as he grabbed her and hugged her.

'Well now, if you want me to keep me word we'll have to make this wedding quick. What about tomorrow?'

'Tomorrow!' She poked him playfully in the chest. 'Don't talk daft,

Tom. It takes a while to organize a wedding.'

He gripped her shoulders again and the playfulness left his voice. 'I mean it, Bridget. How soon? This week? This month?'

'I suppose it could be arranged within a month,' she said, screwing up her forehead as she tried to clear her mind. 'I'm that dizzy with everything happening so fast. There are things we'll have to discuss first.'

'Fine, we can discuss them while I take you home.' He turned abruptly to get her cloak from the bed.

'Saints in heaven!' Bridget clapped her hand to her mouth. 'Haven't I forgotten all about the time! Me auntie'll be thinking I've had a mishap.'

'Or that I'm keeping you out late to dally with you. And I want her to think I'm a nice fella if I'm going to live with her.'

Bridget frowned. 'The flat's right tiny and just one bedroom. You wouldn't care for it, Tom. I mean, we could squeeze in another bed but we couldn't be alone much.'

Tom put her cloak round her shoulders and threw on his greatcoat. 'We can talk about that in the hackney.'

'The hackney! Why, I can take the tram alone like last night.'

Without a word he went back to the bed, retrieved a leather pouch from under the pillow and tucked it in his coat pocket. 'Not tonight, even if the trams were still running this late. Come on.' He took her hand and led her to the door. 'It must be well nigh two in the morning.'

'Great heavens!'

The fog enveloped them in a soggy blanket and she rested her head against his arm, allowing him to lead her down the back lanes and across the deserted streets to the station.

The carriage lamps of two waiting hackney cabs greeted them. 'Forty Conyers Road, Byker,' Tom said to the driver of the first.

The man grunted and shook himself.

'We woke the poor bugger up.' Tom grinned as he helped Bridget up and settled beside her on the leather-covered bench.

She stroked the polished leather. 'Dear me! I feel so grand. You're spoiling me rotten.'

He took her hand and pressed into it the pouch he'd taken from the room. 'Here,' he said. 'Put this in your pocket.'

She weighed the heavy bag in her palm. 'But Tom! This is money, a great deal of it. I can't take your money.'

'It's *our* money now, you daft thing. I want you to hand in your

150

notice at the shop tomorrow and to leave as soon as the boss finds somebody else. Then I want you to start looking for a flat with two bedrooms. Maybe I'll learn to like your auntie a lot, but I fear never enough to share me bedroom with her. A man and wife need some privacy.'

'*Two* bedrooms,' Bridget squeaked. 'But Tom—'

He drowned her protest. 'And get any more furniture you need, and clothes, and whatever it is that women have a need of when they get wed.'

'But me auntie wouldn't want to move from Byker, Tom. All her friends are there. And she can't get about much.'

'I don't give a tinker's damn where we live, so long as we live together,' he said with fervour, then gave her a sly sideways look. 'Oh, aye, and when you make the arrangements for the church, would you find out about those lessons I've got to take.' He chuckled as her head jerked towards him. 'Mind you, I'm not saying as I'll believe all that rubbish definitely in me heart, but I'll go to church with you, and I'll be a model Catholic father when the time comes.' He gripped her hand and his voice sobered. 'I can't give you your little lad back, but I'll give you more bairns, Bridget. As many as you want.'

Too moved to speak, she leaned her head on his shoulder and tried to stem the tears, but little hiccup-like sobs shook her.

Tom searched her face in the gloom. 'Good God, Bridget! What are you bubbling about now?'

'Nothing . . . nothing. I'm just so happy!' She bawled louder and he laughed.

'God's truth! I never could make you out, Bridget Brannigan. How am I going to know when you're sad or when you're happy?'

'You will, Tom,' she said between sniffs. 'Because I'm not ever going to be sad again, I swear.'

The clatter of hooves on the cobbles slowed to a stop and the driver's face poked upside down into the back of the cab, 'This is Conyers Road but I can't see no numbers.'

'It's the last one on the left,' Bridget told him, and the horses took up a trot again.

'Will you tell your auntie I'm that sorry I kept you out late, but that I'll apologize in person when I meet her the morrow.'

'That soon?'

'Aye, I'll pick you up from work and come home to meet her. Then I can ask for your hand formal like.'

151

Bridget felt cocooned in a warm glow. 'She'll be right thrilled, Tom. I can't wait to tell her the news.'

The carriage slowed to a stop again and Tom jumped out and helped her down. He bent and kissed her softly on the lips. 'Goodnight, Bridget. And don't stay up talking too long. You'll need some sleep for work the morrow.'

'And you and all, Tom Banks. But I don't know as I can sleep at all, I'm that excited.'

'Aye, me and all. I'm just going to lie in me bed and keep me eyes open. If I go to sleep I might wake up and find out tonight was only a dream.'

'It's real.' She stood on tiptoe and kissed his cheek.

She waved until the carriage lamps disappeared into the gloom, then darted through the door, ran down the dark passage and burst into the kitchen.

'Bridget! Oh, thank the Lord!' Annie's white, strained face peered out from the blanket she was huddled in beside the waning fire. 'Are you all right? I've been that worried.'

Bridget knelt at her feet and lifted a radiant face to her. 'I'm sorry I gave you cause for worry, Auntie. But I'm grand. Indeed, I've never been grander in me life. Just wait till you hear me news . . .'

'Eey, my! Eey, my!' Annie's old eyes glowed almost as bright as Bridget's by the time the story was unfolded. 'Now that's happenstance for you! And, by God, you deserve some good fortune, lass. The Lord hasn't forgotten you. I can't hardly believe it. I never thought I'd spend me last days in such style, and with me own family, and grandbairns sooner or later.'

'Aye, Auntie.' Bridget's eyes lost their sparkle for a moment. 'I'll never forget me little Anthony. But I'll have more little ones . . . and they'll be Tom's and mine. I know it's too much to ask to have everything you want in life, and now I've got everything I could ever want but one. I'm more fortunate than most.'

'You are that, hinny. But now you'd better get some sleep.'

'Sure, it'll give me great joy to tell Mr Nunn I'm leaving.' Bridget sighed with pleasure before clapping her hand to her mouth. 'Dear me! In all me excitement I left me work dress and the fish at Tom's. I'll have to wear this good one to work tomorrow.'

Annie raised herself by the chair-arms and clasped her shawl tighter. 'Never mind, luv. You can get better than that now. Tom said to buy

152

whatever you need, didn't he?' She pulled a wry face. 'And to tell the truth I'm not sorry we won't be having fish the morrow.'

'Me neither! And just think, Auntie, we won't ever have to eat fish again, except on Fridays of course.'

Chapter Fourteen

The following Sunday, the last day of February, Mrs Kennedy was coming to visit. Bridget could hardly wait to see her and of course surprise her with the news about Tom. On her aunt's visits to Bridget at Nellie's, Annie had made friends with Mrs Kennedy and was as excited as Bridget.

When Tom and Bridget returned from mass he sat by the fire, smoking his pipe. The women bustled about cooking a special joint of mutton with turnip and roast potatoes and laughing at his observations on the holy ceremony. He shook his head in amazement. 'I tell you! I've never seen such a palaver in all me life. All that Latin rubbish nobody understands anyway. I hope they don't expect me to learn that at me lessons. I felt like a bloody sheep just following what everybody else did – kneel, stand, sit, kneel, stand, open me mouth and pretend to sing.' More head-shaking. 'And I felt even dafter when Bridget gave me a nudge that would have felled a horse and pushed me back on me knees. How was I to know I couldn't go to the altar with her? Everybody looked.'

Bridget stopped peeling the turnips and grinned at Annie. 'Sure, I told him before we went he couldn't take Holy Communion till he's finished his lessons and been converted, but he got up to follow me.' She gave Tom a fond look. 'Anyway, you did grand for your first time.'

Tom slumped down in the chair and sucked on his pipe. 'Aye, I suppose I can get used to anything if I have to. Though I'll never understand it, mind you, lessons or no, it'll always be gibberish to me.'

Bridget smothered a giggle. 'I swear Mrs Kennedy'll drop dead when she sees you sitting there like the cock o' the roosters. And she'll drop dead again when she hears you're being converted.'

He puffed on his pipe, then grinned. 'Aye, well, she'll have to rise

154

again from the dead twice, won't she?'

The front door knocker rapped. Bridget jumped, pushed back the loose curls about her face, and smoothed her new grey dress and white apron. She calmed herself with effort. 'Now, I'm going to greet her as if nothing's unusual.' She took measured steps down the passage, but at the door flung herself at the waiting figure. 'Oh, Mrs Kennedy, it's grand to see you! It's been that long.'

'Eey, by! It has. Let's have a look at you then.' Breathless, Mrs Kennedy took her by the shoulders and gazed at her. 'My, but you look fine.'

Bridget tried not to smile too widely. 'Come on in now. What is it I'm doing keeping you out here in the cold?'

Mrs Kennedy indicated over her shoulder. 'I've tethered the horse to that lamppost. Such nosy neighbours you've got – all peering out behind their curtains. You'd think they'd never seen a horse and trap afore.'

'Aye, they're nosy all right. Not much happens to get excited about round here.' Bridget almost pushed her along the passage and into the kitchen.

'Man alive! It's Tom!' Mrs Kennedy looked as if she'd seen an apparition.

With an expansive grin, Tom stood up and took her hand. 'Aye, it's me, Mrs Kennedy, in the flesh. How're you doing?' He relieved her of the small carpet bag she carried and set it by the door.

'Why, it's right nice to clap eyes on you again, lad.' She looked from one to the other. 'I see you two've got back together. And about time.'

'It's thanks to you,' Bridget said. 'We've got lots of news to tell you.'

Annie rose from her chair at the table, her face as welcoming as the fire in the grate.

'Eey, Annie!' Mrs Kennedy flapped her hands in excitement. 'I didn't see you sitting there, I was that taken aback at the sight of this lad.'

Annie smiled. 'Aye, it's nice to see you and all, Kate. Let me take your cloak and bonnet, then go and have a sit-down by the fire. Our Bridget's forgetting her manners.'

As Annie removed the cloak Bridget noticed that Mrs Kennedy was no longer stout. Her black dress hung from her shoulders like a coat from a hanger. She searched her face. It was the colour of dough, the cheeks deflated and ridged, the eyes deep in their sockets. She chastised

155

herself for being so wrapped up in her own excitement that she hadn't noticed how ill the woman looked.

She took her by the elbow. 'Come and sit by the fire. How thoughtless I am! You're looking poorly still, and you've gone right thin.'

Mrs Kennedy wheezed as she lowered herself into an armchair. 'Aye, the influenza nearly knocked the living daylights out of me, but I'm starting to eat again and I'm getting some of me strength back. I'd have got it back sooner if the old witch hadn't planned all those house parties when she knew I wasn't well enough to get up. I just had to drag meself around and get on with it. I'd have been to see you long afore now if I'd been up to it.'

Bridget sat on her knees beside her and took her bony hands. 'Indeed, I know you would. You shouldn't have made such a long journey so soon. Did you see a doctor?'

Mrs Kennedy pulled an unladylike face. 'Aye, the mistress had her own physician to me – that worried she was that she might have to do some organizing around the house. He said I was lucky it didn't turn to pneumonia. But it's left me bronchial pipes clogged. I can't get me breath the way I used to. Anyways, I'll get over it, hinny. Me da always said I had the constitution of a horse.' She turned to Tom. 'And that reminds me. The horse needs a drop of water, and a little rub-down wouldn't hurt. Would you mind?'

Tom jumped up. 'Why aye, I'll do it now.' He took the water bucket, and an old towel from the line on the mantelpiece, and crossed the room in a few steps.

Mrs Kennedy's eyes followed him. 'He's grown into a fine man, Bridget. I'm that glad you're back together. Does he know?'

Bridget nodded. 'Aye, he knows everything. I've got loads to tell you. But how's me little lad?' She was unable to contain the question any longer.

Mrs Kennedy gave her a heartening smile. 'He's doing fine, hen. I see him every day. And since the snow and rain stopped the new nurse has been taking him to that old copse you used to go to. Anthony begged her to.'

Thrilled, Bridget jumped to her feet. 'I could go to see him. Nobody ever goes there.'

'Aye, I thought that and all. But you'll have to be careful nobody sees you, especially her. Would you mind giving Tom a shout to fetch the box I left in the trap when he comes in? In me eagerness I forgot it.'

Annie got up from the table where she was mashing the turnips. 'I'll go,' she said. 'You two've got a lot of nattering to catch up on.' She set the pan back on the trivet and left the room almost at a trot. In her newfound happiness at times she almost forgot her pain. Her voice resounded down the passage as she bellowed to Tom to bring in the box, and she returned as fast as she'd left.

Bridget smiled at Mrs Kennedy. 'There's no need to tell you me auntie's feeling better.' Then, with a lurch of her heart, she knelt again and threw her arms around her friend. 'Oh, it's so grand to hear about me little lad, and to think I can see him again. So many wonderful things are happening at once, I swear you're not going to believe all our good news.'

Annie bent to the oven and pronged the joint with a fork. 'Aye, the Lord's been right generous to us. But wait to tell her till Tom gets back.'

Tom returned with the bucket and towel in one hand and a round box in the other. Mrs Kennedy waved him away as he held out the box to her. 'Nah, it's for Bridget, lad.'

'A present! Oh, you shouldn't have. 'Tis present enough for me just to see you.' Nevertheless, Bridget took the box eagerly and, still kneeling, set it on the floor. Her eyes grew large as she pulled out an elegant grey felt hat. The side brims curved upward, a cluster of feathers adorned one side, and a dark grey veil floated from the downturned front brim. 'Now isn't that beautiful – a real lady's hat.' Bridget held out her prize for everyone to see.

Mrs Kennedy coughed and wheezed. 'It's not a fancy present, luv. It's a common-sense one. It's for you to wear when you go to see Anthony. Nobody'll recognize you with the veil down. And you know Anthony mustn't see you. It'd only mean trouble. Promise me you'll wear it.'

Bridget's expression grew solemn. 'Of course I will. I'll keep it special for those occasions.' She kissed Mrs Kennedy on the cheek. 'You're that thoughtful – and sensible. Thank you, indeed.'

Annie clapped her hands for attention. 'Dinner's on the table. You can get on with your news while you eat.'

After dinner, replete with food and overflowing with happiness at the news of the imminent wedding, Mrs Kennedy leaned back in her chair. Tears wound their way down the new crevasses in her cheeks. 'Well, well! This has been the best day of me life for a long time. Have you set a date yet?'

Tom made a good-natured grimace. 'If I had my way it would be the morrow, but you know *her*. He inclined his head towards Bridget. 'Everything's got to be done proper like and I've got to finish me conversion first.'

'It'll only be six more weeks on Saturday,' Bridget said to Mrs Kennedy. 'Can you manage another day off?'

She puffed out what was left of her substantial chest. 'Wild horses couldn't stop me. And I'll bring Nellie and the bairn. Jack'll be working of a Saturday. Eey, I'm all of a dither. It's so much to take in at once.'

Annie stood up. 'Why, now we're all going to sit by the fire and relax. The dishes can stay there the rest of the day for all I care. This is a special occasion.'

Hands entwined, Bridget and Tom sat on the floor between the women. Bridget thought how perfect the day was . . . except for one thing.

That night, lying in bed beside Annie, she planned her first visit to Anthony. Mr Nunn had already found someone to take over at the shop. Tomorrow Bridget was to train her. Afterwards her days would be free to organize the wedding, and to find a larger flat and set up a real home. Weather permitting, she would go to see Anthony the following day.

Excitement at the prospect kept her awake most of the night. And when she did sleep, she dreamt she was sitting on the grass in a green and sunny clearing in a wood, the grey felt hat in her lap. A small bird alighted on a bare branch nearby and stared at her with bright yellow eyes. She held out her hand and it flew towards her. But it rested on the hat brim beside the brown and grey feather cluster which, as Bridget watched, turned to an iridescent blue like the bird. She stretched out a finger to stroke it, but it fluttered back towards the branch, chirping Brid-jet, Brid-jet. When it alighted it was joined by five more identical blue birds and they chirped in chorus, Brid-jet, Brid-jet. She awoke in the dark, silent bedroom and forced herself to sleep again.

On Tuesday morning she got up early to catch Mr Jones' cart. She would arrive in time to pay Nellie a quick visit before Anthony's afternoon outing. As she would miss the return journey that day, she would stay overnight with Nellie.

It was cool and misty but there were no signs of rain clouds. She sat in the cart fingering the unaccustomed hat and ignoring the stares from

158

the other passengers. They obviously wondered why a woman of means was travelling in such a lowly fashion. Although her black coat didn't match the hat, it was in good condition. She decided to buy a grey cloak next time.

It was a happy reunion with Nellie and Lizzie. Nellie was overjoyed to hear the news. 'Eey, Bridget! I can't believe me ears. I'm that glad for you. Do you hear that, Lizzie? You're going to have a new uncle.' She danced Bridget around the kitchen. The occasion was marred only by Lizzie's repeated demands to see Anthony.

At two o'clock Bridget left, giving herself plenty of time to skirt around the west side of the grounds and approach the copse from the opposite direction the nurse would take from the house. It felt strange having to dart from bush to bush, tree to tree, like a criminal in hiding. But her goal kept her moving. As she neared the clearing she took slow, stealthy steps, avoiding fallen branches and twigs that might snap under her feet. The leaves, already disintegrating into the earth to complete their cycle, formed a moist carpet to muffle her footsteps.

A sudden scurrying sound sent her running for the cover of the nearest tree. She stood rigid and held her breath. A squirrel scampered past her and disappeared up a tree. She breathed again and moved on. Yes, she thought, as she saw the light of the clearing ahead, she must get a grey cape that would blend better with the trees. She stopped. Not a sound.

She inched a few yards further and hid behind a large oak. As she pressed herself against the tree's crust she felt as if a strange energy flowed out from its core into her being. She hugged it and pressed her face against its damp bark, inhaled its earthy smell. Somehow she felt as she did when taking communion, full of awe at being so close to God, and yet calmed. From here she had a good view and would be invisible. It seemed forever she stood, straining for the sound of footsteps, Anthony's voice.

A crackle from beyond the clearing made her heart skip. Only another squirrel? No! The noise was followed by Anthony's laughter. She put her hand to her mouth lest she forget and cry out his name.

'Over here, over here.' The sound of his voice brought tears. She dared to peek around the tree. He stood at the far edge of the clearing, tall and straight, beckoning to a black-cloaked figure behind him. Bridget summoned all her strength to resist her instinct to run to him, hold him close, whisper his name. Instead she stared. How he'd grown!

And how beautiful he looked in his fine tweed jacket and breeches! A matching cap sat on top of his curls, grown almost to his shoulders now.

'What is it then?' The nursemaid's voice intruded on Bridget's few moments alone with Anthony.

A large woman approached him, carrying what appeared to be a knitting bag. Bridget could see by the face under the black bonnet what Mrs Kennedy had meant. Anthony would certainly not get his own way with her. It was a stern face, though not cruel. She thanked God for that at least. But the mistress had obviously chosen someone cold and impersonal to avoid Anthony forming an attachment that excluded her.

'Look! Look!' He raked the crumbled leaves at the foot of a large oak with a stick. 'Acorns . . . lots of acorns. It must be a squirrel's nest. I want to collect some.'

'No, Anthony,' the woman said firmly. 'They're too old now, and besides, you wouldn't steal the squirrel's food, would you?'

Anthony looked disappointed for a moment then cheered up and raked the leaves back. 'He might come for his dinner while we're here.'

'Aye, maybe.' The woman stood stiffly in the centre of the clearing. 'But we can't stay long. I'll never understand why you like this place so much. There's more room in the meadow for you to play. And you can make your letters by the stream.'

Bridget's heart almost burst. He still made the letters she'd taught him! Part of her was still with him.

Anthony thought for a moment. 'Please, can we play hide and seek first? Please? There's nowhere to hide in the meadow.'

'Not today. I'm too tired.' She turned with no further word.

Anthony's expression was one of silent resignation. Bridget knew that expression so well, knew that it masked the burning frustration of a child helpless against the iron discipline of adults. Anthony's will was strong. Some day it would burst its chains and he would flout adult authority. At the thought, she quailed, and prayed that he wouldn't attempt to assert his spirit too soon. Yet even more she dreaded the thought of his 'parents' moulding him to their likeness.

He gave in and followed the woman, dragging his feet. 'All right, but please, tomorrow?'

'Now, now! Stop your wheedling.'

Bridget's gaze followed them until they disappeared among the trees. Then, as before, she slipped from one tree to another until she reached the meadow side of the copse. From here she could still get a

160

good though more distant view. Anthony squatted by the side of the stream, idly throwing pebbles into the rushing current. The nurse sat on a log, knitting.

Bridget merged her body into a gnarled tree trunk. It was narrower than the other. She tightened her cloak, made herself thin. Although the distance was further than in the copse she was more likely to be spotted across the open view.

Anthony tired of throwing pebbles. He flattened the grass with his feet and began to arrange the stones in patterns. Bridget strove without success to see what letters he was making. Lost in time for a moment, she was sitting beside him again, guiding his hands to make the letter A, then N, then T.

As he played he began to sing, almost under his breath, until, carried away with his game and his song, his voice rose to full strength. Tears of delight blurred Bridget's eyes, as piercingly sweet, his words filled the air:

> When I'm at home I am a nice man
> For rumour-mongers I don't much care
> When I'm at home I am a nice man
> And gossip too's not my affair
> When all the local lads go sporting
> Devilment is in the air
> Then I go back to my old nursemaid
> And I rock the cradle for her

A pleased expression crossed the nursemaid's face. She put down her knitting. 'Well now, I haven't heard you sing that one afore. What's it called?'

'"The Nursemaid".' Anthony gathered more pebbles into his pile.

'Is that what you'll do when you're a grown man? Come back to your old nursemaid? Now that would be nice, wouldn't it?' She nodded with satisfaction and resumed her knitting.

This time he didn't answer, but bent his head and began making another letter.

Bridget closed her eyes, her joy at his singing now mixed with sorrow. When she'd sung that song to him she'd believed he would indeed come back to see her, that the song had been written especially for them. She felt a surge of jealousy, anger even, at this woman who'd done her no harm. She asked God's forgiveness for her sin.

161

She started as she heard the woman's voice, loud: 'All right, now. I'm getting chilled to death out her. Time to go in and have some tea.'

'Five minutes more,' Anthony begged.

'Didn't you hear me the first time?' Her tone brooked no argument.

'Yes, I did.' His voice was small, resigned. He stood and wiped the dirt off his hands on the seat of his trousers.

'Now how many times do I have to tell you not to do that.' The woman dusted his trousers with her hand. 'What would your mama think if she saw you going into the house looking like a ragamuffin?'

Bridget dug her fingernails deep into the tree bark until it crumbled in her hands. She smelt the sweet dankness of the fleshy wood beneath as she watched the retreating figures. Anthony followed slowly in the woman's wake, scuffing his toes in the grass. Again she fought the wild impulse to run to him, to pull him back, hold him to her and say, 'It's me, Anthony! It's Bridget! Bridget!'

She waited until they were out of sight before running to the spot where he'd played. She caught her breath. On the grass, neatly laid out in grey pebbles, were the letters ANT. He remembered everything! She knelt to stroke the stones he'd touched and, heedless of lingering in the open, finished his name with pebbles from his pile. She sat back and gazed at her work for some time before adding X underneath. 'A kiss to you, me darling boy,' she said aloud as she rose to go.

Weary, she climbed down from the cart. Of course it had been wonderful to see Anthony and to visit Nellie, but now she felt drained. She trudged up the steep street, telling herself she must look for the new flat in a less hilly area, easier for her aunt to walk. But her heart lifted and her steps quickened as she neared the flat. Tom would be coming after work . . . only a couple of hours.

Annie's hand flew to her mouth as Bridget opened the kitchen door. She sat hunched at the fire. 'Oh, it's you, Bridget!' Her voice was faint with relief.

'Of course it's me! What's wrong, Auntie?' Bridget stared at Annie's face in the gloom. Her left eye was black and swollen, the cheek bruised. 'Dear God, what have you done to yourself?' She knelt beside her and took her hands.

Annie burst into tears. 'It's *him*. He's been.'

'Oh, no!' Bridget stiffened with fear and anger. 'How? What happened? Did he hurt you anywhere else?'

Annie sniffed and shook her head. 'No, he just bashed me face

162

in. But he said he'd do more next time.'

'Saints in heaven! How did he find you?'

'I was feeling lonely like, so I went to Nellie's ma's for a bit of a chinwag. He saw me coming out and followed me. I never dreamt! It being Tuesday, I thought he'd be at work. He waited till I got home then came pelting through the door.' With a loud moan, she covered her face with her hands. 'Eey, bad as he is, I never thought he'd stoop to this . . . and now he knows where I live.' She turned a frightened face to Bridget, who still knelt by her.

'Not for long, Auntie.' Bridget rose with determination and dampened a towel from the mantel line in the bucket. She placed it over Annie's eye and bruised cheek. 'Now, just you hold that there for a while and it'll ease the pain. I have to go out for a bit.'

Annie sobbed again as she held the towel to her face. 'He said any woman that deserts her man deserves to go to hell, and that's where I'm bound. He says I broke me marriage vows I made in the name of the Lord and that it's a mortal sin.'

Bridget tipped the last of the coal from the bucket on to the fire. 'That's rubbish, Auntie, and you know it. 'Tis a mortal sin he's done to you. Now you just sit there and stay warm. I promise I won't be long. I'm going to get some bolts and Tom'll fix them on the doors tonight. That man won't get near you again, I swear to you. And we won't be here much longer anyway.' She cursed herself for not thinking of bolts earlier.

'I'm that sorry, Bridget, to cause you all this trouble,' Annie began, then sat up straight. 'Eey, and I'm that full of me own woes, I never even asked if you seen the bairn.'

'Yes, Auntie, I saw him. I'll tell you all about it when I get back.' Bridget left hurriedly for the ironmonger's. She hated to leave her aunt alone even for a few minutes, but better to leave her now than have that man come back after he'd been to the pub. Once again, she thanked God for His mercy in giving her Tom.

Chapter Fifteen

The next few weeks were hectic. Bridget spent most of her time hunting for a larger flat, without success, until in desperation she advertised for an exchange. Only one reply came. Most people who had the luxury of more than one bedroom made extra income by taking in lodgers, but the applicant, a widow in her late seventies, was happy to find smaller, less expensive accommodation. She no longer had the energy to look after lodgers.

Frank had paid no further visits to the old flat. And Bridget and Annie felt nothing but relief when Nellie's mother and Annie's old neighbour, Bella Brown, ran all the way to Conyers Road one Monday morning to deliver the news about Edie Devlin. Edie, the barmaid from the Bull's Head, was well known for favouring her customers with more than the odd free pint.

'That slut's moved in with him lock, stock and barrel,' Bella blurted out the moment she flung open the back door. Her three chins wobbled with excitement as she spoke and, despite an attempt to anchor her grey hair in her bun, most of it flopped about her face like a worn-out mop. But her green eyes were alight with mischief. Bridget always smiled when she saw Bella. There stood Nellie thirty years from now.

Annie only nodded at the news and went on slicing a cabbage on the kitchen table as if she'd been told her husband of thirty-five years had bought a new suit. 'Come in and have a sit-down and get your puff back, Bella,' she said.

But Bella needed no invitation. She'd already closed the door and was hanging up her coat. 'Aye, I can't stay but a minute though.' Bridget and Annie exchanged amused glances. They knew Bella's idea of a minute.

'I knew Edie was staying the night sometimes,' Annie said. 'I saw some of her things lying about the flat. And I'm glad for the both of them if she's moved in. She'll be in it for the free rent and him for her free services.' She stopped slicing to pick a slug off the cabbage, threw it on the fire and went back to her work. 'Knowing her, though, I don't know as she'll see much to his needs out of bed.'

'Aw, from the size of her that one likes her belly as much as she likes her men.' Bella toddled to the fire and lowered her bulk into an armchair with a grunt of satisfaction. 'There'll be grub in the house where Edie's around.'

Annie scooped the cabbage into her apron and dropped it into the pan of pork bones simmering on the trivet. She straightened and rubbed her back. 'Aye, well, that's a comfort. Bridget and me's getting tired of keeping him fed and clean. I was going over to take him some of this soup later on.'

Bridget, kneading dough on the other side of the table, felt relief circling her like a warm breeze. 'I hope that means he won't come round bothering Auntie any more,' she said.

'Aye, she'll see to that. He'll have his work cut out pandering to her needs.' Bella revealed her large yellow teeth in a leer that was meant to be a grin. 'She's getting on a bit – must be fifty if she's a day – but she still can't get enough.'

'Well, she chose the right one in Frank,' Annie said without emotion. 'She knows what she's getting into. They've been having it off for years.' She scooped the inedible remains of the cabbage from the table into her apron and dumped them into the fire. The hot coals sizzled. She stood watching the flames splutter and die before poking them back to life. 'God forgive me, but I was glad of her then and I'm even more glad now.'

'She's not looking after the place the way you did, though.' Bella twitched her freckled nose in disapproval. 'You should've seen the colour of her washing yesterday – grey, it was.' She nodded sagely and settled herself more deeply into her chair like a hen preparing to roost. 'Aye, it's true what they say – you can tell a woman's morals by the colour of her sheets. And ten o'clock before she got them on the line! Now, if she's doing the washing – in her fashion, mind you – that tells you she's moved in good and proper, doesn't it?'

Annie gave Bridget a sly wink as she took the salt jar from the dresser and put two pinches into the pan.

Bridget smiled. Bella's own washing was the cause of much tittle-tattle in the neighbourhood. Nellie hadn't picked her slovenly habits off the ground. But though Bella Brown liked a good time and wasn't the most scrupulous of housewives, nobody could say a word against her morals.

'Aw, Bella,' Annie went on, putting the lid on the pan. 'I'm just glad his sheets've got dipped in water at all and that his belly'll get filled by somebody else.'

Bella seemed to notice Bridget for the first time. 'How's the wedding preparations coming then?'

'Grand.' Bridget plopped the dough on to a baking tin. 'I'm off to Shields Road this afternoon to get meself a new dress and cape.'

'*New!*' Bella looked impressed.

Annie lowered herself into the chair opposite Bella. 'Aye, Tom said he didn't want her to stint herself for her wedding day. It's the first brand-new dress she's ever had, except for her uniform dress. I'm that happy for her.'

Bella nodded affirmation and this time showed Bridget her yellow teeth. 'Me and all. You've fallen on your feet all right, pet. And not afore time.'

'I have indeed, and I thank God every night.' Bridget gave Bella a long look. She wondered if Nellie had told her mother about Anthony or if the remark simply referred to her age. At almost twenty-one, she was approaching spinsterhood.

But Bella's face gave nothing away.

'Aye,' Annie said, 'she'll never have to struggle the way *we* did. We're moving to the new flat on Friday. I'm that excited.'

Again, Bridget scrubbed, cleaned, whitewashed, and moved Annie into their new home. This time, she sang as she worked. The flat was spacious compared with the last one. Two small bedrooms led off to the left and the kitchen was built out into the yard from the end of the passage. It took up a large portion of the yard, which looked like an L-shaped passage itself. There was just enough room for the privy, against the lane wall, and the two coalhouses underneath the flight of stone steps leading to the upstairs flat. The water pump was outside in the lane and, as usual, four houses shared it. But the extra bedroom was an asset.

On the day they'd moved in Annie and Bridget were out inspecting the yard when a stringy middle-aged woman emerged from the privy.

She introduced herself dourly: 'I'm Betty Gray. I live upstairs.' Not a trace of a smile lit her long, grim face, her mouth running straight across the lower half like a large buttonhole below her clothes-peg nose. 'I'm glad to see there's only two of you. Me ladies don't like noise.'

'Your ladies?' Bridget enquired.

'Aye, four of them, me lodgers.' She placed her hands on her bony hips and surveyed Annie and Bridget through grey eyes, glazed and lightless like slate.

'This is me Auntie Annie and I'm Bridget. And I'm getting married next week, so there'll be three of us. But we're very quiet.' Bridget smiled, hoping to soften the flinty face. To no avail.

'Married! I suppose that means hordes of bairns screaming the place down afore you can say Jack Robinson.'

Annie's temper rose. 'Aye, we're hoping for bairns all right. Nothing like a big happy family to keep you young and sprightly.'

The buttonhole mouth seemed to sew itself up.

'You're invited to the wedding. It's on Saturday,' Bridget said with the sweetest smile she could muster.

'Thank you, but I'm not one for weddings.' She stalked to the stairs. 'Parties and bairns,' they heard her muttering as she climbed the steep flight.

Annie ushered Bridget inside and closed the door with a bang. 'Well, a right frosty one that! She's just a frustrated old maid. Don't let her get to you, hinny.'

Bridget didn't. Nothing and nobody could spoil her happiness.

The afternoon before the wedding, the cleaning and decorating finished, Tom took a couple of hours off work and carted his furniture on one of the company's wagons. Bridget helped him carry his single bed into Annie's bedroom, the smaller of the two. She giggled as they heaved the horsehair mattress over the spring bedstead, nervous at the thought of sleeping with Tom in the double bed the next night. 'That's a nice comfy bed for Auntie,' she said. 'But I hope she won't be cold all on her own.'

'Nah, this'll keep her nice and cosy.' Tom threw his patchwork quilt over the mattress and took Bridget in his arms. 'Look, you know I like your auntie, and I've no objections to her living with us, but I draw the line at bringing her into our bed,' he said with a chuckle.

Bridget turned pink. 'Now, Tom Banks, behave yourself. You know I wasn't meaning—' But Tom's lips pressed against hers and silenced her.

It was a warm, affectionate kiss, with only a hint of the passion she knew burned inside him. She marvelled again at how, since that night he'd vowed he would hold his manliness in check, he'd done no more than kiss her softly and hold her close. She pressed her hands playfully on his chest and pushed him away. 'Now what are we doing wasting time when there's work to be done?'

He let her go. 'Aye, let's get it over with. We'll have all the time in the world after tomorrow.'

Bridget blushed again. During the past few weeks she'd thought with delight of every aspect of marriage with Tom, except one. She couldn't wait to share his life, cook his meals, wash his clothes, even have his children. But being his wife in bed! She dreaded going through that ordeal again, even with Tom.

He hailed her from the door. 'Come on then, don't stand there like one o'clock half struck!'

'You're getting that bossy, Tom Banks,' she said, smiling. 'Remember, I'm still me own woman, and I could change me mind if I had a will to.' She picked up her skirts and followed him down the passage.

'Aye, you're still your own woman all right,' Tom muttered over his shoulder. 'And I don't think getting wed's going to change you. It's just as well I know aforehand what I'm getting meself into.'

He pulled down one of the heavy stuffed armchairs from the cart, hoisted it over his big shoulders and lumbered back down the passage.

'Eey, my! Isn't that grand!' Annie clapped her hands in excitement as he set the chair between the two that flanked the fire.

Tom scratched his head and looked around the small kitchen. 'There's another one outside. Where do you want it?'

She pointed to the empty wall next to the dresser. 'Over there and we can pull it up when we have visitors.'

He scratched his head again. 'And where do you want the extra dresser and table and chairs then? It's starting to look like a second-hand furniture shop in here.'

Bridget appeared in the doorway, a kitchen chair under one arm, Tom's prized mahogany mantel clock under the other. She took control. 'The dresser can go in the bedroom to put our clothes in, and the table next to Auntie's bed. Now she won't have to stoop to the floor for the candle.'

Annie's eyes lit up like a cat's in a creamery. 'Well, I'll be! I've never had such comfort in me life.'

Bridget set the wooden chair at the table, the clock on the mantel, then surveyed the room. She wrested her gaze from the clock. She couldn't hurt Tom by telling him she hated clocks. Time passed fast enough without hearing every second ticking away in your head. She dismissed the thought and put a smile on her face. 'Look you, Auntie, there's a chair at the head of the table for Tom and *two* for visitors.'

Annie clucked with pleasure. 'Aye, or little ones soon enough.'

'Now don't you be rushing me, Auntie.' Bridget's spirits sagged. She couldn't cast Anthony out of her mind like throwing away an old frock simply because she was going to have a new one. But she couldn't dampen Annie's delight at the prospect of having a family.

The furniture all arranged, Tom proudly retrieved his coffee jug and packet of coffee from the dresser. He waved them in front of Annie. 'Now, I'm going to give you a treat, Annie. I'll make us some coffee afore I go.'

Annie, settled in her chair by the fire, peered suspiciously at the brown packet. 'Coffee? What's wrong with a nice cup of tea then?'

'Nowt, Annie. Just stop being so old-fashioned and try some.' Tom kissed her cheek as he bent to put the jug on the fire.

Tired but excited, Bridget smiled as she sat opposite Annie. 'It takes the roof of your mouth off, Auntie. But it's right reviving, and we've got a lot to do still.'

'Aye, lad, you'd better skedaddle after you've had it,' Annie said to Tom. 'You're not supposed to see the bride the night afore. And we've got a lot more cooking to do, and Bridget's got to have her bath.'

Tom stretched himself out in the remaining chair, lit his pipe and grinned. 'Well, I wouldn't mind staying to watch the bath, but don't fret yourself, I'll be off after me coffee. The lads at work are giving me a send-off at the pub. I'll doss down for the night with one of them, seeing as I've got no bed to sleep in.'

Annie wagged her finger at him. 'And just you remember, we don't want no hungover bridegroom.'

'Nah, I think I'll get a skinful the night. The morrow's going to be all old crows and cups of tea from the sound of it.' He chuckled.

'You get a skinful, Tom Banks, and you'll have to find another lass to walk up the aisle with you.' Bridget smiled, and he gazed at her with love and longing in his eyes.

'Only one more night and we'll be man and wife, Bridget. I still can't believe it.'

'I can't either.' She hesitated before reaching for his hand.

'Everything's so wonderful. Except . . . Oh, Tom, am I selfish to want Anthony as well? I went to see him again yesterday and it fair broke me heart when he walked away with that woman. I know he'd love you. He'd be so happy with us.'

Tom's face lost its look of contentment. He squeezed her fingers in an awkward attempt at reassurance. 'I wish I could give him back to you. But you know yourself, what's done's done.'

Bridget lowered her head and mumbled into her chest. She didn't want him to see her eyes wet on their wedding eve. 'Oh, if only you could've seen him yesterday, Tom. He played at nothing else but making his name. He said he wanted the "little people" to come back and put a kiss under each one. He remembers everything I ever taught him.'

'Well, that means he hasn't forgotten *you* neither, now doesn't it?' The gruffness in Tom's voice revealed his anger and frustration at his helplessness. Tom was a man who settled things, but fighting the law was beyond him. He loosened his grasp on her fingers and stroked her hand roughly.

Despite herself, Bridget gave him an affectionate smile. When at a loss, Tom always stroked her hand. 'Aye, Tom. I know he hasn't forgotten me,' she said with a sigh. 'And that's gratifying. But 'tis hard to have me own little lad think I'm a leprechaun when I'm standing there in the flesh but a few feet away. I put kisses under all the names he'd made. That's the closest I can get to talking to him.' She didn't mention that she'd put a B after each cross. That was her own little secret she would hug to herself.

'Aye, I know it's hard on you.' Tom's voice was soft and coaxing. 'It might be better if you didn't go to see him, if it upsets you that much.'

'Never! As long as me legs can move under me I've got to see how he's getting on.'

The coffee bubbled and Tom stood to attend to it, a perplexed look on his face.

Annie, who'd been twisting her apron as if wringing out a dish rag, tried to calm Bridget. 'Don't fret on your wedding eve, luv. It'll get easier seeing him.'

Bridget nodded dumbly and rose to go to the dresser. 'Aye, maybe,' she muttered after a few seconds. Head bent to hide the sorrow veiling her eyes, she poured milk into three mugs and added sugar. But she squared her chin as she carried them to Tom. 'Now what am I doing dampening everybody's spirits on such a happy day? Wait till you taste Tom's coffee, Auntie.'

Tom's face regained its merriment. He winked at Bridget as he filled a mug and handed it to Annie. 'Here, drink up, it'll warm your cockles.'

Annie sipped, spluttered, and screwed up her face to a likeness of a beaked bird. 'Dear God! I've had better-tasting medicine!' She thrust the mug at Bridget, still sucking in her lips in disbelief.

Tom looked crestfallen, but Bridget persevered. She added more sugar and milk and handed Annie the mug. 'Go on, try it now.'

Annie sipped again, clicked her tongue in noisy distaste and placed the offending beverage firmly on the hearth. 'None of your fancy airs and graces for me, thank you. I'll stick to me tea.'

Chuckling, Tom strode to the door and fumbled in his overcoat pocket. He returned with his hands behind his back. 'I'm sorry you don't like me coffee, Annie. But I know you like these.' He bent to kiss her cheek and laid a box of chocolates on her lap. 'A little wedding-day present for me best girlfriend . . . and one for me blushing bride.' He gave Bridget a loud smack on the cheek and presented her with a box. Then he sat back with his coffee in his hand and a very pleased expression on his face.

Annie looked as if he'd just presented her with the crown jewels. 'Eey, for me? Nobody's ever given me a box of chocolates in me life.'

'Well, somebody has now.' He drew his pipe from his pocket and looked with contentment at each of them.

'Tom, you know you shouldn't,' Bridget said. 'They're that expensive!' But she knew she'd never be able to train Tom to be careful with money and, after all, his generosity was one of the things she loved about him. She smiled from one to the other. It was going to be wonderful living with two people she loved. Again she reminded herself that she mustn't spoil what she had by dwelling on what she'd lost.

The next day, the seventeenth of April, dawned bright and cold. At the little square of mirror hung near the kitchen window, Bridget put the finishing touches to her hair.

Annie, dressed in her new Sunday frock, fussed around her. 'Eey, I've never seen a bonnier bride. Now here's your hat and cloak. You couldn't have got a better match.'

Bridget neatened the military collar of her new blue dress, pinned on the grey felt hat on top of her swept-up curls, then allowed Annie to

171

fasten the new grey cape round her shoulders. She looked down at herself. 'Indeed, I feel like a fraud, Auntie – all dressed up like a lady.'

Annie tied her bonnet ribbon under her chin. 'What rubbish you're talking! Fraud indeed! It's what's inside a woman that shows what she is, not the frippery outside. There's many a dressed-up "lady" with the soul of a guttersnipe.'

Bridget pulled a face that didn't befit her appearance. 'Aye, you're right there. There's one I can think of straight off.'

'Eey now, I shouldn't have made you think about her on this day. This is the happiest day of your life.' Annie looked at the clock and changed the subject. 'Half past eleven! I can't think where them two's got to. It'll be time to go soon.'

'Stop fretting, Auntie. We've got half an hour yet. And I know it's Nellie kept them late. She's never on time.' Bridget pulled on her new grey cotton gloves and eyed the table one last time. It held a simple array of cold mutton sandwiches and jam tarts. She wondered if there'd be enough.

The clatter of high-heeled boots down the passage interrupted her thoughts. A flustered Mrs Kennedy bustled in and hugged them both in turn. 'I'm that sorry we're late, luv. It was *her*, of course.'

Nellie, breathless as ever, dumped the two baskets she carried on a chair and swung Bridget round. 'Aye, it's always me,' she grinned. 'You can blame Nellie for everything. I'm used to it. Lizzie had to go poe-poe twice on the way, and that's *my* fault and all, I suppose.'

Lizzie was dressed in her Sunday clothes and bonnet and scrubbed to a shine. She left her mother's skirts and helped herself to a slice of mutton.

'And get off that food, Lizzie, or I'll clout you one,' Nellie said. Lizzie opened her mouth to wail and Bridget intervened.

'It's all right. You can have it, and more later when we come back from church.'

Lizzie tugged with her teeth at her treasure, then looked up at Bridget with a puzzled expression. 'Where Anthony?' she asked with her mouth bulging.

Bridget's eyes misted. 'He can't come, sweetheart.'

Mrs Kennedy jabbed a warning finger at Lizzie, who quickly climbed on to the nearest chair and munched in silence. 'Now you eat that up and be quiet, or else . . . And I'm going to have meself a few minutes' rest. Me old bones don't sit so well on the cart the way they used to.' She massaged her buttocks before sinking into Tom's chair with a sigh.

Bridget scrutinized her from head to toe. 'You're that thin still! Are you feeling no better?'

'Aye!' Annie screwed up her old eyes to peer at the woman. 'And you look pasty and all.'

Mrs Kennedy dismissed their concern with a wave of her hand. 'Nah, I'm doing better. Me chest's just taking a while to clear up. When the weather gets warmer I'll be fine.'

Nellie rolled her eyes. 'Why aye, man, she's got more puff than I have. She's been ranting at me the whole way here.' She took Bridget by the shoulders and examined her from the crown of the grey felt hat to the pointed toes of the new black boots. 'Honest to God, you look like the Queen of Sheba!'

'Aye, you're a sight for sore eyes. Tom'll be proud of you.' Mrs Kennedy nodded approval at Bridget, then glowered at Nellie and pointed towards the baskets. 'And it's no good just dumping those things on a chair.'

Nellie unloaded the baskets on to the table and smacked Lizzie's thieving hand as it shot out to grab a cake. Her face puckered as she opened her mouth to protest. But Nellie forestalled her. 'And none of your whingeing or you won't get none when you come back.' The threat worked. Lizzie stuck her finger in her mouth and devoured the table with her eyes.

'What's that?' Annie poked her nose to within an inch of an elegant platter piled with dark sliced meat and garnished with greenery.

Mrs Kennedy chuckled as she explained, 'That's venison, and the green's parsley. They had a big do last night and I told cook to save everything she could.'

Annie looked impressed. 'Well, I'll be! I haven't never seen venison. And what's all this stuff?' She poked her index finger at the various plates Nellie had set down.

'That's duck liver pâté,' Mrs Kennedy told her. 'You eat it with those little bits of toast, and the cakes are called rum babas, made from the King of Poland's own recipe, so Cook says.' She preened herself, enjoying the array of awed faces.

'My, but it all looks grand,' Bridget said. 'Though you shouldn't have gone to all this trouble.'

When Nellie lifted the white towel from the second basket and revealed two red bottles, Mrs Kennedy giggled like a schoolgirl. 'Why, the food was no trouble. But I had a job getting those.' She pointed to the bottles. 'In forty years I've never taken me ration of booze at Christmas so I decided they owed me some. I helped meself from the cellar.' She clasped her hands on her belly and sat back with a satisfied grin.

Unable to hide her dismay, Annie lowered herself on to the nearest kitchen chair. 'But we haven't got no glasses. I thought we were just having tea. I borrowed mugs from Nellie's ma.'

Nellie stepped in to cheer Annie. 'Aw, mugs is fine. Who do you think's coming anyway? Me ma would drink it out of the bottle if she had her way.' She sat down beside Annie and lifted the unusually silent Lizzie on to her lap. For the first time, she looked around the kitchen. 'Comfy little nest you've got here.'

Bridget beamed with pride. 'Thank you. We've been working hard to make it nice.'

'Now don't you start settling yourself in,' Mrs Kennedy said to Nellie. 'Be off with you now and get your ma and the rest. We'll see you at the church.'

Nellie rose with an injured expression. 'All right, all right, keep your hair on. Nobody even said I look nice, and I spent hours titivating meself so I wouldn't show you all up.'

Bridget had noticed Nellie's unusually neat appearance and smiled at her in appreciation. 'You look very smart, Nellie.'

Nellie curtsied, flung back her cloak and pirouetted to show off her grey Sunday dress. Not a stain to be seen. And the black bonnet and cloak had obviously been brushed with a damp cloth. 'They're only me old Sunday things but I sponged them down and ironed them.'

'You look fine. And now get off with you, I say.' The rising note in Mrs Kennedy's voice finally ejected Nellie from the room.

'All right! Ta-ta. See you there.' She dragged Lizzie behind her and with a swish of black cape was gone.

Mrs Kennedy made an exaggerated grimace. 'I swear that girl'll never grow up. I'm fair worn out with her chatter all the way.'

'Aye, you take a few minutes to rest then.' Annie sat opposite her, her movements more agile than they'd been for months. 'And why don't you take the weight off your feet for a few minutes, Bridget?'

'No, I'm too excited to sit.' Bridget looked through the window and peered up at the sky. 'Sure, it's turning into a lovely day. The clouds are breaking up.'

'Aye, the sun's going to shine on you the day, Bridget,' Mrs Kennedy said. 'Your troubles are all behind you.' A bout of coughing overcame her, and it took several minutes before she managed to stifle it. Bridget and Annie looked on in alarm.

174

'Dear Lord! You need to do something about that cough. Have a tot of this.' Bridget opened a port bottle and tipped some into a mug, but Mrs Kennedy waved it away and, still wheezing, pushed herself up.

'Nah, never could stand the stuff. Let's get a move on. We'll take a nice slow trot to the church.'

But Bridget first had to enquire about Anthony. 'How's me little lad?' she asked. 'I saw him two days ago. 'I . . . I wrote his name again and another kiss.' Once more she didn't mention adding her initial. 'How's he getting on with *Madam* now?' It was like probing a sore tooth.

Mrs Kennedy took her by the shoulders. 'Fine, hen. Nurse says he's behaving himself better. Madam sees a bit more of him now. And the master's just got him his first pony. He's right proud of it. But he still seems more excited about the "little people" by the stream. Nurse told him it was just one of the staff playing a game with him, but he won't have it. He says they're real fairies from far away, that Bridget told him about them.'

'He said me name . . .' Bridget said to herself. Sadness and joy floated about her like snowflakes. She brought herself back to the moment and picked up her skirts. 'Well, now, let's be off. I can't be keeping Tom waiting on our wedding day.'

Looking very smart in his new navy blue suit, Tom already stood at the altar as Bridget walked up the aisle on Annie's arm. The back of his neck was red to his ears and Bridget's heart rushed out to him. She knew the religious ceremony was an ordeal for him. Yet he'd suffered patiently the trial of his conversion. And all for her! She lifted her head with pride. She was a lucky woman to be taking such a caring man for a husband.

When they neared the altar, Annie knelt in the front pew and Bridget completed the last few steps alone. She glanced sideways at Tom and smiled encouragement. One eye met hers and one corner of his lips twitched. She felt an unseemly desire to giggle.

But the service went smoothly and Tom managed to say 'I do' on all the right occasions, though his voice sounded high-pitched. Bridget didn't see him full face until he placed the ring on her finger. He was like a peony from neck to forehead. She longed to stroke his face and tell him how much she loved him and how she cherished all the sacrifices he'd made for her. Instead she made a little kissing movement with her lips. He flushed deeper.

175

But as they walked arm in arm down the aisle, man and wife, he regained his confident manner, gripped her hand and grinned down at her.

At the flat, the merrymaking was a sight to be seen – and heard. Bella Brown, well under the influence of the port, slurred at regular intervals, 'Here's to the bride and groom.' On each occasion her raised mug grew less steady.

Mrs Jackson, one of the turnout of Annie's old friends and neighbours, not far behind Bella in her port consumption, added her piece, 'Aye, health, wealth and happiness to both of you. May you always have a pot to piss in.'

Tom, in his element as the centre of attention in a crowd of old women, returned the toast with a grin, 'And a healthy long life to all you lovely ladies. If I wasn't a respectable married man, I'd have a job deciding which one of you to dally with. But you understand I've got to be faithful to me lovely wife from now on.' He and Bridget were seated at the head of the table and he took her hand. She felt warm all over.

'Tom Banks,' she said, 'now tell the truth. You're only keeping your hands off the ladies because you know their men would be after you.'

Bella Brown gave one of her yellow grins. 'Aye, I'm that glad the men are at work the day. I can make a spectacle of meself without our Jim yelling at me to button me lip.' She whooped as she raised her fifteen stones from her chair and took the centre of the floor. 'Time for a singsong! And here's one for our Tom.' Without waiting for agreement she launched into song. Her raucous voice filled the air like a market vendor, while her fat arm waved time with her mug:

> Aw's a broken-hearted keelman,
> an' aw's overheed in luv,
> Wiv a yung lass in Gyetshead,
> an' aw calls her me duv;
> Her nyem's Cushy Butterfield,
> an' she sells yalla clay,
> An' her cusin is a muckman,
> an' they call him Tom Gray.

Everyone but Bridget joined in the chorus, though she tried to memorize the words:

She's a big lass, an' a bonny one,
an' she likes her beer;
An', they call her Cushy Butterfield,
an' aw wish she was here.

At the final chorus Mrs Brown lifted her skirts, stamped her worn-out boots on the floorboards, did a few heel-toes followed by some high kicks, and crashed into an armchair like a carthorse shot through the heart.

Everyone clapped and asked for more.

But she puffed and fanned herself with her work-grimed hands. 'Nah, I'm done in. It's Bridget's turn. Our Nellie says she sings like a lark and dances like a butterfly.'

After only a little coaxing, Bridget took the floor and sang 'The Irish Girl', Tom's favourite. Her audience hushed as her sweet voice filled the room, causing many a tear to be wiped away by a gnarled knuckle.

At the cheers and applause, Tom puffed with pride and begged her to dance an Irish jig for them. Since nobody knew the tune and she couldn't sing and dance at once, she started without accompaniment, hands on hips, toes pointed, taking intricate steps and hardly moving from the spot. But as the audience picked up on the six-eight rhythm they clapped time, faster and faster, until she hopped and twirled herself to a standstill and flopped into Tom's lap.

He accepted the applause as if to himself. 'There now!' he said when the noise had stopped. 'Haven't I got meself a talented little wife? She kept me waiting long enough, mind you, but it was worth it.'

Bridget had never felt more loved. Not even her grumpy neighbour's periodic knocking on the ceiling could mar her joy.

At six o'clock the presents were opened and admired – a new rolling pin from Annie; a white china teapot painted with pink roses from Mrs Kennedy; a red and white striped linen tea towel from Nellie; and from Annie's friends, who'd clubbed together, two fine-weave cotton pillow cases.

When the guests had trickled home to feed their families and Mrs Kennedy and Nellie had set out for the long ride back to Morpeth, Annie insisted that Bridget and Tom take a walk in the fresh air while she cleaned up.

Arm in arm they strolled up and down the hilly streets to Byker Village, which was still separated from the rest of the township by

177

fields containing six farms. Here was a different world. There was still grass cropped by cows, and a country atmosphere, some pretty cottages and farmhouses, and a few elegant houses fronting an expansive meadow. It was a relief to get away from the dingy brick terraces of the out-skirts.

Bridget breathed in the musty smell of the earth as they walked on the soft meadow grass. 'Wouldn't it be nice to live here one day, Tom? It makes me homesick for the farm.'

'Aye, it would,' he agreed. 'But no farm job would pay what I'm earning now. Of course, one of these days I might save up enough to buy one, or maybe one of them big houses there.' He grinned down at her and she laughed and leaned her head on his arm.

'You? Save up? Sure, not at the rate you've been spending your money on me. But it was a grand wedding day indeed. Only it went so fast. I swear there were no minutes in the hours.'

He gripped her arm. 'It's not over, Bridget. It's just beginning.'

She froze, then giggled to hide her nervousness. 'Mrs Tom Banks! For the rest of me life! I'll never get used to being married.'

He turned her homeward and said with a grin, 'You'd better learn. There's no getting out of it now.'

When they returned, the kitchen was cleaned and Annie already in her new bed. Concerned, Bridget looked in on her. 'Auntie, what are you doing in bed so early? Are you all right?'

'I'm feeling fine,' Annie said with exaggerated weariness. 'Just tired. It's been a hectic day for an old crow like me.'

Bridget kissed her forehead. 'All right then. If you want anything, just shout.' She tried to hide the tremble in her voice. She knew Annie had gone to bed to leave Tom and her alone on their wedding night. There was no putting it off any longer.

'She's all right – just tired,' she told Tom when she returned. He was stretched out in his chair, smoking his pipe. She sat in her accustomed place, hoping her anxiety didn't show. 'Would you be wanting some tea . . . or coffee?' she asked. Anything to ward off the moment.

'Nah, I just want you. Come and sit here, Mrs Banks.' He laid his pipe on the hearth and patted his lap.

She obeyed. He held her close and nuzzled her hair. She smelt the newness of his suit mingled with tobacco smoke and the familiar warm smell of his skin. That always comforted her. She pressed her face into his neck and savoured the accustomed feeling, again trying to delay the moment when the thing she couldn't allow herself to think about would begin.

If Tom sensed her anxiety, he didn't show it. He lifted her chin and kissed her lightly, as always, on the mouth. She wound her arms round his neck like a child seeking solace.

His hands stroked her back for a long time before he tilted her chin again and kissed her, longer and harder this time. She wanted to pull away but knew that this was the comfort he needed, that he'd needed for so long and that, as her husband, was his right. She submitted. After a while his kisses grew more urgent, travelled over her face, her neck. But she jumped when he kissed her ears. What a strange place to be kissed! And what a strange feeling!

His head was buried in her throat, his hands touching her waist, almost spanning it. 'Oh, Bridget, Bridget,' he whispered. 'I've dreamt about this for so long. You *know* I love you.'

She made a sound with her lips that seemed to say yes. She knew what he was trying to tell her and loved him for his understanding. But words couldn't help her. She attempted to reassure him by kissing him back on the mouth the way he'd kissed her. She would learn to be the sort of wife he needed.

His response overwhelmed her. The pressure of his lips became almost fierce. His fingers explored her body, her breasts. She jerked as a physical pain shot through her. Tom's big hands held her breasts gently, yet she felt again those grasping paws kneading cruelly into her.

He seemed to know. 'Bridget, it's me, Tom.' His hands, still now, lay lightly over her breasts. She made herself feel his hands, touched them with her fingertips. Then she increased her pressure. At this permission, he groaned and fumbled with her bodice buttons. She steeled herself. His lips grazed her throat, her bare breasts. She wanted to cry out but instead bit hard on her lip.

With a moan, he nuzzled his head in her bosom again. 'Oh, Bridget, you're so lovely, and I love you so much.'

'And I love you, Tom.' She tried to relax. He mustn't feel her shaking.

Still holding her, he stood and carried her down the passage to their bedroom. His boots resounded on the floorboards. Bridget stiffened with fear and embarrassment. It was about to begin. And Annie would know. She would hear his footsteps.

She thanked God the room was dark but for the faint reflection of the streetlamp through the window. When he laid her on the bed he whispered gentle words she couldn't quite hear. The springs whined. She froze again. The noise would go through the wall. He began to take off her dress. She tried to make her body go loose. Her breath was coming in little spurts. Then he removed her petticoat, her stockings. Dear God! He was taking off all her clothes! She was naked as the day she was born! She felt her neck and face go scarlet. Even a husband didn't have that right. 'Tom! Me nightdress! I got it special.' She strained to fumble under the green coverlet, under the pillow.

But he picked her up as tenderly as a mother and slipped her under the blankets. 'No, please, I want to be as close as I can to you. There's no harm in it. And I'll keep you warm.'

Bridget held the sheets around her chin, eyes closed. She couldn't tell him she wasn't cold, that she was burning all over despite the chill night air. Quick, rustling movements and the soft noise of garments falling to the floor told her he was undressing – she prayed not completely.

She heard him move around the bed. The springs groaned at his weight and, as he moved closer, the mattress sagged in the middle. His arm stretched under her neck and drew her to the dip in the centre. The full length of his body pressed against hers. Dearest Lord! He was as naked as she. When he kissed her she couldn't hear his gentle words, only the screaming in her head. His kisses and his touch stayed gentle for a long time, until the screaming in her head became a mere whisper. At last she put her arms round him and touched his naked back. He quivered all over.

'Oh, Bridget, I love you so much.' He kissed her neck and down to her breasts again.

She felt his hand stroking the length of her body and stiffened once more, but only for a moment. This was Tom, she repeated over and over in her head. She kept her arms round him. The contours of his back were so familiar, but it was strange to feel his skin. It was smooth and warm. She explored further, ran her hands the length of his spine, felt his muscles ripple and run like the flanks of a horse. He groaned with pleasure. She wanted to please him more and continued stroking, across his shoulders, down his sides to his waist. And the touch of his skin against hers, his body against hers, began to feel strangely comforting.

Suddenly he moved over her. She tensed again. He whispered her name as he pressed his legs between hers. She almost cried out. She wanted to beg him to stop now. Just for tonight. To give her time. But he'd already given her so much. She must give to him now.

He was kissing her forehead, moving all the while. She felt his body touch hers in *that* place and gritted her teeth. But he stayed still for some time, whispering words she couldn't hear for the pounding in her head. Then he began to move again, slowly, gently. She took a deep breath and forced the tautness within her to relax, forced her body to accept him. It wasn't exactly a pain, just a tight, uncomfortable sensation.

Tom groaned and moved faster. She gripped his back. If this was all it took to please him, she could do it. She screwed her eyes tight and thanked God. She could please the man she loved and feel no pain. She even felt some joy at being able to give her body to Tom. She braced herself against his rising passion, but it was only a mild discomfort. Then he cried out, loud. She hushed him with her hand over his mouth, aware still of Annie's proximity. His cry fell to a whimper and he lay to her side.

The room was silent but for the sound of his breathing. It seemed strange and heavy. He drew her closer, his arm round her shoulders. 'Oh, Bridget, Bridget,' he said at last. 'Did I hurt you? Was I too rough? I tried to hold back. But I wanted you that much.'

She pressed a finger to his lips. 'Shhh, Tom Banks. You were kindness itself. And long have I kept you waiting.'

Tom strained his eyes to peer at her in the dimness. 'You . . . you did it just for me?' His voice asked more than his words.

'No, Tom, I liked pleasing you.' She ran her fingers down his cheeks.

'I was that scared you wouldn't like me to do it . . .'

'Don't you ever say that. You're me husband and I love you. Sure, 'tis me pleasure to be a good wife to you.'

'Your pleasure – not just your duty?' He still sounded uncertain.

'Me pleasure, Tom, a great pleasure indeed.'

'I love you, Bridget Brannigan.'

She smiled in the dark. 'Bridget Banks, Tom. *Mrs* Bridget Banks, you daft thing.'

'Oh, aye, I'll have to keep reminding meself.'

He threw himself back on the pillow and they lay wound together in a comfortable silence, until his breathing grew heavier. She slid his arm from under her and tucked the blankets up to his chin. His sleeping face looked so peaceful. She closed her eyes. It was wonderful to know that married life with the man you loved wasn't frightening at all. After a while she fell into a happy doze.

181

Her eyes fluttered open as Tom's arm across her chest awakened her. It was still dark. He pulled her to him. 'Dear Lord,' she whispered, 'you scared the life out of me. And what is it you're doing awake again? Aren't you tired?'

He chuckled. 'Not any more.' Kissing her, he ran his hands over her as he'd done before, but this time he seemed different, his movements more confident.

Surprise jerked her wide awake. 'You mean . . .?'

'Aye, that's what I mean.' He kissed her again, and this time something deep inside Bridget began to stir – that feeling she used to get all those years ago whenever he'd kissed her. She returned his kiss and the feeling grew bigger. They kissed and stroked, kissed and stroked, until the feeling became a yearning . . . for what, she didn't know.

When he took her again, she felt herself moving, unsure at first, as if learning a new dance step. Gradually she moved with him like one, carried along by a current of feeling. Her head began to spin as, deep inside her, little ripples started. After a while they swelled out in a circle like water disturbed by a pebble. She felt Tom at her core, and then her being seemed to escape from her body. When he cried out, long and loud, she didn't even think to quieten him. She lay, incredulous, tears trickling down her face.

He collapsed over her, and the dead weight of his body seemed amazingly light. After a few moments, he felt the wetness between their cheeks. He raised his face. 'Bridget, me little Bridget, I've made you cry.' His voice was hoarse with dismay. 'And I thought it was so wonderful.'

'Oh, it *was*, Tom! It was so wonderful I can't believe it.'

He lowered his head into the pillow and snorted a deep breath of relief. 'Lord! You scared me.'

She pressed her cheek back against his. 'I had no idea it could be like that. Indeed, I've never felt anything so beautiful in all me life.'

'You felt that different, that marvellous,' he murmured, 'I couldn't believe it neither. You were scared the first time, weren't you?'

She nodded.

'And you won't ever be scared of me again?'

Forgetting the thin walls, she laughed. 'Never, never, Tom Banks. But I swear if you don't get off me I'll die of suffocation.'

He rolled off her and chuckled. 'That would be like killing the goose that lays the golden egg.' He drew her to him again and she pressed her head into his chest.

After a while, she said, 'Tom, I never dreamt being wed could be so, well, you know . . .'

He chortled. 'Pleasant, like?'

'Sure, a lot more than pleasant. God didn't make a word for it. I felt as if me soul left me body and floated up to heaven.'

He gave her an affectionate squeeze. 'You're a funny little thing. You make it sound like dying. I wouldn't be in such a hurry to go to heaven if I was you. I don't know as they do it up there.'

'Indeed they must,' Bridget protested. 'The priest says heaven is eternal bliss, so they must do it all the time.'

The springs rattled and squeaked with Tom's mirth. 'Well, in that case I think I'll go on ahead and warm the bed up.'

Bridget's heart chilled like a stone in a stream. 'Don't you dare, Tom Banks! Do you hear? Don't you dare go to heaven before me, not even for one minute.'

Chapter Sixteen

Summer came and went. For Bridget there were no days in the weeks, no weeks in the months. Each morning she'd get up at five thirty and, while the oven was heating from the newly laid fire, make stotty cakes for Tom's sandwiches. She would split the hot, flat loaves, sprinkle them with sugar or jam and pack them in his tin. Her initial fear about his job had subsided. She was glad he spent the day with his horses in the fresh air instead of down a pit or in a dirty factory.

He'd dismayed and delighted her with his extravagant purchase of two brand-new bicycles, and they'd joined the recently formed Newcastle Bicyclists' Club. On Sundays they rode up the Great North Road or the Military Road, finding different turn-offs each time to explore the country lanes and cart tracks that unravelled like string throughout the countryside.

Twice a month she visited Anthony and played her little game with him. Now he could imitate his entire name, and it was sprawled a dozen times with increasing neatness along the stream bank. So far, no one had spotted her, and she'd become less nervous on her visits.

Late in autumn, though the weather had turned as cold and grey as wash water, Bridget glowed with happiness. Today she glowed especially bright as she waited for Tom to come home. She flung herself into his arms the second he appeared in the back doorway.

He laughed at her impatience. 'By God! What a welcome! Can't you let a man get his coat off first?'

She clung to him, her arms round his neck, her feet kicking the air in excitement. 'Tom, I was sick this morning.' She lowered herself to the floor and watched his face with bright eyes.

But he just stared at her. 'Have you eaten something bad?'

Impatient, she shook his coat lapels. ''Tis not poorly I am, you silly thing. It's happened!'

He scratched the back of his neck as he always did when at a loss. 'Are you sure it's that?'

'Positive.' She giggled at his half-stunned, half-incredulous expression.

He closed his open mouth, gripped her shoulders and stared again at her face as if looking for a tangible sign of her condition.

She stood on tiptoe and kissed him before undoing his coat. 'All right, you can take it in slowly. First, get your things off and sit down. I went out to get you a jug to celebrate.' She smiled as he stood, still stupefied, and allowed her to remove his coat and cap and lead him to his chair.

'I can't think of any words,' he said when he was seated.

Bridget skipped to the table, poured a mug of ale and wrapped his hands round it. 'Then just make a toast, you idiot. You look as if I'd told you I was going to have a litter of puppies. And isn't it only a baby we're going to have, that's all!' She slipped on to his knee. 'Go on, make a toast.'

He grinned and raised his mug high. 'Cheers, then! Here's to you . . . and it!' His other hand rested on her belly almost with reverence.

Annie returned from the privy where she'd tactfully disappeared before Tom's homecoming. 'You've heard the news, I see.' Her toothless smile cracked her face in two.

'Aye!' Tom patted Bridget's belly as if to assure himself there was indeed something in there. 'I'm that thrilled! I'm going to be a da!' He puffed out his chest with pride and took a long draught of ale. Then he gave Bridget an almost accusing look. 'When? You didn't say when.'

Affectionately she combed his hair with her fingers. 'I've been over and over working it out and it's got to be in May, round about me own birthday.'

'Well, now that's a nice birthday present I've given you, so you won't need another one when the time comes I suppose.' He sucked the last of his beer and grinned at Annie as she sliced bread at the table. 'What do you think of that then? You're going to be an auntie all over again!'

'Aye, I can hardly wait,' she said. 'All me life I've wanted a little one around the place.' She shuffled to the stove and bent with difficulty to fork the potatoes. Bridget jumped off Tom's lap and scolded her.

'Now, Auntie, I've told you to sit quiet by the fire. I'm seeing to the

185

supper.' Annie gave in and eased herself into her chair. Bridget sighed. The cold and damp were taking their toll on Annie's joints again, the only shadow on her own happiness.

On the nineteenth of May, one week before Bridget's twenty-second birthday, Patrick Thomas Banks was born. He grew into a roll of butter, with Tom's blue eyes and yellow hair and a laugh that could be heard at the other side of Byker. Inevitably, he became 'Tommy'.

Tom was a proud and doting father and Bridget never tired of watching him with the child, so gentle in his clumsiness. If only Anthony could know a father's love like Tom's!

She'd been unable to visit Morpeth for several weeks, but when Tommy was one month old she felt well enough to travel and take him with her. At Tom's insistence, she took the passenger coach instead of Mr Jones' cart, though the fare of one shilling and threepence was an extravagance.

At ten minutes to eight she reached the Haymarket, paid her fare, and climbed on to the coach with Tommy in her arms. She sat with a sigh of relief on one of the wooden passenger benches, her eyes taking in the enclosed wooden sides and roof and the window openings with leather blinds that closed when it rained. This was luxury.

While the driver collected the fares from the boarding passengers, the four greys, immaculately groomed, snorted as if impatient to be off. Bridget was happy to be among those travelling inside. The less well-off travelled on the open top for ninepence. The coach made no deliveries and only three stops for passengers, reaching Morpeth at ten o'clock. This allowed her plenty of time to spend with Nellie before Anthony's afternoon outing. And she would return by the Alnwick stage which stopped at Morpeth at four. Now she wouldn't have to spend a night away from Tom.

By the time the coach reached Morpeth the June sun had broken through the early morning clouds and the day turned emerald green, royal blue, and gold. Nellie saw her coming down the track and waited at the open door. She grabbed the white bundle from Bridget without even a greeting. 'Eey, now! Let's have a look. Ooh, isn't he lovely! The spitting image of his da. I bet Tom's tickled.' She cooed at the placid pink face, the bright blue eyes.

'Indeed, you'd think he was the first man in the world to father a child,' Bridget said with pride. 'Now aren't you going to ask me in?'

'Why aye, come on, luv. It's grand to see you. I've got a surprise for you – in fact I've got two surprises.' She cooed again at Tommy and carried him into the kitchen.

Bridget followed and gave a little jump of pleasure. Mrs Kennedy sat by the fire. 'Hello, luv,' she said with a grin. 'Nellie made me hide. When she told me you were coming the day I fibbed to Madam, said I had to go to the market. I couldn't wait to see this little fella.' She stood and took the baby from Nellie, examining him with oohs and ahs. Tommy chortled back at her. 'My, he's a bonny little lad,' she said. 'Just like his da!'

'Aye, he's always got a smile on his face like Tom and all.'

'And how're you feeling?'

'Grand. What about you?' Bridget kissed her on the cheek and set her basket on the table. It was a few minutes before she became accustomed to the gloom. Mrs Kennedy looked thinner and paler than ever, her cheeks cavernous, her eyes unnaturally bright. 'But it's poorly you look still!' She couldn't hide her dismay.

'Nah, I'm doing better now.' She managed a smile, but her breath was laboured as she sat down on a dining chair with Tommy in her arms. 'I've just had another bout of the bronchitis. It's taking me a while to get over the winter. How's Annie?'

Bridget sat in an armchair, her joy and excitement at seeing Anthony momentarily forgotten. 'She's not getting much better either. I'm that worried about the pair of you!'

Nellie had poked the kettle over the fire and was unpacking Bridget's basket with unabashed delight. 'Now stop worrying about *her*, Bridget. It's nowt the warm weather won't cure – and a nice long rest would help. I keep telling her to take a few days off and stay with us for a break. We're getting another bed anyway.' She smoothed her crumpled apron over her belly and gave Bridget a wide grin. 'I haven't told you me second surprise. I've fallen again. I mean *really* this time. I was beginning to think I'd dried up afore me time.'

Though Nellie had been overjoyed to learn Tommy was on the way, Bridget knew that her friend longed for more children herself. Since Lizzie's birth she'd had two miscarriages. Bridget jumped up and hugged her. 'Ooh, that's wonderful! When?'

Nellie shrugged. 'Ask me! I think I've missed three months in a row, but I've been missing that many lately. I know this one's taken though. I've been sicking me insides up every morning for the past two weeks.' She unpacked the basket as she spoke. 'Eey, looka here!' She spread on

187

the table a jar of jam, a dozen home-made scones and a packet of tea. 'And Mrs Kennedy's brought a chocolate cake. Lizzie's asleep and I'm not getting her up till we've had ours in peace.'

While Nellie bustled about setting the table with chipped brown mugs and plates, Mrs Kennedy began to cough, gagging sounds that grew to a fitful hacking, like a dog choking on a bone. Tommy opened his mouth to wail and Bridget jumped up to take him from her. 'Get her a drink of water, Nellie.' She watched in dismay as the pale face turned red, then purple.

Nellie tipped a mug to Mrs Kennedy's lips and she managed to suck a few drops before a fresh bout of coughing took her.

The sound hurt Bridget's ear like a knife twisting in it. It was some minutes before the fit subsided. Mrs Kennedy still laboured for breath but her colour began to return. She dabbed at her eyes and mouth with a white handkerchief. 'Eey, it's a bugger,' she said through her handkerchief. A few breaths later she noticed Bridget's white face. 'Come on, hen, don't look so worried. It's nowt. It just gets to me now and then.'

'And how often is that?' Bridget's voice was almost angry. 'Why didn't you let me know you're still poorly?'

Mrs Kennedy flapped her hand. 'Aw, you can't do nowt about it. And I can still get around and do me work.' She pulled a wry face. 'Madam makes sure of that. She's even had her own doctor to me again to make quite certain I don't pop off and leave her to find somebody else, so I'm in good hands.'

'I hope so.' Bridget tried to hide her concern. The baby whimpered and she returned to her chair at the fire. 'He's hungry. That's the only time he cries. And he shuts up as soon as you stuff food in his mouth. He's like his da in that and all.' Her face softened, as it did whenever she mentioned Tom. She put the baby to her breast. But as he sucked, she watched his glowing cheeks and felt a tide of sadness wash over her. If only one child could wipe out the need for another. 'Have you seen me little Anthony?' she asked. 'I wish he could see his baby brother.'

Lines furrowed Mrs Kennedy's forehead. 'I went up to see him yesterday, hen. He's fine. Bonnier than ever. They got a new tutor last week and he's started his lessons. He's a bit stiff and starchy but he knows a bright lad when he sees one. Anthony'll get a gentleman's education.' The forehead lines receded as she stretched her wrinkled lips in an encouraging smile.

Another stranger in Anthony's life! And another starchy one at that! Bridget hugged Tommy tightly to her. 'Aye, at least he'll get an education.'

After tea Bridget took her usual route round the west side of the grounds. She trod softly through the woods. The mulch of winter leaves and twigs smelled dank like a basement despite the June sunshine straining through the trees.

Before she reached the copse she froze. A sound like running feet, too heavy for a rabbit or squirrel. She flattened herself behind a large beech tree. The noise drew closer. She pulled her cloak about her, tilted her hat brim over her face and adjusted the veil. The sound stopped.

She strained her ears – a hard snap like a branch giving way, then slow footsteps and another sound like a broom sweeping. Mentally Bridget made the sign of the cross. Please God, let it be no one she knew! The steps grew nearer. She glued herself to the tree. Suddenly a large beech branch swept the ground beside her and caught in her skirt. Her eyes travelled up the branch in dismay, then stopped. Anthony's hazel eyes stared at her veiled face with curiosity. She trembled with fear and delight. He seemed to be alone. Why?

'Who are you? What are you doing here?' he asked with the confidence of one secure on his own territory.

Bridget struggled to keep her voice low. 'I . . . I was passing through and got lost in the woods.'

'I never get lost. I play here all the time. That's my house up there.' He indicated the direction of the house with his free hand, long and slender now.

He hadn't recognized her. Although relieved, Bridget also felt a sadness akin to a physical blow.

His voice became eager. 'Where are you going? If you wish, I can show you the way. I know everywhere around here.'

'Thank you. I . . . I was trying to find the road to Morpeth.' His fluting tones rang like bells in her head. He was so tall, a schoolboy already. Though his face hadn't changed much – the same wide-eyed expression, as if constantly discovering something new and amazing, and yet sad as if he'd just lost his puppy. He interrupted her thoughts.

'It's this way.' He turned back the way she'd come and she forced her shaking legs to catch up with him. He swished the branch in front of him as he walked. 'I'm sweeping the path,' he told her.

'And why would you be doing that?' She felt heady with joy to be

189

talking to him and at the same time desolate that she couldn't say, 'Do you remember me? I'm Bridget. I'm your mother.'

'I clean the path the way the gardeners clean the drive. I'm going to be a gardener when I grow up.'

'Now, that would be a fine thing to be.'

'But I have a long time to wait. I'm only five and a half.'

'Indeed, and your mother lets you come to the woods on your own?' The question had been nagging at her.

Anthony lowered his head. 'Not really. My nurse took a nap after lunch and she didn't wake up for my outing, so I went out the back way. I've done it before. I like to be out on my own.'

'Won't you get into trouble?'

'Yes, I always do. But it's worth it.'

Bridget was about to ask what sort of trouble, but they'd reached the edge of the clearing and he stopped and pointed with his branch. 'If you take that path to the end it leads to the Morpeth Road.'

'Well, thank you—' She was about to say his name.

'I'm Anthony.'

''Twas very nice to meet you, Anthony.'

'What's your name?'

'. . . Mrs Banks.'

'Will you come back again?'

'I . . . I don't know. Perhaps. If I get lost again.'

'I'm going to catch tadpoles now and watch the baby ducks on the stream.' He hesitated, then looked up at her with eager eyes. 'Would you like to see them?'

'Sure, I'd love that, but I have to go to Morpeth,' she said, though her mind screamed, *Oh yes, yes! There's nothing in the world I'd like more.*

He seemed as reluctant as she to part. 'I'd like to go to Morpeth.'

'Would you now?'

'May I come with you?'

She resisted the urge to take his hand, tell him he could come with her forever, and run all the way back to Byker with him. 'That would indeed be lovely, Anthony. But I think your nurse would be angry. Why don't you go home now? If you go in the back way again perhaps no one will even know you went out, and you won't get punished. And you mustn't say you met a lady. That'll be our secret.'

He bowed his head and made circles with his branch on the grass. 'You won't tell anyone?'

'Not a living soul.'

He looked up, relief on his face, and raised his cap like a gentleman. 'Good day to you then, Mrs Banks.'

Bridget watched his back until he disappeared into the woods. Then she walked on, pretending to take the path to Morpeth. Tears blurred her vision but took the edge off her pain like cool water on scalded skin.

Chapter Seventeen

Bridget bore Tom three more sons before her longed-for daughter arrived. Six-year-old Tommy stood by the bed with his brothers – Mick, four and a half; Dan, three; and Joseph, almost two. All stared solemnly at their new sister as Bridget pulled back the sheets to show off the bundle in her arms. She smiled at the four towheads, grouped like a carelessly arranged bunch of chrysanthemums. As always she felt a surge of love and pride. Their father's sons. Every one a miniature Tom.

Tommy peered at the baby and screwed up his nose. 'She's red.'

Bridget smiled. 'And so were you when you were two hours old.'

'What's she called?' Mick glanced at her without much interest.

'She's going to be called Maureen. Now isn't that a pretty name?'

Dan, like his brothers in looks but with a streak of the devil in him the others fortunately lacked, poked his finger into the baby's wrinkled cheek. 'She looks all screwed up like Auntie Annie.'

Bridget chuckled. 'What do *you* think of her, Joseph?'

Joseph stuck his finger in his mouth and sucked noisily, his bright blue eyes fixed on the baby in a puzzled stare.

Dan dug his hands in his trouser pockets and gave Bridget a pleading look. 'Can we go out to play again?'

'All right, all of you, out! Give your auntie a bit of peace before your da gets home.' She waved them away with her free hand, glad to have another hour's rest before greeting Tom with her surprise.

He was a wonderful father to the boys, like a child himself when he played with them, yet a model of adult virtue when necessary. He attended mass with them every Sunday even though, as he regularly said to Bridget, he still couldn't take all that palaver seriously. But Bridget was content that he made the effort and thought God would be satisfied too.

* * *

After a few minutes Annie shuffled in, her shoulders hunched almost double, her pale eyes glazed but a wide grin on her gnarled face. 'I brought you some tea, hen. Tom's stew won't be long. I'll feed the lads afore Tom gets home and he can have his here with you.' She handed Bridget a mug, her fingers as skinny and brittle as twigs on a winter tree.

Bridget took the tea gratefully. 'Thank you, Auntie. You look fair worn out yourself. Why don't you have a cup with me? The lads are too much for you.'

Annie eased herself on to the side of the bed. 'Nah, I've had some. And them lads'll never be too much for me. It's them that's keeping me going. God kept me waiting till the end of me life before he gave me bairns to love.' She cackled with pleasure as she peered at the sleeping baby. 'But He's making up for lost time. I can't wait to see Tom's face when he sees it's a bonny little lass. And like her mother for a change!'

A shadow crossed Bridget's face. 'Yes, she's the double of Anthony when he was born.' She gazed down at the dome of chestnut fuzz above the high forehead, the turned-up nose. She stroked the long fingers clenched in a fist.

She hadn't seen Anthony for several months. She closed her eyes and recalled her last visit. He'd been riding his horse, tall in the saddle, his riding habit expensively tailored to his slim body. The autumn term would have started by now and he'd be off to Rugby. She'd been distraught when Mrs Kennedy had told her they were sending him away to school. That would be Madam's doing, no doubt. Now she could see him only on school holidays. It would be even more difficult to find a free day with her choice so limited. Annie did her best to help, but she was too frail to handle the children for long.

In a few months Anthony would be twelve. Was it really that long since she'd first looked into his newborn face as she now looked into her daughter's? She'd spoken to him once more, two years before. Trotting his pony on the track to the west of the copse, he'd surprised her before she could take cover. Again she'd pretended to have lost her way, and he'd flashed her a strange look as he gave directions. She wondered to this day if he remembered their first meeting in the woods.

Annie peered at her. 'You look tired, pet. Why don't you have a nap afore Tom gets home?'

Bridget nodded. 'Are the lads behaving themselves?'

She chuckled. 'Aye, they've hardly been in the house. They're that newfangled with them iron hoops Tom got them. They're making a right old racket in the front street clanking along the cobbles.' She pulled a face and looked up at the ceiling. 'Her upstairs's been out to them umpteen times threatening to set the coppers on them.'

Betty Gray had become increasingly frustrated with the arrival of each child. But Bridget only smiled. She'd long since given up worrying about the woman's dislike of children and their inevitable noise. In fact, Bridget felt she was providing her with a necessary service. Without something in her life to complain about, 'Stick Face' as the children called her, would have no reason to live. Besides, the many friends Bridget had made in the street more than compensated for one grumpy neighbour.

Annie eased herself up from the bed with a grunt. 'I'd better get me old bones cracking and get their teas ready afore their da gets home.'

With mixed happiness and sadness, Bridget watched her shuffle off. Happiness that her aunt had never been in brighter spirits, and sadness that she now suffered her aches and pains year round. Since leaving Frank, the only time Annie had shed a tear was at his funeral – not, she'd claimed, that she felt any loss, only sorrow for his soul. As she'd always predicted, his drinking did indeed cause his end. His mistress found him dead in bed one morning, drowned in his own vomit.

Bridget dozed until a heavy movement on the bed awakened her. She opened her eyes. Tom sat staring at her in awe. He bent to kiss her cheek. 'How you feeling, luv?'

'Grand!' She was wide awake. 'Look, Tom!' She held out the bundle still sleeping in her arms. 'A daughter at last!'

He beamed. 'Aye, I know. The lads told me. Can I hold her?'

He took the baby and cradled her in his huge hands. 'She's a bonny one. And a *little* one like her ma. Now I've got two lady-loves.' He kissed the pink nose and Bridget's eyes misted.

'I thought I'd call her Maureen after me sister.'

'Aye, that's nice.' The baby puckered her face and whimpered. Tom handed her back with a grin. 'I think she wants her tea.'

Bridget put the baby to her breast. 'Why don't you have a wash now? Auntie says she's bringing your tea in here.'

He bent to kiss her cheek again. 'She went out to get a jug for me to

194

celebrate and all. I'll have it after me wash. I'm that proud of you, Bridget Banks!'

'Be off with you! I couldn't have done it without you.'

He stood and squared his shoulders with a satisfied air. 'Aye, I'm a dab hand at it, if I say so meself.'

Bridget smiled as he strutted from the room like the cock of the farmyard. She settled back against the pillows and watched the baby suckling. She felt so loved, so contented.

The following morning Annie rushed into the bedroom waving an envelope. 'This just came for you, luv.'

'It must be from Mrs Kennedy.' Bridget sat up and took the envelope. 'No, 'tis not her hand.' The envelope was printed in large, awkward letters, as was the letter inside. Puzzled, she read the signature. 'Nellie! Now why would Nellie be writing to me?' She read aloud to Annie, her voice rising, falling, and crumpling in dismay:

Dear Bridget

Our Jacks ritin this down for me. I am that sorry to tell you that missus Kennedy died sudden like yesterday, she was only poorly for a few days but then she was took. The doctor said it was water on the lung or sumthing. She didnt suffer long tho, she was hear to see me only last week. He said it was cos her chest was allready weak that it took her so bad and so quick. I did as she allways told me to do if she was took bad. She sent one of the lasses over and I went strait to see her but I was to late. You see she didnt want to worry you aboot it but she told me where her savings was hid in her pillow and if anything happened to her she wanted me and you to share it. But when I got there she was allready gone and they wouldnt let me see her. I aksed the girl who come to open up her pillow if she got the chance an I was goin to give her some of it but the mistress had allredy made them lay the poor ould sole out in a closed cofin and burn her bedin and clean her bedroom with carbolic cos what she had was catchin, two of the upstairs maids got coffs and she sacked them. Madams gone off to a place called Bath to take the waters till the house is clean again and shes complainin like mad that missus Kennedy didnt give her enuf notice. The butler's got to find a new housekeeper wile madams at that place. Im that sad and that sory Bridget that I didnt do things as she wanted at the end. Shes being

buryd the day, I know its your time and you cant come. Ill mis her
as much as you. I hope your well with the babby and that its here
by now. Its luky that Antonys away oot of it.

luv Nellie

PS. Ill put sum flours on her grave from you.

Bridget clenched the hand that held the letter and stared at the wall.
She felt as if her blood had been drained out of her. An anguished moan
escaped from deep in her throat.

Annie sat on the bed, tears meandering down her cheeks like melting
wax on a candle. 'Eey, luv, don't cry. You'll upset your milk. Mrs
Kennedy wouldn't want you to cry over her, especially not with the
baby. At least it's a comfort to know she went quick.'

Bridget nodded. 'Quick, yes, and then boxed away so nobody could
even pay their last respects.' She raised her eyes to heaven. 'The
mistress's got a lot to answer for! May the Lord forgive me but I hope
she catches the sickness – or something more painful and long-drawn-
out.' Her face crinkled and she wept, long, deep sobs of loss – a feeling
she remembered too well. At last she stopped and gulped a breath. 'Oh,
why? Why? Why is it that God's always taking the people I love away
from me?'

Annie patted Bridget's clenched fist. 'There, there . . . He's given
you plenty to love as well. Now just look at that little thing!' She
nodded at the sleeping baby next to Bridget. 'The Lord gives and the
Lord takes.'

Bridget picked up the baby and gazed at her through her tears. 'Aye,
one comes and one goes. If only she'd got a chance to see this one
before she died.' She kissed the baby on the forehead. 'I'm going to call
her Kate – Katherine Maureen. It just seems right! Me little sister'll
understand.'

Annie nodded. 'Aye, she will. And them's two bonny names.'

196

Chapter Eighteen

More than five years had passed. Bridget sang as she sponged two-year-old Eileen's face and hands. She sat her on a kitchen chair and wagged a finger at her. 'There's me birthday girl! Now I want you to sit there and stay clean till I get meself ready. Just look how good Kate's being.'

Kate sat dangling her legs next to her younger sister, her face shining clean, her chestnut curls neatly brushed down her back below her Sunday bonnet. At five, she was a model child and the only one in the family to take after her mother. Eileen, as rambunctious as her brothers and, but for the long blonde curls hanging past her shoulders, indistinguishable from them, wriggled in her chair in frustration. She hated Sundays. Neither staying clean nor sitting still was in her nature.

'You'd better do what Ma says or you'll have to get washed all over again before the party,' Kate told her.

The threat worked. Eileen froze like a marble statue, though she pouted, impatient to be out with her father and brothers in the front street. Tom was keeping an eye on the already scrubbed boys while Bridget saw to the younger children.

She handed Eileen's Sunday bonnet to Kate. 'Here, luv, put this on her, then take her in to see Auntie. I've still got to feed the baby, and he's filled his nappy again. I swear we're going to be late.'

Kate tied Eileen's bonnet under her chin and led her to Annie's bedroom. Though July, the weather was cool and Annie was having one of her bad turns. But Bridget knew she'd get up for Eileen's birthday party in the afternoon. Annie wouldn't miss that if she were on her deathbed.

After changing Sean – another roll of butter like his brothers and Eileen – Bridget put him to her breast. She enjoyed the peaceful time after all the activity of the morning. When he'd finished, she wrapped him in his light shawl and laid him back in the cot before the fire.

She combed her hair in front of the mirror and pinched her cheeks to give them colour. Her face had changed little, the only difference two small smile lines that used to be dimples at each side of her mouth. She took her grey cloak and hat from the doornail. The original garments had long since been replaced with almost identical ones. She ruffled the hat veil upwards around the brim and placed the hat on her head, secured it with a hatpin, then fastened her cape round her shoulders. She sighed with relief. She was ready.

Sean, now sweet-smelling and well fed, slept. She picked him up and joined Tom in the front street, Kate in her wake leading Eileen by the hand.

Tom caught the football Mick had kicked before it flew through the front bedroom window and with a grin threw it inside the door. 'All right, lads. Time for church.'

Bridget inspected the four pink faces, still looking freshly scrubbed. 'Are their hands clean?' She gave Tom an accusing look.

'Aye, I only let them kick the ball.'

She looked down at their feet. 'Their boots are scuffed, Tom Banks. Now didn't I tell you no games till after church? Are you ever going to grow up?'

'I'm sorry, luv.' He pulled a contrite face then grinned and stood to attention for inspection. 'Am I clean enough for you?'

She smiled. 'Come on with you or we'll be late.'

Tom hoisted Eileen on his shoulders and marched ahead down the street, singing, '*Humpty Dumpty sat on the wall, Humpty Dumpty had a great f-a-l-l.*' At the last word he lifted her legs high and dangled her down his back.

She screamed with delight. 'Again, Da! Again!'

'Aw, go on, drop her, Da,' the boys shouted as they ran behind.

It was a familiar Sunday morning routine.

'Ma,' Kate began in a serious tone. 'I . . . I did something bad today. Will I have to tell God in church?'

Bridget tried not to smile. 'Indeed, and what did you do?'

'I opened the box with Eileen's dolly in it and had a look.' She gazed up at Bridget with penitent eyes. 'But I put it back and wrapped the tissue paper round it again. I didn't harm it.'

'Well, if you didn't harm it I don't think God would call that a real sin. Sure, I think He's already forgiven you that one.'

Kate's elfin face relaxed. 'Can I help Eileen open it at the party?'

'If she'll let you.'

Tom trotted backwards towards them, Eileen still on his shoulders. 'Come on, you lot,' he shouted. 'Put a step in it. You're like the donkey's tail, always behind.'

Kate giggled. 'If we're the donkey's tail, you're the donkey. Gee up, Donkey!'

'Hee haw, hee haw!' Tom galloped ahead and Eileen, whooping with fear and delight, tightened her grip on the thatch of hair below his Sunday cap.

Bridget shook her head in despair. 'Tom Banks, this is Sunday. Have you no respect?'

He continued to trot and she watched his clownlike movements with affection. Tom would never change. Though his outdoor work had creased his face like soft shoe leather, his hair was still the colour of the five blonde heads that surrounded him, his eyes as blue.

In church she thanked God, as she did daily at home, for the wonderful husband and family He had given her. And she prayed for Anthony. But she would see him on Tuesday. Rugby's summer holidays had just started and she'd arranged for Meg, one of her friends and neighbours, to keep an eye on Annie and the two girls, the only ones not yet at school. As the boys' holidays started the following week, it could be her only chance to see Anthony this summer.

She wondered what he looked like now – at sixteen and a half, approaching manhood. She sighed. Her first-born, and she'd missed so much of his growing up! It was almost a year since she'd seen him, her life being too busy and the fare too expensive with such a family to look after. But they were always clothed, shod and fed. They wanted for nothing. Tom saw to that. And Bridget saw to it that Tommy and Mick spent a full day at school. The extra money they could have earned working half-days would have been useful, but not as useful as an education would be later.

After the midday meal Bridget helped Annie get up and dress for the party. Seated in her chair by the fire, her brittle bones wrapped in a wool shawl, she beamed a toothless grin at the group round the table, all decked out in the bright paper hats Bridget saved year after year for Christmas and birthdays.

Though Annie's skin was as tough as tree bark, her eyes rheumy and sunken deep in their sockets, her joy shone through like light from a shrouded lamp. She directed her grin at Eileen. 'Eey, now, isn't that a lovely cake your ma made for you? And you've got your hat on and all!'

Eileen nodded, overawed, and torn between the desire to open the two boxes set in front of her and to blow out the two candles on the cake.

Tom took control. 'Come on then. We'll sing "Happy Birthday" first and blow out the candles. Then you can open your presents and we'll have the cake after, in that order.'

While everyone sang 'Happy Birthday' he stood her on her chair and puffed with her, and when the flames flickered and died they all clapped.

Kate made to slide off her chair. 'I'll help you open your presents, Eileen.'

But Eileen grabbed the larger of the two cardboard boxes and screamed, 'No, me do it!' She tugged off the lid and tore at the tissue paper. Hey eyes widened. 'A dolly!'

Bridget watched her reaction. She'd longed to get her a china doll but they were too expensive. ''Tis a rag dolly? Isn't it nice now?'

Eileen held it up by one of its stuffed pink arms, pulled at its yellow wool hair and stared at its blue button eyes. Then she hugged it. 'Nice dolly. What she called?'

'Anything you like,' Tom said. 'How about Dolly?'

Bridget smiled. 'Your da's that original!'

Tommy, bored with the present-opening preliminaries and impatient to get to the cake, said, 'Call her Dolly and have done with it.'

'No! Buttons! She got buttons for eyes.'

'Good! That's a nice name.' Tom was as eager as the children to sample the cake. 'Now open that one. That's from your Auntie Annie.'

Eileen sat the floppy doll on her lap. 'Now you be good girl,' she said, wagging a finger as she'd seen her mother do.

Bridget recognized herself and smiled.

'What this?' Eileen picked up the small box and opened it on her lap. 'A red ball!' She tried to pick it up with her free hand but it fell to the floor, bouncing and rolling under the table.

In a flash Tom dived under the table and came up on his knees with the ball in his mouth. 'Wuff, wuff!' he went, the ball still in his mouth.

Eileen giggled and tugged at it.

'Aren't you going to give Auntie a kiss for that nice ball?' Bridget said. 'And then we'll cut the cake.'

Doll in one hand, ball in the other, Eileen squirmed from her chair and planted a resounding kiss on Annie's cheek.

'Eey, now! That was a nice smackeroo!' Annie's chortle of delight sounded like dry leaves being crushed underfoot. 'Give us another one.'

Mick groaned. 'Aw, let up, Auntie! Let's get on with the cake.'

On Tuesday Bridget alighted from the coach at Morpeth with Sean cradled in one arm, over the other a basket with scones and jam for Nellie, clean nappies for Sean, and a bunch of sweet peas for Mrs Kennedy's grave. She'd been buried in St Robert Newminster churchyard at Morpeth and Bridget always stopped to pay her respects on her way to Nellie's.

She approached the grave, set down the basket and knelt. Sean whimpered and she rocked him. As always, she read the inscription on the small headstone and, as always, thanked Tom for sending Nellie the money to have it erected. The words still looked freshly etched in the grey stone: *In Loving Memory of Catherine Margaret Kennedy, Gone But Not Forgotten. Born 1831. Died 1892.*

Bridget picked up the familiar jam jar, today filled with wilting daisies – Nellie had obviously been here recently – and walked through the cut grass to the tap. Sean, sleeping, lay heavily in her arm as she emptied the daisies into the waste basket and filled the jar with fresh water.

Kneeling at the grave again, she placed the flowers in the jar with her free hand and made the sign of the cross. She prayed for several minutes before easing herself up under Sean's weight and trudging towards Nellie's house. But at the thought of seeing Nellie and Anthony her steps grew lighter.

Too laden to lift the latch, she kicked the door gently. 'It's me, Nellie!'

In a flash Nellie yanked open the door and engulfed Bridget, baby, and basket in her arms. 'Eey, it's grand to see you! I was that excited when I got your letter. Let's have a look at him then.' Lifting Sean and holding him high, she laughed with delight. 'You did it again, lass. Another little Tom!'

Bridget walked past her and set the basket on the table. 'Aye,' she said with a smile in her voice. 'Except for Kate, it seems like Tom makes the dough all by himself and all I do is bake it for him.' She laid her hat and cloak on a dining chair. The room was empty. 'Where's *your* lot then?'

'At their granny's. I took them over this morning so we could have a natter in peace. Lizzie didn't want to leave when she heard you were coming, but Jimmy and Bobby wanted to go to the market. Their granny always buys them winkles.' She stood in front of the fire rocking Sean. 'Eey, I wish I fell as easy as you. All these years married and I've only got three to show for it. It's still not enough to keep us in comfort in our old age.'

'You've got time for more. But in the meantime, count your blessings.' Bridget sat at the fire with a sigh of relief. 'I'm run off me feet day and night.'

Nellie lifted her head and twitched her nostrils. She handed a puce-faced Sean to Bridget. 'Aye, I see what you mean. He's filling his nappy by the looks and the stink of him. You can have him now.' With a grin she plopped the baby on to Bridget's lap. 'I'll make the tea.'

By the time Bridget had changed and fed Sean, Nellie had removed the dirty breakfast dishes from the table and stashed them on the floor by the water bucket to wash when she felt in the mood. She'd made the tea and set scones, jam and a plate of ginger parkins on the table.

'I see you've been baking.' Bridget looked at the ginger biscuits with surprise.

Nellie yawned. 'Nah! Me bake? Not if I can help it. Jack's ma sent these. I've got better things to do with me time.'

Bridget smiled as she looked around the grubby room, the dirty dishes on the floor, the unwashed windows, and a pile of washing in one corner still waiting to be ironed. She always wondered what Nellie did with her time. 'I'm so glad you never change, Nellie,' she said.

Sean left in Nellie's care, Bridget trod warily as she neared the outskirts of the grounds, keeping her eyes peeled for any unexpected sign of Anthony. But for the odd beech tree or clump of rowan or gorse bushes, there was little cover over the rolling land until she reached the copse. And now that Anthony was older he roamed the area at will. Once she'd seen him jumping his horse across the ditch that bordered the neighbouring estate. But at some point in the afternoons he always came to the copse and the stream, as if paying homage to a shrine.

Bridget breathed in the sweet country air, unsullied by acrid smoking chimneys, belching factory stacks or smouldering pit heaps. Her heart quickened as she reached the cover of the west side of the copse. Perhaps Anthony would already be there.

As usual she made her way from tree to tree, treading lightly on the soft mulch, stopping like a deer sniffing the air for danger at the slightest sound. A white-tailed rabbit bobbed in the undergrowth to her left, a starling flapped its wings and alighted on a nearby branch. It began to sing, an exultant song that echoed in Bridget's heart.

She moved on until she came to the old beech tree she'd adopted over the years as her best cover. As she leaned against it she felt the relief of a lone sailor in a storm finding a familiar harbour. The peace of the copse enfolded her. She closed her eyes and listened. After a while it seemed as if she could hear a multitude of small sounds usually inaudible to the human ear, the sigh of a single leaf in the breeze, the footfall of a butterfly alighting on a branch, the private life of the woods, unperturbed by human intruders.

The thud of galloping hooves on turf rent the stillness. Bridget stiffened. Excited yet nervous, she peered round the tree to the clearing. Two horses crossed the meadow, their riders reining them in to water at the stream. Dear God! The master was with Anthony! Although she hadn't seen the man for twelve years, his portly figure was unmistakable.

They were less than twenty yards from her. She panicked and for a moment thought of running. But common sense prevailed and she remained behind the beech, embedded in the trunk as if she were one with it. She didn't dare peer out but heard Richard Hayward's voice in the still air.

'Well, another excellent term report, Anthony! I'm proud of you. At this rate you'll be up for a first at Cambridge.'

A small silence, then Anthony's voice, not quite a boy's but not yet a man's. 'It's a long way to look ahead, Father.'

'Of course you'll do it. You've got brains – more than I had at your age.'

And even now! Bridget thought. An unchristian feeling for this man coursed through her veins when Anthony addressed him as 'Father'. And yet, she reminded herself, that *was* his God-given title.

Richard's voice again, 'It's funny that despite your brains you're so inclined to the arts. You're the first in the family.'

'Yes, sir. If I do get to Cambridge I'd dearly love to continue to read music.'

'Music! Bah! Not fitting for a man! It's all right for a boy or a woman to play silly instruments and sing for their friends at gatherings. But a man? No, me lad, you stick to your studies.'

Anthony didn't reply.

Her first panic having subsided, Bridget dared to peer round the tree. They'd tethered the horses to a nearby willow and sat on the bank, their backs to her. She was glad they came no closer to the copse, yet she dearly wanted to see Anthony's face. Even sitting he looked taller than his father.

He began to pick up pebbles and idly skim them across the stream. Though he no longer wrote his name, the first one she'd finished for him and signed with her initial remained, still clumsily framed in pebbles by his childish hand. Each time she saw it she was touched anew that he continued to tend it and plucked the grass around the little stones, now anchored deeply in the earth.

Richard's voice broke the silence. 'We should be getting back. The Cranstons will be here before tea.'

Bridget thought she saw Anthony's shoulders slump.

'Do I have to join them, sir?' His voice was half pleading, half resigned.

'You know what your mother's like when she's set her mind on something. You must pay your respects to them before the ball.'

Anthony bowed his head. 'I wish she wouldn't organize so many parties when I come home. She knows how I hate them. And I particularly dislike Melissa and Mirabelle. I have nothing to say to them, nor they to me. They're so . . .'

Richard threw back his head and a raucous laugh thundered from his throat. Bridget realized it was the first time she'd heard him laugh. 'They're silly, you mean? What do you expect, boy? They're girls! You'd better get used to it. All women are silly, that's how God made them. And you'll thank Him for it one day. He made them nice in other ways, though, custom-tailored for a man, by jove! It's time you learned how to appreciate them.'

'I don't think of girls that way, sir.' Anthony's voice was stilted, as if he were holding himself back.

Another of Richard's laughs. He slapped his thighs. 'By God, you're a slow starter! When I was going on seventeen there wasn't a pretty filly on the estate I hadn't dallied with, nor in the county for that matter. You're spending too much time with boys at that school!'

'At least I can talk to them about things that interest me. I'm not good at social chatter with girls.'

'Well, this summer's going to bring out your manhood, I'll be bound. Your mother's laying on enough parties with plenty of fillies to keep a battalion of soldiers happy. There's sure to be one of them that tickles your fancy.'

Anthony remained silent for a while. Then he spoke slowly. 'I shan't

204

be seventeen till Christmas, sir. I've got time. One day I'll meet a girl I like. I don't think they're *all* silly.'

'Aye, you're right.' Richard's voice sounded almost grudging. 'But stay well clear of the clever ones, me boy. I'd rather take a six-foot fence on a wild stallion than ride an intelligent woman.'

Anthony picked up a dead willow branch and trailed it back and forth in the water. 'I don't think I could, as you say, "ride" any other kind of woman, sir. I should have to be able to talk to her as well . . . I mean, not just party talk.'

Richard snorted. 'Ha! We shall see. Wait until you clap eyes on all those pretty faces your mother's got lined up. I'll warrant you'll be eating your words before you go back to school. I only wish you could stay for the hunting season.'

'You know I don't miss that, sir.'

'Aye, well, you'd better start learning to like it, me lad.' Richard's voice now held a note of irritation. 'Before long you'll be master of this place and all that goes with it. And that means carrying on the traditions. You'll be master of the hunt whether you like it or not!' He stood up abruptly as if to indicate that this was his final word.

'Yes, I'm aware of that.' Again, Anthony sounded quiet, resigned.

Richard dusted off his trousers. As he turned, Bridget saw that his face was as red as a cock's comb. Was it anger? His jowls, also red, and heavier than ever, hung over the collar of his riding habit. She shuddered.

But her heart leapt as Anthony sprang to his feet and strode to the horses. She swallowed hard at the sight of him. So handsome! Such a young gentleman! His face did indeed show the first signs of manhood – long and finely chiselled, yet his jaw firm, his eyes dark pools against his ivory skin, his hair curled neatly about his ears. She drank him in.

After giving his father a hand up he untethered both horses and swung his long leg over the saddle with the ease of youth. As Richard turned his horse Bridget noticed that his movements were heavier and stiffer than of old. Anthony nudged his mount, not directly round as Richard had, but veering towards the copse, circling it as if to delay his return to the house.

She withdrew her head and pressed herself into the tree. She longed to peer out to gain a closer look, though caution forbade it. But after a few moments her desire overwhelmed her. She slid her head round the tree like a snake. Richard was well ahead now, Anthony, still appearing reluctant, trailed his horse. It neighed as it neared the tree. Bridget trembled. Could it sense her? Please God, no! They were at least a dozen yards off. It neighed again. Anthony glanced to his side and paused. Bridget drew back her head like a frightened turtle, heart pounding. Had he seen her? She dug her nails into the bark and stood like that for what seemed an eternity. The horse neighed once more but the sound was receding.

She heard Richard boom from the distance. 'Come on, boy, stop your dallying! What's the matter?'

'Nothing, only a deer in the woods.' Anthony's voice sounded thin, barely audible.

She dared to peer out once more. He was looking back. She withdrew her head again, beads of perspiration on her face.

After a while she heard his horse's hooves speed up to a canter. The small thuds on the turf resounded in her ears until they only echoed in her head. The meadow was silent. Shaking, she clasped the tree for a long time before she turned back.

Chapter Nineteen

A sunny Monday the following May, Bridget and Annie ate with the children as usual when they came home from school. Afterwards Bridget sent them out to enjoy the light spring evening before bedtime. She washed the dishes and, as always, covered Tom's dinner plate with a lid and set it on a pan of hot water to keep warm. She sat down for a rest until he arrived.

Waking with a start from a shallow doze, she glanced at the clock. Half past six! He always told her when he'd be late. She checked his dinner. It was drying up. She took it off the stove and went to the back lane to bring in the children. Kate loved to push Sean up and down the lane in his pram; it always lulled him to sleep.

Within a few minutes of Bridget's summons, Kate had wheeled the worn-out carriage round the block to the front door, Eileen at her heels.

Bridget manoeuvred the pram into the narrow passage and carried the baby to his cot in the kitchen.

'Where's Da?' Kate asked.

When Bridget laid Sean down his face puckered and he let out a wail. She sighed and picked him up again. 'Your da's late. I don't know what's happened to him. And he'll be tired when he gets home. Would you sponge Eileen's hands and face and put her to bed while I feed Sean?'

Kate climbed on to a chair to get a flannel from the mantel.

'No!' Eileen screamed. '*Ma* do it!' She flattened herself against the wall as Kate advanced with the wet flannel.

'I'm busy,' Bridget said. 'If you let Kate do it I'll tell you a story in bed.'

Eileen submitted and Bridget sat down to feed Sean. Her forehead creased in a frown.

'Oooww! Soap in me eye!' Eileen clapped a hand over the offending eye and slid along the wall out of Kate's reach.

'If you'd stay still it wouldn't go in your eye.' Kate advanced again. 'Where's Auntie Annie?' she asked as she collared her victim and attacked her once more with the flannel.

'She's gone to bed early, luv. When you've finished with Eileen, why don't you clean yourself up and both of you go in and keep her company? I'll come in when it's sleepy time and tell you a story.'

The sleeping arrangements were crowded but comfortable. The boys slept heads to tails in the double bed Bridget had squeezed in with hers and Tom's. The space between the two was so narrow you had to walk sideways to get into bed, but there was room for the dresser against the back wall. After Eileen's arrival she'd bought a bigger bed for Annie and the girls.

Bridget's eyes returned to the clock. *Quarter past seven.* She put Sean back in his cot and went to the lane to call the boys, hating the harshness in her voice. 'Come on, you lot. It's getting dark. Time to come in.'

Despite their grumbles they were all washed and sipping their cocoa by eight. Kate joined them after getting Eileen off to sleep.

The children were unusually silent. Had they picked up on her mood? Bridget tried to sound cheerful. 'When your da gets home I think he deserves a box on the ears for not telling us he was going to be so late. What do you think?'

Mick grinned. 'Aye! Can I give it to him?'

'Nah, *me*, I'm bigger!' Tommy squared his shoulders to assert his superiority.

Bridget smiled. 'No, neither of you. I'll be keeping that pleasure to meself.'

By nine o'clock all the children were in bed. Bridget sat by the fire, glanced again at the clock, and stood. She retrieved her sewing basket from under the baby's cot and sighed at the pile of mending on top. She sat down once more and picked up one of Tom's work shirts.

Five minutes later she still sat, shirt in hand but no needle, when Annie shuffled in.

Bridget jumped. 'Auntie! You startled me. What are you doing up at this hour?'

'I just thought I'd sit a bit with you, pet.' Annie also checked the clock, then eased herself into the opposite chair and pulled her shawl round her. 'I bet you've got a right mouthful ready for him when he gets home.' She looked closely at Bridget.

'Aye, I have that!' Bridget placed Tom's shirt over the chair-arm, scooped the pile of mending on to her lap, and searched in the basket for the pincushion. She withdrew a needle but didn't thread it.

Annie started to push herself up. 'Would you like a cup of tea then?'

'No, no thank you.' Bridget stuck the needle back in the pincushion and set the basket on the floor. She kept the pile of mending on her lap, Tom's shirt over the chair-arm.

'Them bairns went off like little angels. It makes a big difference when they can play outside a bit at night.' Annie clenched and unclenched her skinny hands in her lap.

'Yes, they were good.' Bridget glanced at the clock.

'He's all right, lass,' Annie burst out. 'He just forgot to tell you the lads was having a do at the pub after work.'

'Yes, something like that.' Bridget threw the mending to the floor and stood. 'I'll make some cocoa.'

The kettle had just started to hiss when a loud knock sent her flying down the passage. She squeezed past the pram and opened the door. In the gaslight she could see two dark figures.

'It's Tom, hinny. He's had an accident.' The voice belonged to Matt Henderson, one of Tom's workmates. He gripped his cap in his hands.

Bridget put her hand to her head. 'Where is he? What's happened?'

'He's in the cart, luv.'

'Dear God! He's hurt! How bad?'

Matt shuffled his boots on the step and looked down at them. 'He's dead, missus.'

The two shadowy figures swayed in front of her eyes. She pressed her hand against the doorpost. 'Dead?'

'It was a bad accident. The cart blew up. He can't have felt a thing, it must've been that quick.'

No . . . no . . . not dead. Not her Tom. She saw his face, smiling, as he'd bent to kiss her goodbye that very morning, then she felt herself sliding down the doorpost. Matt Henderson stepped forward and put a hand under her elbow. She heard Annie shuffling behind her, crying, 'Dear God! Dear God!'

'Hush, Auntie! The bairns! Go back to the kitchen.' It was her own voice speaking, and her Tom was dead. She rubbed her forehead with both hands and drew herself up. 'Can you bring him in?' she said to the men. 'And can you be quiet?'

'Aye, missus.' Matt pushed his cap back on his head and cleared his throat. 'He's wrapped up, but there's bloodstains.'

'It's all right.' She inched the pram closer to the wall, then found herself back in the kitchen. She cleared the table, still set for Tom's supper. The men's boots clattered down the hall as they staggered in under Tom's weight. He was bound in a blanket tied with rope.

'Where d'you want him, missus?'

Bridget put a finger to her lips to quieten them. 'On the table.'

'Dear God! Dear God!' Annie kept repeating. She stood, shoulders hunched, hands clasped to her cheeks, her sunken eyes staring at the men's burden. Then she sobbed.

'Whisht, Auntie. And sit down.'

Annie sat in her chair and clapped her hands over her mouth, stifling her sobs to a pitiful whimper.

Bridget watched, transfixed, as the men laid their large bundle on the table. Tom's charred boots stuck out of the blanket and over the table edge. She turned a dining chair round to rest his feet on the back.

Both men stood, caps in hands, eyes on the floor.

'Why's he all bound up?' She got a towel from the line and dabbed at the bloodstains on the blanket. They were dry.

The younger man spoke for the first time. 'We had to, missus.'

'I'll need to undo him to wash him.'

Matt shuffled to where she stood, by the chair Tom's feet rested on. He put a hand on her shoulder. 'Nah, hinny. Leave him be.' He patted her shoulder clumsily. 'He was in a bad way. We had to . . .'

Annie's sobs grew to a wail.

'Sshh, Auntie!' Bridget passed her hand over her forehead. 'What happened?'

Matt dropped his arms awkwardly by his side. 'He collided with one of them newfangled horseless carriages. The cart toppled over and smashed it. There was an almighty explosion. The driver's dead and all, and the horses.'

Bridget moved to the top of the table and looked down on Tom's mummified body. Her teeth dug into her lower lip till it bled. He's not all in one piece then?'

'He was in a bad way,' the younger man, Jack, repeated.

Bridget stroked the blanket over Tom's chest. She mustn't give way to the anguish that churned inside her. 'He was always so careful,' she said in a flat voice.

Matt shook his head in a hopeless gesture. 'Aye, it's a downright shame. This morning he was in a bit of a rush like. Old Bill came in coughing and wheezing and was having trouble getting his load on, so Tom loaded for him and set him off afore he started on his own.'

Jack twisted his cap in his hands. 'Aye, I offered to help him when I'd done mine but he said there was no point in making everybody late.'

Bridget pulled out another chair and sat facing the table, hands folded in her lap. Her eyes never left Tom's body.

Matt coughed nervously. 'D'ye mind if I have a seat, missus?'

For a moment Bridget took her eyes off the table and waved to the armchairs. 'Please sit down. I'm sorry. I haven't even thanked you for your kindness.' She turned a lifeless gaze on Annie. 'Auntie, do you feel up to making a cup of tea for the gentlemen?'

Annie nodded and pushed herself up. Her face was distorted with grief, her eyes screwed shut.

'Did anyone see it happen?' Bridget went on.

Matt lowered himself heavily into a fireside chair as if still carrying his burden. Jack took Tom's chair. Matt spoke. 'There was two witnesses, an old man and woman who live nearby. It was just outside Fellburn. Tom was racing, they say.' He paused, obviously embarrassed to admit that Tom had been breaking the law. 'And the motor carriage came from the left to the crossroads, but it stalled in the middle of the road just before Tom turned. He was cornering too fast and it was too tight for the motor carriage and all. He tried to whoa when he saw it, but the cart tipped over on top of it and took him and the horses down with it. There was only the driver in the motor, thanks be to God, and him and Tom must have gone like lightning, and the horses.'

Jack nodded. 'Aye, he couldn't have suffered, missus, except for being scared just afore.'

Annie poked the kettle over the flames and tottered to the dresser for mugs. They rattled in her hands as she stared helplessly at the overloaded table.

Bridget stood. 'I'll do it, Auntie. You go and sit down.' She laid the cups on the hearth and made the tea, her hands working without her bidding.

'The old people who saw it went to the police station,' Matt continued, 'and the police rang the office. It took them a while like, 'cause they couldn't identify the cart. It all happened that fast, the old people didn't see much afore the whole thing went up.'

Bridget placed a mug of tea in Annie's hands and stroked her arm as she would a child. Then she gave a mug each to the men. They grunted their thanks.

Matt took a large gulp before he went on, 'Then the local police had to go through the Newcastle police. They held the bodies there for a long time. Jack and me didn't know nothing about it till we got back from our rounds. Aye, and when we heard we went straight to the police station. We knew as Tom would want to come home.' He rested his mug on the chair-arm. 'The other fella didn't come from these parts it seems. Nobody's come to claim him. And there was nowt left to identify him.'

'It was kind of you to bring Tom.' Bridget sat again at the table, her eyes fixed on the blanket. 'Your wives'll be worrying.'

'Never mind about them, missus. They'll be all right.'

'I'm indebted to you.' Bridget rose. 'I'll have to go and get me neighbour to take the bairns. I don't want them waking up in the morning and seeing their da like this.' She hesitated, reluctant to impose on their kindness. 'Would you mind just waiting with me auntie till I get back?'

Matt nodded. 'Aye, missus. Anything we can do.'

'Can I give you a hand with the bairns?' Jack set his mug on the floor and stood.

'Thank you, I can manage them. But I'd be glad if you'd go and warn me friend that I'm coming. I don't want her to show her upset in front of them. It's straight across the street, number forty-one. Would you ask her to keep them till I come for them tomorrow? I'll bring some extra clothes.'

She glanced into the cot to make sure Sean was still sleeping, then went to the boys' room. She collected their clothes and shook the bed gently in the dark. 'Come on, lads, we've got visitors that'll be sleeping the night. Up you get, you'll have to go to Meg's. Just stick your feet in your boots and wrap yourselves in a blanket each. And whisht, now!' she said at their muttered protests.

In Annie's room, Kate's eyes opened wide as Bridget shook her gently and told her what she'd told the boys. 'Can't Eileen and me get in with you and Da?'

'No, and hush or you'll wake Eileen.' She heaved up Eileen's sleeping weight, wrapped her in the coverlet and carried her to the door. 'Come on, Kate, get a blanket round you – and bring both of your clothes.' Puzzled, Kate silently obeyed.

The boys grouped at the front door. 'Did Da bring some people home then?' Mick asked.

'Yes.'

'Who?'

'Nobody you know.'

'But why can't we just sleep on the floor?' Tommy complained. 'It'll be the floor at Meg's anyway.'

'Just mind your business and do as I say.' Bridget crossed the road with her shadowy followers.

Jack stood with Meg in her doorway. There were tears in her eyes as she glanced at Bridget in the lamplight, but a smile in her voice as she welcomed the children. 'Come on, you lot! Let's see where we're going to put you all, eh?'

When Bridget and Jack returned, Annie and Matt were sitting in silence staring into the fire. At the sight of Bridget Matt put his hand in his pocket. 'I nearly forgot, missus. The boss gave us this for you.' He pulled out a crumpled brown envelope.

'Thank you.' Bridget opened it and sat by Tom's body again. 'It's a letter of condolence and five pounds,' she said dully.

Matt nodded. 'Aye, it's not much, hinny. If it'd been their fault they'd have given you more. But they say it was his own negligence, you see.'

Bridget put the letter and money in her apron pocket and stood. 'I'm indebted to you both. You must get back to your wives now. I don't want to be worrying them more than's necessary.'

Matt scraped back his chair and joined Jack, who still stood in the doorway. 'We'd be happy to help with the funeral arrangements,' Matt said. 'We'll come after work the morrow, won't we, Jack?'

'Aye, after work.'

'But it'd be wise to have a box made first thing, hinny.'

Bridget nodded. 'I know. I'll be seeing to that in the morning.'

She saw them to the door and returned to Annie, who sat huddled in her chair, silent. Bridget stroked the straggly grey hair. 'Come on, Auntie, I'm going to get you into bed.'

Annie shook her head with surprising vehemence. 'No, I'm not leaving you!' Then she wept again. 'Oh, me poor Bridget, me poor Tom!'

'Sshh, Auntie, you'll wake Sean.' Bridget continued stroking Annie's hair. 'Now Tom wouldn't want to see you getting into a state over him, would he? But stay if you must.'

'Oh, me poor bairn, and the little ones!' Annie rocked to and fro as she wept. Bridget bent to kiss her cheek. 'I know, I know.'

She went to the table and, kneeling by Tom's body, made the sign of the cross and prayed. She had no idea how long she'd prayed, but when she got up, Annie's head had nodded on to her chest in a fitful sleep.

Filled with a fathomless fear, Bridget returned to sit by Tom. She laid her head on the blanket over his chest and for the first time allowed her anguish its head. She wept, long, low sobs that rippled like convulsions through her body. She felt the quickening life in her belly and placed her hands over it.

It was morning when she raised her head.

Chapter Twenty

Her vigil over, Bridget pushed herself up from the chair. She rubbed her aching back. Annie still slept by the fire, her chin on her chest, her bony hands knotted in her lap.

Swept along by death like a twig in a stream, Bridget rushed through her morning chores. The ashes were still warm from the night before and the fire took quickly. While the kettle boiled she changed and fed Sean. He looked up at her with his father's eyes and her heart wept. He had a lifetime ahead of him, without Tom's love. He wouldn't even remember him. The one in her belly would never know him. And the others? And Anthony? He'd never had a real father. She seemed to have a flair for bringing fatherless children into the world. Her loved ones flitted in and out of her life like birds in a tree.

For a long time after Sean had finished suckling she held him close, till his hair grew wet with her tears.

She opened the curtains a crack and closed them again. It was a sunlit day with only a thin veil of cloud, yet she shivered. Kneeling by the bucket, she splashed her face and hands. The cold water stung and numbed her. She bent lower and immersed her face, splashed her throat, the back of her neck.

Patting herself dry, she shook Annie by the shoulder. ''Tis morning, Auntie.' Her voice was as lifeless as the bundle on the table.

Annie opened her eyes and closed them again. Bridget hated forcing the reality of the day on her. She kissed her withered forehead. 'Come on, have some tea, then I'm going to get you into bed. You shouldn't have sat there all night.'

Annie uncreased her body and clicked her gums. She buried her face in her hands. 'Oh, why couldn't it have been me! An old bag of bones no good to nobody.'

Bridget poured the tea brewing on the hearth and wrapped Annie's

215

hands round a mug. 'What nonsense you're talking! Indeed, you're a grand help to me. I want you to have a proper rest in bed and take Sean in with you while I get Tom's coffin seen to. Drink your tea.'

'Aye, of course, hinny.' The mug shook as Annie raised it to her lips.

Bridget moved a dining chair to the fire and set it with bread and butter. 'Now, you eat, Auntie. You need your strength.'

'Nah, I can't eat. But you'd better feed that bairn inside you.'

Bridget stood before the fire, her back to Tom's body. 'I'm having some tea. I'll eat later.' Sean whimpered. She set her mug on the mantelpiece untouched and bent over him. 'There now, me little one.' She picked up the clothes-peg doll hanging from his cot and stuffed it in his fist. He rammed it in his mouth and it soothed him. She must remember to get more teething jelly when she went out.

After helping Annie out to the privy, she tucked her in bed and laid Sean beside her. 'I'm off to make the arrangements now. Mind he doesn't fall out.' He was too heavy for Annie to lift but she could rock him and soothe him.

'Don't worry, luv. I'll see to him.' Annie's eyes watered as Sean turned his wide eyes on her and chortled, 'Da-da, Da-da.'

Bridget stared at them both for a moment. So many people to comfort! But it helped to keep her own grief at bay. She returned to the kitchen for her hat and cloak and said a prayer over Tom's body before leaving.

By eight fifteen the sexton and the joiner had arrived to measure the body and make the arrangements. By noon they had returned with a rough-hewn pine casket and a white shroud. The black-clad sexton spoke. 'Would you mind stepping out, missus? And would you open the curtains afore you go?'

'No, I'm staying.' Bridget opened the curtains and stood by the window. She had to see Tom one last time.

The sexton shrugged. Then the pair undid the ropes that bound the blankets to re-wrap him in the shroud. The blanket stuck to his flesh. Bridget retched as they uncovered what had once been Tom's face. Hands clasped to her cheeks, she ran out to the privy. There she vomited and wept, vomited and wept, until it seemed all the life fluid was gone out of her.

An hour later Tom was sealed in the coffin and arrangements made for his funeral in two days. Due to the manner of his death the burial had to be soon.

'That'll be four guineas, missus.' The sexton, hat in hand, didn't look at her. His voice was apologetic. 'You pay for the burial and service at the time.'

Without a word Bridget reached for the jar on the mantelpiece and counted the money. She handed it to the man with a shaking hand. 'Thank you. You've been very kind.'

They shuffled out and she counted the money left in the jar. Five pounds and sixpence. She wondered how long she could put off paying the rest of the fees.

Annie was still in her bed with Sean. Before getting her up and going to Meg's for the children, Bridget scrubbed the floor. She emptied the dirty water in the yard and half filled the bucket from the tap. The corner by the window would be a good place, she decided. She set it there, almost out of sight, topped it up with hot water from the kettle, then shaved carbolic soap from the bar and swished it into the water. The children mustn't know the smell of death.

She closed the kitchen curtains, lit two candles and placed them on each side of the coffin. Finally, she filled a jam jar with water and arranged the pansies she'd bought on her way home from the sexton's. She placed them at the foot of the coffin and made the sign of the cross.

After taking Annie a bowl of soup she changed and fed Sean and tucked him back in bed beside Annie. His belly full, his eyelids fluttered, then closed. Bridget straightened and rubbed her back. 'I'll be off to tell the bairns now, Auntie. Will you be all right till I get back?'

Annie nodded.

As she crossed the road, Bridget prayed for help to deliver the news. Meg saw her coming and met her at the front door.

'Oh, hinny! I'm heart-scalded for you.' Her eyes filled as she hugged her, enveloping her in her mounds of fat like a feather bed.

Bridget released Meg's arms. 'Please don't be crying or you'll set me off for sure. And I don't want to blubber in front of the bairns.'

'Aye, you're right.' Meg wiped her eyes on her apron and ushered Bridget inside. 'They're in the back lane playing. Right thrilled they were to have a day off school! I told them you said they could for a treat. I'll call them in now.'

'Thank you.'

They'd reached the kitchen and Bridget sat in a fireside chair while

Meg waddled out to the yard. Her voice, like a cracked bell, rang up and down the lane.

Bridget felt like a ship without a captain. But she composed herself and sat calmly as the children trickled in, Kate first with Eileen in tow. They threw themselves at her.

'Ma,' Kate burst out, 'Mrs Jackson let us have her clothesline for a skipping rope and Eileen did five skips in a row.'

Eileen tugged Bridget's hand. 'Come see.'

Bridget shook her head. 'Later, sweetheart. I've got something to tell you all first.' She lifted Eileen on to her lap and Kate perched on the chair-arm. Bridget clasped her arms round them.

Meg hustled the boys in and grouped them on the clippy mat before the hearth. 'Now all of you, sit down and be quiet. Your ma wants to talk to you.' Though it was a command, her voice was gentle and her great jowls wobbled with emotion.

Tommy ignored Meg's instructions and sat on a chair at the table. 'What do you want to talk about, Ma? Have the visitors gone?'

'Yes.' Bridget couldn't answer the first question yet.

Meg puffed her way down to the mat and put an arm round the youngest boys, Joseph and Dan. Everyone's gaze turned on Bridget. She stared at the six faces, scrubbed and polished by Meg, looking like living angels. Her throat was too dry to speak. Joseph squirmed on his bottom to her feet. 'Mrs Jackson's making me a birthday cake with seven candles for tea. Can we have it here?'

She nodded.

Dan, fourteen months older than Joseph, but slower than the others, gave his brother a scathing look. 'Your birthday's not till tomorrow. You're daft!'

'Listen who's calling *me* daft. Dafty! Dafty! Everybody knows you're a dafty.' Joseph poked Dan in the chest.

'That's enough!' Mick, the second eldest, asserted his authority. 'Quiet, both of you. Ma wants to talk to us.' But he turned to Bridget and went on, 'It's nice sleeping here, and Mrs Jackson made us sausages for breakfast. Can we stay the night and all?'

Again all eyes fixed on Bridget, and again all she could do was nod. She strove to remember her planned words. But they wouldn't come.

Tommy swivelled in his chair and straddled it as he'd seen his father do. He was tall and broad for his eleven years. 'Who were the visitors then? And why did they have to stay?'

Bridget's voice was small but controlled. 'They were friends of your da's. They brought him home.' Eileen shifted in her lap. Bridget stroked her head and went on. 'He had an accident at work.'

'Is he hurt?' Mick looked up at her with frightened eyes.

'He's in no pain, sweetheart.' She continued stroking Eileen as she prayed for the strength to say the words. '. . . God decided He wanted him with Him in heaven.'

There was a hushed silence as six mouths opened like small dark holes and six pairs of uncomprehending eyes stared at her.

'He's dead?' Tommy jumped up from the chair and stared at her in disbelief.

Kate and Eileen began to cry. Bridget drew Kate down from the chair-arm and squeezed her on to her lap next to Eileen. She clasped them to her and rocked.

'He's with God,' she said.

A chorus of wails rent the air. Meg clutched Joseph and Dan, who bellowed into her bulging bosom.

Tommy, dry-eyed, still stood staring at Bridget as if accusing her. 'Why didn't you tell us? I want to see him.' He ran to the door.

'Stay here till I've finished.' Bridget gave him a look that begged forgiveness.

He leaned against the door, his face twisted. Suddenly he let out a screech like a dog in pain and the tears were loosed. 'It's not true, Ma! It's not!'

Bridget nodded. ''Tis true.' She felt as if she were cutting out her heart. 'That's right now, have a good cry, all of you. Let's do that here, before we go home. Sure, you know your da would want you to be happy for him that he's gone to heaven.'

'Da's dead!' Kate finally understood what her mother was saying. She screamed and struggled, setting Eileen off. Bridget grasped them tighter.

The boys continued to sob into Meg's bosom. Bridget took a deep breath. Dear God, give her strength! 'You've got to remember that he's happy in heaven, happier than anyone could ever be on this earth. We're not crying for him. We're crying for ourselves 'cause we'll miss him.'

Still weeping, Tommy left the support of the door and trailed to the back of her chair. He put his hands on her shoulders. Then his face crumpled and he broke down, burying his head in the back of her neck. She slipped her arm from round Eileen and reached back to pat his head. Then Eileen screamed again. She clasped her once more.

219

She closed her eyes. Her ears rang with the children's wails. She mustn't give way. She tried to soothe them but no believable words would come.

Two hours later Bridget and Meg took the children home. As they passed Annie's bedroom she appeared at the door, weeping. 'Please stay in bed, Auntie,' Bridget whispered. 'Don't let them see you crying.' Annie sniffed and went back to look after Sean.

Tears spent for the moment, the children allowed Bridget and Meg to group them round the coffin. They fixed their eyes on the wooden box in horror and awe.

Tommy broke the silence. 'Why did you do that, Ma? Why did you box him up? Now we can't kiss him . . . and we're supposed to. Jimmy Best kissed his da. And the whole class kissed Father Davie's forehead.' Tommy looked as if he were about to cry again. But Bridget had prepared her answer.

'Now wouldn't your da have wanted you to remember him when he was alive? 'Tis only his body there now. And that's just to carry our spirits around in till God calls us.' She watched their faces, but their eyes never left the coffin. She moved to the head of the box and stood facing them. 'But you can kiss his coffin. Come on, who'll be first?'

'I'm first.' Tommy stepped forward to assert his seniority.

'And I'm next,' Mick said.

The others took their cue from their older brothers and filed in order of age to kiss the rough wood above Tom's head. Joseph managed to reach on his own but Bridget had to lift Kate and Eileen. Meg stood throughout, hands clasped, toothless mouth moving in silent prayer. Bridget touched Meg's arm. 'Would you mind keeping them till the funeral on Friday?'

Meg didn't answer but gathered the young ones to her and beckoned the others with her head. 'Come on, you lot. We're going to have tea now and then I'm going to make that birthday cake for the morrow. Your ma and your auntie'll come over later.'

At the sound of the front door closing, Bridget went to the bedroom. She must see to Sean and comfort Annie.

'Ashes to ashes, dust to dust . . .' Father Gantry's words pelted Bridget like hailstones. She shivered by the graveside. Ashes! Her dearest Tom! The sky, as cold and grey as ashes, threatened rain. She shivered again but felt the pressure of Tommy's hand tighten in hers, then Mick's on

220

her other side. Purpose overwhelmed her. Her children were her life now. And they needed her more than ever.

They stood round the grave with the mourners. Tommy had insisted on saying his final goodbye to his father like an adult, and Mick, unwilling to admit that eighteen months made him any less grown up, had also begged to come. Bridget thanked God for Meg, who was taking care of the others.

'In the name of the Father, and of the Son, and of the Holy Ghost, Amen.' After the final prayer the group turned to leave.

The boys' eyes were wet, as were most others. But Bridget continued to do her crying inside. She held her head up and, Tommy and Mick on each side of her, followed the procession back to the house.

Meg had left the children with her married daughter and was there to welcome the guests. By the time Bridget and the boys arrived the kitchen was thronging with neighbours and Tom's workmates.

Meg held out a mug to Bridget. 'Have a little nip of this, luv.'

Smelling the pungent odour of port, Bridget shook her head. 'Sure, I'll just have a cup of tea. And one each for the lads and all, please.'

Meg bustled to the stove and Bridget mingled with the guests to accept their condolences.

Mr Gardner, the man Tom had helped on that fateful day, stretched out a mottled hand and tugged at Bridget's sleeve. 'Eey, I'm that sorry, missus! I feel that guilty! If he hadn't stopped to help me out he might still be alive.' His face was pale beneath its weather-beaten skin, his rheumy eyes begged forgiveness.

An unusual emotion welled up in Bridget. She asked God's absolution for the bitterness she felt towards this stranger and took his hand. 'Sure, if he hadn't been helping you it would've been someone else,' she said softly.

Meg poured the port and tea while Annie served the mutton sandwiches, sausage rolls and jam tarts they'd baked the previous night. Everyone sang Tom's praises

Matt, one of the men who'd carried home Tom's body, had brought his accordion and soon everyone accompanied him in song. Bridget sang Tom's favourite, 'The Irish Girl', not for the guests, but for Tom. He would be smiling up there, that proud smile that cracked his face whenever she sang for visitors.

When the last guest had left, Bridget put the children and Annie to bed but kept Tommy and Mick up. Tommy sat in Tom's chair in front of the fire, Mick in Annie's. Bridget made them cocoa and joined them. She thought of her mother's words: 'The family needs a man to steer it.' But she attacked the thought. 'You know why I've kept you up?'

The boys nursed their mugs and nodded.

'Aye. How much have we got, Ma?' Tommy's voice suddenly sounded deeper.

Bridget sighed. She could protect them from this no longer. 'Two pounds, one shilling and tuppence. And I still haven't paid off all the funeral.'

'Don't worry, Ma. We'll both go out looking the morrow. I bet we can find something to start next week.' Mick's voice was eager and despite herself Bridget smiled. He hated school.

'We could move to Benton or somewhere near. There's money in the pits,' Tommy said. 'Seth Blake's been down since he was nine and he makes three and six a seven-hour shift. They want little lads as can get into small spaces. We could do it, Ma.'

Bridget's mouth set in a tight line. 'Indeed, you're not going down the pits, and that's that! You've got *some* education, you're going to use it.'

'Aw, Ma,' Mick said. 'Book-learning doesn't put food in your belly.'

Bridget pushed herself up and paced the floor. 'No, but you can get a better job than the pits . . . something where you can use your head as well as your hands. Jim Barts got work as a chippy's apprentice in Jarrow Village. He'll end up a carpenter and could start his own business some day. I want you to learn a good trade.'

Mick nodded. 'Aye, I'd like to work with wood and all.'

Tom sneered at him. 'Men sleep outside factory gates waiting for those jobs, man. We'll not find anything as cushy as that.'

'Yes, you will, or better.' Bridget stopped pacing and turned to them. 'You've got some time because while you're looking, I'll be working at the New Hawk Inn. Mr Cox has offered me a night job as a barmaid.' Unconsciously, she measured her belly with her fingers. She could barely feel the rise. Knowing that Mr Cox wanted her as much for decoration to please the male customers as for her ability to pull Bass, she hadn't told him about her condition. But she could still pull Bass from behind the counter when she showed. 'I can probably work five or six months,' she went on, colouring a little. But they were the men of the family now. She had to tell them. 'I'll be giving you another baby sister or brother round about then.'

They stared at her, surprised and puzzled.

'How d'you know?' Tommy finally asked.

Bridget tried to think how to phrase her news. Though she'd given them many brothers and sisters before, she'd never told them in advance. 'Your da gave it to me before he died,' she said. 'Sure, I know when it'll be coming.' She couldn't bring herself to say more.

Mick's surprise turned to dismay. 'Another one!'

'What of it?' Tommy said in his mother's defence. 'One more won't make much difference. But who'll look after the bairns and Auntie when you're at the pub, Ma?'

Bridget sat again with a sigh. 'Kate'll have to do what she can. You'll all have to learn to help yourselves more. And Meg said she'll keep an eye out for you.'

Tommy looked thoughtful. 'Why don't you want Dan to work, Ma? He's old enough, he just acts young for his age.'

'He's too stupid,' Mick said. 'He never gets anything right.'

'Indeed, that's quite enough!' Bridget's voice was sharp. 'And how many times do I have to tell you? He's not stupid! He's just a bit slower than the rest of you. But anyway, I'm not about to be sending any eight-year-old of mine out to work. He needs the schooling more than any of you.' She took a sheet of notepaper from the mantelpiece and handed it to Tommy. 'I've looked in the paper and asked around the street. Here's a list of all the best firms to begin with. You can start looking in the morning. Off to bed with you now.'

PART II

Chapter Twenty-One

Anthony trailed down to the morning room. He hated this room. Everything was dark green – the upholstered chairs, the walls, the velvet curtains. He didn't feel like breakfast. The banquet from the previous night lay heavily on his stomach. Mildred and Richard sat at the long oval table, the rosebud china and silver sparkling against a white damask cloth.

'Good morning, Mother, Father.'

Richard grunted and Mildred acknowledged his presence with a scowl.

Anthony stood before them, tall, slender, and strikingly handsome. The chestnut curls of his childhood were trimmed, though not completely tamed, the planes of his face finely chiselled, as if the carver had whittled and modelled as far as he dared. Yet it was a strong face.

Harold, the butler, new since Anthony's Christmas visit home, pulled out a chair for him with white-gloved hands and poured his tea. A few seconds later he returned with two steaming silver platters. Anthony waved them away, and Richard waited until the liveried figure had glided backwards to the buffet and dissolved into the woodwork before he spoke: 'What the devil got into you last night? Upsetting your mother like that when she'd gone to all that trouble for you!'

Mildred dabbed at her mouth with her damask napkin. She was plumper than ever. Her bosom, hoisted by her stays, puffed up like rising dough. She raised her round face to Anthony. In its displeasure, it looked as if it were pressed against a windowpane. 'How dare you embarrass me in front of all those people! And I invited them in your honour!' Her chin, quivering with indignation, sent vibrations down her jowls.

Anthony shifted in his chair. 'I'm sorry, Mother, I know you went to a great deal of trouble, and it was a splendid ball. I'm just not used to

227

three parties in a row. I get tired of them.' His voice was soft, distant, like music floating in from another room.

Mildred snorted and was about to say more, but Richard cut in. 'Tired, indeed!' He also had grown outwards and downwards. He wagged his domed head, now as bald as a croquet ball but for a fringe of grey hair above his collar. 'Begod, boy, when I was your age!'

'I know, sire, but I'm not you.' Anthony's tone was respectful, but it didn't appease Richard.

'Well it's time you leaned to be more like me! You're a grown man. One of these days you'll have to fill my shoes.' Richard's bull neck looked as if it would burst out of its tight collar.

'More bacon, Harold, and more toast!' Mildred called to the butler. There was silence as he served four rashers from the silver platter, refilled the toast rack and floated back into the woodwork.

Mildred sawed at her bacon. 'The next time I hold a party, whether it's in your honour or not, you shall stay until the last guest has left and say your goodbyes formally. No more disappearing to bed like a ten-year-old in the middle of the evening! Indeed!'

'It was midnight, Mother.'

'Don't answer me back! The guests didn't leave till four. What a time I had, making excuses for you again. No more, I'm warning you. And those two nice Misses Pringle! They were quite upset when you disappeared. It gave the impression you didn't like them.'

Anthony made circles with his cup in the saucer. 'But I didn't care for their company, Mother.' He longed to go out into the sunshine, to get away from this scene – one of so many similar.

Mildred spread marmalade on her toast and sighed. 'Indeed, and what was wrong with them? They're two of the most eligible young ladies in the county.'

'I agree, there's nothing wrong with them. I just didn't like them as prospective . . . partners. They bored me. Their chatter was so . . .'

'Silly?' Richard threw his napkin on the table. 'It seems you think that every female in the damned county is silly! What the devil do you expect in a woman, boy?'

Anthony looked his father in the eye. 'Nothing, sir. That is, I don't wish anything of a woman for the moment. I'm content to go up to Cambridge in the autumn and commence my studies. I shall be too busy for . . . fillies . . . in any event, and I have no desire for a woman in my life at present. I shall know when the time comes.'

Richard scraped back his chair and jumped up. 'Begod! The time had better come soon! And I mean before you go up to Cambridge. Who'd have believed a son of mine would turn out to be a . . . a sissy!'

Anthony flinched.

Mildred coloured. 'I'm not listening to this language.' She rose, gathered her silk skirts and stalked from the room. Her yellow coiffure, now faded and tinged with grey, bobbed with each step.

The men stood. Anthony sat again as the butler closed the door behind Mildred but Richard remained standing and glowered down at him. 'I'll make a man out of you yet. And soon! You're coming with me to Newcastle for a few days whether you like it or not. We leave tomorrow. And when you come back, we shall see if you haven't changed your tune about women.'

Anthony closed his eyes. He knew what that meant. He knew about his father's frequent excursions to Newcastle. When he opened his eyes only the butler remained, shoulders back, head high, impassive as a tin soldier.

Pushing his horse to its limits, Anthony rode at a gallop in the morning sunshine. He had to escape the confines of the house, feel the breeze on his face, the wind in his hair. The horse's hooves seemed to spring from the grass, green and fresh from the previous day's rainfall. Out of habit Anthony turned towards the copse. But he needed a long ride today. He skirted the wooded area, crossed the path to the Morpeth Road and took the bramble hedge bordering the neighbouring property.

Once off his father's land, he felt free. He'd been a boy when he'd last trespassed on the Flagdon Hall estate. Suddenly he felt like a boy again. The meadowland was less flat here, the undulations dotted with patches of hawthorns and clumps of rowans. He guided the horse around the clusters of trees, felt the rise and fall of the shallow hills, and at last turned down towards the stream. He dismounted, let the horse drink, then tethered it to an overhanging willow.

With a sigh he threw himself on his back on the bank and closed his eyes. The June sun, warm on his face, lulled him into a dreamless sleep.

'Are you all right?'

He opened his eyes to see a small shadow surrounded by a bright light bending over him. He blinked and sat up. It was a woman's voice and form, but he couldn't see clearly for the sun behind her. 'I do beg your pardon, madam. I must have fallen asleep.' He jumped up and bowed.

'Thank goodness! You were so still I feared you were dead.'

A faint aroma of violets surrounded her. He could see her clearly now, a slight figure, barely reaching his shoulders. She wore a well-cut riding habit, her silver-blonde hair swept up beneath a narrow-brimmed riding hat. The face underneath held his gaze. He'd never seen a more fetching woman. He realized he was staring.

She laughed and the sound was tinged with silver like her hair. 'My, I'm delighted you're not dead. But you do look . . . dazed. Did you take a fall?'

'Er, no.' His voice trembled and he cursed himself for sounding like a schoolboy.

She took a step towards him and looked him full in the face. Her eyes were violet, like the satin blouse at the neck of her riding jacket, and like the perfume in the air around her. 'May I ask your business here?'

'My business?' Suddenly he realized he wasn't on his own land and remembered the foreign neighbours who for some reason were never invited to the house. 'Oh, I . . . er, was just out for a ride and got carried away, I suppose. Is this your property?'

She nodded, her violet gaze still on him.

He flushed. 'Please forgive me. I didn't intend to . . . it was just such a beautiful day, I kept on riding. I'm Anthony Hayward.' Unconsciously, his head jerked in the direction of the house, invisible in the distance.

'Ah, I see, my neighbour! I do, of course, know of the Hayward family.' Her lips parted in a smile that dazzled Anthony as much as the sunlight. She reminded him of a silver and white ornament from a wedding cake. She held out a dainty gloved hand. 'I'm Adelle Grayson. I'm pleased to make your acquaintance.'

That wasn't the name he remembered. The property must have changed hands. He took her hand and bowed. 'I'm honoured, madam. You must be new here. I'm sorry we were not acquainted earlier.'

She laughed again. 'Oh, dear, no. I was born here, though I lived abroad for many years. I've been back in residence for a year.'

She moved away and Anthony saw that her horse stood tethered by his own. She took its rein and, before he could offer his assistance, had mounted the side-saddle with the grace of a cat. She smiled down at him. 'If you'll excuse me, I'm expected back at the house. But please, feel comfortable if you wish to stay. Indeed, feel free to enjoy my land whenever you wish.' She clicked the reins.

'I'm indebted to you, madam.' Anthony bowed farewell and went on staring long after she was out of sight.

* * *

The ride to Newcastle the following morning gave Anthony his first chance to talk to either of his parents alone. Although he dreaded the impending 'holiday' he took advantage of his father's good humour. 'I met our new neighbour from Flagdon Hall yesterday, sir,' he began.

Richard lounged against the black leather of the new Daimler motor car and raised his eyebrows. 'New neighbour? It's still the Pagnol family estate as far as I know.'

'Yesterday I came across a lady I haven't seen before. She was riding near the property line. But her name wasn't Pagnol,' he went on, 'it was Grayson, Adelle Grayson. Yet she said she'd been born here. She was blonde and very beautiful. Do you know the name?'

'Bah! I don't remember names. But the blonde one was the married daughter – the pretty one. Not a male child in that family for three generations, except for the grandfather and a son who died.' He looked at Anthony with satisfaction. 'I'm glad to say I don't suffer that dilemma.'

'Then what happened to the property?' Anthony wanted to ask about the daughters, but he must proceed with caution.

'The grandfather inherited the French estate and, later, Flagdon Hall. It had belonged to a distant branch of the family – a lateral pass I believe is the legal term. He and his wife spent their time between the two estates. But when their only daughter married a penniless younger son there wasn't even an heir presumptive. The old man got round the problem by willing both estates to the son-in-law – with entails, naturally.' Richard paused but Anthony steered him on.

'What were the entails, sir?'

'As I understand, the properties could never be mortgaged or sold while the daughters or their offspring were alive, whether or not the children be female. They lost the family name of course, but at least managed to hold on to the property.'

'So now the young daughters live on the estate?' Anthony's excitement rose.

'Not young – the married one's widowed and the other's a spinster. But only the widow lives there. She has two children, both girls again, according to your mother.' Richard chuckled. 'But then most of the gossip I hear is according to your mother.'

Anthony's heart somersaulted like a tumbler at a circus and landed in his stomach. She must be the widow's daughter. 'I suppose the children are grown up now?'

231

'No, still children, the daughter only married twelve or thirteen years ago.'

Anthony was beginning to feel exasperated. It didn't make sense. 'Then the person I saw must be a relative or friend.'

'Perhaps.'

Anthony waited for further information about distant relatives. But Richard went on about the mother. 'So now the widow's a landowner, unless she remarries and bears a son. Women landowners! Damned untraditional if you ask me!' He shrugged. 'But what can you expect of foreigners?'

Anthony tried to draw his father away from the widow. 'That couldn't be the lady I saw,' he insisted. 'She was young and very beautiful.'

'Ha!' Richard slapped his thigh. 'Taken your fancy, has she? Well, I'm glad some woman has at last.' Now he slapped Anthony's thigh. 'Don't worry, me boy, there'll be plenty your age where we're going. That one must be nigh on old enough to be your mother.'

His mother? How ridiculous! She looked *nothing* like his mother. Anthony leaned back against the leather, the roar of the engine resounding in his ears. His frustration mounted. He'd succeeded in getting his father to talk at length about the family, yet still he had no idea who yesterday's phantom could be. He couldn't let the matter drop. 'Are there any other relatives you're aware of, sir?'

'No, but your mother would know better.'

'Why did you and Mother have no dealings with the family? I mean, everyone else in the county and beyond is invited to Mother's affairs.'

'Not those foreigners!' Richard took a cigar from his pocket, lit it, and puffed out blue smoke. 'Your mother wanted nothing to do with them and I can't say I blame her. Religious they were. The son-in-law was a Swiss Calvinist and the daughter converted before her marriage. Pity! A pretty little thing as I remember.'

'Are you saying Mother didn't want anything to do with them because they were foreigners or because they were religious, sir?'

Richard's mirth rumbled up from his belly like an erupting volcano. 'Can you imagine?' he said, trying to control himself. 'Bible-spouting Calvinists at your mother's affairs, preaching hellfire and damnation! They didn't drink, didn't entertain, except soirées where people sang songs – in praise of the Lord, no doubt – and recited poetry and drank coffee.' Still chuckling, he wiped his eyes on his handkerchief. 'Ho, ho, no! Not exactly our set, even if they *had* been English. Could you see them at your mother's balls?'

232

'Not if they are as you say, sir. But the lady I saw certainly didn't give that impression.' He closed his eyes and tried to imagine her in black, preaching hellfire. Still he saw only the silver and white image.

Richard flicked ash on to the carpeted floor and stared out of the window.

But Anthony couldn't stop probing. 'If it *was* the widow I saw, she doesn't look at all the stuffy kind to me. And as you say, she's pretty enough. Why does Mother not invite her to her affairs?'

Richard guffawed and choked on his cigar smoke. He wheezed as he spoke. 'You've hit the nail on the head there, boy! A widow! And a pretty one at that! Women don't like widows around their men, pretty or not. They're man-bait. Once they've had it, you see, they feel . . . deprived. Anybody's husband is better than none.' He patted Anthony's hand. 'You'll know what I mean soon.'

Anthony suppressed a shudder at the thought of the ordeal ahead. 'You know that I should prefer to go riding, sir.'

'Ha!' Richard chortled and placed his arm round Anthony's shoulders. 'That's just what you'll be doing, me boy. But riding a two-legged filly this time, eh?'

Folding his arms, Anthony slid down in his seat. The June countryside, bright green and blue, fled past him unnoticed. The next two days were now going to be an even bigger ordeal than he'd imagined. He couldn't wait to find out who she was. His father had certainly got it wrong. A pretty young woman like that couldn't possibly be a widow and mother. She *must* be a cousin.

Anthony blinked in the dimly lit foyer. Purple, everything was purple – purple upholstery, purple carpets, purple satin-covered walls, purple hangings at doors and windows. Such grotesque décor!

A large middle-aged woman bore down on them. 'How nice to see you again, sir. It's been so long.'

'Ah, yes, I've been busy, Molly.' Richard took the proffered beringed fingers and touched them with his lips.

'And you've brought a guest with you!' Molly inspected Anthony with satisfaction. 'Such a handsome one and all!'

Anthony squirmed under her gaze.

Richard winked. 'My son, Anthony. It's about time he . . . er . . . saw a bit more of life. Been closeted up with boys too long at that damned school.'

Though still squirming inside, Anthony took the fat hand Molly

233

fluttered before him and managed a bow. A sweet, cloying smell overwhelmed him. It brought to mind his mother. Lily of the valley! But it was mingled with the stale smell of unwashed clothing.

'Well, now, come with me.' Molly bustled over the purple carpet with a flounce of velvet skirts and led them to an inner reception room. Everything here was red.

They sat on the red velvet chaise she indicated, frock coats flicked aside, top hats on knees.

Molly clucked over them. 'I'll get you some refreshment and bring the girls.'

'That one used to be quite a handful in her day – two hands full in fact.' Richard laughed at his joke. 'Pity she's past it now. They get past it so quickly, makes a man feel old. Wait till you see the girls, though! You've never clapped eyes on such an inviting assortment.' He gave Anthony a playful poke in the ribs.

As if on command, the 'girls' filed in. Anthony froze. Most of them looked old and lifeless despite their painted smiles. Molly carried glasses and a carafe on a silver tray. She filled two glasses and offered the tray. 'Here you are now. A little something to wet your whistle. Just take your time deciding on the girls. The best selection in Newcastle, if I say so meself.'

Richard knocked back his drink. Anthony held the glass. It smelled like port. At least it gave him something to do with his hands other than twiddling his hat.

'And now, whatever takes your fancy.' Molly hovered over them, sweeping her arm along the row of women, some dressed and some in various stages of undress, down to camisoles and pantalettes. Anthony stared again at the sight, his earlier disgust overtaken by a terrible sadness. Such a way to earn a living!

'Come on, boy! Which one?' He pointed to a small brunette at the end. At least she was dressed.

Molly clucked approval. 'Good choice, sir! Mary's one of our best ladies.' She nodded to the girl, who stepped towards the door and waited for Anthony to follow.

In a daze, he set his glass on the side table and, clutching his hat, stepped the hundred miles across the red carpet. In the narrow corridor Mary put her arm through his and led him without a word to a small chamber.

He stared around the room. The bed stood in the centre, festooned with scarlet and gold hangings, scarlet and gold chairs were dotted here and there, and the scarlet and gold walls were almost invisible under an array of Rubenesque paintings. By comparison the purple foyer was in excellent taste.

Mary indicated a high-backed chair and he sat stiffly, hat again on his lap. She posed before him, hands on hips, and he saw her for the first time. Yellow sequins sparkled on her green taffeta dress, gilt baubles twinkled in her dark hair. She was slim, skinny even, her miniature breasts only a slight rise above her gown. She was little more than a schoolgirl.

'What's your pleasure, sir?' Her voice, thin as a reed, pierced his eardrums. He could sit and stare no longer.

'How much do you charge?'

She cocked her head. 'Well, sir, that depends on what you want.'

'I want only to talk.'

'To talk!' Her grey eyes stared at him, puzzled. Then she gave him a knowing wink. 'Oh . . . I see . . . some dirty talk first.' She moved towards him.

'No! Just talk, plain talk.' Beads of perspiration formed on his upper lip.

'Just plain talk, nothing else?' She sat in the adjacent chair and stared at him, her crimson mouth open.

He fumbled in his coat pocket for the wad of notes his father had given him and peeled off five. 'Is that enough?'

Her hand darted forward and clutched the money. 'That's plenty for talking, sir.' She scrutinized him as she tucked her treasure inside her bodice. 'But to tell you the truth, you're the first gentleman in a long time I wouldn't mind doing it with. Most of them are . . . well . . . like the gentleman you were with, sir – with respect.'

Glad that the preliminaries were over, Anthony relaxed his face into a smile. But he must caution this girl. 'The gentleman is my father, and the only reason I'm here is to please him.'

'Oh, dear!' She clapped her hand to her mouth and despite himself Anthony laughed.

'Don't worry, you have my word, not an utterance that passes between us will go beyond this door. Do I have your word also?'

'Oh, yes, indeed, sir.'

'My father must never know that I have a lover, a very dear lover, to whom I could never be unfaithful – even in thought. It would destroy me to keep such a secret from her, and destroy *her* if she found out.'

Mary nodded. 'Oh, I see now, sir. How romantic! Such a faithful gentleman you are! I've never had anyone like you afore.'

Anthony lowered his eyes. Was he strange? Was he, as his father believed, not a real man? Even had he not met that silver and white creature yesterday, the thought of being with a woman he didn't love repelled him. Yes, surely love was the difference. If Adelle were sitting in front of him now he could certainly not feel so cool. But he must make conversation with Mary. He cleared his throat. 'Tell me about yourself,' he said.

The journey home was exhilarating. Anthony sucked in the fresh air rushing through the car windows. The dark, cloistered saloons and gaming rooms of the past two days seemed a million miles away.

Richard appeared satisfied that his son was now a man and had been delighted when Anthony even seemed eager after the first visit to the brothel. But during the ride home Richard was silent much of the time, his manner irritable. Anthony guessed his father was unhappy about his performance in the boudoir, though he'd won fifty pounds at cards. Several times Anthony had congratulated him on his prowess at the tables. But now he too fell silent, dreaming of the following morning when he would again take the hedge that bordered his neighbour's estate and find out who that mysterious creature was.

Chapter Twenty-Two

The horse seemed to want to fly as much as Anthony. Its hooves barely touched the ground before it took the bramble hedge. It was still early, nine o'clock, but Anthony didn't care if he spent the entire day waiting, he mustn't miss her.

He dismounted at the same spot by the stream and lay up the bank on his belly, chin resting on his hands, eyes peeled. This time he would be awake when she approached. The thought that she might not come passed unbidden through his mind.

But he lay alert until the sun was overhead. Still no sign. His stomach felt empty. He'd avoided the chore of breakfast. While considering going home for luncheon and returning afterwards, he heard the thud of hooves on turf. He sat up, took the book he'd brought from his pocket and opened it at random. He must seem to be busy. But his eyes couldn't take in the blurred print.

The hooves sounded nearer. He turned his head. She was coming towards him, riding the same dappled mare. Still holding his book, he stood and clasped his hands behind his back. He waited until she was a few feet away before inclining his head in greeting.

She reined in beside him, looking just as she had that first day, except that her riding habit was now dove grey, her blouse buttercup yellow. No, she couldn't be a day over twenty. Her violet eyes smiled down at him. Was there a hint of amusement in them?

'Good morning, Mr Hayward. I see you took advantage of my offer.'

He bowed deeper. Suddenly it struck him. How should he address her? 'Good morning, Miss Grayson,' he said. 'How could I refuse such an invitation? It's so beautiful here.' She hadn't corrected him. She couldn't be the widow. And she was dismounting! She was going to stay!

He moved to place his hand under her elbow but she'd lowered herself as lightly as a shadow and stood beside him, barely reaching his shoulder. She glanced at the open book in his hand. 'I see you brought some entertainment.'

He shrugged. All the words he'd practised left his head.

She reached out 'May I see?'

Feeling foolish, he handed her the small leather-bound volume.

She took it, still open at his place, and read aloud:

> *Come live with me and be my love,*
> *And we will all the pleasures prove*
> *That valleys, groves, hills, and fields,*
> *Woods or steepy mountain yields.*

She closed the book and her eyes glinted with humour. 'Marlowe's one of my favourites too. Though I learned to like him later in life. He wasn't considered exactly ... well, suitable reading for young ladies at school.'

She held out the volume and he stuffed it in his pocket.

His cheeks burned. How unfortunate it should be open there! 'I'm glad you ... um, learned,' he muttered to his boots.

She turned and strolled towards the water and his blush appeared to pass unnoticed. From behind she could be a schoolgirl, so slight, so straight. He joined her on trembling legs. What to say now? Where were all the words he'd planned? He coughed. 'I'm delighted to have your company. But I'm interrupting your ride. Perhaps I could ride with you?'

Her face seemed to unfold like a flower when she smiled. 'Then I should like to see some of your estate. I've seen it only from a distance.'

Anthony remembered his father's words. Could she be one of the daughters – not a visitor? 'It would be my pleasure,' he said trying to keep the excitement from his voice.

Before he could reach her she'd mounted her mare. He cursed himself for his awkwardness and untethered his horse. She was already ahead of him. He would take her to the gate by the road, the hedge was too high for a woman. But she was off like a gazelle in the direction of the hedge.

He caught up and beckoned towards the gate but she laughed and took the hedge with ease. He followed, then overtook her and made for the copse. He wanted to show her this place, his private spot. Out of breath, he dismounted and tethered his horse to an oak sapling in almost a single movement. This time he would be ready to help her. His hands circled her waist lightly, as if any pressure would snap her in two. He'd never seen such a fragile creature. 'We should walk here to enjoy it best,' he said.

She moved aside an overhanging branch with her riding crop as she walked. 'I used to think ogres and witches lived here. We were forbidden to cross the boundary as children.'

Was she perhaps one of the granddaughters? His father must have been mistaken about their ages. 'We?' He kept his voice calm.

'My sister and I.'

He opened his mouth to ask further, but checked himself. He couldn't let her know he'd been enquiring after her. Instead he laughed. 'Your childish fancies weren't completely wrong. My father can be an ogre at times and sometimes I also believe my mother has a secret broomstick.'

Her laughter bubbled up from her throat and already the sound was wonderfully familiar. They walked in silence for a moment, he at a loss for what to say next and she looking around and picking her way across the carpet of leaves. 'It's so beautiful and peaceful, it's hard to believe that "evil doings" went on here.' She turned her smile up to him.

'Is that what you believed?'

They'd reached the clearing and she sat on a fallen log. He sat so close he could smell violets again.

'My father was very religious,' she went on. 'And from what we understood, your parents were, well, just the opposite. My sister and I were very much under my father's thumb at that time.' She paused and smiled. 'But we outgrew it.'

Her father! Then she *was* the widowed daughter. Anthony's heart slumped to his riding boots. But why should it matter that she was a widow? And his father had mistaken her age. He forced his voice to remain calm. 'Where are your parents now?'

She twisted the riding crop in her hands. 'Both dead, and my brother died very young.'

'But you have other family – your sister?'

'My sister lives on my grandparents' estate in France. She prefers the climate. When I married I moved to my husband's estate in Wiltshire. He died two years ago.'

'I'm sorry to hear that.'

'The property went to his younger brother. But he's an army man,

239

away much of the time. My husband willed that I and my daughters could live there for our lifetimes. But I preferred to come back here. There were too many recent memories.'

'And your children?'

'They love this place as much as I do. I was always happy here.' She caught his puzzled glance and laughed. 'Oh, yes, my father was strict but we were a happy family. And of course my mother was French. She enjoyed life as the French do.' Her violet eyes danced with merriment at his surprised expression. 'You understand, we spent a great deal of time with my grandparents in France and, when there, my grandfather's preference for the good life overrode my father's views.' She drew circles on the ground with her crop and chuckled. It was like the sound of running water.

'How old are your daughters?' The question had been burning inside him. He hoped it didn't sound impolite.

'They're twelve and ten, and growing up too fast.'

Anthony cleared his throat and loosened his collar. 'It's sad to lose a father so young.' He felt he was choking. She must be almost old enough to be his mother. He couldn't help twisting his head and staring. How could she still have the face and body of a schoolgirl?

She must have felt his gaze for she turned, raised her eyebrows and laughed again. This time the sound seemed to fill the copse. 'Yes, most people are surprised. I know I look deceptively young. It runs in the family . . . on my mother's side.' She looked at him, the corners of her mouth turned upwards as if she hadn't quite finished laughing. 'But you're obviously inexperienced at life, or you'd discern its scars. I bear its signs of laughter and sadness.'

Unconsciously, Anthony screwed up his eyes. But he could see none of the traces she mentioned. Her smile widened and he blushed at his crassness. 'Er, let me show you the stream,' he said. 'It's deep and very beautiful here. I used to swim in it as a boy.' He jumped up, eager to show her his favourite spot. Suddenly her age seemed unimportant.

She unfurled herself from the log like a kitten after a nap and joined him. 'You talk as if you were alone a lot. You have no brothers or sisters?'

Anthony cleared a path before them with his riding crop. 'An older sister, but I never brought her here. She married an army officer and lives abroad most of the time.' Margery was due to arrive from London with her husband and daughter that day. He should be back in time for tea. He dismissed the thought and went on, 'As a child, when I left the

240

house it was usually to seek solitude.'

'And now?' She glanced sideways at him, still with that amused expression.

Damnation! Why did he have to blush whenever he caught her eye? 'And now, I've finally discovered my neighbours.' Pleased that he'd turned that corner, he continued, 'I wish I'd been allowed to know them earlier.'

They reached the clearing and she skipped over the grass towards the stream. She stopped at the stones that spelled his name and glanced back at him. 'I see you've placed your stamp here.'

This time he didn't blush but smiled with pleasure as he caught up with her. 'That appeared overnight when I was about four – one of the staff out of bounds. I used to think the fairies did it. Somehow I still can't bring myself to break it up.'

She sat on the bank, her feet almost in the water. 'What's the B for?'

He shrugged before sitting beside her, hands hugging his knees. 'Whoever it was must have signed it.'

'I take it you're home for the holidays.'

Damn! She'd guessed he was still at school. He forced himself to look her in the eye. 'I go back to Cambridge in October.' She didn't need to know it was his first term, that he wouldn't be eighteen till December.

'Ah, the advantages of manhood! I dearly wanted to attend a university. But it wasn't considered feminine. Instead I was sent to a school for young ladies, followed by finishing school in Switzerland. I never cared for the Misses Brontë or Mr Trollope, but I read what I liked in secret. I followed James Clemens' advice.' She threw back her head and closed her eyes as she recited:

> *Happy he,*
> *Who in his home at night.*
> *Finds in his books delight*
> *And sweet society . . .*

She paused and Anthony finished:

> *While he who sees no profit in their use.*
> *Will live a fool and die as great a goose.*

For the first time he felt himself smiling. He was beginning to relax

241

with her. He held out the book. 'Would you care to borrow this? It's a wide anthology.'

She took it and stood. 'Thank you. And now I have to go. I'm expected for tea.'

Dismay written on his face, Anthony jumped up. 'Shall you be out tomorrow? I'd like to see you again.'

'I'm out every day when it's fine.'

'The same time? I mean, er, after lunch?'

She nodded then dusted off her skirts. 'Please don't bother to ride back with me.'

'Then I'll see you to your horse.'

They walked in silence to the horses, where he untethered her mare and offered his hand to help her mount. Her touch on his hand, light as a butterfly, sent a tremor through him. Then she sprang into the saddle and with a wave she was off.

His eyes followed her until she was out of sight. Then, humming, he returned to the house. He would be in time to receive Margery and her family. But tomorrow he would see Adelle again. Nothing else mattered.

He waited by the stream. This time he didn't pretend to read but mounted his horse and joined her as she approached. 'I'm so glad you came.'

She reined in her mare and smiled at him. 'I thought I'd show you some of *my* land for a change.'

Anthony laughed. 'I admit I trespassed once or twice as a boy. But even then I should have preferred such a guide.'

She raised her eyebrows. 'You aren't surprised by a woman owning property?'

He supposed he should have shown some reaction. 'I, er, didn't wish to pry.'

They rode slowly and she told him much the same story as his father had the previous day, except that coming from her lips it sounded like a fairytale.

The sun had shone without interruption for a week and the afternoon was flawless. After two of the most intoxicating hours of Anthony's life, Adelle turned her horse towards the house. 'Would you care to see the family chapel?'

'I should enjoy that.'

She led him to a small stone building that could have been an outhouse. Inside, it was damp and plain, the altar bare but for a wooden cross flanked by two brass candlesticks, the family pews dusty. She ran her gloved hand along the empty prayer book rack near the door. 'Since my father's death there's been no service here. I feel no need. Though sometimes I come to find peace and to think.'

'Then you don't believe in God?' His father had been wrong about that.

Her smile glowed in the gloom. 'I didn't say that. If God is everywhere, as they say, then it shouldn't be necessary to visit a chapel to communicate with Him. I try to worship Him in my own way, in my daily life. To me, our ride today in the countryside He created is a form of worship.'

'I think I understand that.' Strangely, he felt he did.

'Not many people do. But I know my mother felt as I do. She conformed to my father's faith for love, but she worshipped more the joy of life.' She rubbed her hands together to remove the dust from her gloves. 'But now, it's almost teatime. My daughters are expecting me. Would you like to join us?'

'Thank you.' Anthony's head reeled. She was inviting him to her home! He smothered his discomfort at meeting her daughters.

They approached the house, a charming Tudor building, yet small – perhaps a quarter the size of his own. She opened the door herself, he noted, and pulled a bell. A motherly housekeeper in black bustled into the stone-flagged hall and took their hats and gloves. Her round face was wrinkled, though her stout frame was still firm and straight, and her brown eyes looked at Anthony without curiosity.

'Tea's ready in the drawing room, madam,' she said. 'I see you'll be needing another cup.'

'Thank you, Eva.'

No butler, Anthony observed. Yet with three family estates she couldn't be poor. He followed her through an open doorway to the right and found himself in a small but pretty drawing room. The furniture was upholstered in floral-patterned velvet and matching curtains hung at the open windows. The room resembled Adelle – all soft surfaces and gentle colours.

She beckoned him to a long sofa, a tea table in front set for three with pink and white china. 'Please sit down.'

'I feel I'm intruding,' he said, though he sat nevertheless.

'Rubbish, the children will be delighted to have company.'

At that moment two girls charged in, slowing to a stop when they saw Anthony.

243

'This is Michelle.' Adelle indicated the elder. A slight child with spun silver hair like her mother's, her violet eyes stared at him with open curiosity.

'And I'm Arlette.' Dark-haired and rosy-cheeked, the younger girl grinned with total self-assurance.

He smiled at both and Adelle went on, 'This is Mr Hayward, our next-door neighbour.'

They chorused 'How do you do?' and bounced into the opposite armchairs as if they met a new neighbour every day.

Anthony had rarely felt so shy. But he made what he hoped was suitable conversation and tea was an animated affair. The girls were eager to tell him about their impending visit to Newcastle the following day. But he was pleased to hear it would be only for one day. Already the prospect of spending an afternoon without Adelle disturbed him.

Chapter Twenty-Three

The summer sped past. Anthony spent every afternoon at Flagdon Hall and those evenings when he wasn't forced to attend some function, though Mildred nagged him about his constant mysterious absences.

Richard glowered at her as Anthony stood to leave the luncheon table for one of the outings to Morpeth he'd invented. 'Leave the boy alone, woman.'

'I still think we should meet these new "friends" of his.' She frowned and threw her napkin on the table. 'How do we know they're suitable? I can't think of anyone in the entire county we're not acquainted with. If we don't know these people there must be a reason for it.'

'Bah, woman! Let the lad have a fling. He needs to sow his wild oats before he settles down with someone "suitable", as you say. By jove, I sowed many an oat when I was a lad!' He winked at Anthony, who still stood behind his chair waiting to be excused. 'Some of the best days of my life,' Richard went on. 'You go and have a good time, son. I'm glad my little, er, lesson, has given you a taste for the good life at last. It's a nice change not to see you buried in a book.' He belched, then nodded permission for Anthony to leave.

'Thank you, sir.' Anthony exhaled with relief and left.

The mornings at the house dragged until he could be with Adelle again. In the early afternoons he tutored the girls in music and French. But most of his time he spent with Adelle, riding, exchanging books, playing the piano and singing, she in a soprano that went to his head like wine. Every day they seemed to discover some new delight in common. Though she'd invited him to join her circle of friends at Morpeth – intellectual couples who lived in their own world of aesthetic pursuits – he'd declined, jealous of his time alone with her. He loved to share her simple life. But for the children's laughter, the house was so tranquil. The servants were rarely to be seen, except for the ubiquitous

Eva, who appeared to wait on her mistress in every capacity from nurserymaid to parlour maid to lady's maid to butler. He loved Adelle's simple tastes and never thought to question them.

This day, he savoured the prospect of having Adelle to himself after the children's lesson. Seated between the girls at the nursery table going over the last of their homework, he tried to suppress his laughter. 'No, no, Arlette. When a young girl is planning her *épousailles* it doesn't mean she's planning a succession of marriages, only one.'

Arlette chewed on her pencil, a puzzled expression on her chubby face. 'But it's plural, is it not?'

Adelle, sitting by the window with her embroidery, bent her head over her work to hide her mirth.

'Remember, some nouns are used only in the plural?' Anthony attempted a stern look, but failed.

Michelle's violet eyes, so like her mother's, looked with superiority on her younger sister. 'It's the same as *funérailles*, silly. And who would want to have more than one funeral?'

'Quite!' Anthony said. 'That's very good!' He closed his book and stood. The girls jumped up also. But he placed a hand on each shoulder and lowered them back into their chairs. 'Oh, no. I have finished! *You* haven't! I want that translation done by the time I get back.'

Michelle puckered her face. 'It's not fair! You're going riding and we have to do homework. Please, please can we come?'

'No, you can't.' Adelle laid her needlework in the basket at her feet. 'When your Uncle Anthony helps you with your French, the least you can do is show some appreciation. Besides, you rode all morning.'

With exaggerated groans the girls lowered their heads.

Adelle smiled as she took Anthony's arm and led him out. 'You spoil them,' she said when they reached the landing. 'It's so good of you to spend so much time with them.'

'I enjoy it, and besides, the more time I spend with them the more I spend with their mother.'

'You know you need no excuse to do that. I'm always as delighted to see you as they are.'

They retrieved their riding jackets from the hallstand and Anthony watched with undisguised pleasure as she pinned on her hat in front of the mirror. 'You're looking particularly beautiful today,' he said.

'Thank you. But you say that every day.'

'If I do, then it's true.'

246

She took his arm as they walked to the stables. 'Such charm! And such good looks! I shall never understand why you don't have all the ladies in Morpeth after you.'

He smiled secretly. 'I'm happy to say my father believes I do.'

It was August when Anthony began to brood that all too soon he would have to leave for Cambridge. He was unusually sombre as he sipped his after-dinner coffee with Adelle. The children were already in bed.

She glanced at him over the rim of her cup. 'You look so gloomy. Did dinner disagree with you?'

'I was just thinking that soon I shan't be seeing you every day.' He set his cup on the table and looked at her with his soul in his eyes. 'You've no idea how I'm going to miss you.'

She joined him on the sofa. 'I think I have. I shall miss you too. But it's almost another two months away. Why so sad now?'

His hands on his lap plucked at the fine wool of his trousers. He had to tell her. He couldn't hide his secret any longer. 'I'm in love with you.' He couldn't believe he'd actually said the words that had filled his thoughts for the past two months.

She placed her cup beside his and turned to smile at him. 'I know.'

His heart clenched like a fist. 'You know! And you're not shocked!'

'Should I be? You think love is shocking?'

'How did you know?' He stared at her, uncomprehending.

She put her hand over his. 'My dear Anthony, just looking at your face is like reading your diary. It's one of the charms about you I find most endearing.'

He swallowed hard as embarrassment thickened in his throat. But she found him endearing! He could feel her hand burning into his like coals. He grasped it. 'How long have your known?'

'Since the beginning. I feel honoured and proud to have someone like you love me, and to love in return.'

To love in return! His ears were playing tricks. 'Are you saying . . .?'

She nodded. 'Also since the beginning. You made it all too easy, though it was the last thing I had in mind.'

Drunk with exhilaration, he tried to think what to say. But all he could do was stare at her.

She leaned towards him and kissed him lightly on the mouth. It was a long kiss. He closed his eyes at the feel of her lips on his. Every cell in his body stirred, and behind his closed eyelids he saw a dizzying kaleidoscope of colours. His lips followed hers as she withdrew, but she placed a restraining finger on them and sighed. Her breath on his face felt like the night breeze. He'd never been this close to her, so close he could smell the warmth of her skin mingled with the aura of violets that always surrounded her. The intimacy was intoxicating. He opened his eyes to find her gaze on him, unusually solemn.

'I must warn you,' she said. 'It isn't easy for two people like us. Though my own little circle would find our situation intriguing and delightful, I know that most people—'

But Anthony cupped her face in his hands and found her mouth again, like a thirsty man seeking water.

She returned his pressure and a feeling as keen as pain shot through him. His yearning was so strong, to possess her could not fulfil it. He longed to lose himself in her, to *be* her.

Her arms went round his neck, and he clasped her to him, reeling with the multitude of feelings that swept through him. He held her close, yet gently, as if afraid he might break her. They embraced for what seemed an eternity, he kissing her lips, her face, her eyes, greedy to experience her.

At length, out of breath, she eased him away. This time her eyes smiled. 'We're crazy! But I don't care what the world thinks. I do love you. I feel we were meant.'

'We were,' he said. 'It couldn't be wrong. I've never felt so . . . so joyful.' As he spoke, he explored her neck, the little hollow of her throat above her gown, his fingertips absorbing with wonder the soft feel of her skin. Then he buried his lips in her throat and felt a tremor travel up her neck as she moaned. The sound soared in his head like music.

He searched for her lips again, but she pressed her palms against his chest and stood. Without a word she held out her hand. He rose and let her lead him upstairs. He couldn't feel the floor under his feet. She pressed her finger to her lips as they passed the first chamber door. 'The girls' night nursery,' she whispered. 'They wanted to move from the top floor to be near me.' They tiptoed to the end of the passage. Here she opened a door and he followed her inside. So this was where she slept. The summer evening light fell on the blue silk counterpane of a large four-poster bed. His eyes could take in nothing else in the room.

She sat on the bed and beckoned him. He joined her and took her in his arms, pressing her down on the silk coverlet and kissing her with reverence. He'd dreamed of this so often, but the reality was even more dreamlike. His head spun, his senses whirled about him like snowflakes.

Her fingers ran through his hair, then down his coat lapels. She eased them back from his shoulders and he lowered her gown. Within a few moments, as naturally as if they'd undressed each other every day of their lives, they were naked.

He laid her on the bed and knelt by her, adoring her with his eyes, touching her here, there. He'd never seen anything so beautiful. He'd never felt so alive. He lay beside her and they explored each other in silent awe until he could no more stop himself than he could stem the blood flowing in his veins. He made love to her, with wonder, with joy. So this was what it was like to love someone completely!

He heard himself murmuring her name, heard her little cries of delight, the sounds floating in the air like the strains of a distant violin. Then, in the blue-blackness inside his head, stars exploded. A myriad of undreamed-of feelings surged through him and made him cry out with joy. It was as if he *did* lose himself and become *her*.

He lay over her lightly so as not to crush her, his face buried in the curve of her neck as he tried to pull himself back into the world. She stroked his hair as if soothing a child.

'Oh, Adelle,' he finally whispered, 'I love you so much! I can't believe—'

'Sshh.' She moved aside and his body lay beside her, but his head floated far above. Then he heard her voice, saying, 'You must believe it. I love you too.'

He drew her to him and whispered, 'I'd read so much of love, but I had no idea it could be like this. I can never leave you now. I want to marry you. I want to love you like this every day of my life.'

She laughed softly. 'That's a long time. Let's not talk about the rest of our lives. We've got the present. Remember, *Gather ye rosebuds while ye may* . . . but think not of the following day.'

'Herrick didn't say the last part.'

'He meant the same – *Old Time is still a-flying*. My time's flown longer than yours. I've learned not to spoil the present with concern for the future.'

He raised himself on his elbow and looked down at her, her hair tousled over the pillow, her eyes closed. She looked like a sleeping child. 'I won't have you say that. We can get married. I love you. And I love your daughters already. I don't care if people talk.'

She admonished him with a smile. 'Do you think I worry about that? You're so young, Anthony! Your entire life lies ahead of you. At thirty-two, a woman's life is almost over. For you anything is still possible.

You'll fall in love with a girl your own age one day. But I . . .' Her voice trailed to a whisper: '*This same flower that smiles today, Tomorrow will be dying.*'

'Never! Why do you quote only the sad lines? He also says, *Then be not coy, but use your time, And while ye may, go marry.* Marry me! You'll never grow old to me! And I shall age too. We'll grow old together.' His hand stroking her shoulder suddenly gripped it and shook her. 'Marry me, please!'

She sighed. 'You'll know I'm right one day. In the meantime, why make ourselves unhappy talking about tomorrow when we can be happy today? We can go on as we are, being together, loving each other, until . . . whatever.' She shrugged and ran her fingers down his side. 'Promise me you won't bring up marriage again?'

'No. But I'll leave it for the moment.' He lay back on the pillow and drew her into his arms. The thought that she'd loved her husband, had made love to him like this, burned in his mind. She'd never spoken of her marriage except to say it had been successful. Now he wanted to know if she'd loved her husband as much as she loved him. He cast out the childish thought. The past was over. It was enough that she'd chosen him to love now.

The October air held the warning chill of winter and the drawing room fire glowed in the grate. Adelle sat by it, listening as Anthony improvised on the piano. 'You can't stay late tonight,' she said. 'You must be fresh for your journey.'

'I'm not going! I'm not. And that's an end to it!' He thumped down the piano lid and stalked to the fireplace. Hands clenched behind his back, he stood staring into the flames.

'It's only for eight weeks. We'll have the Christmas holidays together.' She gave him a pleading look. 'Be sensible, Anthony! I could never forgive myself if you gave up your education for me.'

'I've got an education. I don't need any more. I need you.'

She rose and took his arm. 'Let's walk in the garden till dinner. The girls will be down in a moment and I don't want them to see you in such a mood.'

She led him through the French windows and into the chill air. Drawing her silk shawl around her, she glanced sideways up at him. His profile was set, rigid. She laughed and tucked her arm in his. 'You look like a schoolboy when you sulk like that.'

'I'm not sulking! And I'm not a schoolboy! And I know my own

250

mind! I'm telling them tonight I'm not going.'

She squeezed his arm. 'Please, please see sense. If you don't go I swear I will go away.'

'Back to Wiltshire? France? I'll find you.'

They crossed the lawn to the gazebo, leaves crunching under their feet. Still with her arm in his, she pulled him down beside her on to the narrow bench inside the railings. 'Anthony, if you love me, please at least go for one term. You can't refuse me that.'

His shoulders drooped. 'Why do you put it that way, as if I'd be doing you a courtesy by going?'

She shook her head. 'You know the last thing I want is for you to leave me. I simply can't let you disrupt your life because of me. Don't you understand how guilty I'd feel?'

'And don't you understand how desolate I'd be without you?'

'Just eight weeks, Anthony! You'll see that your life can be rich and rewarding without me. And I shall write – every day. You can't let your parents down.'

'I don't give a fig about my parents! But I'll go for one term to prove to you that I *can't* live without you. And when I come back you'll marry me.'

Her laughter trilled through the air like birdsong. 'I've never known such a determined young man. One thing at a time! First go, and then see how you feel when you come back.'

'I know how I'll feel.' He stared into the darkness, his lower lip pouting.

She stood. 'Well, that much is settled at least. The girls will be waiting for us. Promise me you won't be morose over dinner?'

He shrugged, defeated, then rose and took her arm. 'I've never known anyone who could extract so many promises from me. But not a day over one term!'

Arlette and Michelle were waiting when they reached the dining room. 'Uncle Anthony,' Michelle said as they sat at the long oak table, 'this isn't the last dinner you'll have with us, is it?' Her face puckered and tears welled.

'No, Michelle, I'll be back quicker than a wink. And by then I expect you to play everything I've taught you – without a mistake and without the music.'

'And to read French without looking at the dictionary.' Arlette said.

'And I'll write to you every day *in* French,' Michelle went on.

251

'Me too!' Arlette was not to be outdone by her sister.

'Splendid! I shall treasure the letters and tie them with a pink ribbon.' He managed a smile. But he was much less animated than usual at dinner and was relieved when Eva announced that coffee was served in the drawing room. This was the signal for the girls to retire.

They flung themselves at him and wound their arms round his neck. It was like being strangled by an octopus. He gave each a peck on the cheek and dismissed them. 'Off with you now.'

Adelle nodded. 'Uncle Anthony has to get up early in the morning. He needs some peace. And it's past your bedtime.'

They strangled him once more before kissing their mother good-night and trailing backwards to the door, reluctant to let Anthony out of their sight.

Adelle and Anthony adjourned to the drawing room and took their usual places by the fire. Adelle picked up her coffee cup and held it without drinking. Like Anthony, she'd eaten little. 'They're so fond of you, they'll miss you almost as much as I shall.'

'That's what's so damned silly! Nobody's going to enjoy it – least of all me. My life is here with you now.'

She placed her cup on the table untouched and sat on the arm of his chair. He inhaled deeply, as if it would be the last time he would smell her closeness. Her arm went round his shoulders. 'Let's give them a few more minutes to get into bed before we go upstairs.'

He pulled her onto his lap and buried his face in her hair. This would be the last time he would make love to her for an eternity.

But when he came back for the Christmas holidays he would be eighteen. A man! Old enough to make his own decisions, to flout his parents' authority. He would announce his intention of marrying Adelle and to hell with the consequences. They could go away, to France or Wiltshire perhaps.

At first he'd thought his love was boundless, yet he loved her more with every passing day. And he loved the girls like a father, and they loved him. He would be patient for a few more weeks.

Chapter Twenty-Four

As soon as Anthony arrived in Cambridge he stopped at a haberdashery and bought a spray of cream silk rosebuds. He had the salesgirl send them to Adelle and enclosed a note saying, 'They will never wilt, my love.'

Determined that the term should fly as fast as possible, he threw himself into his work. His free time he spent writing to Adelle, reading and rereading her letters and writing to Michelle and Arlette. To his parents he'd written that the term was going well and that he looked forward to the imminent Christmas holidays.

The Saturday before examinations week he received another letter from Adelle. He shouldered his way through the throng in the hallway scrambling for the post. He wished to savour her letter in quiet in his room. Sitting on the window seat overlooking the well-kept lawns he read:

My Dearest Anthony,

I had hoped not to have to write such a letter as this, but as you will be here next week you will find out anyway. I wanted to spare your feelings and wait until the news was more certain before telling you of it.

I am carrying your child. And that part of my news is wonderful. The prospect fills me with delight. Unfortunately, I have had some slight bleedings and my physician has confined me to my bed until they stop. Please pray that they do. I want this child more than I can tell you. If my guess is correct, it will be due in late May.

I long for next week to see you and hold you.

Please, please, do not worry. I simply wish you to be prepared before you see me.

253

My love and my thoughts are with you every moment.
Adelle

Anthony crumpled the letter in his fist and stared sightlessly out of the window. Adelle was carrying his child! He would be a father soon. But she was ill. He must be with her, now, and to hell with the examinations. He had no intention of going back the following term anyway.

It was seven thirty a.m. If he hurried he could catch the daily train. And if he made the connections at Doncaster and York he would arrive in Newcastle that day. In a frenzy he packed his bags and took a hackney to the station.

It was ten p.m. when the train chugged in at Newcastle Central Station. Though he'd been cold for most of the journey Anthony shivered as he alighted and ran with his bags to the hackney rank. The rain that had trickled down the train windows all day was now a downpour, the air raw.

The driver gave him a strange look when he asked to be taken to Morpeth. 'Eey, I don't know, sir. It's a bit late to go that far. And I go off duty at eleven.'

Anthony thrust five pound notes into the man's hand. 'Will this do?'

He raised his hat. 'Aye, sir, that'll do nicely.'

With a sigh of relief Anthony climbed in. He wished now for the speed and comfort of his father's motor car.

But the driver, obviously in a hurry to get the journey over, urged the horses and turned them almost at a gallop into Grainger Street. Anthony hung on by the window ledge, glad the man was wasting no time.

Adelle would probably be asleep when he arrived. If so, he would sleep in the study until morning.

Her bedroom light was on. His heart crested like a wave and he thrust another pound at the man for his trouble. There were no lights visible downstairs but he walked round to the back where a narrow beam shone from the basement kitchen window.

He felt his way down the steep flight. His tap on the door brought no answer. He tapped louder, longer, his impatience overcoming his concern at disturbing Eva. At last he heard muffled footsteps, then the door creaked open.

'Glory be!' Eva screwed up her eyes and peered into his face by the light from the kitchen. 'Sir! You startled me.'

'I'm sorry to disturb you so late, Eva.'

'That's all right, sir. I wasn't abed. I was sitting by the fire and I must have dozed off.'

'I've just arrived from Cambridge. Is the mistress still awake? I see her bedroom light is on.'

'I don't know as she's still awake, sir, but I'll go and have a peep. Why don't you sit down by the fire here? The ones upstairs is all out now except for Madam's bedroom. I bank that up for her. You look starved to death.'

'Thank you, I'm fine.' Anthony dropped his bag and threw his wet topcoat and hat over a wooden chair. He stood rubbing his hands together before the fire in the stove. The kitchen, small and scrubbed and cosy like the rest of the house, was as warm and inviting as Adelle. He prayed she would be awake.

Eva returned with a smile on her wrinkled face, her skin draping her bones like worn-out curtains. 'She's awake, sir. She says to go up. And I'll bring you some hot soup.'

He nodded his thanks, bounded up the servants' staircase and ran down the long hallway.

In his haste he forgot to knock. Adelle lay, pale as the pillows under her head, her eyes deeply shadowed. But her face lit up as he hurried to her. For a moment unable to speak, he bent over her and pressed her fingers to his lips.

She released her hands with a smile and patted the bed for him to sit. 'I shouldn't have written. I should have known.'

'My love, as soon as I heard I couldn't wait to see you.'

'You're such an impatient person! I can't deny I'm cross with you but it *is* wonderful to see you.' She cupped his face in her hands and he leaned forward to kiss her cheek. The scent of violets surrounded her, so familiar he would know her presence in a darkened room. He drew away and searched her face. 'I'm so happy and so sad. How is your health?

'My physician says if I stay on my back for a while all should be well. Oh, Anthony, I blame myself. I should have known sooner. I rode before I guessed I was with child. I didn't dream . . . All these years I thought I could never conceive again. It's a miracle.' Tears welled in her eyes.

He gripped her hands so tightly she winced. 'But you're all right? And the child's all right?'

255

'So far, but I must be careful. I almost lost Arlette the same way. I had to spend much of the time in bed before she was born. It was a difficult birth. A surgeon had to be called.'

He chastised her with a look. 'Is that why you wouldn't marry me? Because you thought you couldn't give me children?'

'Only one of the reasons.'

'You know it would have made no difference. And Arlette's a healthy child! This one will be too!'

'Ah, the certainty of youth! But I must be even more careful this time. I'm older now. And I want this child so much.'

'Oh, my darling, and so do I. We'll get married now!'

She pressed her fingers to his lips. 'Dearest Anthony, curb your impatience. Keeping the child must be my only concern for the moment.'

'But we can still get married.'

A smile passed over her lips like the sun glimpsing through a cloud. 'Whoever heard of a bedridden bride?'

'Then as soon as you're well enough to get up?'

She smiled again at the urgency in his voice. 'We'll talk more about it then. Now there's another more pressing matter.'

Anthony's face set in resolve. 'I will tell my parents tomorrow. They can't stop me.'

She shook her head. 'I'm talking about your examinations. If I'd known you'd be so foolish as to drop your studies, I should have kept the news until you arrived. You must return tomorrow while there's still time to complete the term. Your parents need never know you've been home.'

'I'm not going back, I'm not!' He paced the room, then dug his hands in his pockets and stared at her with defiance.

She gave him a look of despair. 'You're behaving like a truculent child, Anthony. I can see once you've made up your mind there's no changing it.'

He sat again on the bed. 'I'm staying with you and that's an end to it.'

Weariness overtook her and she let out a long sigh. 'It seems I can't stop you.'

A knock interrupted them. Eva entered carrying a tray. 'I've brought some soup for Mr Hayward, madam, and some for you and all. It'll help you get off to sleep.' She gave Anthony a meaningful look and he loosened his collar in discomfort. How thoughtless and selfish of him! He must let Adelle sleep.

She raised herself on her pillows. 'Thank you, Eva. And would you mind making up the bed next door for Mr Hayward. He'll be staying the night.'

Eva nodded, placed the tray on the bedside table and disappeared to carry out the command as if her mistress had asked her to bank up the fire.

Anthony handed Adelle a bowl from the tray, ignoring his own. 'And I'll be staying tomorrow night and every night. And when you're well I shan't need another bed.'

She laid her head back on her pillows with a smile. 'I fear I'm no match for such determination.'

Anthony breakfasted early with Adelle. The morning light was less kind to her than the lamplight of the night before. She looked even paler, the shadows under her eyes deeper.

'I beg you one more time to wait to tell your parents.' She placed her empty teacup on the tray and shook her head as he rose to refill it.

'I've waited too long already,' he said. 'And there'll never be a good time to tell them.' He laid the tray on the bedside table and bent to kiss her. 'I'll take your mare.'

He slipped out the back way to the stables while the girls, unaware of his presence, were in the day nursery with their governess. Time enough to see them at lunch.

He didn't even notice the sharp north wind biting into his face as he urged the horse faster. He must get this over with.

According to plan, he arrived as his parents were finishing breakfast. Mealtimes were the only occasions he could be sure of catching them together. He tethered the mare to the rail by the portico and took a deep breath before starting for the house.

When he opened the dining room door Richard and Mildred looked up in astonishment. They sat in their usual places at each end of the long table, now littered with silver and china and the remains of smoked fish.

The butler, startled out of his trance at his post by the buffet, rushed to admit Anthony.

Richard set down his cup with a thud and Mildred let out a squeak.

Richard was the first to find his voice. 'Good God, boy! What's wrong? Why are you here?'

'I've left Cambridge for good, sir. I'm getting married.' He stood by the table between them, straight and determined.

257

'Married!' Mildred leaned back in her chair as if about to swoon.

'To whom? For God's sake, boy, talk sense!' Richard's head jutted forward on his bull neck, his eyes bulged.

Mildred pressed her napkin to her lips and whimpered. 'I suppose you've got one of those harlots you've been cavorting with into trouble. Why on earth—?'

But Richard cut her short, thumping the table with his fist. 'For God's sake, lad! Are you out of your mind? You don't have to marry the wench.'

'She's not a wench, sir, and the fact that she's with child has nothing to do with my choosing to marry her. I made that decision a long time ago.'

Richard waved impatiently towards the buffet and the butler bowed and flitted from the room like a shadow.

'Who is it, for the Lord's sake?' Richard boomed.

'Adelle Grayson, sir, our neighbour. She's the younger of the Pagnol daughters.'

'The Pagnol daughters!' Mildred's screech set the chandelier above the table tinkling.

Richard flicked his hand towards Anthony's accustomed chair. 'Wait a minute! Wait a minute! Sit down, boy, and let's talk about this sensibly.'

Anthony sat stiffly between them. 'There's nothing to talk about, sir. I shall marry her as soon as she's well enough. She's indisposed at the moment.'

'Tell us about this woman.' Richard had adopted a reasoning tone, but his facial muscles twitched with the effort. 'For one thing, how old is she? And is she the widow or the spinster?'

'She's thirty-two, sir, and widowed. She's a lovely and wonderful woman.'

Mildred's bosom jerked. 'Thirty-two! And the widow with grown children! You're out of your mind. I want to hear no more of this nonsense.'

'It's not nonsense, Mother. I've never been more serious about anything in my life. I've given up my studies and I shall marry her as soon as possible.'

'Give up your studies? And marry a widow old enough to be your mother?' Richard's voice had lost its control and the veins in his temples pulsated. 'I will not have it. I'll disinherit you first. And your allowance is cut off as from this minute.'

Anthony knew that disinheriting him was an idle threat, and he could always earn a living in the meantime. Nothing could change his mind about Adelle. 'As you wish, sir. I'm sorry to disappoint you, but I must lead my own life as I see fit.'

'Your own life!' Mildred's chins quivered and her eyes pierced Anthony's like a sword. 'Yes, that's all you've ever been concerned with. Never a thought for your father and me and your responsibilities here.'

'I've tried, Mother.'

Mildred leaned forward like a bird of prey about to swoop on its victim. 'Mother! Don't you call me "Mother"! I am *not* your mother, and I thank God for it now. I could never have borne such a selfish little ingrate.'

Richard's face turned white. 'Mildred, for God's sake! Hold your tongue, woman.'

Stunned, Anthony looked from one to the other.

But there was no stopping Mildred. 'I've held my tongue all these years and now I must speak the truth. You're your father's son, not mine! Your mother was a little slut of a scullery maid. And you're turning out just like her. You've never been a real son to me.'

'Mother?' Anthony jumped up and stared at her in disbelief.

'I've told you! Don't call me "Mother"!'

'Mildred!' Richard shouted again, to no avail. She went on, out of control.

'I've done my best to bring you up like a son to please your father. All he wanted was to carry on the family name. And now look what you've done to it. Dragging it through the mud! We'll be the laughing stock of the entire county. I swear, if you go through with this marriage—'

'That's enough, Mildred!' Anger, like a scar, distorted Richard's features, and Mildred swallowed the rest of her words. She jumped up and flounced from the room, flinging her skirts before her and slamming the heavy oak door.

The chandeliers tinkled again.

'She's just upset. Ignore her. There's no truth to it.' Richard tugged at his high starched collar and avoided Anthony's incredulous gaze. For the moment Richard had forgotten the reason for Mildred's outburst.

'But why would she say such a thing if it weren't true?'

Richard didn't raise his eyes. 'All right! It's true. But you're *my* son. And that's enough for me.'

259

Anthony leaned back in his chair. He should feel desolate, yet the clouds that had surrounded him all his life began to blow away. He wasn't his mother's son. Was that why he'd always felt so alone, so apart from his family? He looked at Richard. 'Then, who *is* my mother? I think you owe me that much.'

'I owe you nothing. You're a Hayward, do you hear? I want no more talk of this.' He leaned over the table in a conspiratorial manner and clasped his hands, his knuckles white. 'Look, just apologize to your mother and forget all this silly nonsense about marrying that woman. We'll overlook this whole business.'

'Never!'

'For God's sake, boy, you're young! You'll meet a hundred pretty women who'll take your fancy. This is just . . . calf love. You'll outgrow it, you'll realize it was only a silly fancy. You'll find a suitable wife one day.'

Anthony wanted to get up, to run away, to think and clear his mind, but he felt rooted to his chair. 'I've found the only woman I shall ever love. I intend to marry her, whatever obstacles you try to put in my way.'

'Just give it a year, boy, and you'll see I'm right.'

'I'm sorry that my choice of wife distresses you, sir. But my decision is made. I shall be staying at Flagdon Hall until my marriage.' He stood to leave. But Richard jumped up with such force that his chair toppled backwards.

'You leave this house now and you leave it for good. Do you hear me, boy?'

'I hear you, sir.' Anthony turned on his heel and marched to the door. He had to get out. Anger and confusion raged inside him. He had to clear his head. So much was happening to him at once. He must compose himself before he returned to Adelle.

In a daze, he walked down the long hall to the front door, oblivious of the servants' curious stares. He let himself out and gulped in the fresh air as he ran down the steps. Adelle's mare neighed as he jumped into the saddle and spurred her to a gallop. The air stung him like a cold plunge.

When he neared the copse he dismounted and made towards the stream. He sat on the bank where he'd sat so many times as a boy, daydreaming, wondering about life. Now he wondered again. Dispossessed of his birthright and his mother in one morning! Though he knew that sooner or later his father would have to change his mind

260

about his inheritance, in the meantime he must earn a living. But who was he? And how was it he'd always sensed that he didn't belong? He must find out who his mother was.

In his absence the grass had grown. He pressed it down and ran his fingers over the stones that spelled his name, the letter B underneath. One of the servants! His mother a scullery maid? Could it be? He would find out. A thing like that could never be completely hidden from the staff. But how to approach them without causing scandalmongering? He rubbed his eyes and tried to think. No, his mind was spinning with all the recent events. He would wait until he felt calmer to form a plan.

Strange, such news should devastate him, yet it didn't. At last he felt he would begin to know himself, no matter how humble his origins. He must tell Adelle. But first he needed to think about the pressing matter of earning a living.

Towards noon, stiff from the cold, he returned to Flagdon Hall.

When he entered the hall the girls darted out from the drawing room.

'Uncle Anthony!' Michelle flung herself at him and he held her tight.

Arlette followed and he took her into his grasp. Her bright eyes gazed up at him with adoration. 'Why didn't you tell us you were coming? We just found out from Mama.'

'I thought I'd surprise you.'

'She said you're staying. For ever and ever! Cross your heart!' Michelle disengaged herself and made a cross over her heart.

Anthony made the required sign and was surprised to find himself smiling. 'Cross my heart! But now I must talk to your mama. I shall see you both at lunch.'

'She's not really ill,' Arlette said, though it sounded more like a question. 'She just has a stomachache and must rest.'

'I know.' He smiled reassurance before taking the stairs two at a time.

As he knew she would, Adelle took the news calmly. 'Like you, I'm sure your father would never risk losing the family name,' she said when he'd finished. 'He'll have to come round sooner or later. And, in the meantime, you're hardly being thrown out on the street. You have a home here. But how do you intend going about finding your mother?'

'The only way is through the servants. Though I haven't worked out how yet.' He bent to kiss her cheek then took her hands.

Her eyes looked past him for a moment. 'Eighteen years . . . a long time. But I'm sure Eva could help.'

'Eva?'

She pulled him down beside her. 'She's been with my family for thirty-five years and friendly with your cook for almost that long. They still visit one another occasionally in the evenings. If Eva doesn't already know something, she could find out.'

'But we would have to let her know.'

'Not necessarily, but in any event I would trust Eva with my life. She was present when I was born in this very room and is as fond of me as a mother. You of all people should know how discreet and loyal she is. She's a great blessing.'

'Well, I'm certainly aware that she's . . . er, unusual for a servant.'

'A servant? She hardly feels like one to me. This house and my family are her life. Have you never wondered why she insists on serving us personally day and night when there are maids downstairs?'

'I simply assumed you wished to economize on staff.'

'My dear, I have money enough for a battery of servants, but I have no desire for such and no need. It's Eva's joy to serve me and my pleasure to have her. Even in my absence she keeps this house as if I were to return any day. She'll keep your secret equally protected.' She paused and gave him a searching look. 'But are you quite sure you're prepared for whatever you might find?'

'You mean that my mother was or is a lowly servant?'

'That and, well, she may not wish to be reminded of her past or may not be a likeable person.'

Anthony chewed on his fingernails, thinking. 'I have to run that risk. What should I say to Eva?'

'Leave it to me.'

He kissed her hands. 'Thank you. I wouldn't know how to approach such a delicate subject.' He stood and stared out of the window. 'And now that I'm penniless I have other pressing matters to deal with. I must first think what I can do to support you.'

An amused smile touched her lips. 'Support me? My dearest, I need no support. Granted, I'm not as wealthy as your parents. But the estates bring in over three thousand pounds a year, and there's my husband's allowance from the Wiltshire estate.' He swung round but she went on before he could speak. 'I know you would prefer to be independent, but surely you could subdue your pride until your father is forced to change his mind.'

Anthony made a face. 'I've just remembered what he had to say about your grandfather having to transfer the property to your father's name. And he can't abide Margery's husband. I know he has no choice. Though he could certainly cut off my allowance for the moment.'

'But you wouldn't need an allowance, you—'

He broke in, 'Do you think I intend to live off you? I have an education. I can always teach. I can save your governess expense by tutoring the girls and I will find work in Morpeth.'

At his determined tone Adelle settled back on the pillows with a resigned expression. 'I understand your need to do something with your life, and the girls would love to have you tutor them. But whatever else you choose to do, please don't do it for the sake of income. Teach only if you would enjoy it.'

'I should. And I must.'

'Then you will.' She beckoned him to sit again and reached out to stroke his cheek. 'But I'm feeling a little tired now and my physician's due at any moment. Would you mind taking lunch with the girls? I've told them only that you'll be staying here from now on. Please say no more at present. They know nothing of the child yet. I wish to spare them as much as possible.'

'Of course! I promised to take lunch with them anyway. But I shall be back as soon as your physician leaves. You rest, my love.' Her eyelids fluttered with weariness as he bent to kiss her brow.

After lunch Anthony sat in the drawing room facing the open door. He would catch the physician as he left. Twenty minutes later he hurried to the hall as Eva ushered the elderly man out. Anthony stood before him. 'Sir, may I have a word with you?'

The man looked over his gold-rimmed spectacles. 'You must be Mr Hayward. Dr Kingston.' He bowed his head.

'I'm pleased to make your acquaintance.' Anthony beckoned him into the room. 'I wish to know how she is,' he said when the man was seated by the fire.

Dr Kingston's opaque blue eyes again surveyed Anthony over his spectacles. 'I must be honest, I don't know. Only time and rest will tell if she can carry the child to its full term.'

'I'll make sure she gets plenty of rest.'

'Yes, I understand you will be . . . er, living here.'

'We shall be married as soon as she's well enough.' A thrill of pride ran through Anthony at his words.

263

'As you'll be, er, with her a great deal I look to you as well as to Eva to let me know immediately should she start bleeding again, or should she feel unwell. And even if she feels well enough to get up, please keep her in bed until I say so.'

Anthony's face grew pale. 'How likely is it that she will bleed again?'

'As I said! These things are impossible to know. But at the moment she's doing well.' Dr Kingston took out his pocket watch and raised himself by his cane. 'And now, I have another patient to call on.'

Anthony saw him to the door and returned to the drawing room. He sat deep in thought for some minutes before going up to see Adelle. He would read poetry to her to pass the time. He would keep her entertained and happy during her ordeal.

Though he'd imagined it would be difficult to be close to her and contain his passion – and on occasion desire rose in him like a rending pain – his affection overwhelmed his physical craving. In her illness his overpowering need was to comfort her. And when she was well again there would be endless nights of lovemaking.

Chapter Twenty-Five

Early the following morning Eva had just set the tray on the bed when Anthony joined Adelle for breakfast.

'Morning, sir,' she said. 'Mr Hayward's downstairs to see you. I've shown him into the drawing room.'

Anthony's smile froze. 'Thank you, Eva. Would you please tell him I'll be down presently.'

'Yes, sir.'

He bent to kiss Adelle. 'I shan't be long, my love.'

She cupped his face in his hands and pleaded with her eyes. 'Make your peace with him. You know he could never let his only son go, and not only for the reason you think. In his own way, I'm sure he loves you, though he has trouble showing it.'

Anthony sank on to the bed, the feeling of freedom he'd enjoyed since the previous day ebbing out of him. 'I suppose he shows it in the only way he knows. He's always done his best for me – as he sees it. And how could I not feel something for him? But there'll be conditions attached to any truce. And besides, I have no desire to go back. We could never be happy there.'

She took his hand in encouragement. 'There would be no need to go back immediately. You can make conditions too. But he's getting old, at least give him the reassurance that he can count on you when the time comes.'

He stood and squared his shoulders. 'You're always right, my love,' he said with a smile. 'Though sometimes I wish you weren't.'

Richard sat by the fire, his head bowed, the flames reflecting on his bald dome. Suddenly he looked old and tired. A pang of sorrow shot through Anthony as he crossed the room and stood before him. He couldn't let his father down. But nobody could stop him from marrying Adelle. 'You wished to see me, sir.'

Startled, Richard looked up. His ruddy face was pale in patches, his eyes dull. 'I need to talk to you.'

Anthony took the opposite chair. 'If you've come to change my mind about marrying, your journey was fruitless.'

'No, no, boy. I know when I'm beaten. You always were a headstrong lad. I know you'll do what you want with or without my blessing.' Richard took out his handkerchief and mopped his forehead. Then with pain in his eyes he looked at Anthony. 'If you must marry this woman, so be it. Even though she's a foreigner she *is* at least of good stock and is giving you a child. Your mother and I will accept her.'

Anthony raised his eyebrows. His mother? He resisted the temptation to bring up that subject for the time being. 'I'm glad to hear it,' he said.

'And the question of your inheritance . . . I spoke in anger yesterday. You will of course resume your position as my son and heir.'

'If that's your wish. But I must make it plain that I intend to remain here for the moment.'

The pain in Richard's eyes turned to astonishment. 'Remain here?'

'Yes, sir. And after my marriage I shall live here with my wife until such time as . . . my return is necessary.'

Richard leaned forward in his chair, a flicker of anger now in his eyes. But he sat back, powerless. 'I suppose you mean until I—?'

'I mean until you need my assistance. You and Mother enjoy a good life at the house. My presence with a wife and young family would, I think, be an intrusion for you at the moment.' His shoulders dropped with relief. He'd managed to put it tactfully, though what he'd really wanted to say was that he could not tolerate the prospect of spoiling his happiness with Adelle and subjecting her to his family life.

Richard looked around the small drawing room, its simple furnishings, its cottage-like air. 'You can't be serious that you would rather live in this place.'

Anthony ignored the remark. 'I shall of course visit you, and you're welcome here.'

Richard grunted and ran his hand over his smooth head. 'I never did understand you, boy.'

'I've rarely understood myself, sir, until now.' This was the time to bring up the subject. 'But learning of my . . . birth yesterday makes me wonder—'

'That's enough!' Richard rose to leave. 'I won't have that subject brought up again. You're *my* son, and that's an end to it.' His voice had

266

regained some of its authority, and Anthony decided to spare them both further argument. He would settle that matter alone.

When Richard reached the door he turned and said as if in afterthought, 'Your mother will need to discuss the wedding plans with you.'

Anthony's mouth tightened. On this subject he would stand his ground. 'The wedding will be a quiet affair from this house, sir. Of course, you're invited. But we will make our own preparations when Adelle is well enough.'

A flush of anger spread over Richard's face, then he shook his head in obvious defeat. 'You know your mother will be very upset at such an arrangement.'

'Yes, I know, but it's my fiancée's wish and mine.' He was surprised at how calm he felt, how strong.

Richard opened the door slowly. It seemed that all the bounce had gone out of him. He turned again before leaving and his voice was almost humble. 'You'll pay your respects to your mother?'

Anthony nodded. Now that he'd won his victory he felt sorrow for the old man who'd lost his power over him. 'I shall bring my fiancée to meet you as soon as she's well,' he said, his tone gentle.

He rejoined Adelle for breakfast and related the event. She was pleased he'd made his peace with his parents.

'And now I have some news for *you*,' she said when he'd finished. 'I spoke to Eva yesterday and she herself remembers talk of a scullery maid who left and returned as nurserymaid. The reason given for the unusual promotion was that the girl was the housekeeper's niece, though for some other reason that fact had been kept secret until then.'

'Nurserymaid?' Anthony shook his head. 'It couldn't have been my nurse. She was old enough to be my grandmother.' Then a faded memory fluttered through his mind and his voice became eager. 'But I had another nursemaid before her. She left on my fourth birthday. I remember the day because I was so unhappy. I loved her. And she left me without even telling me she was going.' He ran his hand over his head as memories flooded back. 'She used to sing to me – Irish songs. I still know them. What else does Eva know? What—'

Adelle raised her hand. 'Calm yourself. That's all she knows. I didn't tell you yesterday until she'd had a chance to talk to your cook. She says Cook was delighted to rake over old gossip but she couldn't remember the girl's name. Though she did say your old housekeeper used to visit her niece at Newcastle after that.'

Anthony's shoulders slumped. 'The old housekeeper died six years ago. How do I find a nameless woman in Newcastle?'

'Be patient! Cook's coming over to visit Eva on Monday, her next evening off. Eva will try to jog her memory again. You understand, she had to listen to Cook's ramblings about every happening in the house worthy of the servants' notice over the past thirty or so years. Eva couldn't press too hard on that one incident. But rest assured, if there's any more to find out she will.'

'I'm grateful to her. But you know patience is not my strong point.' A smile stole up on him uninvited. He moved the breakfast tray to the side of the bed and leaned over to kiss her cheek. 'Women and their ways! What story did you concoct for Eva?'

Adelle fastened a button on the cuff of her nightgown sleeve. 'None. I simply asked her to find out that information for me. When you've known Eva longer you'll understand what I mean. She sees and hears all but says nothing. I told you she's a blessing.'

Anthony picked up a piece of cold toast, screwed up his nose and placed it back on the rack. 'Maybe if I take down this cold rubbish she'll bless me with a fresh breakfast.' But as he picked up the tray a thought occurred to him. 'I suppose Cook also indulged in the latest morsel of gossip – about my staying here?'

'That was top priority. But what does it matter? We couldn't hide the fact for long.' Adelle smiled and twirled a wisp of hair on her forehead between her fingers. It was an unconscious gesture she often made when amused. 'Just think what a stir you're causing among the house staff!'

'And I intend to make an even bigger stir as soon as you're well enough.' He chuckled as he carried out the tray.

The next few days passed pleasantly. Even Anthony's visit to his parents had gone smoothly. Richard's forced geniality and Mildred's aloofness were more tolerable than the overt anger Anthony had expected.

On Monday he took the children to Morpeth to buy Christmas presents. Afterwards the gardener delivered the Christmas tree and they helped him carry it in with great ceremony and stood it by the fire in the drawing room.

Arlette brimmed with excitement as Anthony hoisted her on to his shoulder to place a silver star on the top of the tree. 'This is going to be the nicest Christmas we've had since Papa died . . . except I wish Mama could get up,' she added, frowning. 'It seems like her stomachache will go on for ever.'

The star in place, Anthony dropped her to the floor. 'I was going to keep it a surprise but I talked to Dr Kingston today and he's pleased with her progress. He says it would be all right for her to be brought down on Christmas Day, providing she lies on the sofa. I shall have the pleasure of carrying her downstairs myself.'

Michelle stopped sticking candle holders on the branches and flung her arms round him. 'Then it *will* be the best Christmas since Papa died.'

'The first of many to come,' Anthony said. 'Now I'm going up to see your mama and when I come down I want to see that tree finished and both of you in bed. I'll come in to say goodnight.'

The girls pounced on the boxes of tinsel streamers and glass ornaments surrounding the tree and embarked on their assignment.

Bursting with happiness, Anthony bounded down to the cellar. For him it was going to be the best Christmas he'd ever had. He heard Cook's voice through the closed kitchen door and remembered – it was Monday evening. She was visiting Eva. He resisted the temptation to listen outside the door, selected a bottle of claret from the dusty shelves and sneaked back up to the dining room. He set the bottle with glasses on a tray and carried it upstairs.

Adelle, propped high on her nest of pillows, put down her book when he entered. 'Are the girls wearing you out?'

'Yes, and I love it. The tree's almost up, the presents are wrapped, except for some secret ones of mine, and it's time for a celebration.' He placed the tray on the bedside table and poured the wine.

Adelle held up her glass in amusement. 'What are we drinking to?'

'To what is going to be my happiest Christmas ever.' He sat on the bed and touched her glass with his.

'And your birthday! Don't think I've forgotten that.'

A shadow crossed his face but passed in a second. 'I know. I'll pay my parents a visit on the day, I promise. But for tea only. I intend to be back for Christmas dinner with you and the girls.'

'Yes, the girls! I'd thought of telling them they're going to have a little sister or brother – and father – as a sort of Christmas present. But I've decided to postpone it until the Easter holidays.' She sipped her

269

wine and her eyes twinkled. 'That's long enough notice or they'll be truly impossible to deal with.'

He gazed down at her belly, hidden under the thick eiderdown, and fluttered his hand over it, too awed to exert even a finger's pressure. 'It's such a miracle! I still can't believe my child is growing in there. And to think that by next Christmas we'll be a family of five. Quite an achievement for a man of my age!' Grinning, he walked to the other side of the bed and stretched out beside her, his back supported by the high pillows. 'You've wrought so many miracles in my life.'

'And you in mine.' She sipped from her glass and set it on the bedside table. 'Now hold me, please.'

He put his glass on the floor and slipped his arms round her. As always when he held her, he felt himself stirring at the touch of her body, the smell of her hair, but he shut his eyes and contented himself with her closeness. If he had to he could spend a lifetime just being with her like this.

A knock on the door interrupted the moment. He jumped up and smoothed back his hair.

Eva stood on the threshold. 'I'm sorry to disturb you, madam, but you asked me to come up when Cook left.'

Adelle nodded. 'Ah, yes, please come in, Eva. Did you discover any more information?'

Eva stood before her, hands folded. 'Well, yes and no, madam. She went on about a million things afore I could steer her back to that, er, business without her getting suspicious. But all I could get out of her was that another scullery maid who used to be a friend of this girl had the nerve to get one of the servants to search the old housekeeper's room after she died. It was like robbing her grave, Cook said. But the little minx – *Cook's* words, madam – didn't get nothing 'cause the mistress had burned the contents of the room to kill the disease. Anyway, she did say that the person still lives nearby 'cause she sometimes sees her at the market. Cook snubs her, so she says. That's all, madam.'

'You did well, Eva. But I know you won't let the matter rest there. You may go now.'

Before leaving, Eva's mouth flickered – the closest she ever got to a smile.

Anthony paced the room, hands behind his back. 'Another scullery maid! And she lives locally! Where does that get us? How do I go hunting around Morpeth looking for ex-scullery maids?'

Adelle patted the bed for him to sit. 'Patience, Anthony, remember?

270

That virtue you so sadly lack! Every little snippet of information could help – like putting together a jigsaw puzzle. Now you've got another possible contact. And Eva will continue to pursue the matter.'

He took a deep breath and nodded. 'You're right. My lack of patience has plagued me all my life. Perhaps with your help I shall acquire it. But now I must go. I promised to say goodnight to the girls. I'll be back.' He kissed her tenderly on the mouth.

'Anthony,' she called after him as he reached the door, 'whether or not you ever achieve patience, your other virtues outweigh that particular flaw.'

'Ah!' he said. 'But I must attain perfection to be worthy of you.'

When he returned Adelle's face glowed from the wine.

'You're looking better,' he said, reclining again beside her. 'Perhaps it's time you had your friends to visit to alleviate your boredom.'

She turned to stroke his cheek. 'I have all the company I need to keep me happy. Besides, I saw much of my friends while you were away. I've written to them of my condition but until I'm on my feet again I'm content with my family.'

'Family!' He savoured the word. 'I can't wait for us to be legally a family.'

She admonished him with a frown. 'Your impatience is rearing its head again. You know we can't make the marriage plans yet, but if it would cheer you up we could at least decide where to go for our wedding journey. Just the two of us – after we've spent some time with the child.'

Anthony's eyes glowed with excitement. 'Anywhere! Anywhere in the world you want. London? Paris? Rome? All three?'

But she shook her head, the corners of her mouth lifting in a slow smile. 'There's only one place I should dearly love to visit. But I'm afraid you'll laugh at me.'

He raised his eyebrows. 'And where is that?'

'The Isle of Skye.'

He did laugh, with mirth and delight. 'Then you shall, my love.'

'I've read so much about its wild beauty,' she went on. 'I'd love to take a cottage there and experience it for myself.'

Anthony was still chuckling. 'I fear it will be less comfortable than Europe but in its own way more exciting. It's a marvellous idea. What an unconventional and wonderful creature you are!' He kissed her cheek.

271

'Then you don't find it strange?'

'Splendidly strange! And now that we've at least settled that matter I must let you sleep. Otherwise Eva will be up to chase me out.'

Chapter Twenty-Six

January brought snow. Heavy white cotton decked the fields and trees and drifted high against the hedgerows. Daily chores changed. Life became a constant battle to keep roads and cart tracks clear. It was a losing battle. Few roads remained passable for long before another fall landed like a swarm of silver bees. No newspapers got through, no post, and only those with urgent need attempted travel.

But the silent white wilderness delighted the girls, and Anthony. He romped with them in the snow, built snowmen, had snowball fights, and to their utmost delight took them sledging.

After an afternoon's sledging they returned to take tea upstairs with Adelle. Their faces glowed and their eyes sparkled.

The girls ran to their mother, their white wool stockings flashing under their skirts. In their wake, Anthony grinned like a schoolboy.

Michelle's silver hair, sparkling with snowflakes, mingled with her mother's as she pressed her cold lips against Adelle's cheek. 'It's such a shame you can't go out in it, Mama. It's so much fun.'

'I swear we went twenty miles an hour,' Arlette said through chattering teeth. 'And Uncle Anthony tipped us over twice on purpose.'

Adelle smiled at the three pink faces. 'I'm delighted you had fun. But you all look frozen. Have some hot tea now.'

Michelle, who enjoyed her temporary role as hostess, skipped to the table Eva had set by the fire and poured the tea. 'We sledged all the way down to the stream and we didn't tip over once.'

As always, Anthony marvelled at this intimate, unconventional family life – the children allowed to sleep on the same floor as their mother, take their meals with her, share with her their games and their lessons. How he wished he'd been surrounded by such affection! He sat on the bed and pressed his cold hands to Adelle's cheeks. 'Feel the fresh air, my love. You missed a treat.'

273

She shivered and pulled her pink bedshawl tighter about her. 'I think I'd rather enjoy it from my window.'

A slight pout replaced Michelle's smile as she placed the bed tray between Adelle and Anthony. 'Do we really have to start studies tomorrow? It's not fair. The schools are still on holiday.'

'I thought you were looking forward to studying with me,' Anthony said, passing a cup to Adelle.

Michelle's pout grew. 'Well, yes, but not when it's snowing.'

'You start tomorrow, and that's final!' Adelle's twinkling eyes belied her stern tone. 'There'll be time for sledging after your lessons. Now go by the fire and have tea, and afterwards your piano practice.'

Defeated, Michelle trailed back to the table.

Screwing up her nose at the hot buttery pastries, Adelle waved away the scone plate Anthony held out. 'Just tea, please.'

His eyes, though still sparkling from the cold, filled with concern as he looked at her. He kept his voice low so the children wouldn't hear. 'You hardly ate anything at lunch. Remember, you must eat for two.'

'I'm doing my best. It's difficult to acquire an appetite lying in bed.'

'I know how boring it is for you but time *is* passing, my sweet.'

Adelle sighed. 'Another four and a half months! It seems an eternity . . . though I long for the outcome.' Her face softened, then she glanced towards the table. But the girls, attacking the scones with frost-sharpened appetites, were too preoccupied to take an interest in grown-up conversation.

'I promised to dine with my parents this evening,' Anthony said. 'But I'll excuse myself as soon as I decently can.'

Despite her condition, Adelle's laugh was as vivacious as ever. 'You *always* excuse yourself early. But don't worry, I shall entertain myself with Mr Wordsworth in your absence.'

He picked up a scone and threw it back on the plate. 'Damn! I wish they could meet you, only once, and then they would understand why I love you. You've no idea how hard it is for me to sit there for an entire evening and listen to them talking as if you didn't exist.'

She tilted her head as she always did when thinking. 'You know it doesn't trouble me. But if it would make you happy why not invite them for tea tomorrow? I could receive them in the drawing room. It wouldn't hurt for me to lie downstairs for an hour. I was fine at Christmas. And a change of scenery would be welcome.'

'That would be wonderful! I know they think I'm insane, that I've fallen in love with an old dowager. When they see that you're young and beautiful, and would be an asset to any man as a wife, they'll soften.' As he leaned forward to stroke her cheek, a worried frown creased his forehead. 'But promise me you won't let it upset you if Mother's cool to you. It may take a while for her . . . you know how she is.'

'Indeed I do,' she whispered, pressing her finger to her lips to remind him of the children.

'But I'm sure Father will be pleasantly surprised when he meets you,' Anthony went on in a low but more confident tone. 'And though he doesn't mention it I know the fact that you're carrying his grandchild secretly pleases him. He'll be praying – in his fashion – for a grandson.'

'I wish I could promise that. But I shall try to make my condition conspicuous without being too unladylike and do my best to, as you say, "soften" them.'

Anthony felt relief and fear – relief that the meeting would formally establish his relationship with Adelle but fear that his parents' hostility would upset her.

She seemed to know his thoughts for she changed the subject. 'It's almost time for the girls' music lesson.'

Despite his worries, he grinned. 'I've got a Beethoven étude planned for them today. They're going to hate all the practice but I think they're ready for something more challenging.'

Anthony returned from his visit home excited yet anxious. His parents had accepted the invitation for the following day. He ran upstairs to Adelle's bedside. 'They've agreed to come tomorrow,' he said, panting. 'I'm sure this will be the beginning of better relations with them, my darling. Even if they're only civil to you it will make life easier.'

'I'm glad they accepted.' Her voice was strangely quiet, her face even paler than usual.

'Oh, my sweet!' He sat slowly on the bed. 'Are you too tired? Will it be too much for you? We can make it another day.'

She smiled and placed her hand over his. 'No, tomorrow will be fine. Though I do feel tired tonight. I took your advice and tried to eat for two at dinner. I'm afraid it disagreed with me.' She laid her other hand on her stomach and grimaced.

'Can I get you anything?'

'No, Eva gave me a strong dose of peppermint linctus. And she also gave me more news. Your cook came for a visit after dinner and mentioned that affair without Eva bringing it up. It seems she saw the woman who in your cook's own terms "tried to steal from the dead". She was on her way back from the market when she saw the one in question turning down that disused cart track off the Morpeth road. It struck Cook as strange because she'd seen your old housekeeper taking her trap down there. She said Mrs Kennedy kept herself to herself and never associated with the servants outside of the house, so she's convinced there's another scandal just waiting to be unearthed.'

Anthony looked thoughtful. 'I know of that track. There's nothing down there as far as I'm aware. But when the snow clears I'll take a ride and find out.'

'And if she does live there? How will you explain your visit?'

'That's a problem. But if she is, or was, a friend of my real mother and of her aunt then I'm sure she knows anyway. And if she's kept quiet all these years she has at least been loyal to them. I'll think about it further and devise a way to approach her. But her being a friend of Mrs Kennedy could be reason enough for my curiosity. The woman was more like a second mother to me than my own nurse.' He smiled and patted her hand. 'And I've no doubt you'll think of some ingenious woman's scheme before the time comes.'

'I shall think on it. But now I need to sleep, my dear.'

He looked contrite. 'Forgive me. I'm thoughtless and selfish as well as impatient. Those are two more virtues I must improve on. You sleep, my love.' As he bent to kiss her, her forehead creased and she let out a sharp breath. He stood up in alarm. 'Did I crush you?'

Her face relaxed again. 'No, sweetheart, it was just another touch of the dyspepsia. Would you please ask Eva to bring me some more peppermint linctus. Tomorrow I shall be more careful what I eat.'

A thumping on the door roused Anthony from a deep sleep. Without waiting to be admitted, Eva rushed in carrying a lamp before her. 'Sir! Sir!' she said. 'You must go and get Dr Kingston. Madam's not well. She's in pain and she's bleeding, sir.'

Anthony shot out of bed, uncaring that he was in his nightshirt. 'How badly?' As he spoke, he groped in the dark for his clothes on the valet stand.

'Badly, sir, please be quick. I was going to get the coachman but I know you'd be quicker. You know the house, sir. It's on the corner of Market Place and Bridge Street.'

'Yes, yes, I know it.' He was already pulling on his socks, his head racing. He would have to take his horse and ride back in Dr Kingston's

276

automobile. But the roads were still bad. Any form of travel would be slow. Suddenly he thought of the new telephone his father had recently had installed. But the fields were impassable. He would have to go via the Morpeth road to get to the house in any event. It would be quicker to go straight to the doctor.

From the hall stand he grabbed his greatcoat and muffler but ignored his gloves, still soaked from snowballing. Great flurries of snow like goosefeathers blanketed him as he made his way to the stables behind the house, slipping several times on the frozen slush. He saddled his mare. It was quicker than waking the stable hands. The horse snorted clouds of vapour into the freezing air as he urged her out with unaccustomed harshness. He started at a near gallop along the cleared path to the front drive and down the private turn-off to the Morpeth road. His numb hands could barely feel the reins.

The half-moon shed scant light but reflected off the high banks of snow packed against the ghostly hedgerows. The cleared road was dotted with treacherous patches of black ice and the new fall was concealing the patches fast.

Anthony could feel the tautness of the animal's body beneath him, her hooves hesitant and unwilling, but he urged her as fast as he dared and soothed her with soft words. If he pushed her too hard and she fell it would take him an hour on foot. He found himself praying aloud to a God he'd until now only read about and discussed with intellectual curiosity, 'Dear Lord, don't let Adelle die! Don't let her die!'

He reached the house without incident, his face wet with perspiration despite the cold. Lights shone from the fanlight above the door and from a downstairs window. Thank God! The man was at home. He pounded on the heavy oak door with his fists.

After a few moments it creaked open and an elderly woman peered at him in the hall light. She hugged a black shawl over her nightgown. 'Be quiet, be quiet. You'll wake the whole house. Don't you know what hour it is?'

'I wish to speak to Dr Kingston immediately.' Forgetting his manners Anthony pushed past her into the hall.

'He's out on an emergency and I'm not supposed to let nobody in without his say-so.' The woman's tone was respectful now. From his speech and dress he was clearly a gentleman.

Anthony closed his eyes and clapped a hand to his forehead. 'When will he be back?'

Before replying she shut the door against the icy draught. 'That I don't know, sir. He hasn't been gone but ten minutes. That's as why I'm still up.'

'Where? Do you know where he went?'

'I can't say, sir. I know it's an old man yon side of town was took ill sudden and somebody came for Dr Kingston just like you. The poor doctor hasn't had a full night's sleep since this bad weather. Everybody's being took ill.'

Anthony covered his face with his hands to think. Should he stay and wait for the doctor or should he ride to the north of town to look for the man's motor car? It would surely be parked in the street. But even if he found him, a physician couldn't leave one patient to attend another.

Tears of desperation blurred his eyes as he looked back at the woman. 'Do you know where Dr Wilson lives? He's my mother's physician. I'll go there.'

'Aye, I know where he lives, sir, but he's abroad on holiday. That's one of the reasons as Dr Kingston's that busy.'

'But surely there'll be a doctor on duty at the hospital.'

'Nah, they don't make house calls from the hospital, sir. And I wouldn't recommend that place in any case from the tales I've heard about it. But if it's that serious you could take the person there.'

'No, she can't be moved. And certainly not in this weather.' Anthony wound his soaked muffler tighter round his neck. It would do no good waiting here. He must get back to Adelle. 'Would you bring me pen and paper so I may leave Dr Kingston a note to come as quickly as possible. It's Mrs Adelle Grayson of Flagdon Hall, she's severely ill.'

'Aye, come in here, sir.' Huddling her shawl about her she led him to a room on the right. It appeared to be the doctor's surgery.

Anthony hurried to the leather-topped desk, grabbed the pen and scribbled on the pad by the telephone. He thrust the sheet at the woman. 'You *will* give it to him immediately he returns.'

'Aye, sir. I'll wait up for him anyway to make him a warm nightcap. He'll need it if he's got to go out again. I'll give him the message straight away.'

Heedless of leaving the mare out in the cold, Anthony tethered her to the post in front of the house and took the stairs three at a time. Filled with apprehension he knocked on Adelle's door. He heard Eva running to open it. Her jaw dropped when she saw him alone. 'Where's Dr Kingston?'

'Out on another emergency. I've left a message for him to come

278

immediately. How is she?' He stood on the threshold, straining to see Adelle's face. But Eva stepped outside and closed the door behind her.

'Not good, sir. I've raised her legs higher to help stop the bleeding but it's not doing much good and she's in pain. You stay downstairs till Dr Kingston comes. This is women's business.'

'But I must see her. Please, please, let me see her.'

'I'll ask her if she feels up to it, sir.' She closed the door behind her and a few seconds later returned.

'You can come in, sir, but please don't stay long. Don't tire her.'

He followed Eva into the familiar room. He felt like an intruder. Adelle lay in an unnatural position, flat without a pillow, her legs supported under the eiderdown almost as high as the bed rail. Filled with fear and tenderness he knelt by the bedside. Her face was ashen, her eyes full of pain as she turned her head to him.

A lump formed in his throat. 'How are you feeling, my darling?' Shaking, he took the hand she held out.

A wan smile touched her face. 'It'll be all right, sweetheart, don't worry. I can feel the child, it's not harmed. And Dr Kingston will stop the bleeding.' But her face creased in pain and her grip on his hand tightened.

Eva ran forward. 'You'd better go now, sir. It looks like another pain coming on. Please wait downstairs for Dr Kingston. Cook's up, she'll get you something hot.'

'No, I want nothing.' Anthony trailed downstairs in a daze.

After stabling the horse he returned to the drawing room and left the door open. He sat in the dark by the dead fire, still in his soaked greatcoat, his ears peeled for the sound of an automobile.

Tears trickled down his cheeks. He was responsible for Adelle's pain. If he hadn't made love to her . . . He would never risk this happening again, never. He would learn control. She couldn't die, she couldn't! And their child? Once again he prayed to his unknown God: 'Please, Lord, if anything goes wrong let it be the child, not Adelle, *please* not Adelle.' A strange feeling ran through him – hatred for their unborn child. If it weren't for the child . . . He shook his head. Enough of these terrible thoughts. Dr Kingston would be here soon. All would be well.

He had no idea how long he'd sat when he heard Eva's running steps down the stairs. When he reached the hall she was halfway down. She stopped and clapped her hands to her cheeks. Then, her voice trembling, she said, 'She's gone, sir. Dear God, she's gone.' Her mouth quivered and tears gathered in the dark cavities under her eyes.

Anthony's scream sliced the night like a lancet. He gripped the banister for support then raced up the stairs, crying, 'No! No!'

Eva followed. 'Please, sir, the children,' she whispered, as they neared the night nursery.

He gagged himself with his hand and hurtled on down the hall. When he reached the bed he stopped, stunned. Adelle lay as if sleeping, her silver hair tousled on the pillow as though she'd suffered nothing more than a restless night.

Groaning, he flung himself over her. He cried out her name, then kissed her mouth. Her lips were still warm. But he felt the stillness of death. No tender pressure returned his. He took her by the shoulders as if to shake life back into her. 'No, my love, no! Don't leave me, please don't leave me.' He laid his head on her bosom and wept. But the tears had no healing power, his agony no end. He'd killed her with his love as surely as if he'd pierced her heart with a sword. But she had wanted his love! Had wanted the child! How could he have prevented this? How could he have known? After some time he felt a light touch on his shoulder.

'Please, sir,' Eva said in a broken voice. 'I've got to see to her now.'

He looked up but scarcely noticed that the woman's eyes were as red, her face as desolate with grief as his own. He rose and slumped into the chair by the bed. 'Hell and damnation on that man! If only he'd got to her!'

Eva wiped her eyes on her apron. 'He couldn't have done nothing, I'm sure, sir. The child came. There's nothing anyone could have done.'

'The child! Hell and damnation on the child as well!' He put his head in his hands and rocked back and forth.

'I'm sorry, sir, but you'll have to go while I see to her.'

'No,' he said in a whimper. 'I can't leave her.'

Eva put her hand under his elbow and coaxed him, all traces of formality gone from her voice. 'Come on now. I'll just take you next door to your room and you can come back as soon as I've finished.'

He felt his body rising at her command and allowed himself to be led to his room. She left him standing in the doorway and lit the lamp. When she returned he stood in the same position. She put her hands on his shoulders and ushered him to the bed. He sat, his eyes staring before him but seeing nothing.

'I'll be back when I've finished, sir,' she said as she left.

An hour later when she came back he still sat staring, his eyes like red coals in his white face.

'She's ready,' Eva said. She had to touch him on the shoulder before he moved. And then he started as if out of a deep sleep.

'Why don't you stay here and lie down, sir. I'll sit with her till morning.'

He stood. 'No, no. I must be with her. You get some rest.' He felt his legs moving under him, and then he was at the bedside.

Adelle wore a fresh lawn nightgown and her hands, like delicate ivory carvings, lay crossed on her chest. The silver rope of her hair, plaited in the fashion she wore to sleep, reached almost to her waist over a white coverlet. She looked like her own reflection in a still pond.

He knelt to kiss her forehead and shuddered. She was cold. This was his Adelle, so full of the joy of life even in her illness. Suddenly he realized how fleeting and precious life was, not constant and unchanging as he'd believed in his youth. A deep sigh rose from the depths of his being. His youth! He'd grown up so quickly. And now grown old overnight. His life was over. His beautiful, warm, living angel was dead. She'd always known. She'd warned him – *Gather ye rosebuds while ye may.*

He stroked her alabaster forehead. He couldn't let her lie alone in the cold, dark earth. He would go with her. If they couldn't be together in life they could be together in death and share whatever lay beyond the grave. There were in any case no rosebuds left on this earth for him to gather.

He sat on the chair, his hands hanging limp in his lap. Tears flowed again but he blinked them away. He wanted to see her clearly, unwilling to miss a moment of his precious time with her before—

He felt a heavy hand on his shoulder.

'I'm sorry I got here too late.' Dr Kingston stood at his side, Eva behind him.

'Yes, too late,' Anthony repeated.

'I left as soon as I got your message but my motor skidded into a drift. I had to walk home and get a carriage.'

'You can't help her now.' Anthony heard his own voice and it sounded disembodied, as if he'd already gone to meet Adelle.

'I would have been of no use anyway,' Dr Kingston went on. 'I couldn't have stopped the child from coming. I feared this might happen.'

281

'Yes, no use.' Anthony echoed the man's words again, unable to form his own.

'I'm going to get Dr Kingston some hot broth,' Eva said. 'I'll get some for you, sir. Please come downstairs.'

'No.'

'Sir!' Her voice held a pleading note. 'It'll be daylight soon and the children'll be up for breakfast. You'll have to pull yourself together and tell them, sir. Please come down.'

'The children.' Anthony blinked. In his own grief he'd forgotten the children. How could he tell them such news? But he had to. They would need him. He couldn't possibly think of joining Adelle while her children needed him. He must summon the aunt in France. He rose stiffly. 'I'll come down. I need to make the arrangements.' He looked at Adelle before he left, and whispered, 'I'll stay for them while they need me, my darling.'

He couldn't swallow any broth but, though feeling as numb and lifeless as his beloved in the darkened bedroom, he forced his leaden legs to move, his heavy head to think.

Before the girls came down to breakfast he'd written a telegram to their Aunt Eleanor in France to announce the melancholy event and to ask her to come with haste. The snowfall of the night before had spent itself. Though unless there was a sudden thaw he feared the aunt's journey would be delayed.

After the letter he wrote the required obituary for the newspaper and dispatched the coachman to Morpeth to take the telegram to the post office and the obituary notice to the newspaper office, though few newspapers were being delivered. The final call was to request the undertaker, the joiner and the sexton to call later that morning.

His immediate chores over, Anthony couldn't bring himself to wash or shave but changed into a dark grey suit. Eva had placed a black armband on the bed. He pulled it over his sleeve. So often he'd seen men wearing mourning bands but he'd never known how it felt to lose a loved one. He dreaded his next ordeal. He sat by the fire in the drawing room planning his words, waiting for Eva to bring down the girls. He longed to sit with Adelle again, to drink in every last moment of her earthly presence until he could join her. But he must first perform his duties.

One on each side of Eva, Michelle and Arlette arrived dressed in white, the customary mourning attire for young ladies. Their faces were puzzled.

Michelle ran to him and his heart welled with sadness as he took her hand. She tilted her head in enquiry. 'What's happening today, Uncle Anthony? Why did we have to dress up? Eva was a meanie. She wouldn't tell us anything. Are visitors coming?'

Arlette followed her sister slowly, the corners of her mouth turned down. 'Whatever it is I suppose it means we can't go sledging today.'

Anthony patted each arm of his chair and they sat. He held them. He couldn't speak for the lump in his throat. Eva remained as he'd requested. She stood, sombre-faced, her hands clasped against her apron so tightly the knuckles were white.

'I'm afraid I have some unhappy news for you, my dears,' he finally began, though his words sounded strangled and hopelessly inadequate. 'Your dearest mama was taken to heaven last night.'

'To heaven?' Michelle still looked puzzled. Then her eyes widened and she stared at him in horror. 'You . . . you mean she's dead?' Her lips trembled and she burst into tears.

'Yes, she died without pain, in her sleep.' The lie came out as he'd planned, giving him the courage to go on, 'And it's not sad for her. She's very peaceful and happy.' If only he could believe his own words!

Full realization finally hit Arlette. She crumpled her face and let out a scream. 'No, Mama's not dead! She can't be! She's only got a stomachache.'

'No, she's in no pain now. I told you, she's peaceful and happy where she is.'

They wailed in anguish and he drew them to his chest like a mother. Through their wool dresses he could feel their sobs rippling like convulsions through their bodies. 'That's right, my dears, cry as much as you need.' He clenched his eyelids to stop his own tears but despite his efforts he broke down, and the three clung together like one, sharing their grief.

After a while he took a deep breath and stilled himself. He must try harder to remain calm and strong for them. His voice trembled as much as theirs as he went on, 'You know, I share your grief. I loved your mama as much as you did. We shall all miss her.' But his words were drowned by the sound of their suffering.

His outburst of emotion had calmed him for the moment, and he rocked the girls in silence until, their first rush of agony spent, they gulped in air and whimpered like hurt puppies.

'You'll be safe with me, and Eva. And your Aunt Eleanor will be coming soon,' he said, still rocking them.

Arlette let out a choking sound before vomiting into his chest. Eva rushed forward. 'I'll see to her, sir.' She raised Arlette's racked body and half led, half carried her from the room.

Anthony rubbed at his jacket with his handkerchief and continued to rock Michelle.

'I'm going to be sick too,' she said in a strangled voice. He scooped her up to carry her out. But she fainted in his arms.

Anthony sat by the girls' bedsides and comforted them. Yet all the while his impatience grew inside him. He longed for his tedious earthly duties to be over so that he could be with his beloved for ever. He chastised himself for his selfishness.

At eleven o'clock Eva returned with hot milk for Michelle and Arlette. 'The men are waiting in the drawing room, sir,' she said.

He nodded and rose. 'I'll be back soon,' he told the girls. Their red eyes followed him to the door as if afraid he would leave them for ever as their mother had.

The sexton and undertaker stood self-consciously in the drawing room, top hats in hands. The joiner stood beside them, his cap in one hand and a tape measure in the other. They jumped to attention when Anthony entered. The sexton introduced himself and the others.

Anthony nodded a greeting and stared at the tape measure. 'Thank you for being so prompt. *Must* you take measurements?'

The undertaker looked at the floor. 'Yes, sir.'

But Anthony was unwilling to let strangers touch her. 'I can tell you that she was barely five foot three, and slight. Surely, that should be enough.'

The joiner coughed. 'Aye, sir, I can go by that. What sort of coffin would you be wantin', sir?'

'Not elaborate. Her tastes were simple.' He thought for a moment. She liked mahogany and the colour violet. 'Please use mahogany and line it with violet satin.'

The joiner nodded. 'I could have it ready by tomorrow mornin', sir.'

'I suggest the funeral be held two days after that, sir,' the sexton said. 'We've already got one for ten o'clock, so say at eleven? You'll need at least a couple of days to inform relatives and friends. I'll organize a service to be held first in the chapel.'

A service? She didn't care for formal services. Anthony couldn't ignore custom completely but he *could* modify it to her tastes. 'A very short and simple service then,' he said.

'Any special hymns or anything you'd like, sir?' the sexton went on.

Anthony rubbed his brow. He only knew her favourite poetry. 'No hymns,' he said. 'After the service I shall read a short elegy myself. And then I'd like the organist to play Beethoven's "Ode to Joy".'

The sexton stared at him with disbelief. He cleared his throat. 'As you say, sir.'

'And what about the engraving on the tomb, sir?' the undertaker wanted to know.

Anthony pulled a folded paper from his pocket and handed it to him. 'I've prepared it.'

The man slipped it into his own pocket without reading it. 'Thank you, sir. Then that'll be all for now. We'll be back with the coffin in the morning.'

Anthony returned to sit with the girls. Though they'd been unable to hold down their morning milk, by one o'clock their stomachs were calm enough to take the hot broth Eva brought them.

'Would you like to see your mama tomorrow?' Anthony's voice was hesitant. Though custom decreed it he was unwilling to inflict such an ordeal on the children unless they wished it.

Michelle whimpered, 'I want to see her now.'

'And me.' Arlette always followed her sister's example, though there was fear in her eyes.

He looked to Eva, who sat by the fire. She nodded affirmation. Like Anthony, she'd remained with the girls through their torment, leaving them only when necessary to direct the servants at their chores. She helped Arlette out of bed and dressed her in her wool dressing gown. Anthony dressed Michelle and, his arm round each of them, followed Eva down the hall. As they neared the bedroom he feared his legs would crumple under him.

The girls walked unnaturally, like clockwork dolls. In the doorway they burst from him and ran to the bed. But they stopped short and stared in awe at the white marble statue that only yesterday had been their mother.

Adelle looked as she'd done the night before, though the stench of the burning tarpot and the saltpetre-soaked papers drying in the fire grate filled the darkened room. Only a single lamp burned by the bed.

Anthony gulped down his desire to vomit at the smell and stood between the girls. 'Would you like to kiss your mama goodbye?' he whispered, quelling his own urge to throw himself over Adelle and let his grief pour out of him.

Dry-eyed, Michelle nodded and he held her, her body shivering despite her warm dressing gown, while she bent to place her lips against her mother's forehead. When she raised herself she fainted again in his arms.

'I'll take her back to bed,' he said to Eva. 'And you come too, Arlette.' He tried to keep his voice matter-of-fact.

But again Arlette followed her sister's example. She freed herself from Eva's grasp and kissed her mother's forehead. 'Mama! Mama!' she sobbed as Eva led her away.

Back in bed Michelle moaned and blinked herself awake. She pushed away the smelling salts Eva held to her nose. It was hard to believe that her eyes, dull and filled with fear and sorrow, were the same eyes that had sparkled with excitement in the snow only yesterday.

Anthony tucked the covers round Arlette and took up his vigil beside the two once more.

'I'll get them another hot drink, sir, and you and all,' Eva said.

Anthony looked up at the woman who stood over him, as pale and red-eyed as all of them. For the first time he realized that Eva, like him, had suffered a cruel loss and a sleepless night. Again he rebuked himself for his selfishnesses. 'Thank you, Eva,' he said. 'And afterwards you must have a rest. You've done much more than your duty.'

'Don't worry about me, sir. I'm all right.' Eva squared her shoulders and walked from the room as straight and vigorous as ever.

Anthony felt humble. He now understood how true Adelle's words were. Eva was indeed a blessing.

She returned with the hot milk and announced as if in apology, 'Mr and Mrs Hayward are downstairs, sir.'

He started, then squeezed his eyes shut in despair. He'd forgotten his parents' visit. That it should be this day of all days!

'I showed them to the drawing room, sir. They asked why the curtains were closed but I didn't say nothing.'

'Thank you, Eva. I'll go down. Please stay with Michelle and Arlette.' He dragged himself up and trailed down the stairs.

They sat at each side of the fire in the lamplight, Richard wearing a blue suit and Mildred an emerald velvet gown decorated with a lace

286

fichu and jewels. A matching green feathered hat sat on top of her elaborate coiffure.

'Good afternoon, Mother, Father,' Anthony said stiffly.

Mildred inclined her head around the room with a look of distaste. 'I didn't expect to be received in such a fashion. Have you forgotten you invited us? It looks like a mourning room in here!'

Anthony was too drained to feel anger. 'It *is* a mourning room, Mother. My fiancée died last night.'

'Oh!' Mildred's bejewelled hand flew to her mouth.

Richard jumped up and gripped Anthony's shoulders. 'My dear boy, I'm so sorry . . .'

'How unfortunate!' Mildred rose to kiss him on the cheek. 'Please accept my condolences.'

Anthony felt a wave of disgust wash over him like dirty water. Did he imagine it or had their first shocked expressions changed to relief? Richard lowered himself back into his chair and Mildred sat on the edge of hers.

Anthony told them in a monotone, 'The child was born too early, last night. I apologize I didn't get word to you in time to cancel your visit.'

Richard shook his head. 'Damned sad news! I'm sorry to hear it.'

'And I.' Mildred rose again and this time kissed Anthony on both cheeks. 'If there's anything we can do . . . to help you make the arrangements.'

Yes, he thought, she enjoyed organizing affairs of any kind. Could it be that she would especially enjoy this task? His tone was curt. 'Thank you, no. The matter's in hand. I'm sorry I can't receive you today as planned. Again, please accept my apologies.' He walked to the door.

'Well, I . . .' Mildred began, then seemed to think better of it and followed.

In the hall he helped them into their outdoor clothes with no apology for the lack of a butler.

Richard shook Anthony's hand in his man-to-man fashion. 'I know how unhappy this must be for you, my boy, but—'

'Yes, sir,' Anthony interrupted. He couldn't take any of his father's platitudes today.

Mildred fussed with her hat at the hall mirror as if she were going to a ball. 'Now don't forget, if there's anything we can do?'

'There's nothing. Thank you. The funeral will be on Thursday morning at eleven.' He had to tell them, but he couldn't bring himself to invite them formally.

The chauffeur, resigned to a long wait, had wrapped himself in blankets in the front seat of the car. He jumped out in confusion when they appeared in the doorway.

Anthony closed the door behind them and lay against it. He could almost hear their relieved discussion on the way home – the errant son's return to the fold. But he had his own plan, and he would carry it out as soon as the time came. In the meantime he must return to the nursery.

When the girls, exhausted from their day of torment, finally fell asleep for the night with the aid of a sedative, Anthony at last went to sit with Adelle. He'd taken nothing but two cups of tea all day.

Again he choked when he opened the door. In a frenzy he drew back the curtains and threw open the windows. The freezing night air bit into his face. He collected the burned saltpetre papers from the grate, stuffed them in the tarpot and flung it through the window. It landed upside down in the snow with a thud. He felt a great release. At least his love was no longer imprisoned in a foul-smelling cell.

He stood by the bed and gazed at Adelle. 'Feel the fresh air, my love,' he murmured. And suddenly it came to him that he'd spoken those very words to her only yesterday, in joy. Tears stung his cold cheeks as he stroked her fingers. But he jumped. He'd never felt such chill. The unrelenting chill of death.

Unaware that he was almost as chilled himself he slumped into the chair and gazed at her. Tonight he couldn't just sit and stare. He would entertain her as he'd done so many times sitting in this chair. He recited to her, her favourite poems, beginning with the one that had caused her to smile on that first day, and had caused him to blush: *Come live with me and be my love, And we will all the pleasures prove.* 'I'll be coming soon, my love,' he finished.

He didn't hear the knock on the door. 'Sir, the windows!' Eva's voice was shrill with shock. 'Sir, you can't do this. Let me close the windows, and *please* come downstairs or go to your bed.'

'No, Eva. I'm staying here tonight. And I want her to smell the fresh air. That other smell is even worse than death. She would have hated it.'

'Oh, sir!' For the first time Eva's voice sounded as if she were about to break down. Then she raised her chin. 'Very well, sir. But I'm bringing you some hot soup and blankets and I'm going to light the fire.'

'There's no need,' he said, but she'd gone.

A few minutes later he submitted as she tucked blankets around him, though he refused the broth she held out.

She sighed as she went to the fireplace and began twisting papers to start a fire. When she'd finished she stood by him with a worried face. 'With respect, sir, we don't want nobody else to be took ill in the house. Please go to bed after a while. I've put a hot water jar in your bed.'

'Thank you, Eva. But I shall stay here.'

'Then I'll be back to keep the fire going,' she said, defeated.

But Anthony didn't even notice her quiet comings and goings in the night.

It was morning when he stood, stiff and blue. The girls would be awake soon and would need him. He left the curtains and windows open. 'Enjoy the daylight, my darling,' he said before leaving.

Chapter Twenty-Seven

By ten o'clock the following morning Adelle rested in her coffin, cushioned on violet satin. But when the undertaker and the joiner placed the lid over her Anthony cried out, 'No! Not yet! Take it off.'

'I'm sorry, sir.' The undertaker cleared his throat. 'But she has to be closed up now. You understand, sir?'

Anthony's face distorted in agony. He knew they were right. He knelt to take one last look at his angel. He couldn't bear to see her when she . . . He couldn't even form the thought. He placed the leather-bound volume of poetry that had first brought them together on one side of her pillow, on the other the spray of cream silk rosebuds he'd sent her from Cambridge. He then nodded permission to the men.

The lid in place, the men hoisted the coffin on their shoulders and Anthony led them out along the snow-cleared path to the little chapel in the grounds. She would rest with her parents and brother in the family crypt.

When she'd first taken him into the crypt he'd examined with interest the marble tombs in the little room off the chapel and memorized the names of her ancestors on her mother's side. He'd wanted to know every detail of her life. The thought that one day her name would be inscribed on a similar tomb had never occurred to him. And that day had come so soon.

The men laid the coffin on the altar steps, where it would remain for the funeral service.

Anthony checked inside the crypt. The workmen had carried out their task with speed. A shiny new tomb was in place, the lid propped against the stone wall. Through misted eyes he read the simple inscription he'd ordered: *Adelle Marianne Grayson, born 10 April 1865, died 12 January 1898. Beloved By Her Family and All Who Knew Her. Her Time Flew Too Swiftly.*

He bit his lip. She'd warned him her time would fly before his. Suddenly a painful thought seared through him. Should he have arranged for her to be buried beside her husband in Wiltshire? Still he couldn't bear to think that she'd loved another before him, though he tried to quell his childish jealousy. But now yet another painful thought came uninvited. If there were indeed a life beyond the grave she would be with her husband again. He would have to share her. He banished the excruciating idea. But he reassured himself that he'd made the right choice. In any event the weather would have made a funeral procession to Wiltshire impossible. And this was the home she loved most.

The sexton coughed and startled Anthony out of his reverie.

'Will that be all, sir?'

'Thank you, yes. The service is organized as I asked?'

'It is, sir.'

'Then you may go.'

Anthony returned to the chapel and sat in the front pew where Adelle had sat so many times before. The place had been dusted and swept, no doubt on Eva's instructions. He tried to feel the peace Adelle had found here. He'd only been in churches at weddings and funerals and had always been moved, always wondered what it was like to truly believe. Could it be that there was some beneficent being or power up there that loved him, that he could turn to for solace?

As he gazed at the simple altar, still adorned only by the wooden cross and empty brass candlesticks, he began to feel calmer. He knelt and bowed his head. He didn't pray, but closed his eyes and let the silence seep through him.

Half an hour later he still knelt, as if hypnotized, when light footsteps sounded on the flagstones behind him.

'I'm sorry, sir,' Eva said softly. 'I didn't know you were here. I didn't mean to disturb you.' She was dressed in her black cloak and bonnet and carried a basket on each arm, one laden with white chrysanthemums and the other with two white candles and two crystal vases.

'Don't apologize, Eva. Thank you for getting the flowers.'

'I got white like you asked, sir, but I could only get chrysanthemums this time of year. I know she liked them though. And the shop's delivering the wreath.'

He nodded and stood. 'Let me help you arrange these.'

Together they worked, not as servant and master, but as teacher and pupil, she showing him how to arrange the tall blooms in the centre, the smaller ones according to size around them. Handling the flowers proved soothing and he felt rewarded by the pleasing result of his efforts.

They each placed a candle in the holders and she handed him the matches. He lit one and was about to light the other when he paused and blew out the match. He gave the box to Eva. 'You light one for her. I know how much you loved her.'

'Thank you, sir.' Eva's eyes welled with tears and her hands shook as she struck a match and held it to the candle.

It was the first time since that terrible night Anthony had seen her give way to her emotions. He felt shame at his own lack of control and selfishness. He placed his hand on her shoulder. 'Why don't you stay for a while if you wish? I'll go back to the children.'

'I left Cook with them, sir. But she has to get on with the food for the funeral. I'd better go.'

'No. I'll relieve Cook. You stay. There's little else I can do now.'

Throughout the short service Anthony remained dry-eyed, gripping the children's hands on either side of him. They wept quietly. He shivered only once, when the bearers carried the coffin to the crypt to lower it into the tomb. As the mourners followed, the organist played 'Ode to Joy'. A few heads were raised in surprise then bowed again.

When the coffin was in place and the men eased the marble slab over the top of the tomb Anthony had never felt anything so final. He placed his arms round the girls' shoulders and they buried their faces into him. They also felt the finality of the sealed tomb. When the music stopped, in a voice full of emotion, he recited the few lines he'd taken from Oscar Wilde, one of Adelle's favourites:

> *Lily-like, white as snow,*
> *She hardly knew*
> *She was a woman, so*
> *Sweetly she grew.*

> *Coffin-board, heavy stone*
> *Lie on her breast,*
> *I vex my heart alone,*
> *She is at rest.*

At the house the ghostly figures of the mourners gathered in the

292

drawing room. Couples, single women, single men, introduced themselves and offered their condolences. Some still wept. So these were the people who'd known and loved Adelle, the people he hadn't wished to meet in his jealousy at sharing her. Though he knew no one, none showed surprise or puzzlement at his role of chief mourner.

The housemaids served hot punch and he took a glass mechanically. He found himself circulating and murmuring appropriate responses as if some invisible puppeteer were pulling the right strings.

But he froze in surprise when he saw his parents in a far corner of the room, cradling glasses yet distancing themselves from the guests. No doubt they didn't consider Adelle's friends suitable company. Though dressed in dark colours, their unconventional fashions and demeanour betrayed them as intellectual modernists.

He wove towards his parents. 'Mother? Father? It was good of you to come.'

Richard wore a grey mourning suit and Mildred a fur shawl over a black velvet gown. She held out a gloved hand. 'Please accept my deepest sympathy, my dear.'

Richard nodded gravely. 'And mine, my boy.'

'It was a very nice, er, very unusual service,' Mildred went on. 'I'm sorry we can't stay. I already had a luncheon arranged for today. But we thought we'd pay our respects.'

Richard wasted no time with his question. 'I take it you'll be coming home soon then?'

So that was why they'd come! To find out his intentions! 'I have no plans as yet,' Anthony said. With relief he heard Eva announcing that luncheon was served. He gave a stiff bow. 'If you're not staying for luncheon you must excuse me. I should attend to my guests.'

He led the group into the dining room, Michelle on one arm, Arlette on the other. Richard and Mildred remained in the corner. They would have to see themselves out. Eva and the maids were occupied with the other guests. Well, it wouldn't kill his parents to find their own coats, he thought wryly.

The meal was simple roast beef, the conversation subdued, the ordeal interminable. Afterwards Eva took the girls upstairs for a nap and the party adjourned to the drawing room for coffee.

At three o'clock, groaning inside with relief, Anthony bade the guests goodbye and went to his room. Now he could be alone. Though he felt exhausted he had no desire to sleep. Whenever he closed his eyes recurrent dreams of Adelle tortured him: After he'd struggled to prise

293

the marble lid off her tomb, her face, iridescent and eyeless, rose up to him. Or she was hanging by her hands from a ledge above a dark ravine and, when he seized her arms to pull her up, she slid from his grasp into the blackness.

Aunt Eleanor arrived four days later, having taken a mixture of trains and stage coaches after her long voyage, and a hackney to the house.

Eva knocked on the door of the day nursery, where Anthony was reading to the girls in French. Though it was too soon to impose formal lessons on them, he tried to occupy every minute of their days.

He looked up from his book. 'Yes, Eva.'

'Miss Pagnol is downstairs, sir.' Eva's eyes were wet.

Of course! It suddenly occurred to Anthony that Eva had known both sisters from birth and was probably as fond of Eleanor as she'd been of Adelle. He jumped up, flustered by the suddenness of the aunt's arrival even though he'd been expecting her.

Michelle tugged at his sleeve. 'Please may we see Aunt Eleanor?'

'Yes, please, please?' Arlette looked at him with such imploring eyes that he relented.

'All right. You may spend five minutes with her and then she and I must talk. Eva will serve your tea here afterwards. Soon you will have all the time in the world with your aunt.'

They flew from the room, down the stairs and into the drawing room like leaves in a gust of wind. Anthony followed slowly, reluctantly. He didn't wish to intrude on the family reunion.

Aunt Eleanor sat by the fire in the drawing room. She rose when the girls entered. They ran to her and wept with joy and sorrow. Her hair was dark like Arlette's and drawn up in a tight coil on top of her head, which was bent over the children. The severe coiffure and the black bombazine frock she wore in her mourning gave her a formidable appearance. She wept with her nieces for some minutes before she held them at arm's length.

From the doorway where he waited in discomfort, Anthony could see that her face was not formidable. It was strongly carved, like Greek statuary, but her full mouth quivered with emotion and her eyes, like dark pools in her grief, gazed with tenderness on the girls. 'My poor children,' she said in a voice heavy with feeling. 'I'm here now. I'll look after you as your dear mother did. There's no need to fear any more.'

Michelle sniffed and wiped her eyes on her pinafore. 'Uncle Anthony's

294

been looking after us. He's very kind and he loves us very much. And we love him.'

'Yes,' Arlette added, 'and he tutors us and plays with us. We've never had a tutor who plays with us. He's wonderful.'

'Indeed,' Eleanor said, 'and where is this new uncle of yours?'

The girls looked behind them and Eleanor's gaze followed. Anthony, still in the doorway, coughed in embarrassment. 'I . . . I wished to give you a few moments alone,' he said. 'I apologize if I appeared rude. And I apologize also that I didn't send the carriage for you. I had no idea when you'd arrive.'

'I understand.' She inclined her head though no smile of greeting crossed her face.

He walked towards her and bowed. 'I'm pleased to make your acquaintance.'

She nodded but didn't hold out her hand.

An uncomfortable silence followed. Anthony spoke to the girls. 'Eva will have your tea ready now. You may come down at six. I'm sure your aunt's tired and will need a rest after tea.'

'Half past five, please?' Michelle begged.

'Six.' Anthony didn't waver.

Knowing better than to press further the girls filed out.

Eleanor still stood, forcing Anthony to remain standing. His legs felt like blancmange. This woman had every reason to hate him, and from her cool appraisal it seemed she did.

At length she sat and motioned to the chair opposite. He sat with relief.

'My sister wrote much about you,' she began, after what was to him an interminable pause.

'I loved her deeply, you understand,' he blurted out. 'We were soon to be married.' Was he excusing his behaviour? No! Whatever this woman thought of him, his love for Adelle was beyond reproach. He raised his chin, ready for any blow she might deliver.

She sighed. 'I know she felt deeply for you also. But I feared nothing good could come of it. You must realize it's difficult for me to . . .' She dabbed at her eyes with a black lace handkerchief. 'When, but for you, she'd be alive today.'

The blow was mortal. Anthony covered his face and sobbed.

'Oh, forgive me,' she said quickly and dabbed at her eyes again. 'I hadn't planned . . . I allowed my own grief to run away with my tongue. I can see you're as heartbroken as her own family.' She gave him a searching look and Anthony felt she could see through to his bones. She went on, her voice softer, 'My sister was childlike and impetuous – most endearing qualities. But she was also a sincere person. I know she couldn't have fallen in love lightly. Of course, it was only natural at first to think that if this hadn't happened . . . But what's the use now? You mustn't hold yourself to blame.' She sniffed and used the handkerchief again.

He looked straight at her, his lips trembling. 'You can't know how much I wish it had been *my* life!'

She turned her dark eyes on him, so unlike her sister's bright gaze, but her expression was warm now. 'I begin to see why she gave her heart to you.' She rose and smoothed down her skirts. 'We must talk more after dinner. Now I should like to go to her tomb alone, if you don't mind. And then I shall take a rest. I've had a tiring and distressing journey.'

Anthony stood and bowed again. 'Of course, Miss Pagnol.'

But she raised her hand in restraint. 'Please, call me Eleanor. We were, after all, almost family.'

He nodded.

'I understand Eva is preparing tea,' she said. 'Would you mind asking her to bring mine to my room when I return from the chapel.'

'As you wish.'

He watched her as she left, tall and statuesque. Though opposite from her sister in appearance and manner, she had the same distinction he'd noticed in Adelle that first day – a regal quality he'd seen in no other woman. He sighed with relief. Michelle and Arlette would be in good hands.

After dinner Eva packed the girls off to bed and Anthony and Eleanor withdrew to the drawing room for coffee.

They sat again by the fire, facing each other. Though in the firelight her face looked softer and younger, it held none of the girlish, ephemeral quality that had drawn him to Adelle. It was hard to believe there was only four years' difference in their ages.

She sipped her coffee and set the cup on the chair-arm. 'I shall take the girls back to France as soon as I've made arrangements.'

His stomach suddenly felt like a tight ball of string. Why had he imagined the aunt would remain here? That the children would be brought up in the place their mother had loved, and they loved also?

'They like it there,' Eleanor continued, 'and the weather is kinder.

296

Besides, this place holds too many unhappy memories for them at the moment. I know they're fond of you. I will of course allow them to correspond with you. And you'd be welcome to visit them if you wished.'

'Thank you,' Anthony said automatically, while his head spun with dismay and confusion. His sadness at the thought of not seeing the girls again surprised him. He hadn't even considered them while making his plans. Yet they'd be distraught if he left their lives as their mother had. How could he deal them another blow of bereavement? But he longed to end his life and join Adelle. Was he being totally selfish? Would she wish him to live and comfort her children? He felt Eleanor's eyes on him and forced himself to speak, though the words didn't seem to come from him: 'Of course I should like to write to the girls and visit them. I love them as if they were my own.'

That was true. How could he desert the only two people left in his life he held dear? They'd lost their father, then their mother, and now looked on him as family. He ran a hand over his head. He was being pulled in two directions, he felt torn apart.

Eleanor peered at him with concern. 'Are you feeling ill?'

He must compose himself, give her his full attention. 'No, forgive me. I was distracted for a moment.' He straightened in his chair and forced himself to look at her.

She met his gaze levelly. 'I understand that you must put the pieces of your own life together again. Adelle told me of your responsibilities, your family estate. But if you told the girls you will visit them from time to time it would make their parting less distressing.'

The words came out: 'Yes, yes, I will.'

'Of course, I shall keep on this place as Adelle did. It's the girls' inheritance, this and my home in France.'

'It's comforting to know they're well provided for.'

'Yes, financially! But emotionally I fear they've been terribly deprived. I intend to do my best to be a mother to them, inadequate though I feel.' She sighed and rose. 'And now you must excuse me. My journey has tired me more than I thought and I have many arrangements to make tomorrow. I'll tell the girls in the morning. But I'll soften the blow with the news that you'll visit them.'

Lying in bed Anthony remembered Eleanor's words. Put the pieces of his life back together! What pieces? He could never go back to his house now. And Eleanor had elicited that commitment from him! He

297

couldn't break his promise to Michelle and Arlette. At least – a thought occurred to him – not for a while, not until they'd had time to adapt to their new life. Children were resilient. They would form new friendships and need him less.

In the meantime he would go away. Far, far away. And be alone. Truly alone without another living soul around him. All his life he'd been alone yet surrounded by people. Now he wanted absolute solitude, endless loneliness, infinite silence – to think, to remember, to decide.

He sat up in bed as the idea came to him. The Isle of Skye! Adelle's dream of visiting it! He'd go and experience it for her, and share it with her. He'd fill his days and nights only with Adelle. She'd show him which path to take in his wilderness.

Chapter Twenty-Eight

Within two days Eleanor had organized the journey to France. The girls were cheered by the impending trip but sad at leaving their favourite home – and Anthony. While the carriage waited to take them to Newcastle, the first leg of their long excursion, they hung round his neck.

'Goodbye, Uncle Anthony,' Michelle said through her tears. 'You *will* visit us soon, promise?'

'Promise? Promise?' Arlette begged him with wet eyes.

'I promise.' He unravelled their arms from his neck and straightened. 'And now, your Aunt Eleanor's waiting.'

He took the gloved hands Eleanor held out and she gave him her now familiar level gaze. 'We shall all look forward to your visits.'

He felt warmed that she'd included herself. In their brief acquaintance he'd grown to like this woman. Beneath her strong exterior he'd discovered the same kindness and gentleness he'd loved so much in Adelle.

The driver bundled the girls into the carriage and helped Eleanor in. When he nudged the horses to a trot three hands waved out of the back window. A lump formed in Anthony's throat. He waved back, feeling his final aloneness like a sharp pain.

He returned to the house to find Eva furiously rearranging cushions in the drawing room. For the first time she didn't attempt to hide her tears.

He tried to comfort her. 'They'll be back, Eva.'

She nodded and sniffed, still plumping cushions. 'Aye, sir, I know.'

'I've made my own arrangements and I'll be leaving tomorrow,' he told her.

She punched the cushions harder and sniffed again. 'I'll be that sorry to see you go, sir. But I'll keep this house going just as I always did.' She straightened and looked him in the eye. 'Begging your pardon, sir. I know it's not my place, but if you ever want to come back here . . . for any reason, I'm quite certain Miss Eleanor wouldn't mind.'

Again he felt touched and put his hand on her shoulder. 'I know that too, Eva. Thank you. I'm going to say goodbye to my parents now and I'll be leaving first thing in the morning.'

'It would give me pleasure to pack your bags, sir.'

'Thank you.' The lump in his throat started again. He left the room hurriedly. He had so much to thank Eva for.

'The Isle of Skye!' Richard leaned forward in his chair by the main drawing room fire, his eyes popping in amazement.

Mildred's mouth opened and closed like a landed fish before she managed to get her words out: 'Whatever for? Live in that . . . that wasteland? With those Scottish barbarians? When you've got a comfortable home here?'

Anthony rose from the sofa and stood between them, hands behind his back, chin forward. 'I didn't say I was going to live there for ever. But I need to get away for a while. And Skye is my choice.'

'For God's sake, for how long?' Richard's eyes were back in their sockets but his face was still incredulous.

'I have no idea, sir. For however long it takes me to discover what I must do with my life.'

'But you know what you must do with your life! Your life is cut out for you here. You have responsibilities!' Though Richard's voice rose in anger Anthony remained calm.

'I'm aware of my position here, sir, but I must get away to clear my mind. I have decisions of my own to make.'

Mildred fluttered her lace handkerchief. 'Decisions of your own! You're thinking only of yourself again. Don't you think it's time you thought of your duty to your father?'

'I have thought of that. But I know that the best thing I can do for myself – and everyone – is to be alone for a while. I leave first thing in the morning.'

'Oh! The morning!' Mildred's handkerchief fluttered again.

Richard grunted and stood with his back to the fire. His hands at his sides clenched and unclenched but his expression was resigned, even sad. 'Well, it seems there's no stopping you, boy. I suppose you'll need money for the journey.'

'Thank you, but I have more than enough for my needs, sir. I've

300

spent little of my allowance over the past months.'

The luncheon gong sounded and Mildred rose. She crumpled the handkerchief in her hand. 'Would it be too much to ask you to stay to luncheon? You've spent little enough time at home lately. At least honour us with your company on your last day.'

She'd said 'us'! Her tone didn't sound sarcastic. 'I'd be delighted to stay, Mother,' he said, smiling. At least he would make his parting as congenial as possible.

Richard had insisted his driver take Anthony to Carlisle for the first stage of his journey. From there he would take the train to Inverness via Perth and would travel by stage to Kyle of Lochalsh, his last stop on the mainland.

After the luxury of the motor car the cold, soot- and smoke-filled train ride was only the beginning of his uncomfortable journey. Yet his bodily discomfort proved a balm to his mental anguish. He endured the overnight stops at dubious inns, eating food of doubtful origin and unutterable flavour with no thought of complaint. It was as if these physical trials were a necessary part of his greater ordeal – that of finding, or losing, his soul.

The final road, or rather track, to Kyle of Lochalsh was steep and rutted and the 'stage' an open cart. The only passenger on the last lap of the journey, Anthony hung on to the side rail for support while his bag careened around the floor.

The driver whoaed the horse and yelled, 'This is it, sir. Best you walk from here. I've stuck me cart once too often in this weather – that boggy it is.'

Anthony shook himself. He stared at the scattered grey stone cottages surrounded by fog-soaked moors, volcanic rock and shadowy hills. Ahead lay what appeared to be a wide bay but it was difficult to decide where the dark grey water stopped and the sky began. Though late morning, the light was wan and weird, like dusk before a storm.

The driver jumped down and broke into a knowing grin. 'The last bit of civilization you'll be seeing, sir.'

Anthony alighted and stared again at the melancholy landscape while the driver fetched his bag from the cart. 'I don't get many wanting to go this far, sir,' he said, setting the bag beside Anthony. 'Especially no at this time of year.' He nodded towards the water. 'That there's the Sound of Sleat, separates the island from the mainland.'

301

'Where do I take the ferry to Skye?' For the first time Anthony wondered if he was doing the right thing. Isolation he longed for, but this was desolation. Despite its weird beauty the starkness of the place and the swirling fog round the ghostly peaks filled him with a sense of impending doom. And the people? Were they 'barbarians' as his mother had said?

The man pointed a dirty finger at a clump of cottages. 'The pier's yon side of there, though the ferry'll no be going today I think.' He pushed back his cap and scratched his head. 'But auld Hamish might take you for a special price or a dram of whisky if you've got one on you. His is the hoose yon side of the landing.'

'Thank you. How much do I owe you?'

He stroked his bristly chin. 'Och, let's say fifteen shillings, sir.'

Knowing the price was outrageous for a twenty-five-mile cart ride, Anthony couldn't help smiling at the man's artless robbery. He handed him eighteen shillings. After all, he'd been the only passenger for most of the journey.

The man raised his cap. 'Well, didn't I know you were a gentleman just. Thank you indeed, sir.'

Anthony picked up his bag and waved to the driver before making for the cottages. His fine leather shoes and spats, already muddy and scuffed from his multiple ordeals on the journey, sank into the slippery bog. Yet strangely his spirits rose again. It didn't matter what the place was like. At least here he would find his solitude!

As he neared the cottages doors opened and figures surged towards him – men, women and children clad in shabby, torn clothing, jerseys over jerseys, scarves and shawls on top, and scarves round their heads. Even the men and boys wore scarves over their caps.

'Good day to you, sir,' the man in the lead said. His face was covered in at least a week's growth of black stubble and his beaked nose shone from somewhere in the middle of the black mass like a beacon on a moonless night. His smile revealed a set of teeth the colour of the boggy landscape. 'Can we help you, sir?'

Anthony returned the smile hesitantly, overwhelmed by the natives' tribal welcome. 'Well, er, I'm looking for the ferryman.'

'Aye, that's me! Hamish's the name.' He held out a hand encased in a moth-eaten wool glove.

His followers gathered in a circle and inspected the visitor with undisguised pleasure and curiosity, taking in his finely tailored greatcoat, incongruous top hat, and inadequate city footwear.

302

Anthony lowered his gaze under their scrutiny. 'I'd like to go today, now, if possible.'

Hamish pulled on his porcupine chin. 'The noo, eh? Well, I was no planning on going today.' He looked up at the torpid sky. 'But the wind's no too bad. If you don't mind it a little choppy?'

'No, no, I don't mind.' Nothing could be worse than the ordeals he'd already endured.

'It'll cost you.'

'I know that. How much do you want?'

'Five shillings,' Hamish said without hesitation.

Again Anthony found himself smiling. Already he was beginning to understand the local people. If they weren't barbarians they were at least rogues. He knew the crossing was no more than fifteen minutes. 'Five shillings it is,' he said, putting his hand in his pocket.

Hamish's beady brown eyes widened with surprise and delight as he snatched the money. Anthony wondered, was he expected to bargain?

'Why, noo, I no mind putting meself oot for a gentleman. Come with me, sir. We'll take Wee Peggy.' Hamish turned towards the pier.

Anthony followed him. 'Wee Peggy?' He wasn't expecting another passenger.

'Aye, Wee Peggy's the little boat, no point in taking Big Peggy oot for one passenger.'

The ancient rowboat creaked and groaned as Hamish stepped in and held out a helping hand. Anthony noticed with dismay that the floor was covered with at least three inches of water. He hesitated with one foot on the passenger bench. 'Er, isn't the boat leaking?'

'Och, aye! She's taken in ever since the day I got her but she hasn't gone under yet. You'll stay dry if you keep your feet up on the bench just, and your bag. And if you wouldn't mind bailing a bit with that pail.' He eyed Anthony's elegant footwear and shook his head. 'You're going to need some gumboots if you're bent on staying long. Them's no proper clothes you're wearing for the likes of here.'

Anthony realized he should have thought of that and wondered what Eva had packed for him. He braced himself across the bench, knees bent almost to his chin, and for the hundredth time on his journey thought of Adelle. She would have suffered even this hardship with amusement.

'That's right,' Hamish went on, 'and noo, see, I'll stow your bag under your knees so it'll be anchored just, and won't that leave your hands free to bail?'

It was a tortuous position but Anthony took the zinc pail Hamish held out and began scooping and twisting to dunk the water over the sides. Soon he was caught up in the rhythm. He needed the physical activity after so many days travelling. But the black water glowered up at him and he grimaced. The River Styx! Would he ever reach the other side? And if so, would he return?

'So it's a relative you're visiting, eh?' Hamish shouted over the thrashing of the waves as he pulled on the oars. 'And who might that be?'

'No relative. I wish to rent a cottage.' Anthony's voice came in gasps as he contorted his body over the side once more.

Hamish stopped rowing for a second and the boat, left to the mercy of the waves, bobbed even more perilously. 'Well I'll be!' He pulled on the oars again. 'Och, man, this is no a place to rent a cottage. And, begging your pardon, but why would a gentleman like you want to come all the way oot here if you've no got kin here?'

'I simply wish to live alone for a while and to see the island.' Anthony hadn't even given a thought to the local people's reaction to his strange sojourn. But he didn't care if they thought him odd.

Hamish gave him a curious look and went on, 'Well, noo, if you've no kin I'll get you straight to Megan. She takes in the odd visitor in the summer. She doesn't use the room herself since her family went.'

'But I don't wish to be a guest,' Anthony insisted. 'I want to rent a cottage.'

'Och, man, that's easier said than done. Families live in the cottages, have done for generations. Excepting Jock's cottage's been empty a year nigh on, since he went to Glasgow to work. But it's up for sale, not to rent.' He furrowed his brow till it looked like a ploughed field. 'But I'll get Megan to sort you oot.' He chortled and wiped his mouth with the back of his hand. 'If ever a woman can sort anybody oot it's Megan.'

At the landing stage a crowd had already gathered to greet the new arrival. Dressed like their neighbours on the mainland, they were if anything even more curious and welcoming.

A wizened, chinless little man, almost invisible under his mountain of clothing, was the first to speak. 'Och, noo, I see you got a passenger, Hamish.' He removed his clay pipe from his mouth, the only clear definition between his face and his neck, and conferred on Anthony a grin that seemed to slit his throat.

In return Hamish again exposed his dung-coloured teeth. 'Aye, I've

304

got a passenger all right, Ally.' He tied the boat and helped Anthony step on shore. 'And he's looking for a cottage to rent. What do you think of that?'

Ally pushed his wrinkled face close to Anthony's, scrutinized it, then surveyed him from top to toe. 'My, well, that's something noo!'

Even more curious at the mention of a stranger renting a cottage, the islanders closed in and examined Anthony further. He shuffled from one foot to the other.

Hamish bellowed over the crowd. 'Would anybody know where Megan is?'

A woman's voice boomed from the rear, 'Aye, I'm here, Hamish.' The crowd parted as Megan surged forward like a battleship breaking waves. A barrel of a woman, her layers of thick jerseys and shawls over her numerous skirts accentuated her roundness. Her sea-grey eyes considered Anthony. 'I suppose it's a room you're needing?'

'Well, actually, I'm looking for a cottage to rent.' This time Anthony anticipated the crowd's astonished expressions.

But Megan smiled and her face turned into a maze of cheerful wrinkles. 'Och, man, there's no a cottage for rent but I can rent you the room and feed you like a king.'

Anthony persevered. 'I thank you for your offer but Hamish tells me there's a cottage for sale. Perhaps the owner would let me rent it until such time as he sells it.'

'Jock's cottage?' Megan looked disappointed, then went on unwillingly, 'Aye, I suppose he'd be glad to earn a bit on it in the meantime. But you'd be more comfortable with me. That dump hasn't been lived in nigh on a year and it was no too clean when he left it neither.'

'That's no problem,' Anthony said quickly. 'I can clean it.'

Megan looked at him as if he'd said he would burn the place down. 'Och, that's no a man's work! And certainly not a gentleman's! If you're bent on taking it we'll clean it up for you.' A murmur of assent spread among the women. 'But first you come to my hoose and I'll give you a bite and a sup of tea. You look half frozen.'

'Thank you.' Anthony sighed inwardly with relief. He could certainly use something to eat and a hot drink. And after that – his own private place. It hadn't been so difficult after all. Suddenly it occurred to him that he hadn't introduced himself. He must seem rude. He'd noted that the people used only their first names. 'I apologize for not introducing myself earlier. My name's Anthony.' The unaccustomed informality felt strange.

305

Megan nodded. 'Aye, an English name. You'll get to know this lot in no time.' She waved her arm towards the crowd and made no attempt to present them.

Ally picked up Anthony's bag and started inland. Anthony followed, as did everyone else, even Hamish. Here the cottages were spread out, each on its own croft of land. Shepherds waved and shouted incomprehensible greetings while their dogs barked. Women leading tethered cows stopped their chores and joined in the chorus. Doors opened and a miscellany of men, women and children ran from cottages to join the party.

Anthony hoped the empty cottage would be more isolated, and as if in answer to his thoughts Megan pointed north towards a wide bay. 'Jock's cottage's up yonder by the bay,' she said. 'A bit blustery but it's no a bad spot if you don't mind having none but the gulls and sheeps for company.'

'That sounds fine,' he assured her.

They approached one of the cottages and Megan pushed open the creaking door, the iron hinges rusted from years of sea air exposure. 'Come on in just and make yourself comfortable while I brew some tea.'

Anthony had to bend his head to enter and found himself in a small kitchen furnished with a wooden table and chairs and a recessed bed in one corner. A hen clucked on one of the chairs and Megan shooed it off, grabbed a rag from one of the seemingly hundreds of nails on the walls, flicked it over the chair and moved it closer to the fire. The furniture and floors were speckled with white guano.

Ally and the rest of the entourage squeezed into the little kitchen, sitting on the bed, the chairs, the floor, chattering among themselves.

Megan unwound her headscarf and revealed a dishevelled mound of grey hair anchored precariously with a mass of black hairpins. She advanced on him. 'Noo, I'll take your coat and hat and you set yourself beside the fire just.' Before her words were out she began undoing his greatcoat.

Though embarrassed at being revealed in his frock coat and high starched collar in such casually dressed company, Anthony submitted to her attentions and sat on the dusted chair by the fire. This was obviously Gaelic hospitality and he didn't wish to appear rude. But they stared with only mild disapproval at his attire and said nothing.

Megan hung her outer shawls and scarf on a nail on the wall and Anthony's on another. Then she put the kettle on the black stove which like the rest of the room was speckled with white. She began setting the table with a platter of scones and loaves and two of the women helped, taking down mugs from the ubiquitous nails. Anything and everything hung from nails – clothing, kitchen utensils, fish and bacon.

'I'll pop over home and get some more mugs, Megan,' one of the women said.

'Aye, and your teapot and some more bread and stuff.' Megan poked the peat in the stove under the kettle and a cloud of smoke filled the room. 'But don't you lot think we're having a ceilidh the noo, there's work to be done yet.'

'A ceilidh?' Anthony asked. What could these people be planning?

Ally removed the clay pipe from his mouth and a gaping hole appeared in his face at Anthony's puzzled expression. 'Aye, you English would call it a party, but a ceilidh's what it is.'

Anthony tried to hide his dismay. 'A party! That's very kind of you but I really—'

'Och, man,' Megan cut in. 'We can't welcome a visitor without giving him a ceilidh. Just a wee one seeing that you've had a long journey just. But it'll perk up your spirits no end. And here you are, so will this.'

Anthony accepted the mug of strong sweet tea she handed him. For this he was grateful. But how could he get out of a party? When the time came he would plead a headache from travelling.

Handing him the scone platter, Megan asked the question he'd been expecting. 'And noo, tell us what brings a handsome young gentleman like you oot here where there's no a thing of interest to you? We only once had a visitor stay a long time – an auld schoolteacher who came to write a book, no like nothing of your kind.'

Anthony was grateful she'd supplied him with a ready answer. He couldn't tell these people that he'd come to lose himself in his despair, to let his thoughts and his memories take him where they willed. 'Um, as a matter of fact I'm also here to write a book,' he said, not looking at them. 'And I was also, er, *am* also a schoolteacher.'

A murmur of excitement travelled around the room.

Ally puffed out a cloud of smoke that smelled like the peat burning in the stove. 'Well, noo, I could see you was a writing man. What have you come to write about?'

Feeling guilty at his deceit, Anthony lowered his eyes again. 'I, er, I'm not quite sure yet.'

Luckily, attention was diverted to the door as the woman who'd left returned with a second teapot and a basket full of loaves and 'hame-made' blackberry jam.

Soon the tea and simple but delicious fare restored Anthony's energy. He set his mug on the table. 'That was very kind of you. But now I'd really like to see the cottage and settle in.'

Megan jumped in horror. 'Och, I told you that's no a job for a man! The lasses'll do that – right noo.' She looked meaningfully at the women and girls in the group and they jumped up at her command.

'Aye, we'll have it done in no time.' It was the woman who'd brought the teapot. She seemed to be Megan's second-in-command.

Anthony stood as she began leading out her troop. 'Thank you, er—?'

'Big Morag, that's me,' she said with a grin that scrunched up her weather-beaten face like a withered apple. 'And this here's my lassie, Wee Morag.' She looked up with pride at the girl beside her, who towered head and shoulders above her. Wee Morag, about Anthony's age, lowered her eyes and smiled shyly. Her comely face glowed with health and even her thick layers of clothing couldn't disguise her shapely build. Her brilliant red hair was pinned up haphazardly like all the women's. Anthony had never seen so many red heads in one room – shades ranging from burnished copper to orange to almost pink.

The women and girls thumped out in their gumboots across the bare floorboards while the men settled themselves more comfortably, obviously intent on staying the rest of the day.

But Megan had other plans for them. 'And you, Rory, give back Jock's gumboots and oilskins. You've had them long enough and Anthony'll be needing them. And Bruce!' She wagged a finger at a round-faced, red-headed youth. 'He'll want the bedding you took and your Mary's got the pots and pans. See that all the stuff's put back as it was. You can't expect a tenant to move into a stripped hoose.'

'Aye, aye, calm yourself, Megan.' Bruce rose from his position on the floor, where he'd snuggled up to Wee Morag throughout the tea party, giving her knee a sly stroke now and then. He stretched and ran a hand through his tousled copper hair before picking up his outdoor jersey from the floor. 'Aye, don't fret, we'll get the things right away, Megan. Come on, Rory.' Rory, a tall, heavily bearded man in his forties, muttered his unwillingness into his orange whiskers. But he heaved himself up from the floor and followed Bruce.

Megan addressed the remaining men and boys. 'And don't think you lot are getting oot of it. Them windows needs the cracks stuffing up and

308

the door's that swollen with no fire being on you'll have to hammer it open and shave a bit off. And all them that took Jock's peat had better bring some back.'

Nodding and mumbling agreement, the men stood. Anthony was amazed by the way everyone obeyed Megan. She gave her commands with calm authority and an air of absolute confidence that her word was law. 'And you, Alistair, me lad!' she said to Ally, who still sat by the stove puffing on his clay pipe. 'You'd better get a move on and get the cart. Anthony'll be needing some things from the shop.' Ally rose at her bidding and they trussed themselves up for the elements as if about to embark on an Arctic expedition.

Anthony found himself putting on his greatcoat and following them. He'd been taken over, he thought wryly. Yet he couldn't resent it. This was obviously a traditional welcome for strangers. But as soon as he was settled in he would have that quiet little cottage on the beach to himself – and the rifled contents. Again he half smiled as he wondered how Adelle would have reacted to such thieves – and such a reception. His smile grew as he realized she would have been charmed by these people, as he was. He also noted with pleasure that after he'd introduced himself no one had addressed him as 'sir'. He was pleased to be accepted as one of them.

Ally, it appeared, was Megan's husband. He disappeared round the back of the cottage and returned with a horse and cart – the cart of the same rustic variety in which Anthony had travelled on the mainland but the horse a fine young dray.

Again Anthony gazed around at the grim landscape and marvelled at the cheerful contrast of its people. They crossed a burn spanned by a rickety wooden bridge. Halfway over he noticed that the central support was splintered in two, bound only by a fraying rope. The bridge groaned and swayed under the weight of the cart. Ally laughed at Anthony's astonished expression.

'Och, man, dinna fret aboot the bridge. That rope's held it up this five year or more and it'll do a bit longer.'

Nevertheless Anthony was relieved when they rumbled to the other side. From there it was only a five-minute ride to the 'shop', which turned out to be a croft cottage like the rest. The enlarged front window displayed an assortment of necessities – bags of tea and sugar, jars of jam, cakes and various-shaped loaves. Arranged around the walls were churns of milk and sacks of flour and grains, and from the nails on the walls hung slabs of meat and fresh and smoked fish. Anthony's

309

nose twitched at the concoction of smells.

Predictably, Megan took over. 'Bonnie,' she said to the old woman who emerged from a back room, 'this is Anthony and he's come to rent Jock's cottage for a while. He'll be needing some things.'

'Well I'll be!' Bonnie stood behind the wooden counter, tilted her monkey face and gazed at him with the curiosity of a two-year-old.

But Megan gave her no time for questions. She pulled a piece of unidentifiable smoked fish from a nail and sniffed it. 'This the best you got?'

'I smoked it meself last week,' Bonnie said without a trace of offence.

'Last year more like it. It's as tough as me auld gumboots.' Megan hung the fish back on the nail. 'I've got some fresh haddie'll do better.'

Bonnie shrugged. 'It needs slow cooking, that's all.'

'Nah, I'll just have a pound of sugar, tea, flour, butter, and . . .' Megan poked her nose into a churn of milk. 'If this is today's I'll have a jug.'

'Aye, I milked Bessie meself this morning just.' Bonnie had set the prepacked bags on the counter and was cutting a slab of butter from a half-round. She slapped it on to a piece of paper and threw it on to the scale.

Megan peered at the weights as they dropped half an inch below the butter. 'It's short.'

'I know, I know, give me time noo.' Bonnie added another pat and the weights levelled.

Megan looked satisfied and Anthony watched in amusement as she helped herself to bread from the window display, punching each loaf with her knuckles to make sure it was fresh.

He pointed to a bowl of eggs on the counter. 'And I'll need some eggs,' he said.

'If you must.' Megan screwed up her nose in disapproval. 'But them's those fancy incubation things from the mainland. No a bit like fresh eggs.'

'They'll be fine,' he insisted.

She nodded her permission and examined the assortment of bags and packets on the counter. 'You forgot the milk,' she said to Bonnie. 'And we'll be needing some whisky – three flagons if you please.'

Anthony protested. 'But I don't care for whisky.'

'Och, you'll learn, me lad. You can't get through the winter months withoot a wee dram to warm your insides noo and then.'

Suddenly Anthony understood. She was stocking up for the party. He would try to postpone the obviously inevitable event but would keep silent until it was mentioned again.

'That'll be all for noo then, Bonnie,' Megan said when the milk and whisky had been added to the collection.

Bonnie surveyed the goods, nodded at each item in turn and moved her lips silently as she added up the cost. 'That'll be fourteen and six altogether.'

'Ten and six, Bonnie.'

'Aye, all right.'

A chuckle rose unbidden from Anthony's throat as he pulled the money from his pocket. So overcharging and haggling were obviously expected. The women grinned happily at one another, each pleased with her bargain.

The cart loaded, Ally flicked the reins and they took off for the cottage. This time Anthony's sigh of relief was audible. *His* cottage – and peace and quiet.

But not yet. On the return journey Megan lectured him on the do's and don'ts of buying from Bonnie. 'Never buy anything from her you can't get fresher from me or somebody else and that's just aboot everything excepting the dry goods. I've got fresh bread and milk daily and Ally's catch comes straight oot the sea, no setting on a shop counter for a week.'

Anthony assured her he would take her advice and Ally pulled up outside their cottage again. Megan jumped down with surprising agility for one of her bulk. 'I'm getting some more food and stuff just,' she shouted over her shoulder.

A few minutes later, the cart loaded with Megan's fresh supplies and Anthony's bag, they started for Jock's cottage. The moment he had longed for!

The cottage was a mile north of Megan's, and as they neared the coast Anthony was delighted that the area became less and less inhabited. Ally pointed to a grey outline in the growing dusk. 'There she is – Tigh-na-Skart.'

Anthony leaned forward to get a better view. 'What does the name mean?'

'Hoose of Skart, that's a shag – a green cormorant.'

Cormorants! How beautiful, he thought. Built of the same grey stone

311

as the rest of the island's cottages, Tigh-na-Skart squatted in sublime solitude at the far tip of the bay.

'A person could die here,' Megan said, 'and nobody would know till a crow spied it oot.'

Anthony's shoulders slumped with relief. That must mean they would leave him in peace after their welcome ceremony. The muddy road approached the cottage from the side and he could see two windows like opera glasses trained on the stage set of sea and sky. In front was the neglected croft, converging on the wasteland. A plethora of carts was parked outside the cottage. The people mustn't have finished their work yet, he thought. But he didn't care. It shouldn't take them much longer. And he was here.

Ally slowed the cart and Anthony jumped out, eager to inspect the beach. From the tideline he could see that at high tide the sea crashed no more than fifteen yards away. He stood transfixed, staring at the grey and white pulverizing waves.

Megan's voice hailed him. 'Och, come on, man. You can see all that in the morning. Get inside in the warm noo.'

She was right. His overcoat, soaked with fog, offered little resistance to the penetrating sea breeze. Tomorrow he would explore his terrain alone.

Inside, the cottage bulged with people. The kitchen, almost identical to Megan's, was scrubbed clean except for the dried-on hens' droppings, which seemed to be accepted as a form of decoration. A kettle puffed steam on the glowing stove, an array of loaves, butter, smoked fish, cold meats and sticky buns littered the wooden table – the centrepiece a clump of whisky bottles. From the inevitable mass of nails on the walls hung a conglomeration of mugs, pots, pans, kitchen utensils and the visitors' clothing.

Clutching the bottles Megan had loaded on him, Anthony gaped around in astonishment. 'Thank you all,' he forced himself to say.

Megan answered for all of them. 'Och, it's no any trouble.' She dumped her bundles of food on the table and relieved him of the bottles. 'And noo you'll be wanting a wee look at the place.' She took his arm and led him to the door off the kitchen. Bodies moved to clear a path. 'This is the room,' she said, 'but you'll be warmer sleeping in the kitchen.'

This was the room with the sea view. A large bed in the corner was made up and laden with blankets, on top of it a heap of infants and toddlers, some sleeping, some sitting up and cramming their faces with food. When he'd got over his surprise, he said with determination, 'No, Megan. I don't wish to sleep in the kitchen. I prefer this room.'

Megan shrugged. 'Please yourself. But you'll soon find oot. And noo, I'll show you where the wee hoosie is.' She led him back through the kitchen and along the side of the house to a small hut. She opened the creaking door to reveal a scrubbed wooden bench with two holes in the centre. 'I suppose you'll be needing it after all this time,' she said, pushing him inside and closing the door on him.

Anthony stood in the dark, stupefied. She was right. In all the activity since his arrival he hadn't even had time to think of such things. He felt embarrassed. Was she waiting for him outside the door? Dear Lord! Was there no privacy at all in this place? But his need overcame his inhibitions. Afterwards he opened the door and peeked out. She'd gone. He braced his shoulders to face the throng in the cottage. There was obviously no way of getting out of this ceilidh, or whatever they called it. But after tonight he would insist on his privacy.

The tea and whisky were already flowing when he returned, the women cutting thick chunks of bread and covering them with meat or fish, the older children who were allowed to stay up helping themselves to sticky buns.

Ally waved a bottle of whisky in one hand and a tin mug in the other. 'Take your coat off, man, then what you need's a wee dram to warm you up.'

'Er, no, thank you, but I'd appreciate a cup of tea.'

Ally looked at him as if he'd blasphemed in a house of God. 'No take whisky! Och, you can't celebrate withoot a wee dram.' He poured a generous serving into the mug and pressed it into Anthony's hands.

With a shrug of resignation Anthony thanked him and took it, though he sidled to the teapot and filled the mug with the hot black tea.

'You no like it neat, I see,' a female voice behind him said. It was Big Morag, grinning at his subterfuge. 'And would you like some sugar and milk in it?'

'Yes, please,' he said, feeling foolish.

'Come on noo, make way for our host.' Megan appeared with a stacked plate in her hand and led Anthony to what was obviously the place of honour – an empty chair by the fire.

Suddenly he felt grateful. The sea air had made him ravenous and the fire looked enticing. He must show appreciation and join in the party spirit. 'What a wonderful welcome, thank you,' he said to everyone

313

as he sat, the heaped plate on his lap and the spiced tea in his hand. He waved the mug around the room, 'Health, wealth and happiness to one and all.'

Countless raised mugs preceded a cacophony of replies.

After most of the food and half of the whisky had disappeared the party truly began. There came a burst of song from Wee Morag, who perched on the edge of the table dangling her gumboots: *Sean suine cha ghagh mi idir*, she began, and everyone joined in with an equally unintelligible chorus.

Anthony looked stupefied, and Ally, sitting next to him, translated in his ear: 'It's aboot a young lassie singing that an auld man's not for her.'

'Thank you,' Anthony whispered, 'but don't worry, I like to listen to the sounds.' He'd never heard Scottish Gaelic and was carried away by its music and Wee Morag's sweet soprano. He noticed that her eyes frequently travelled to Bruce, who looked back at her with an expression Anthony recognized with the pain of loss. The pair were in love. But the joy of the music and the warmth of the whisky soothed his sorrow.

One after another people stood up to sing or dance until an unknown voice from the corner shouted, 'It's Anthony's turn noo.'

'Aye, aye, come on, Anthony,' Megan urged.

He smiled, knowing he must obey Megan. 'I'm afraid I don't know any Scottish songs but I do know some Irish and English ones.'

'Aye, them's fine then,' Ally said. A general murmur of agreement followed.

Anthony sang 'The Irish Girl' and a strange feeling ran through him. His real mother had probably taught him that song, just as these people handed down their own songs to their children.

After the applause Big Morag approached him with a bottle in her hand and a wicked grin on her face. 'My, that tea's wetting your whistle just. That's a fine voice you have. I'll fill you up a wee bit.' He protested but she tipped the bottle into his mug and winked again.

Time seemed to fly and yet stand still. When the first guests began to straggle out Anthony glanced at his pocket watch. Two in the morning! He said his goodbyes and thanks to each departing group, sleeping children over shoulders, and he was assured by all that he was a fine host and gave a wonderful party.

Ally remained glued to his chair, his eyes staring into the fire, his head nodding. Megan wound his scarves round his neck and tied two jerseys round him. 'Drunk as a lord,' she said. 'Would you mind giving

314

me a hand to get him oot?' There was no note of reproach in her voice. Together they loaded him into the back of the cart and laughed as he landed on the boards with the easy thud of the drunk.

'G'night then,' he managed to say.

'Goodnight to both of you, and thank you.' Anthony waved and felt overwhelmed by relief.

He sat by the fire. The day had been unbelievable. He smiled as he looked around the room, littered with dirty plates and mugs. His own mug stood on the hearth, barely touched. What a strange wedding party it would have been for Adelle! And yet, he told himself again, she would have enjoyed it.

He groped his way into the bedroom. Too tired to unpack his bag, which he suspected Ally had left in the cart anyway, he threw off his frock coat and waistcoat, removed his footwear and tumbled into the bed. The sheets were starched and fresh. He stared through the twin windows at the blackness, listened to the thrash of the waves, and ran his hand gently over the empty space beside him on the bed. If only Adelle could have been here with him!

Chapter Twenty-Nine

Anthony awoke to the unaccustomed daylight shining through the bare windows, the waves crashing on the shore. He closed his eyes again. He hadn't slept so soundly since that awful night. And he hadn't had his nightmares of Adelle's death. Instead he'd dreamt she was running along the beach with him, holding his hand, laughing.

He blinked as the memory of the evening before rushed back. Those strange and wonderful people! But he stretched with pleasure at the thought of his final solitude in his own cottage. And the day ahead, the first since Adelle's death when he could simply be himself, have no one's feelings to consider but his own. Such luxury!

Footsteps in the kitchen catapulted him out of bed. He threw on his jacket and crept to the door in his stockinged feet. Megan was bent over the stove, shrouded in underwear hanging from the mantel line.

She extricated her head from what he now recognized as a pair of his own long johns. 'My, but you gave me a start. Good morning to you.'

'Er, good morning, Megan.' He couldn't keep the surprise from his voice, the dismay even.

But she appeared not to notice and with a wide grin pulled down his underwear, a pair of socks and a shirt from the line. 'I brought these for you and aired them. Ally left your bag in the cart all night. And I thought I'd get you a bite of breakfast while I was at it.'

Turning pink, Anthony took the proffered garments. 'Thank you but you shouldn't—'

She flapped her hands at him. 'Och, man, you're always saying that. You get dressed just and go to the wee hoosie. Your breakfast'll be ready in a wink. I brought you two nice kippers.' She picked up his riding boots from the hearth. 'And I aired these. They're better than those things you had on yesterday but you'll fare better with Jock's gumboots when Rory decides to give them up.' She pointed to his riding habit hanging on the wall. 'And them things is more sensible than that fancy suit.'

He collected the clothes and disappeared into the bedroom. Filled with dismay he dropped the riding clothes to the floor and sat on the bed, the underwear dangling over his lap. He was being taken over again, even his most personal needs monitored. Today he must be firm. In the freezing room he changed into the clean clothes. He was glad Eva had packed his riding habit.

Megan's round rear was again bent over the stove as he slid unobserved outside. When he returned, the teapot and chunks of bread and butter were already on the table. She set down a plate of steaming kippers and pulled out his chair. The kippers smelled inviting and he noted that the mess from the night's revelry had been cleared up, the remainder of his clothes hung up. 'You're spoiling me, Megan,' he said. 'I can't let you do this any more.'

'Why, man, I like to look after people.' She sat down and poured two mugs of tea. 'That Ally'll be like a dead man all day, sleeping off his booze.'

Anthony was about to sip from his mug when a loud snort from the recessed bed startled him. He slopped most of the tea on the table and stared at the bed. Almost invisible under a heap of blankets lay a figure. The balding grey head at the top he recognized as Donald's, one of the previous evening's guests.

'Take no heed of him, man.' Megan mopped the tea with her apron. 'It's only Donald. He must've lost his way home and come back last night. He'd had a barrelful as usual. He'll sleep it off just and be on his way.'

Anthony attacked the kipper in silence. So this was the aloneness he'd looked forward to waking up to! It appeared he had a self-appointed live-in housekeeper *and* an uninvited guest. He chewed the kipper vigorously and ungraciously. He'd go out for the day to explore the island and if the cottage weren't empty when he returned he'd have something to say about it. But for now he must hold his impatience. 'Is there a horse on the island I could rent?' he asked Megan.

'Aye, man, anybody would rent a nag for money lessen they're using it. Ally'll no be good for nothing all day. You can have Betty.'

Anthony remembered the fine dray. 'Does she ride well?'

'Like an angel! She's had every bairn on the island on her back since she was a wee pony. I'll take you back with me in the cart and you can have her.'

'How much for the horse for a day? And how much do I owe you for yesterday?'

Megan looked only half insulted. 'Och, you paid for the things at the shop. The rest was for the ceilidh – in your honour.'

'Well, thank you. You're very generous.' Anthony was surprised. Perhaps he'd misjudged these people.

'But it'll be a shilling for Betty and, let's say, four and six for the rent.' She rested an expectant gaze on him.

He smiled. So that was it! The islanders drew a sharp line between hospitality and business. He wondered how much of the rent his unknown and unknowing landlord would get, if any. If he didn't conform to this particular custom he'd be penniless in no time, and he had no desire to ask his father for further funds. He raised his eyebrows. 'That's five and six all together! Shall we say four shillings?'

Megan nodded with a satisfied grin.

No sooner had he placed the money on the table than she'd skimmed it up, lifted her jersey and hidden it in some unknown niche deep in the folds of her skirts.

Breakfast over, Anthony put on his greatcoat over his riding habit and accompanied Megan home. At her cottage they unharnessed Betty from the cart and Megan slapped the horse's sides. 'There you are noo! She's a trusty auld girl.'

Anthony opened his mouth to ask for her saddle, then sealed his lips. It seemed he was expected to ride her bareback, not even a bridle. He smiled as he swung himself over the huge animal and felt her warm flesh between his thighs. As a boy he'd often secretly abandoned his own saddle, and now the ripple of the animal's muscles as it inched forward at his command brought back some of his happier memories.

'You watch where you're going noo,' Megan said. 'Some of them bogs is deep enough to get stuck in.'

'I'll be careful.' He nudged Betty with his knees and turned her with gentle pressure on her mane back towards the beach – his beach. He wanted to see that first. Megan had been right. The animal was obedient and docile, obviously used to riders.

But Megan wasn't ready to let him go. 'You can no go off for the day with nothing on your head, man.'

'Please don't worry,' Anthony said. 'I like to feel the wind in my hair.' But he halted. It would be rude to leave when she was trying to be kind.

318

'Wait a minute just.' She disappeared into the cottage and returned with a cloth cap and a wool scarf. Both suspiciously resembled Ally's.

'Here you are then. These'll keep you nice and cosy.'

He relented, wound the scarf round his neck and placed the cap on his head. It was too large to be Ally's. He wondered with a smile if it belonged to his invisible landlord.

The morning was brighter than yesterday, the sky a paler grey. Only a slight sea mist hung in the air. He urged Betty to a gallop and, once out of sight, stuck the cap in his pocket. But the muffler was welcome. Oh, the freedom! The solitude! The barren wasteland! It was like riding over the far side of the moon. The muddy road looked like a slimy snake slithering across the sinister landscape, but Betty was used to it and sure-footed.

When he reached the beach it was like an embrace. He dismounted and led Betty by her mane. First he wanted to enjoy the sensation of the soft sand beneath his feet. He flung stones into the waves and collected sea shells until his pockets were full. He would decorate the cottage with them. He stooped to unearth a crab shell half buried in the sand, shook it clean and gazed with awe at its splendour, sadness at its emptiness. He knew how it felt to be a fleshless shell. How Adelle would have delighted in this beach!

He rode all day, disregarding the hunger pangs that taunted him by midday. Occasionally he returned the greeting of a lone shepherd with his sheep and dog, a cottager come out to wave to him, but he stayed as far away from signs of human life as possible. This place was what his soul needed. Adelle must have known.

By three thirty it was growing dusk. He wound his way back, making a circle from the way he'd come. Betty speeded up. She knew she was going home. But as he was about to cross an unkempt meadow with a burn at the far side she stopped and neighed. He clamped his knees tighter. 'Come on, Betty, you need another drink.' She snorted and refused to budge.

Curious, he dismounted, picked up a heavy rock and threw it into a dark, grassless spot. It disappeared in seconds. One of the deep bogs Megan had warned him about. He patted the horse's neck. 'Good girl, Betty. You've got more sense than I have.' Strange, he thought, what funds of innate knowledge animals had, whereas people had to be taught almost everything they knew. He remounted and wound along the cart track towards the burn. He would return Betty and walk the mile to his cottage.

Megan and Ally greeted him at the door. 'Dear Lord, man!' Megan said. 'We thought you'd got lost or stuck in the bog. Come on in and have a warm drink and a bite.'

This time Anthony was adamant. 'It's very kind of you but I really must get home.'

Ally gave him his cutthroat grin. 'Och, just wait till you see what Megan's made for you. Dinna be in such a hurry to get back to a freezing empty cottage, man.' He led Betty round to the back and Megan steered Anthony inside.

The kitchen was warm and something on the stove smelled wonderful. He smiled. He'd enjoyed his day alone. It wouldn't hurt to be sociable for a short time and to warm up and eat something hot. He hadn't realized how chilled he was. These people were kindness itself. 'You're spoiling me again,' he said.

Megan helped him out of his greatcoat and ushered him towards the fire. 'Why, it's a wee bit of hospitality just. I hate to think of you being all alone oot there. It's no right for a man to live alone.'

Now was a good time to remind her of his supposed mission. 'I certainly appreciate your hospitality, but you forget I came here to be alone . . . to, er, write.'

'Write?' Megan chastised him with a look. 'Nobody in their right minds would put work before having a good time. Work and pleasure – you've got to balance them oot.' She poked the steaming kettle further over the fire.

'But I must,' Anthony insisted. 'Otherwise I shall never finish what I came to do.' Despite his words the corners of his mouth twitched into a smile. Obviously work was not a priority for these people.

Ally returned and shut the door behind him. 'There's time enough for work tomorrow. Betty's fair wore oot. Always on the go you are! Relax a wee bit, man.' He poured whisky into three mugs.

'Tea will be fine for me, thank you,' Anthony said.

But Ally continued to pour. 'You've still no acquired a taste for it, I see.'

Megan took a rag from the mantel line and lifted the kettle from the stove. 'I'll make you a nice hot toddy with it. Even a two-year-auld can drink that.' She poured hot water into one of the mugs, added sugar and thrust it in his hand.

Anthony thanked her and took a sip.

'There noo, isn't that fine just! Warms your innards!' She glowed with pleasure as she watched him drink.

'It does indeed,' he said. And it did. Perhaps he was acquiring a taste for it after all.

Ally sat beside him, knocked back his whisky and filled his pipe, his face a picture of contentment. 'I bet you've never tasted mutton stew like Megan's,' he said, as she thrust herself between them. She bent at the fire, her round bottom again in its full-moon position, and ladled the chunky mixture into three bowls.

Ally was right. Anthony had never tasted mutton stew like it. After three helpings he waved away Megan's fourth offering. 'You're a splendid cook, Megan, but no more, thank you.'

'Didn't I know just you'd be half starved? Oot all day and nothing in your belly since your breakfast!'

'Please let me pay for this,' Anthony said. 'I can't possibly accept all this hospitality without returning it.'

'Och, aye!' Ally puffed on his pipe, which exuded an overwhelming odour like burning manure. 'That was a fine ceilidh you gave last night and you can give plenty more. How aboot tomorrow night? After you've got some of your work done.'

Anthony groaned inside. 'I will indeed, but not tomorrow, I'm afraid. In the meantime please let me pay you.' He put his hand in his pocket but Ally shook his head.

'Nay, man! You can have it the next night then. I haven't got over last night's yet anyway.' He rubbed his hand over his wrinkled forehead and pulled a face.

Anthony remembered the thud of Ally's dead-drunk body as it collapsed into the cart and marvelled that any man could even be on his feet after such a binge. 'Thank you again, and now if you'll excuse me?' He stood. But they both got up.

'You're no going to walk back in the dark,' Megan said. 'We'll take you in the cart, won't we, Ally?'

'Aye, it's a raw night for walking.'

Anthony knew better than to argue. 'If you insist.' He put on his greatcoat. Tomorrow he would walk around the island. Much as he loved riding Betty, at least he wouldn't be at the mercy of Megan and Ally.

At Tigh-na-Skart he climbed from the cart and thanked Megan and

Ally again. But Megan was down as fast as he was. 'I'll show you how to light the fire just. I'll bet a fine gentleman like you's never lit one in your life, and peat's hard to get going.'

Anthony was about to say he could manage but swallowed his words. Again she was right. He'd seen how the wood and coal fires were built at home but had no experience of peat. After this he would be independent.

The cottage was freezing. Megan busied herself immediately laying fresh peat in the grate, lighting it here and there and fanning it with her apron, then another layer and more fanning. Finally, on hands and knees, she puffed and blew until the room was filled with smoke, but a faint glow had started in the hearth.

In the meantime Ally was warming up in his own way. 'Cheers, then.' He raised a mug he'd filled with whisky and knocked it back. Megan straightened with a grunt and he filled a mug for her. Then to Anthony's disbelief and dismay they sat by the fledgling fire.

Megan sipped her whisky. 'Aye, just a wee dram to warm up, and then we'd better leave Anthony to his work.'

Two 'wee drams' later Megan stood. 'Come on, Ally, we'd best let Anthony get on noo if he's going to have time for that ceilidh.' She turned to Anthony as she pulled on her outdoor jerseys. 'I'll set the word around. You can expect us just before dark.'

So it was considered planned! How could he get out of it without being discourteous? And just before dark here meant about three in the afternoon! 'I'd really rather make it another day,' he said, feeling guilty.

Megan only smiled. 'All right then, Friday? You'll be needing a break from all that work by then.'

Anthony nodded. Friday it would be.

Alone in the now warm kitchen he did in fact write. Eva had packed his diary. He hadn't made an entry since Adelle's death, his days' events and his thoughts and nightmares too terrible to record.

He sat at the table and opened the expensive red leather cover, the matching fountain pen clipped inside. Every Christmas he received a new one from his mother. He thought of Mildred. She wasn't his mother. He chewed on the pen then banished the thought. It would do no good to contemplate that matter now.

He started to write, skipping the blank pages from the time of Adelle's death. He began as if writing to her, commencing that day:

You would not believe this place, my darling, and its people. They are so simple, so friendly, so real. They have little, yet live every minute of their lives to the full. When I think of my parents' rich but empty life it is difficult to imagine that these two realities exist in the same world. I wish that even once I had seen the same look of simple pleasure and joy of life on my parents' faces as on Megan's and Ally's tonight.

I came here to wallow in my grief, to make my decision on what to do with my life, but they won't give me time to brood. I even find myself smiling with them, real smiles, not the kind I have been giving to Arlette and Michelle since you left us. But I must not allow them to take me over. I still have my mission here, and I shall now have my privacy until Friday, when I have been coerced into giving another party.

You would have loved my unusual ride today. I thought about you every moment, yet strangely, mostly about small insignificant things we said or did – the time you laughed and chastised me for cursing when I tripped and fell over that tree root in the woods. I was angry because I felt so unmanly, and you delighted in my ridiculous posture. Finally, I laughed with you. Do you remember? You taught me so much. And, different as these islanders are from you, I find a similarity. You share the same simplicity and optimism. I haven't yet learned that. I wonder if I ever shall? Perhaps you will teach me yet, or perhaps it's too late for me to learn. But whatever happens, I know you will be guiding me.

Suddenly feeling chilled, he put down his pen. He'd forgotten the fire. He grimaced at the dark mass in the grate and chided himself for being so helpless and spoilt. But it was almost time for bed anyway. He would have an early night and get up at dawn tomorrow. He retrieved a nightshirt Megan had hung near the fire and smiled. His nightwear had probably amused her. He couldn't imagine the islanders going to bed in anything but their jerseys and gumboots.

Remembering the shells in his greatcoat pocket, he arranged them on the bedroom windowsills. Without the kitchen fire and the warmth of human bodies of the previous night, the room was frigid. He pulled his nightshirt over his underwear and huddled in the damp bed. A sharp breeze blew in from the stuffed cracks around the windows. The lamp flickered. He'd forgotten it – and the kitchen lamp. Shivering, he got up and crammed the hay around the window frames more tightly, blew out both lights and climbed back into bed.

Again he stroked the empty place beside him and recalled the wondrous nights with Adelle in his arms. But despite the chill bed his eyes closed with weariness from the day's exercise and the sea air. He dreamed again of Adelle running and laughing on the beach with him.

He awoke early, still cold. Pulling on his greatcoat over his nightshirt he made his pilgrimage to the 'wee hoosie' and then knelt to light the fire. How was it Megan had done it? However it was, his efforts were less effective. But within half an hour he'd created a faint glow. Except for the smoke-filled kitchen and his stinging eyes he would have been elated with his success. Coughing, he filled the kettle from the water pail and set it on the trivet. Puny though the fire was, the sooner the kettle got started the sooner he'd have a hot drink inside him, and breakfast. He stared at the various smoked fish on the dresser but had no idea what to do with them. He would try eggs.

In the bedroom he flung on his clothes of the day before. He needed a bath. A zinc tub hung on the wall outside. But he could never boil that much water. He would settle for a hot wash later when the kitchen had warmed up. First something to eat.

He unhooked a frying pan from a nail, eased the kettle to the edge of the stove and set the pan beside it. Black smoke engulfed it. He wafted the smoke away and took three eggs from the bowl. As a boy he'd seen Cook breaking eggs. She held them in one hand and hit them against the edge of the pan. He tried one. Half the shell and half the white and yolk spluttered in the smoke-blackened pan, the other half disappeared into the flames. He tried with the second egg. This time he used both hands and, though he managed to get it all into the pan, the yolk oozed and mingled with the white. He decided not to attempt the third.

A few minutes later, picking out the splintered shell from the flesh, he tried to swallow some of the leathery omelette. He gave up and settled for a chunk of bread and butter. Well, it was his first attempt, he reasoned, though he thought with nostalgia of his feast of kippers the previous morning.

A woman's laughter outside jerked him out of his chair. He ran to the window. Bruce approached, pushing a garden wheelbarrow. Wee Morag reclined inside, her gumbooted legs dangling over the edge. Bruce tipped the barrow this way and that while she clung on, her childlike giggles as sunny as a May morning.

Anthony couldn't help smiling. Then he ran a hand over his brow.

More visitors! He withdrew to the side of the window out of sight. If he didn't answer their knock they would think he wasn't at home. The giggles grew louder, followed by a piercing shriek. He sneaked a glance out of the window and withdrew again. Bruce had dumped Wee Morag outside the door in the dirt. There she sat, helpless with mirth.

Though charmed by their innocent fun Anthony pressed himself against the wall. Was it too much to ask for one day to himself? The expected knock came, succeeded immediately by a crash. The door burst open and, still laughing, they thundered into the room. Wee Morag recovered herself enough to speak.

'Och, there you are! A good morning to you, Anthony.'

'Aye, and a fine one, isn't it?' Bruce straightened his face but only for a moment. He grinned again and nudged Wee Morag in the ribs. 'I think the weather's gone to her head. There's no controlling her today.'

Wee Morag's laughter broke afresh. It seemed to rise from her gumboots. 'Away with you, man. You're the one started it.'

'I see you found a good use for the wheelbarrow,' Anthony said. Though a twinge of envy shot through him he pushed it aside and smiled at the pair of happy faces. To make amends for begrudging them their happiness and resenting their intrusion, he indicated the table. 'Would you like tea?'

Wee Morag nodded. 'Aye, that would be lovely. Ma sent you some girdle scones, fresh baked this morning.'

'Girdle scones?'

'You know, made on the girdle, no in the oven.' She looked at him with disbelief. 'Don't tell me you've never had girdle scones?'

It was Anthony's turn to grin. 'Ah, yes, griddle scones. Where I come from a girdle is something quite different.'

'I'll get them,' Bruce said. 'You left them in the barrow, you dumb-cluck.'

Anthony poked the kettle back over the fire but Wee Morag snatched the poker from him. 'Och, that's a woman's work. I'll see to the tea.'

Relieved, he sat at the table and watched as she bustled about emptying the teapot into the slop pail and setting mugs on the table. She peered at his uneaten breakfast and picked up the plate. 'What's this then?'

'Fried eggs,' Anthony confessed. 'My first effort. I'll do better next time.'

'I hope so.' Screwing up her nose, she scraped the congealed black and yellow mess into the pail. It fell with a plop into the cold tea remains. She gave him a pitying look. 'It's a sad sight to see a man fending for himself. I'd be glad to cook for you.'

Anthony waved his hands. 'Thank you for your kind offer but I need to learn. Perhaps you could give me a few tips though.'

'Aye, I'll do that then, if you're bent on it.' She leaned over the hissing kettle, her shapely rear view a far cry from Megan's enormous globe. Anthony stifled a chuckle at the contrast.

'There you are noo!' Bruce dumped a plate covered with a tea towel on the table. 'Her ma makes the best girdle scones you've ever tasted.'

Wee Morag giggled as she carried the teapot to the table. 'Don't let Megan hear you say that noo.'

The scones were delicious and the tea tasted like tea. Anthony wondered how from the same leaves and water he'd managed to make such a flavourless brew.

Bruce smacked his lips with relish and wiped his mouth with the back of his hand. 'We thought we'd take you to collect some driftwood. That's why we brought the barrow.'

'Aye,' Wee Morag said, 'we're getting some ourselves anyway. If you stack it by the side of the stove till it dries oot, it helps to keep the peat going.'

Surprised, Anthony heard himself saying, 'Thank you, that's a wonderful idea.' The thought of having some exercise on the beach pleased him and he could certainly use something to help with the fire.

They stayed out until it was almost dark, Anthony diligently collecting driftwood, the lovers spending most of their time cavorting on the beach like young mules let out to pasture.

Bruce galloped up to him with Wee Morag on his back. With one of her legs he pointed behind Anthony. 'You missed a fine piece there,' he said, as if chastising him for his inefficiency. 'And it's time we got back the noo. Me belly's rumbling.'

Wee Morag wriggled from his back. Three large fish dangled from her neck, tied by the tails with string.

She laughed at Anthony's expression. 'We met auld Mac up the beach and he gave us these for tea.'

Anthony smiled. Of course, it was inevitable they would invite themselves back. He and Bruce pushed the unwieldy barrow over the sand until they reached the cart track. Here it was easier to manoeuvre and Wee Morag, giggling as usual, climbed on top of the wood heap. She sat astride, her legs spread in a most unladylike fashion, the fish

326

dangling down her bosom like a grotesque necklace. 'Gee up!' she said. 'Let's get this horse to the stable.'

'Lazy beggar that one!' Bruce gave a hopeless shrug, and he and Anthony put all their strength into pushing their heavy load.

At the cottage the men stacked the wood allotted to Anthony while Wee Morag danced about the room in a sudden fit of industry. She encouraged the failing fire and began the meal. Instructing Anthony all the while, she scrubbed potatoes and boiled them in salted water, gutted the fish, rubbed in salt and set them in a pan of sizzling lard. 'There, noo,' she said. 'It's easy, see.'

Inevitably, after the wood was stacked, Bruce set to work on the whisky. This time Anthony accepted his own neat. He coughed at the first sip but afterwards it numbed his throat and he swallowed it with increasing pleasure. When he set down his empty mug Bruce looked on with approval. 'Why, man, you downed that like a true Scot.'

Anthony smiled. 'I'm a fast learner.'

The fish turned out to be herring and Anthony ate voraciously. He'd never eaten such plain yet delicious food as in the past few days.

After the meal Wee Morag and Bruce helped themselves to more whisky and sat with their mugs by the fire. Anthony joined them. He'd given up expecting anyone who visited to leave before bedtime. Besides, he'd lost his initial envy of their love and enjoyed breathing in the happiness in the air around them.

Wee Morag's freckled face, glowing from the whisky and the fire, turned to him. 'Megan's coming round to give you a hand with the ceilidh tomorrow. And Ma and me'll come as well.'

The ceilidh! He'd forgotten. 'Oh, yes, of course,' he said. After all, he *had* agreed to it. But in any case he'd now accepted the probability that he would have visitors every day, invited or not.

When the lovers had made their noisy exit Anthony sat at the table with his diary and again wrote to Adelle of the day's events.

Afterwards he put down his pen and stared into space. So far he'd done none of the contemplation he'd planned. He'd done nothing but eat, drink and enjoy other people's happiness. Even though his pleasure was vicarious, he was beginning to *feel* again. He'd thought that impossible. And in such a short time! Was he being disloyal to Adelle? He shook his head at the thought. No, she would have wanted him to feel. Since her death, although he'd gone through the motions of caring

327

for the children, he'd been numb, had felt nothing but duty.

Suddenly he saw Adelle as on the first night they'd made love, wagging an admonishing finger at him and saying, 'You've got your whole life ahead of you.' Had he? Was there still a life for him to live? He sighed. When he'd arrived his soul had been like this island – barren, windblown. It was still, but now, again like the island, it was inhabited. The islanders had created life out of their wilderness. Was it possible that he could one day do the same? He could never love another woman. That place in his heart had been buried with Adelle. But he'd discovered he could share in others' love, and lives. Yet his grief was as sharp as ever.

He was too tired to think any more. He'd go to bed and hope he'd dream again of Adelle on the beach.

Chapter Thirty

Day followed day and Anthony grew stronger in mind and body. He'd learned to milk Megan's cow, had tended old Amos's sheep when a broken leg had confined him to his cottage, and had generally offered his services whenever he could be of use. But his most difficult though enjoyable task had been taking over the schoolhouse. Aggie, the schoolteacher, had suffered a prolonged bout of prostration after eating undercooked wild rabbit. Without Anthony's help this would have meant the school's closing for the duration.

That first day, full of confidence, he'd addressed his assortment of pupils, ranging in age from six to thirteen. 'Good morning to you all.'

'Good morning, teacher,' they'd muttered back. He'd anticipated their unwillingness. They'd been delighted at the prospect of an additional school holiday while Aggie was indisposed. But Aggie had prepared him for their recalcitrance and instructed him in his teaching duties.

He called the register and gathered the older ones at the front of the class. 'Now you, Jimmy and Mac,' he said to the two brightest, 'you're going to help the juniors with their writing while I give the seniors arithmetic.'

Jimmy pulled at his jersey and crinkled his freckled nose. 'Aggie knows I no like teaching the wee ones.'

'Yes, she told me. But she also told me you're very good at it when you put your mind to it. And you're going to do that, aren't you, Jimmy?'

He gave up playing with his jersey and wiped his nose on his sleeve. 'Aye, if I have to.'

'Good, then you give out the writing books while I start the arithmetic class next door.' Anthony closed the folding-door partition and separated the schoolroom into two classrooms. He'd need strength to get through the day. Never had he seen so many reluctant faces at once.

* * *

He spent his days supervising the classes, darting from one to the other to call order whenever a fight or a game broke out. His task was not only to cram knowledge into their unwilling heads but also to give them some sense of the importance of learning. Both jobs proved more difficult than he'd imagined.

'What do I need to learn reading for?' young Willy McDonald had wanted to know. 'When I grow up I'm going to look after me da's sheeps and I'll no be reading to them.'

The class tittered but Anthony kept his face straight. 'Obviously not, Willy, but you can read books that will give you pleasure. And there are other benefits that will help you in your life, such as . . .' There he was stuck. The islanders were happy and self-sufficient enough without learning. Though it would add another dimension to their lives their existence didn't depend on it. But he pushed on, 'And what if you decide to do something other than being a shepherd one day? Or what if you simply decide to pay a visit to the mainland. You can read street signs to help you find your way, you can read coach and train timetables if you decide to travel, bills of fare at inns.'

'Aw, you've got to have money to travel, man,' Charlie, Willy's younger brother, said. 'And where are we going to get that noo?'

Anthony was losing ground. But he persevered. 'Well, Charlie, if you can read and write you can get good jobs and *earn* money if you want to. You could even become a schoolteacher and take over from Aggie one day.' He smiled as the ten rows of faces contorted in horror.

Charlie's face wasn't simply contorted, it was positively disfigured with disgust. 'Phweeeoo! I'd rather clean oot the pigsties every day of me life till I die.'

Anthony gave up. 'All right! For the moment let's just say it's something you must do, like it or not – the same as cleaning out the pigsties. But later you'll look back and thank Aggie for all she's taught you – even if you only read one book for pleasure or learn how to add up money so you can bargain better.'

Willy McDonald's voice came from the back row: 'We knew how to do that before we started school, man.'

Again, Anthony was defeated. Willy was right. Even the older people with no education had an uncanny ability to count money. He gave the class a hopeless smile. 'Enough chatter now! Back to the lesson.'

* * *

330

He wrote to Arlette and Michelle every week. They were delighted with his accounts of life on the island, especially with his anecdotes about its inhabitants. His letters to his parents were fewer and more sober. Yet in their replies they both remarked that he sounded in better spirits. They'd now accepted his strange sojourn but in each letter enquired about his return. To that he'd given no thought. He lived one day at a time. Still, he had no desire to look ahead.

But his nightmares hadn't returned. He had only happy dreams of Adelle, though his sadness when he awoke without her remained boundless.

Spring arrived and with it peat-cutting. April and May were the best months. This allowed the peats time to dry before the inevitable wet spell at the end of June. Talk of the peat-cutting had been going on for a couple of weeks. But at a meeting in the schoolhouse the previous evening, even though the rain sheathed the windows like a glass bead curtain, it had been unanimously decided the next day would be fine. The time was right.

The next morning *was* fine. Anthony rose early and dressed in his riding habit – his 'work suit'. He pulled on three pairs of socks. They were necessary to fill his landlord's oversized gumboots. Megan had procured them from the temporary unauthorized owner.

After a quick cup of tea and the luxury of two fresh eggs, courtesy of Megan, he left to join the party at the appointed spot. He selected a pick and shovel from the assorted tools in the 'wee hoosie' and slung them over his shoulder. The sodden earth squelched at each step as he followed the track through the glen. He was to meet the others at the moorland reserved for peat-cutting.

Ahead of him a crowd was gathered, enjoying the obligatory gossip before commencing any work. Anthony smiled at the diverse transport parked off the track – carts, garden wheelbarrows, converted perambulators and home-made crates on wheels. The islanders' inventiveness, begot by their poverty, never ceased to impress him.

Anthony had been allotted his landlord's peat glen, a devastated area disfigured with dark ponds and marred by peat hags. Rights to peat glens were handed down through generations. He'd learned from the squabbling during the previous day's meeting that it was a crime tantamount to murder to poach from another's hag.

Megan had appointed Wee Morag to help Anthony in his peat-cutting ignorance. She bounded up to him as he neared the crowd, a collection of tools over her shoulder the way most women carried parasols. Her red hair flamed in the spring sunlight. 'A good day for the peats, eh?'

Anthony smiled. 'Good morning, Wee Morag. I wouldn't have believed it yesterday but you were right.'

'Aye, after a while you learn to smell the weather. But if the wind drops the clegs'll eat us alive.'

'Clegs?'

'Aye, like a horsefly, but a bite like the horse itself. They'll be hatched noo.' The crowd ahead began to disperse and she hooked her free arm in his. 'Come on then, time to get started. And I can't think why you brought that pick and shovel. It's well seen you've no cut peat before. The barrow's here just. Leave them there.' With her tool handles she pointed to Bruce's barrow parked among the other vehicles.

She was always right. He dumped them by the barrow and pushed it on to the track. It was difficult to manoeuvre in the mud and Wee Morag guffawed at his clumsy effort. 'What you doing that for, man? The barrow's no for the peat-cutting. It's for Bruce to take me and the tools home. He's cutting with Ma.'

But he stood his ground. 'Then I'll give you a ride to the hag in it.'

She guffawed again. 'Well, if you want to, man! But first swear you'll no dump me in the bog.'

'I swear.'

She climbed in, straddled her legs, and eased the tools across her lap. As always, Anthony smiled at the sight of Wee Morag in the wheelbarrow, arms and legs dangling over the sides like a baby grown too big for its perambulator.

They turned off the track towards his hag, nodding greetings, shouting greetings, waving greetings. But despite the interruptions Wee Morag gave a running commentary on her forthcoming wedding plans. Her mother, it seemed, had finally persuaded her grandfather to move in with them, and the newlyweds would have their own cottage.

Anthony listened to her happy chatter while his eyes took in the scene. Jet-black hills contrasted against the light blue sky, the white burns still rushing down their craggy sides from the previous day's torrent. The sun and breeze spurred the damp bog cotton to puff out its down. Though he'd long since grown to love the strange beauty of the island he'd never found it so breathtaking as on this spring morning.

Wee Morag deviated for a moment from her wedding plans. 'It's a right good job the worst bit's done on your hag. That's no a job for a woman.'

'Yes,' he agreed, 'stripping's heavy work.' His muscles ached at the memory. With Bruce's assistance, he'd stripped off the dense matted layer of turf and heather roots and uncovered the soft black peat. Bruce had been proud to help him for this traditionally was a man's job.

But Anthony still didn't understand this particular division of labour. He'd noticed that a job's being heavy didn't necessarily mean it was considered 'man's work'. In fact it was mostly the women who did the heavy carrying and lifting. And not only did they appear to accept this as their lot, they also prided themselves on it.

The women would happily welcome their husbands' chivalry in relieving them of a full shopping basket or an armful of driftwood, yet thought nothing of the same husbands' looking on while the wives loaded their own backs with heavy sacks of meal or potatoes.

Anthony had been forced to accept the islanders' standards. To do otherwise would have been rude. And rudeness was one thing they wouldn't tolerate, not even from an honoured guest such as he.

'Bruce said you worked like three women on the stripping,' Morag said.

Anthony wondered whether or not that was a compliment and decided it was. 'He flatters me,' he said.

'Whoa!' she yelled when they reached his hag. 'We'll start here and you mind what I tell you.'

Once again Anthony found himself in the role of pupil, Wee Morag or Megan his teachers. She took off her gumboots and socks and hitched her skirts to her knees, unabashed at exposing her legs. He removed his own gumboots and socks and rolled up his breeches.

'I'll cut and you throw,' she said. 'Stack it flat and no too high so the sun'll dry it.'

Anthony guessed that cutting must be the heavier work but decided to agree to stack until he learned what the entire operation entailed. His guess proved correct.

Wee Morag squelched into the hag almost up to her knees, cut a slice out of the soggy brown mess and threw it at him. Taken unawares, he grabbed at it too late and it smacked him in the chest. Already doubled up, she collapsed almost flat with laughter. 'Och, noo, did I forget to tell you you're supposed to catch it first, then stack it?'

She'd done it deliberately. Though Anthony was accustomed to the islanders' sense of fun, it was impossible to predict when a bout of

333

lunacy would overtake them. He grinned and threw the sodden slice back at her. She caught it expertly, still laughing at her joke.

'That was a dirty trick, Wee Morag.'

'Aye, dirty's the word. Look at your coat just!'

He ignored his coat. He knew he'd be a lot dirtier before the day was over. 'All right! Now I've seen how to do it, I cut and you throw, or catch, or whatever you prefer to call it.'

It was a back-breaking, messy job, but Anthony found himself caught up in the rhythm and companionship of teamwork. As he sliced and tossed he wondered, would he be there to use the peat when it was dry? Suddenly it occurred to him that it was the first time he'd asked himself such a question. But he couldn't answer it.

At midday they returned to the meeting point and joined Megan and Ally for a meal of bread and cheese washed down with milk.

Megan eyed Anthony's ruddy face, his shoulders straining his jacket seams. 'You're looking more handsome by the day, lad. Nothing like good food and fresh air to put a bit of colour in your cheeks and some flesh on your bones.'

'It must be more than that,' Anthony said. 'I've had good food and fresh air all my life.'

Ally nodded. 'Aye, it's the whisky.' He pulled a flask from his pocket. 'How aboot a wee dram to boost your energy?'

Megan snatched it from him. 'Boost your energy! Put you flat on your back more like.' She stuffed it in the pocket deep among her skirt folds, her secret hiding place for just about anything. 'You'll no get a drop till we're finished or you'll flake oot on me as usual. I'm no getting any younger meself.'

Anthony smiled at their domestic tiff, a regular occurrence always followed by Ally's chinless grin. That all marriages should be as happy as theirs! Anthony thought. And that all elderly people should be so healthy and energetic! Was it despite their hard life or because of it? The islanders sustained themselves mainly by their own efforts. Money was a prized possession to be used only to buy what they couldn't produce. Yet he'd noted that once they'd acquired it, it didn't stay in their pockets long. Always, it was a wonderful excuse to celebrate.

The inevitable ceilidh followed the peat-cutting. It was held at Aggie McLaughlin's cottage. A double celebration. She was back on her feet after her prolonged prostration and ready to take school again. Like Megan, she was past her prime, but not even illness could quell her energy and spirit. Still not quite strong enough for peat-cutting, she'd spent the day cooking and preparing a magnificent feast for the workers.

She welcomed them at her open door. Her grey hair was pinned up even more untidily than Megan's. A bird could have nested in the matted mound on top of her head. 'Eh, you look done in, lad,' she said when Anthony arrived with Wee Morag in the wheelbarrow. 'Come on in just. You should've let that lazy lump walk.'

Her husband came behind her. 'Aye, have a wee dram to get your strength back.' Rory McLaughlin, a tall, leathery old man, had a habit of moving his head from side to side with the air of someone looking for a place to sit.

Anthony thanked them and sat on the floor, the chairs being occupied by the early arrivals. Unconsciously he scratched the back of his neck.

'Aye, I see the clegs got you.' Rory handed him a half-filled mug. His idea of a 'wee dram' was the same as Ally's. 'A strange thing noo,' he went on. 'They can be buzzing all aboot me and I've never been bitten yet.'

Aggie grinned down at Anthony. 'It's no strange, man! The beasts have a nose for alcohol. They know one sup of his blood and they'd be on their backs with a hangover for days.' She handed him a plate piled high with chicken sandwiches.

'Chicken?' Anthony remarked. This was a luxury.

Aggie sighed. 'Aye, poor auld Berta! Spring and she's still no laying. She was ready for the pot.'

Anthony had known Berta well. She'd always commandeered the best chair by the fire on his visits to Aggie to go over the days' lessons. For the first time he noticed the feathers and down scattered around the room. Oh, well! He was hungry.

The whisky, the food, and the revelry took Anthony's mind off his sore muscles and irritating red blotches. He'd never felt so tired and uncomfortable. Without a doubt, peat-cutting was the hardest work on the island.

When Ally and Megan dropped him off at Tigh-na-Skart he pulled off his peat-covered clothes, washed in cold water and fell into bed. That night he didn't even dream.

Chapter Thirty-One

June arrived and with it the final preparations for Wee Morag and Bruce's wedding. Anthony was happy for them but couldn't help a twinge of envy and sadness. Had Adelle's child been born in May as expected, they would have been married that month. Still, the couple's excitement at starting their new life had spurred him to think more about his own. Much as he loved this place and its people he couldn't stay for ever.

The islanders had touched him in a way no one but Adelle had. Like her, they'd shown him that life could be rewarding even though it wasn't always easy, and that loss was inevitable. They'd also lost loved ones and had continued to live life to the full. His initial mourning over, he finally understood that Adelle would want him to renew his life, to gather more rosebuds. Though he lacked her natural buoyancy, he discovered an inner strength that surprised him and recovered his will to go on.

He planned to return home after the wedding, but not to his old life. He would pay a short visit to his parents then go to Newcastle and teach for a while. He'd enjoyed his time at the school on the island even more than tutoring Arlette and Michelle. He'd found a deep satisfaction in teaching the basic needs for survival to an unruly mob of ignorant and unwilling children. And it would be even more satisfying to teach less fortunate city children who needed all the help they could get to improve their lives. The Arlettes and Michelles of this world would live in comfort without his perfecting their French verb conjugations.

But his plans were twofold. While at his parents' he would try to unearth more information about his real mother, and when he got to Newcastle he would do everything possible to find her – even if he had to place discreet advertisements in the newspapers. If she couldn't read perhaps someone who knew her could. A strange yearning plagued him to find out who she was. If he didn't, he could never truly know himself.

Wee Morag and Bruce's wedding day proved wet. The late June rain came early. But not even the downpour could dampen the spirit of the occasion.

Outside the chapel Wee Morag's huge father, Robby, lifted her from the horse and trap hired from the mainland. All heads turned as she walked on his arm up the aisle. For once she wasn't wearing gumboots. Her large feet were encased in her grandmother's white satin wedding slippers, her substantial curves attired in her great-grandmother's wedding gown. It was obvious that both women had been smaller than Wee Morag. Her insteps arched high in the narrow pumps. Her new and unaccustomed stays shoehorned her into the dress. But her mother's wedding veil, secured with a garland of wild flowers, floated freely behind her and added an ephemeral touch.

A general 'ooh' of approval issued from the guests – especially from the men. 'Sssshhhh' the older ones hissed. And order was restored. The entire island population, plus some from the mainland, had turned out for the occasion.

At the altar, Bruce's broad shoulders bulged in his borrowed blue suit. When Wee Morag reached him he gave her a look that stabbed through Anthony's heart. But he felt no envy, only joy for the bridal couple and sadness for himself that he could never bestow that look on Adelle.

The ceremony was short, the celebration endless. The schoolhouse had been cleared for the reception. The desks were piled outside in the rain and every cottage had donated its tables and chairs. Though with the partition open the school boasted the largest room on the island, a small marquee had been erected outside the entrance to house the overflow.

Bruce staggered towards Anthony with a glass and a bottle in his hand. 'Come on, man, drink up!' He had his usual happy grin on his face but more than his usual 'wee drams' in his belly. His hand wavered as he tipped the bottle over Anthony's glass and slopped whisky on the floor.

'You're a lucky man, Bruce,' Anthony said.

'Aye, I've got meself a bonny wee wife.' He swayed and flourished the bottle again. Anthony smiled. If Bruce continued at this rate he'd be flat on his back before Wee Morag got him home.

'So there you are, man!' Wee Morag tottered towards Bruce on her high heels, hands spanning her nipped-in waist. Anthony still found it hard to believe this was the same girl he'd only seen in gumboots and jerseys. 'We've got to start the dancing,' she said to Bruce. 'And look at you just! Half-cocked already!' She snatched his glass and handed it to Anthony. 'Watch oot he gets no more, Anthony. This is one night he's going to stay awake.'

Anthony chuckled as he watched her lead her teetering bridegroom to the dance floor. His chuckle grew to helpless laughter at their uncoordinated efforts to lead the circle into the Gay Gordons.

Megan squeezed herself on to the chair next to him, Ally on the other side. She nodded towards Bruce and Wee Morag and shouted above the bagpiper, 'It's aboot time for you and all, lad.'

Now was the time to make his announcement. He shook his head. 'I have other plans. I shall be leaving in a few days.'

They looked at him in dismay. 'Och, why, man?' Ally was the first to find his voice.

Touched by their obvious disappointment, Anthony went on, 'I've had a wonderful stay. But now my time here's over.'

'But you've no finished your book yet,' Megan said.

A secret smile crossed Anthony's face. 'I've finished the first chapter. The rest I plan to work on elsewhere.'

'Aw, man, we'll miss you.' Ally knocked back the remains of his glass as if to help digest the news. Megan puckered her weathered face and sniffed.

'Aye, you'll be a sad loss, Anthony.'

'I'll miss you too, and the island, and everyone. You can never know what you've done for me. You've taught me so much.'

Megan shrugged. 'We've no done anything you've no done for us. And how could we teach a schoolteacher anything?'

'I mean . . . things I could never learn from books, Megan.' To lighten the conversation Anthony smiled and added, 'You know, things like cooking kippers and cutting peat, giving a ceilidh.'

She returned his smile. 'Aye, but them things'll no do you much good back in England.'

He couldn't sidestep the truth any longer. These people were simple but certainly not stupid. They'd asked no questions after that first day, no doubt because they'd sensed his misery and his deeper, unspoken reason for seeking solitude. 'The main thing you've taught me is that I can still enjoy life,' he said.

Megan sighed and nodded. 'Aye, we knew you were in an unhappy state when you come but it was no our business to prod into it. Anyways, it's been nice seeing you come back to life, like a wilted flower after the rain just.'

So they *had* known all along! In their own way they'd left him his privacy, and by disregarding his troubles had helped him overcome them. Affection and gratitude overwhelmed him. He swallowed hard before he spoke. 'I've decided to give a farewell ceilidh. Would you help me organize it?' He knew the suggestion would bring a smile to their faces.

'Aye, that's a fine idea.' Ally grinned in approval and nodded at Megan. 'She'll help you with it, man.'

'You mean *we'll* help, Ally me lad.' She grinned at Anthony. 'The only thing I no have to force him to help with is pouring the whisky.'

Anthony was dragged on to the dance floor several times before the evening was over. It was another of those nights when he tumbled into bed too tired to write in his diary. The wail of the bagpipes echoed in his ears as he closed his eyes.

His farewell ceilidh was the biggest and noisiest he'd yet known. Everyone he'd ever said 'hello' to turned up to pay a final tribute and enjoy the last of his hospitality. Fortunately it was a mild evening, and those who couldn't cram into the cottage sat outside.

When the whisky was depleted by half it was time for the inevitable entertainment. 'Come on, man, give us one of those English or Irish songs of yours,' Bruce said.

'No, I've planned something different for you tonight.' Anthony smiled as he stood and surveyed his audience. He'd borrowed a Gaelic song book from the schoolhouse and memorized the words to some of the tunes he recognized. He began a little hesitantly, but as the faces around him lit up with pleasure, he gained confidence in his Gaelic pronunciation: 'Bheir Mo Shoraidh Thar Ghunnaidh'. The song, 'Take My Farewell Over Gunna', was a poet's lament at leaving Mull, a neighbouring island.

There were tears in many an eye as he finished, but happy applause followed.

A large group was gathered at the ferry when Anthony arrived. Hamish, the ferryman, had brought the small boat again. 'It's a better day than when you came, man,' he said. 'I'll have you there in no time. I brought

339

Wee Peggy just. I know you're a good bailer.'

Anthony smiled at the four inches of water in the boat. He'd be soaked when he reached the mainland and his clothes and shoes were disreputable enough for the journey. He thanked Hamish and turned to the crowd. There were too many to say individual farewells. He swallowed the lump in this throat and waved. 'Goodbye and thank you, all of you. I hope to come back some day.'

After the medley of replies Megan pushed Ally forward. 'He's got a wee present for you, haven't you, Ally?'

Ally held out his pocket flask of whisky. 'Aye, something to cheer you on the journey just.'

Moved, Anthony took the flask and shook Ally's hand. He knew it had cost Ally a lot to part with his whisky, and his precious flask.

Megan stuffed a cloth bundle into Anthony's other hand. 'And here's a bite to eat to go with it.'

His arms full, he couldn't shake Megan's hand but bent and kissed her leathery cheek. She beamed and shooed him away. 'Off with you noo or you'll miss your train.'

He climbed into the boat and arranged himself across the wooden seat as before.

Hamish handed him the pail. 'Here you are, man. You know what to do.'

Anthony started bailing. He thought of his black vision of the 'other side' on his outward crossing. His journey certainly hadn't turned out as expected. Back to civilization, he thought with a smile. Adelle would be smiling too.

Chapter Thirty-Two

'You're going away again?' Richard stared at Anthony across the tea table on the lawn. 'But you've just come home!'

Anthony leaned back in his wicker chair. It was a beautiful day. The last thing he wanted was a family row. But if he'd kept his news from them he would have felt deceitful. 'Yes,' he said, 'and I'm glad to be home. I shall stay for a week or two.' The grass, like green velvet, had been mown that morning. He stroked his foot across the manicured surface, displacing the clippings that had defied the gardener's rake. How could he explain to his parents why he had to do this? The clippings were already turning brown, he noticed.

Mildred forced his explanation. 'Where to this time? And why, for heaven's sake? I suppose you want to play hermit again on another Godforsaken island?' She squinted at him in the sunlight and adjusted her straw hat over her face.

'No, not another island, Mother. I've decided to go to Newcastle and teach for a while. I enjoyed teaching the island children. And I feel the need to make myself of use for a time.'

Richard mopped his damp brow with his napkin. 'Of use? You could be of use here, me lad. It's time you started. You seem to think I'm going to last for ever.'

Anthony was tired of hearing those words but knew that, although his father was as healthy as ever, he'd grown increasingly concerned about his mortality in the past couple of years. 'I shan't stay away long, sir. I simply want to do something different with my life while I can. I've told you, I'll take over when you need me. If I were still at Cambridge I'd be away for another three years.' At the shocked expression on their faces he went on quickly, 'But of course, I don't intend to be away that long.'

'How long then? At least tell us that.' Mildred held aloft a dainty

341

salmon sandwich and popped it into her mouth.

Anthony examined the lawn again. Trying to explain his needs to them was proving even more difficult than he'd imagined. 'I . . . I don't know yet. However long it takes me to feel satisfied that I've done something useful and worked for my living.'

Richard raised his eyebrows. 'Aye, well, that's just what you'll be doing. There'll be no more allowance till you come home.' His voice held no censure, only resignation. 'If you're intent on playing at being a working man, a working man you'll be. You'll find out what it's like to live on a schoolteacher's wages.'

His father's words echoed in Anthony's head – 'playing at being a working man'. Was it simply play? Another self-indulgence like his stay on Skye? No! What he wanted to do was real, even if he couldn't do it for ever. He looked Richard in the eye. 'That's only fair, sir. I don't expect you to continue my allowance.'

Mildred stared at him from under her hat brim. Her powder and rouge stood out more than usual in the sunlight. Her skin looked like cracked plaster of Paris. Anthony rarely saw her out of doors. It came as a shock that she, like his father, was growing old.

'When will you be going?' she asked. 'I hope you'll at least stay long enough for me to organize some functions before you leave. I swear our friends think our son's forsaken us.'

Anthony nodded. 'Of course, Mother.' He owed them that much.

Before dinner he went for a ride. He smiled as he swung into the polished leather saddle. He missed Betty's steamy flesh between his thighs. He made straight for Flagdon Hall. Approaching it, he slowed. The sight of the place that held so many happy and unhappy memories stirred him. That so much had happened to him here! In such a short time! The windows were open to air the house. Adelle had always kept them open whenever weather permitted, until the last vestige of summer faded. Overwhelmed by memories, sweet and painful, he pulled the doorbell.

It took a long time for Eva to answer, and when she did she clapped her hands to her cheeks. 'My! Oh, sir! What a surprise!'

'How are you, Eva?'

'All right, sir, all right. Come on in now.' He followed her into the drawing room, so familiar, yet now for ever removed from his life.

He sat by the French windows and looked out on the lawn. It was scattered with daisies. 'I just came to let you know I'm back, Eva, and to see how you are.' He indicated the window seat opposite.

She eyed him as she sat, hands folded in her lap. 'I'm keeping busy, sir. That's all I can do. And may I ask how you've been, sir?'

Anthony smiled. 'I've come to terms with a lot of things, Eva – about Adelle's death, and myself. I'm sorry now that I was so selfish in my grief.'

'It was hard for you, sir. You stood up well.'

He shook his head. 'No, I leaned on you, Eva. But I've learned to stand on my own feet now. Going to Skye and spending time alone' – he smiled again and corrected himself – 'at least, *some* time alone, was an education far beyond what I could ever have achieved at Cambridge. Have you heard from Michelle and Arlette?'

'Oh, indeed I have, sir, and they were that full of what you told them about the island in your letters.' She rose, obviously uncomfortable at being treated like an equal. 'Can I get you something, sir? Some coffee? A brandy perhaps?'

Anthony patted the window seat again. 'No, please, I simply came to talk to you. You don't need to serve me every minute.'

She sat again and smiled, compressing her wrinkles till her face looked like a giant walnut. 'Serving people's my life, sir. And I like to.'

He nodded. 'Yes, I've discovered, rather belatedly, that it can be satisfying to serve others. I met some very interesting people on the island. But enough of that. Have you learned any more about . . . that business?'

'No, sir. I've tried to probe, but your cook keeps going on about one happening and another. The last I heard about . . . that particular affair . . . was what I told you. You know – the woman who lives down that cart track.'

He tried not to show his disappointment. 'Yes, thank you, Eva. I'll keep you informed of my address . . . and if you do hear more . . .'

'Of course, sir, I'll let you know.'

The next day was cloudless and hot. After accompanying his father on a late morning ride, Anthony rode out to the Morpeth road and turned down the cart track. Eva's information was scant, but all he had to go on.

Towards the end of the track a square grey box of a cottage burrowed into the upward slope of the land. He reined in his horse and stared at the cottage. To his knowledge he'd never ridden this way, yet he sensed a familiarity with the place. Had he been here on one of his errant rides

343

as a child? He nudged the horse slowly and stopped outside the unpainted door. He dismounted and knocked. He would ask for water.

The door opened and an untidy woman with red hair as bright as Wee Morag's, and just as dishevelled, stood before him. She clapped her hand to her mouth.

'Excuse me,' he said. 'I didn't mean to startle you, but I wondered if I may have a drink of water.' His pretext was believable.

She lowered her hand, but a guarded look leapt into her eyes and she backed into the room. 'Aye, aye, I'll get you some, sir.' The door closed in his face.

Had he imagined it? Had there been something else in that look – recognition?

The door opened halfway and she held out a mug of water. 'There you are, sir.'

'Er, thank you.' He took the mug and indicated his horse. 'I'm sorry to impose on you, but my horse also needs watering.'

'Aye, I'll see to the horse.' The door closed again and the woman returned with a bucket of water. Before he could take it from her she'd set it in front of the horse. He stared at her large frame. Was there something familiar about her or did she simply remind him of Wee Morag?

The horse drank eagerly. 'I'm afraid I've ridden her too hard in this heat,' Anthony said, 'and myself! I should have worn a hat. I need to rest my horse before I go on. And I should love something to eat. I'll pay for it, of course.' Country people were known for their hospitality to travellers. But was he pushing too far? From the strange look she gave him he guessed she knew he was no traveller.

'I've only got bread and dripping, and milk,' she said.

'That's fine.' He led the horse to the shade of the wall and looped the reins round a water pipe.

He followed her through the door and forgot to duck. His head struck the low beam.

'Oh, sir, I'm sorry, sir. I should've warned you.' She twisted her apron in agitation.

'My fault for not looking!' He rubbed his head and smiled reassurance. The woman seemed concerned out of proportion to the incident.

Inside, he stopped and stared around the cramped kitchen, the wooden table by the window, two chairs by the stove, a dresser in the corner. He'd been in many cottage kitchens on the island, but had never had this uncanny feeling that he'd been there before. There was a round burn on the table – where a hot pan had stood, perhaps? He'd *seen* that burn before. A heap of clothes on the floor in the corner caught his eye. That too stirred some deep forgotten remembrance.

'Sit yourself down, sir.' She gestured to one of the chairs at the table.

'Thank you.' He watched her across the table as she cut bread and spread it with dripping from a chipped bowl. Again, he knew it wasn't the first time he'd sat there. Her hands shook as she worked. She was nervous. She picked up an earthenware jug of milk to fill his mug. Suddenly he realized he hadn't touched the water.

'You haven't drunk nothing, sir,' she said. The wariness left her eyes and fear replaced it.

He bit on his lip. 'I'm sorry. I've misled you. But please don't be afraid. My name is Anthony Hayward. I live at Hayward Hall.'

She set down the milk jug and lowered her gaze.

'You knew that, didn't you?'

'Well, I . . . er, of course I know that, sir. Everyone about here knows that.'

He cleared his throat and went on. 'I happen to know you were a friend of our late housekeeper, Mrs Kennedy.'

Her eyes remained lowered. 'Well, yes, sir, but what's that—?'

'And of her niece?'

She stopped spreading dripping on the bread and jerked up her eyes. 'May I know as to what all these questions are about, sir?'

Now the only thing to do was to barge in, to let her think he knew more than he did. 'I know about her niece.'

In her obvious confusion she slammed the plate of bread before him. 'What about her niece?'

'I understand you've known her for a long time . . . since before my birth.'

She sat and gripped the edge of the table, the red skin of her knuckles blanching. He mustn't frighten her. 'Look,' he said softly, 'I can assure you I wish no one any harm. I'd simply like some information.' He pulled a five-pound note from his wallet and pushed it across the table. 'I know that I was an adopted child. And I know that Mrs Kennedy and her niece had something to do with my adoption. Please help me. I dearly want to find my real mother. Simply to meet her. I'm at a loss to tell you why it's so important to me, but it is.'

She looked straight at him. 'What makes you think it was Mrs Kennedy's niece, sir?'

So she wasn't going to give in easily, and she'd ignored the money. That was a large sum for a poor peasant woman to scorn. Was she being loyal to her friend? 'I've heard gossip at the house,' he said, 'and I know.' He didn't tell her that he 'knew' mainly by intuition.

'You know!' Her eyes widened and she gripped the table edge tighter.

So he was right! He pursued relentlessly. 'Yes, and I'm determined to find her. Do you know where she is?'

She gave him a pleading look. 'Why do you want to find her, sir? All that business was dead and buried years ago. She's suffered enough.'

'I've told you, I mean her no harm. I simply need to see her, to talk to her.' Though unwilling to bare his soul to this stranger, he knew he would have to give her more reason than that. 'You'll probably think this strange, but somehow I always knew I . . . didn't belong. That I was in some way different from my family. And when I discovered . . . well, perhaps you can understand? I feel the need to know who my mother is in order to know myself.' He stopped. He'd made a fool of himself. But her green eyes were no longer afraid, they were filled with sorrow. She sighed.

'I can tell you that she's a wonderful woman. And that it wasn't her fault. She did everything she could to keep you. What she did was only for your good. She loves you to this day. Leave it be at that. She's got enough troubles without raking up more.'

Anthony was stunned. She loved him to this day? She was in trouble. 'I'm sorry to hear she's in trouble. And I assure you I have no intention of causing more. I'd like to help her.'

The woman shook her head. 'She lost her man this time last year, and then her old auntie three months after. She's having hard times. You can't do nowt about that.'

'Does she have other family?'

'Eight now, and the last one's sickly.'

So *he* also had other family. 'Then at least I could help her financially. Please let me do that.'

'You mean send her money?'

'More than that! I want to see her and help her in whatever manner I can.'

She sighed and rubbed a calloused hand over her forehead. 'Eey, I don't know what to do for the best! She might be mad at me if I tell you.'

The woman was warming to him! In his excitement he jerked forward

346

across the table, his hands clasping and unclasping. 'But you said she still feels for me. Surely, then, she would be glad to see me. And I *promise*! I want to help her. If she's your friend and in distress, you can't deny her help.'

The woman's large bosom swelled as she sighed again. 'Aye, even if I get into trouble for it, it might be worth it.'

'Then you'll tell me where she is?'

She took a pad and pencil from the dresser. 'You can write it down. Her name's Bridget Banks now, it *was* Brannigan.'

'Bridget? Bridget Brannigan?' He paused, pencil poised. The letter B signed after his name on the stream bank! But he mustn't enquire more of this woman. He'd find out the rest soon. 'And where does she live?' He wrote the address she gave him, no need to write the name, it was already engraved in his mind. Then he stood and placed another five pounds on the table. 'I can't thank you enough.'

She pushed the notes back to him. 'I didn't do it for money, sir.'

Was it crass to wish to pay her? He coloured in embarrassment. 'Please accept it as a gift, not as payment. Let's say, a favour returned.'

She stowed the money in her apron pocket. 'Aye, if you put it like that. Thank you, sir. But there's one more thing. I think I should write and tell her what I've done afore you get in touch with her. Give her some warning like. She's had enough shocks lately.'

Anthony bit on his lip. He'd wanted to surprise her. To knock on her door and say, 'I'm Anthony.' Yet the woman was right. It would be more polite for him to write first. But he couldn't put on paper to a stranger what he felt. He had to talk to her, face to face. 'All right,' he agreed. 'You tell her, and let her know I'll be calling on her in a fortnight, less if possible. I'd appreciate that. And if for any reason my visit would be untimely for her, you'll let me know? Perhaps drop off a note at the house.'

'Aye, sir, but she'll want to see you, lessen there's something else wrong I haven't heard about.'

He paused in the doorway. 'May I know your name?'

She looked surprised. 'I thought you knew all about me, sir.'

Anthony smiled. 'Not all.'

'It's Nellie, sir.'

'Well, thank you again, Nellie, for everything.' He bowed, and remembered to duck his head before leaving.

Riding back down the track he repeated the name in his head. Bridget

347

Brannigan! An Irish name! Those Irish songs? There was so much more he would have liked to ask that woman, Nellie. But he'd imposed on her too much. In a couple of weeks he'd find out all he needed to know. Patience! He smiled. Adelle would have been proud of him.

PART III

Chapter Thirty-Three

The night before Anthony's departure Mildred held a grand ball as the finale to her succession of parties in his honour.

He dressed in his black evening suit and surveyed himself in the mirror. He grimaced. He'd been so comfortable in his grubby work clothes on the island. Well, this would be his last ball for a long time. He would be a credit to his parents.

Much to Mildred's approval he arrived at the ballroom even before the first guests. As usual, she was fussing over last-minute details. Despite the light summer evening the galaxy of chandeliers was already lit. The orchestra was tuning up on the raised stage at the end of the hall. Velvet chairs and couches were arranged around the walls 'just so' as Mildred called it, not one protruding half an inch further than its neighbour.

She surveyed Anthony from the top of his immaculately groomed hair to the toes of his patent leather dancing slippers. 'My, the ladies will be fighting over you tonight. You look splendid!'

He kissed her on the cheek. 'Thank you, Mother. And you look very grand.' Grand was the word. Mildred perspired in a heavy taffeta ball gown. She raised her arm to waft her lace fan over her face, revealing a damp stain under the leg-o'-mutton sleeve. When she walked, the largest bustle Anthony had ever seen bounced behind her. A person could have sat on it. 'Your father's late, as usual,' she said, pushing back an errant chair half an inch.

The butler announced the first guests and Anthony followed Mildred as she rustled to greet them. They comprised Lord and Lady Mowbray and their daughter Beatrice, who was in her third season and, judging by the lack of male attention she'd received so far, likely to do more. With them was a small, pretty girl, though she looked too young to have 'come out' at all.

351

After the butler's formal announcement, Mildred effused over them, 'Why, Lord and Lady Mowbray, how absolutely delightful to see you! And looking as stately as ever!' Anthony wondered if his mother referred to the diamond tiara on the woman's head or the size of her husband's waistline. Mildred kissed Lady Mowbray on the cheek and held out her hand to Lord Mowbray.

'Charmed,' he said, and pressed his blubbery lips to her satin-gloved fingers.

Anthony bowed to the parents in turn.

'And my dear Lady Beatrice.' Mildred kissed the third-time-around daughter before surveying the other girl. 'And this must be your cousin, Alice. Absolutely charming!' She took the girl's hand. 'You're not yet acquainted with my son, Anthony.'

He bowed to Lady Beatrice and then to her cousin.

Mildred beckoned a servant bearing a silver tray. 'Won't you take some refreshment,' she said to the group. 'And please excuse us for one moment, we have some new arrivals.' Both girls' eyes followed Anthony as Mildred whisked him off to greet another couple with a daughter in tow. 'Mabel, my dear! And Charles! How nice to see you! And Marian! As pretty as ever!'

Anthony suffered the interminable round of introductions until the ballroom bulged with so many people it was impossible to attend to each individually. But Mildred glued herself to his side. 'Why don't you ask that nice Alice Mowbray to dance? She's very pretty and, I understand, comes from quite an acceptable family in Cheshire.'

He had no desire to strike up a new acquaintance this evening. At least Lady Beatrice was familiar, and an accomplished dancer. 'I agree, Alice is pretty, Mother. But I've danced with her cousin for three seasons because nobody else would, I feel I owe her a duty.'

'If you insist, then be polite for one or two dances, but you must circulate. Besides, she's much too plain and too old for you, titled or not.'

'Yes, Mother, but I feel obligated.' He did feel obliged to show Beatrice some attention, but he also felt safe with her. He knew that, titled or not, his mother disliked the Mowbray family intensely. What was more, they'd lost their fortune. They resided in one quarter of what had once been their stately mansion, and the daughter had nothing but her title as a dowry. Mildred would never push him in that direction.

He led the first waltz, circulated and danced almost every dance, even leading the Sir Roger de Coverley, which he hated. Several times

Richard nodded his approval. When dinner was announced he escorted Lady Beatrice to the dining hall and again felt safe.

The evening seemed interminable, but by four a.m. the last guests had left. Anthony retired for what remained of the night, satisfied that for once he'd pleased his parents.

He fell into bed with a sigh. His fortnight was up. He was leaving for Newcastle first thing in the morning. Another life. For a while at least. What would she be like? He felt reassured that she at least wanted to see him. He hadn't heard from her friend, Nellie.

Richard had insisted on Anthony travelling to Newcastle by motor car, as it was 'so much more civilized than public transport'. But when they reached the station Anthony sent the chauffeur back. It would be ostentatious to arrive in a motor car. He left his bag at the left-luggage counter and took a hackney to Byker. He sat back, nervous at the impending meeting.

As the cab left the dignified city buildings and crossed a bridge, the streets became narrower, the terraced dwellings poorer. The heatwave had passed and the grey muffled clouds did little to cheer the scenery. It seemed the sun had fallen off the edge of the world. Anthony had never been out of the city centre and the stark contrast of grandeur and poverty dismayed him. He leaned forward to see more clearly out of the window. The cab took him down street after identical street of cheerless terraced flats. His spirits slumped. She lived here! In such a poor area! Of course he knew she wasn't rich, but this place was so depressing. Her friend's humble cottage in the country was cheerful compared to this red-brick and cobblestone wasteland. If his real mother hadn't given him away for adoption this is where he would have lived!

He'd chosen to wear a simple sack suit and derby, his most casual outfit, but at the sight of the ragged cloth-capped men, and women in work dresses, mobcaps and shawls, he felt embarrassingly overdressed.

He sat back in the cab, his trepidation mounting. There was so much he wanted to know but he'd planned how he'd introduce himself and no more. He had no idea what to expect. For the first time it occurred to him – what if she didn't wish to see him after all? His visit would surely bring back unhappy memories.

'This is it, sir!' The driver pulled up outside one of the doors. The brown paint was beginning to peel.

Anthony sat, paralysed. 'No, please drive on.' The horses started again. He stopped the driver at the end of the street and paid him. He

353

wanted to walk for a while, to clear his mind before he saw her.

Bridget scrubbed the table until it was almost white. Every day since she'd received Nellie's message in Jack's laboured hand she'd scrubbed and polished, scrubbed and polished. He'd said he would come before the fortnight was up if he could. But it was exactly a fortnight now. He must come today. Fortunately, the boys were at work and Kate at school. The little ones she'd sent to Meg. She prayed Anthony would arrive during the day when the lodgers were also at work. She sighed. If only Tom and Annie were still alive! The only ones who'd known, who could have given her some advice! She didn't know how to deal with Anthony's visit and the conflicting emotions it aroused in her.

After her initial shock and joy at the thought of seeing him, she'd been plagued by questions. Why? Why now? How could he have found out? What was his real reason for wishing to meet her? How should she behave towards him? Not as a mother. Not as an equal. Not as a servant. She would just have to wait and see how he treated her.

She checked eight-month-old Tim sleeping in his cot. His breathing was laboured. Though blond and blue-eyed like his brothers, he didn't have their strong constitutions. And she was to blame. Her misery after Tom's death, followed so soon by Annie's, must have affected the child in her womb. While she'd been happy the others had been born healthy.

She pricked her ears. A knock on the door, so soft she could barely hear it. She ran to the mirror and tidied her hair, smoothed down her black frock and white apron and with a deep intake of breath hurried down the passage.

'Mrs Banks?'

There he stood, tall, handsome, with *her* hair and her eyes. An arrow of joy pierced her, barbed with pain. Her voice was barely a whisper. 'Yes.'

'I . . . er.' He clutched his hat and stared at her.

'Won't you come in.' On trembling legs she led him down the passage to the kitchen. She indicated a fireside chair. 'Please sit down.'

He sat with his hat on his lap, still staring at her. 'Your friend, er . . . told you?'

She lowered herself into the opposite chair, almost immobilized, as if a serpent were coiling around her body. 'Yes, I was expecting you.'

He twiddled with his hat brim. Her gaze fastened on him. His fingers were still long and slender, though his body had filled out to a man's proportions. And his face was a man's, yet had retained the softness of expression she remembered so well from his childhood. Again she saw her own hazel eyes looking back at her.

He must have noticed her scrutiny and shifted in his seat. 'I hope my visit doesn't distress you.'

She wanted to scream out, *No! No! It's the most wonderful thing that could ever happen to me.* Instead, she kept her voice low. 'I'm very happy to see you.' She asked herself for the hundredth time – what should she call him? Better nothing at the moment. To use his christian name would be too forward and she couldn't bring herself to address him formally.

A silence stretched like a taut rope between them. He cleared his throat.

'I know this is as difficult for you as it is for me, but when I found out about my birth it was a shock, yet also a sort of awakening. I felt a strong need to meet my real mother. I'm afraid I used rather dubious means to trace you, but I'm glad I did. I hope I didn't cause any trouble for your friend.'

Without taking her eyes off his face, she shook her head. 'No, Nellie's a good friend. If it was your wish, she did the right thing.' She paused, not quite sure how to phrase the next question. 'How can I help you?'

'Help me?' He shrugged, then continued to play with the hat brim. 'My first thought was that perhaps getting to know you would help me to know myself better. But now I'm here also because I want to help you. I understand you're in trouble.'

She lowered her eyes. 'I'm having hard times. But I'll manage.'

Forgetting the hat, he leaned forward. 'I want to hear all about you, and your life. But to understand better I first need to know who you are. Was it you who wrote my name on the bank and signed it with your initial?'

She nodded. How wonderful that he'd guessed!

'And did you teach me Irish songs?'

And he remembered her songs! Joy fired her blood. She nodded again.

He leaned back in his chair, realization dawning in his eyes. 'You were my first nursemaid! The one who left!'

'No! No!' Her voice was sharp. 'I didn't leave! I was forced to go. But that's all I can tell you.' Near to tears, she averted her head. 'There were . . . others involved, and 'tis not me place to dig up their secrets.'

He threw his hat to the floor and jumped up, towering over her.

355

'There's no need to tell me who. And neither do you need to tell me the details. I can guess sufficiently. But the moment you opened the door you were familiar to me. I can't have remembered your face all those years. I've seen you since, haven't I?'

She looked up at his tall figure, yet he was formless as a dream through her filmed eyes. 'I visited you secretly whenever I could. It fair broke me heart to leave you.'

He clapped his hand to his forehead. 'The woman in grey! And the veil! I remember your voice also.' He sat again and studied her face with compassion. 'It must have been painful for you, only able to visit me secretly, and from a distance. You must have loved . . . that little boy . . . very much.'

'I did . . . I do. A mother never loses the love for her child.' She blinked away the film over her eyes and met his gaze. He lowered his.

'Forgive me. I didn't intend to pry into your feelings. It was selfish of me. I'm greedy for details. At first I thought you mustn't have wanted me.'

Bridget's hands clenched into fists. 'Never! Never! As God's me witness, if I'd had a choice I'd surely have taken it. I even thought of stealing you back.' She shook her head. 'But that wasn't possible. I had to console meself that you'd have a good life and an education, things I could never give you. Please tell me, have you been happy?' She gave him a long and searching look. But again he avoided her eyes.

'Happy? I've known happiness. And, yes, I've had a good life, and an education. But I always felt there was something wrong, something missing.'

Bridget bit her lip. She knew what that 'something' was. But she couldn't say a bad word about his parents. And she couldn't bring herself to enquire if he loved them. 'Do you get on well with your family?' was as much as she could ask.

He looked up and a wry smile touched his lips. 'Better as the years go by. But I'm afraid I was never the son they wanted, nor am I now, though I'm trying harder. I've disappointed them enough.' He shrugged. 'We simply have different tastes, different values. But they've been good to me in their way. I've wanted for nothing.'

Yes, Bridget thought, nothing but that 'something'.

He went on, his voice eager. 'But enough of me! I came to find out about you.'

Suddenly she was reluctant to talk. She stood. 'Dear me! I'm forgetting me manners. I haven't even offered you a cup of tea or a bite.' She

356

poked the kettle over the fire, but he jumped up. She felt his hand on hers, restraining her. At his touch, joy leapt within her like a trout in a stream. How long since she'd held the hand that now held hers! Her happiness seemed to expand inside her, stretching taut her skin, tightening her skull. She burst into tears and, alarmed, he lowered her into her chair. Their hands separated.

'I'm so sorry,' he said. 'My visit *has* upset you. How selfish of me!'

'No! No!' She sniffed and dried her eyes on her apron. She wanted to reach out her fingers and trace his cheek. ''Tis joy that makes me weep. You can't know how much it means to me to see you again, to hear your voice. It's just . . . just taking me a while to get used to it.' She sniffed one last time. 'There, it's fine I am again! Now, please let me make you something. It would give me a grand pleasure.'

He sat back in his chair, still looking anxiously at her. 'If it would please you, I'll take tea, but no food thank you.'

While she busied herself at the stove Anthony took in the room for the first time. How small and shabby! But how immaculate! Suddenly a whimper came from behind him and he turned. He noticed the cot in the corner, the sleeping baby.

She handed him a mug of tea. 'That's me littlest, Tim. He'll be needing feeding and changing. Please have your tea while I see to him.'

He put his mug on the hearth and stood to watch as she picked up the mewling infant. His half-brother! He stared at the blond head, the sleepy blue eyes. His gaze followed Bridget as she carried the baby to another room. Then he sat again, his tea forgotten. She looked so young, and pretty, but so tired! She must have been little more than a child when she'd borne him.

Of course! Very young and very pretty! He knew what had happened. He put his head in his hands. She wouldn't have stood a chance against his father's amorous advances. For a moment he hated the old man. But he chastised himself. Hatred was a destructive emotion, evil in itself. And what part had his mother played in this? Like a bolt of lightning it struck him. His father had needed a son! His mother hadn't given him one! Now it all made sense. It must have been painful for her to accept her husband's bastard as her own. Bastard! The word reverberated through his head. But what did a word matter? And there was nothing he could do to right the wrongs of the past. However, now that he understood everything he could make a difference to the present, and to the future.

357

* * *

Bridget returned and sat with the baby on her lap. 'I'm sorry it took so long. He doesn't take his food well.' She rubbed Tim's back and half smiled. 'Not like the others.' She wanted to say 'and you' but restrained herself. A grown man wouldn't want to be reminded of such things.

'How many others? I want to know everything.'

'Eight, including this one.' Her smile spread at his look of astonishment. 'Aye, my husband used to pride himself on being a dab hand at it. He was a dab hand at everything, God rest his soul.' She glanced at Anthony's mug on the hearth. 'You haven't touched your tea. Let me get you another one.'

He jumped up. 'No, I'll pour two more. You haven't touched yours either.' She tried to raise herself, her mouth open in protest, but he put a hand on her shoulder and eased her down. 'You see to the baby.'

She watched in wonder as he poured the tea. He was waiting on her! Just like Tom used to! She laid Tim in the cot and sat watching Anthony's movements with pleasure.

He handed her a mug and returned to his chair with his own. 'Now,' he said, 'I've talked almost nonstop. I'd dearly love to hear about you. From the beginning. I mean, why you left Ireland . . . and everything since then.' He looked embarrassed for a moment. 'That is, I'd like to hear only what you *want* to tell me. I don't wish to pry.'

She began, haltingly, from her mother's death to the present, but was careful to leave out details that would cast a shadow on his parents.

He listened, saddened yet spellbound. 'But how have you managed since your husband died?'

The cloud over her face darkened. 'I had to take the three oldest out of school, the last thing I ever wanted. But it was either that or the workhouse. Tommy's twelve, he's labouring at Caddy and Lamb's shipbuilding. But he's watching and learning so that one of these days he can better himself. Mick's ten and a half. He's a stoker at Brason's Foundry. Dan' – she paused and looked down – 'Dan's nine, and I hated taking him out of school. He's a bit slow, but not stupid, you understand, and big and strong for his age. He's a labourer at the tar works.' She looked down at the baby in her lap. 'This one's off again. Let me put him down.'

'And the rest?' he probed again when she returned.

She ran a weary hand across her brow. 'Joseph's eight and going to school half days, the other half he works at the nail factory. And I make

358

nails at home.' She sighed. 'When I have the time. With two lodgers and a house full of bairns there's not much of me time left.'

'And the other children are at school?'

'Only Kate, she's seven. Eileen's four and Sean's just a bit over two. They're all over the place so I sent them to me neighbour's today. I knew you'd come.' She smiled, almost shyly. 'To tell the truth I've been sort of hoping every day since I got Nellie's letter. But when the fortnight was up I *knew* it was today.'

He sipped his tea but his eyes held hers. 'Not just today. I'm staying for as long as I can.'

'Staying! But why? You can't stay here!' She blinked in amazement. Where would she put him in the overcrowded flat, even for one night? He was used to such grandeur.

'If I can't stay here then I shall find a place nearby,' he said, a hurt look crossing his face.

She wanted to eat her words. 'Oh dear, I didn't mean . . . I'd dearly love you to stay. It's just that, well, it's only a humble and crowded little flat, especially with me lodgers and all. They're out all day at the laundry, but after work we're all bunched together here like bristles in a brush. And you being used to . . . well. You weren't brought up to it.'

'I've become used to many things I wasn't brought up to. But I understand that you have no room. Perhaps you know of a place close by?'

'Well, me neighbour might take you for a while. But you would eat here, mind you.' Bridget couldn't bear the thought of his living elsewhere, even across the road. 'How long would you be staying?'

'I don't know yet, but I'm going to get a job and do whatever I can to help you out.'

She looked dazed, as if he'd struck her a blow. 'Get a job? You mean live here, not just visit?' Her eyes were deceiving her. She set her half-touched tea on the hearth. 'But you couldn't possibly—'

'Why not? As soon as your friend told me you were in trouble I knew that was what I wanted to do.'

'But your parents. What—'

'My parents know I wish to teach here for a while. That's all.'

She leaned back in her chair. He'd come to help her? Tears gathered like pools in the corners of her eyes. He wasn't only handsome and charming, he was kind, and kind to *her*, after the shameful thing she'd done! She was unable to speak.

He hooked his index finger down his starched collar, giving away his distress at her silence. 'You don't want me to stay?'

The pools in her eyes overflowed down her cheeks. 'Oh, yes, yes, indeed I do! It's just that, well, why would you be wanting to give up your comfortable life to help me?'

'Please, please don't cry. I need to do something useful with my life while I can, and I can't think of anything more rewarding than helping my own mother when she's in trouble – and my brothers and sisters.'

His own mother! He thought of her as his mother. And his brothers and sisters. Overcome, she buried her face in her hands. He jumped up and sat on the arm of her chair, placing his hand on her shoulder. At his touch, she trembled with delight. He'd come back to her. She longed to fling her arms round him, hold him to her as she'd done all those years ago, burrow his face in her bosom. But he was a man now. Instead she placed her hand over his, which still rested on her shoulder. In that touch was all the love and longing she'd held in check for so many years. And he wanted to help her – and his little brothers and sisters. For the first time since Tom's death, hope kindled within her. She had no idea how long they'd sat together, hands touching, when he spoke.

'Perhaps I could stay with your neighbour tonight. Tomorrow I can find something permanent.' He took her hand, still placed over his, and held it.

'Indeed you won't find anything permanent!' Her voice was almost sharp. 'I thought you meant you were visiting for a few days. I'm not having you live elsewhere. I'll give me lodgers notice tonight. But until they go I'm sure Meg, that's me neighbour, would be happy to put you up. Her old mother lives with her but she's staying with her other daughter at Tynemouth for a holiday.'

'That's splendid. I left my bag at the station, I'll collect it later.' He gave her an embarrassed look. 'In the meantime, I do admit I'm hungry now. Perhaps I'll take you up on your offer.'

She withdrew her hand from his with reluctance but jumped up with pleasure at the thought of taking care of her son. 'It's not what you're used to but I've got a pot of stew ready.'

Anthony chuckled. 'I've become used to stew lately, and I like it.' He sat back in his chair and watched her.

Such a gentleman. So polite. He was happy to accept her humble fare. Her hands trembled. She was setting a place for Anthony at *her* table. His voice interrupted her thoughts.

'Afterwards I should go to the station and pick up my bag. I, er . . . didn't like to arrive on your doorstep looking as if I were about to move in. I thought one surprise at a time enough.'

She stirred the stew on the stove and smiled. 'Sure, I don't think anything else can surprise me ever again. I'll take you to the tram stop. And the bairns'll be home when you get back.' The bairns! How would she explain Anthony to them? She'd planned to tell them he was paying her a visit because she'd looked after him as a baby. But now that he was staying she must tell them the truth. Anthony had been kept a secret for too long. She would never feel shame about her past again.

He looked apologetic. 'Er, how would I explain my being here? And how should I address the children? I've no wish to embarrass you. Perhaps I could be a long-lost uncle?'

'No!' She straightened from the stove and placed her hands on her hips. 'You're their long-lost brother. And they're going to know it. Everybody's going to know it.' She closed her eyes. And Tom, and Annie, up there, they would know it and be happy for her.

'If you're sure it won't be an ordeal for you to tell them?' His voice was hesitant.

'Ordeal! Sure, it'll be the *end* of me ordeal. It's been hard denying me own son to meself and the whole world all these years.'

'I can see it has,' he said softly. Then he cleared his throat again and ran a hand through his hair. 'I've, er, been wondering what I should call you.'

Pain flashed through her like a fork of lightning, and passed as quickly. He couldn't call two women mother. But he'd always called her Bridget and it had always sounded like music to her ears. She smiled. 'Bridget would be grand.'

On the tram, Anthony's thoughts tumbled over one another. She was a wonderful woman, and brave. She'd endured so much. He felt humble. He'd been so spoiled and yet dissatisfied with his life. But he'd timed his visit so badly. The schools were about to break up for the summer holidays. In the meantime he must try to find some private tuturing jobs. Now he wished he hadn't told his father he intended to work. His allowance would have been useful in addition to his wages. He had barely thirty pounds left. Tomorrow he must start looking for something, anything.

After picking up his bag he bought a half-pound of mixed caramels for the children and a box of chocolates for Bridget. He wanted to buy more but decided he must hold on to what money he had for necessities until he found a job.

When he returned, two girls and a boy sat at the table. The elder girl was feeding a toddler on her lap. They forgot their stew, put down their spoons and stared at him.

Though Bridget fidgeted with the corner of her apron, her face glowed. 'This is Anthony, the brother I told you about. Now say hello.'

'Hello, I'm Kate,' the elder girl said.

Anthony drew in his breath. She looked so like the photographs of him at that age – and even now. 'And who are you?' he said to the others.

'I'm Eileen and that's me little brother, Sean.' The younger girl pointed to the toddler in her sister's lap.

Anthony smiled at them and turned to the boy next to her, who gave him a puzzled, even suspicious look. 'Me ma calls me Joseph but the lads at school call me Joe,' he said.

'Then what would you like *me* to call you?' This must be the one who went to school half day and worked, Anthony reasoned.

The boy shrugged. 'You can call me what you like.' He lowered his eyes and continued eating.

'All right, Joseph it is. I'm so glad to know you all at last.' Anthony studied them. Except for Kate the others must take after their father. He'd never seen such bright blond hair and deep blue eyes. He felt a profound sadness, and guilt, that he'd had so much and not appreciated it. These were his brothers and sisters, wearing shabby, patched clothing. But their hands and faces were scrubbed, their hair shining.

While he weighed them up Eileen scrutinized him from top to toe. 'You've been away a long time.'

'Yes, too long,' Bridget cut in. 'And now I think Anthony would like a cup of tea.' Her high-pitched tone gave away her nervousness. Anthony knew how difficult it must be to explain him to the children.

'Thank you, I should like some tea,' he said, joining the others at the table.

Sean pointed a chubby finger to the spoon Kate held to his mouth. 'Meat in the stew.'

Anthony smiled. 'Yes, I know. I've had some.'

'Are we having meat again tomorrow, Ma?' Eileen asked.

Bridget's face coloured. 'Now you mind your mouth. And just wait and see.'

Anthony felt a surge of shame. The meat had obviously been a treat for him. He would see to it that they had meat on the table more often.

362

The back door opened and two more blond boys burst in, the elder grimy, but the younger black from head to toe. Bridget wagged a finger a them. 'Now, haven't I told you not to break the door down like that? And where's Dan? Don't tell me you forgot to pick him up again.' She sounded anxious.

'Nah,' the taller boy said, shrugging off his coat. 'He's gone to the privy.'

Bridget looked relieved, and a moment later Dan ran in, dragging his coat with one hand and fastening his braces with the other.

'We've got company,' Bridget said.

Six blue eyes suddenly turned to Anthony. He blushed but managed a smile.

'This is Anthony.' Bridget again plucked at her apron and searched the boys' faces as she went on, 'And he's family, your half-brother.'

Tommy's jaw dropped. 'Half-brother? You're kidding!'

Mick was struck dumb for a moment. 'What's that then?' he asked when he'd found his voice. But Dan simply gave Anthony an innocent and welcoming smile.

'I'll explain properly to you later,' Bridget said. 'But a half-brother's related to you almost like a full brother.' She glanced in confusion from the boys to Anthony. 'He's been away a long time but he's come to stay for a while. And that's all you need to know for now. It's time for your wash. The lodgers'll be home any minute.'

Anthony saw her shoulders drop with relief that the initial ice was broken but knew she would have a lot more explaining to do. He sipped his tea and talked to Kate about school, though he couldn't take his eyes off the three boys stripping off their filthy work clothes to their underdrawers while Bridget filled a bowl of warm water. When they were washed and dried she handed them clean shirts and breeches.

'What's for tea?' Mick buttoned his shirt and studied Anthony.

'Stew.' Bridget placed two bowls on the table.

Tommy screwed up his nose. 'Aw, not fish again!'

'No,' Anthony said, 'it's meat, and it's delicious.'

They sat and eyed him across the table. Tommy frowned. 'If you're our half-brother or whatever you call it, where've you been all this time? Why weren't you here when Da was alive?'

Bridget joined them. 'Sshh, Tommy! How many times do I have to tell you, I'll explain later.'

363

Dan sat next to Anthony and turned his smile on him again. He smiled back. The boy's eyes were so unquestioning, his smile so generous.

Eileen had lost interest in the visitor and climbed down from her chair. 'Can I go out to play?'

Bridget nodded. 'Indeed, and Kate and Sean can go with you, and you and all Joseph if you're not too tired.'

'Nah, I'm staying in,' Joseph said.

Anthony stood. 'May I take the children out?'

A look of pure delight crossed Bridget's face. 'Sure, they'd love that, thank you.'

At Anthony's words, Joseph slipped off his chair. 'I'll go out for a bit then.'

While Anthony was out with the young ones, Bridget joined Tommy and Mick and Dan at the table and told them briefly about their new brother in terms she hoped they would understand.

Tommy gave her a scornful look. 'What do you mean, God gave him to you? Da gave you us. And the lads at work say—'

'I don't want to know what the lads at work say,' Bridget said. 'God has a hand in everything. Of course Anthony had a real father as well, and it was God's decision that he must go to him. I was too young and poor to bring him up meself.'

'Was his da rich then?' Mick asked. 'Is that why Anthony talks posh like that?'

'Yes, his da was rich and gave him a good education. But it doesn't make any difference to you how he talks, he's still your brother.'

'I like him,' Dan said.

'That's nowt! *You* like everybody,' Tommy said.

Bridget placed a protective arm round Dan's shoulders. 'And a fine thing it is indeed to like people the way Dan does! You could learn a lesson from your little brother.' She stood. 'And now the lodgers'll be in any minute. I just wanted to explain some things to you so you'd understand and be nice to Anthony tonight. I'll talk to you again with the little ones before you go to bed. I thought me big men of the family needed a bit more explanation first.'

'Aye, you can say that again,' Tommy said.

Bridget gave him a silencing look.

By the time Anthony returned with the children, Bridget had given the

364

lodgers notice, informing them that her eldest son was returning. She told them no more than that.

The lodgers glared at him, stupefied when they saw his smart suit and refined appearance. Bridget didn't care what they thought. 'This is Anthony, and these are me lady lodgers, Fanny and Mabel.' She pointed to two women ensconced in fireside chairs.

Anthony bowed to the women, both plain and in their forties, with skin like white crêpe paper, though the younger bore a pleasanter countenance than her sister. He looked contrite. 'I apologize that my unexpected arrival has inconvenienced you. You will of course take all the time you need to find other accommodation.'

Mabel, the lodger with the surly expression, stared at him open-mouthed as he spoke in his educated voice. 'Aye,' she said when she'd got over her surprise. 'We'll need plenty of time. It's not easy to find places, and me and me sister want to stay together.'

Kate sat on the mat by the fire and pulled the little ones down with her. Her face shone with excitement. 'Anthony played hoops with us, and bays. Why can't he stay?'

Bridget gave her a warning glance. 'Don't talk daft. There's no room to squeeze a midget in. Come and sit down, Anthony.' She indicated Tom's old chair.

Anthony looked uncomfortable. 'Thank you, but I suppose I should take my things to your neighbour and get settled in first. I don't wish to disturb her at bedtime.' He remembered his presents and his face brightened. 'But first I've got something for you.' He retrieved the sweets and chocolates from his bag in the hall and placed the sweets on the table. 'These are for you to share,' he said to the children.

Dan snatched the bag and peered in. 'Aw! Caramels! Da always used to buy us caramels.'

The others jumped up and gaped at the treats, but Dan clutched the bag to him.

'Dan,' Bridget scolded, 'they're for all of you. You can have two each now and the rest later. But first thank Anthony. Have you forgotten your manners?'

Anthony smiled as they muttered hasty thanks and grabbed their rations. 'And these are for the ladies,' he said, giving the box of chocolates to Bridget. He wished he didn't have to be polite to the other women.

Bridget's eyes filled with tears. 'Thank you, but you didn't have to bring us presents.'

Such simple treats, and such gratitude! Again Anthony felt humble. 'It gives me pleasure,' he said. 'And now I should get acquainted with my new landlady.' He wanted to give Bridget time with the children. She still had a lot of explaining to do. A pity the lodgers were there, but she could always go to another room.

She smiled at Anthony and love spilled from her eyes. 'I'll take you over to Meg's now then. Kate can keep an eye on Sean for a minute.'

When she returned she packed the young ones into bed and called the older boys in. They all sat on the two beds cramped side by side. Again, she didn't quite know how to begin, but once she'd started, the words flowed from her like a river into the sea of upturned faces. She told them a simplified version of the story she'd told the boys and answered their questions as honestly as she could. But Kate still looked puzzled. 'I still don't know how he can be our brother if he's got another da.'

'It's because God had a hand in it.' Tommy repeated Bridget's earlier words and gave her a look that told her he knew better. She ignored him and stroked Kate's hair from her forehead.

'Of course, you know God has a hand in everything. I'm Anthony's ma, just like I'm your ma, so that makes him your half-brother. He's got *my* blood in his veins like you. It's almost the same as being your full brother. And when you get to know him you'll love him as if he was.'

'Is he going to stay for ever and ever, and play with us?' Eileen wanted to know.

'And buy sweets?' Sean added.

Bridget smoothed the coverlet to avoid their eyes. 'He's going to stay for as long as he can, and after that he'll come to see us a lot. Now isn't that wonderful?'

'What I'd like to know,' Tommy said, 'is why he didn't come to see us afore, and help us afore, if that's what he's come for now.' His tone was petulant and Bridget knew he was feeling unsure of his own position as the eldest.

'He came as soon as he found out about us. And isn't it fine that you've got a big brother to help you be the man of the house? You'd like some help now, wouldn't you?' She watched his face closely in the lamplight. She didn't want any jealousy to spoil this new happiness.

'I suppose it's all right,' Tommy said, with only a slight grudge in his voice.

Bridget sighed with relief. She knew that already Anthony – and the caramels – had made quite an impression on all of them. She got up. 'Now it's time you were all in bed. And don't forget to thank God in your prayers for sending Anthony back.'

She returned to the kitchen and was relieved to find it empty. She sat by the fire and stared into the pale embers. Such a day! Happiness drenched her like a rain shower. Though Fanny and Mabel had taken the news badly, she wouldn't allow herself to worry about that. They'd fine somewhere else. And she would have Anthony under her own roof. He didn't seem to mind that her home was so humble. And he and the children would soon love one another like a complete family. God did indeed work in strange ways. He'd taken Tom, but He'd given her back Anthony.

Anthony lay in bed, his mind whirling. He didn't know what he'd expected. But it wasn't this. She had so little money, so many children, such overcrowded housing. This was yet another reality that existed in the same world as his own. Dire poverty and hardship. He'd seen nothing like this on the island. But the hardship he could alleviate, and there was more love in that overcrowded flat than there'd ever been in his own vast home. Adelle would have been charmed by his new family. He would write in his diary tomorrow.

367

Chapter Thirty-Four

By the time Anthony arrived at the flat the next morning the boys and lodgers were at work and Kate at school. Bridget had put Tim in the yard in his pram and sent Eileen and Sean out to play beside their brother. They were safe in the yard. Nevertheless, she peeked out to check on them periodically.

'My, you startled me!' She turned from the window as Anthony came in. 'I was just seeing that those little monkeys weren't up to mischief.'

Her heart quickened as he placed his hands on her shoulders. 'Good morning. I should have knocked. I'm sorry.'

'Glory be! Nobody ever knocks in this house. Now just sit yourself down. I've got your breakfast almost ready.' She set a pan of milk on the stove and made fresh tea. This was the first breakfast she'd made for him. Her excitement at the simple pleasure made her hands tremble as she broke bread into the milk. It was a poor breakfast but he hadn't complained about the plain food yesterday.

He sat at the table and watched her. 'I'm going out to look for jobs after breakfast. Is there a newsagent nearby?'

'There's one just past the tram stop.' She placed his bowl before him and he peered into it. ''Tis only boily, I'm afraid,' she said, hating the apology in her voice.

'Boily?' He looked amused, and the light from the window caught the glint in his eyes.

'Bread and warm milk,' she explained. 'But I've got some dripping if you'd rather.'

He raised his hands in protest. 'No, I'm sure I'll like it.' His face didn't change as he ate but he smiled when he caught Bridget's anxious look. 'I wish you'd stop worrying about my food. This is . . . very tasty.'

Her face relaxed. She poured the tea and sat opposite him. 'Were you comfortable at Meg's?' she asked. Suddenly, she wasn't sure what to say to him.

'Very!' He put his hand over hers across the table. 'And please, also stop worrying about my comfort. I lived alone for a while and took care of myself – more or less.' He chuckled. 'You should have seen my first fried eggs. I'll tell you about my adventure later. But I'm not simply a spoiled rich boy as you think.'

She coloured and lowered her eyes. 'I didn't think—'

He stood and grinned. 'Of course you did. Everyone does.' He placed twenty pounds on the table and his face turned serious. 'This is for you. I've kept some back to pay my rent to your friend, and enough for my tram fares. Please buy whatever you need. I only wish it could be more.'

She stared at the money. 'More! Why, it's a fortune! Sure, I can't take that.' Her eyes filled.

'You can, and you're going to. And there'll be more when I find work.' He bent to kiss her cheek. 'And stop crying. When I come back I'd like you to show me around the area if you have time. And I don't want to take you out looking red-eyed.' At the doorway he turned. 'Oh, and thank you for breakfast.'

Bridget sat, her hand against the cheek he'd kissed as if to imprint that kiss for ever. And he wanted to take her out! How wonderful to walk out with him again. Then her pleasure dissipated like mist in the wind. She had to work that afternoon and most of the evening. But he was out of the front door before she could tell him.

She must see Meg and explain to her about Anthony, but she couldn't leave the children. She opened the back door and shouted to Eileen, 'Would you run over and ask Meg to pop in for a cup of tea, luv. Tell her I need to see her.' Eileen needed no second bidding. She always got a treat when she went to Meg's.

Bridget filled the kettle. She had to tell Meg the truth. But she was undaunted by the task. Meg of all people would understand, as would her other good friends.

At two o'clock Anthony returned triumphant. He bent over Tim's cot and chucked him under the chin. 'Guess what, young man! Two jobs in one morning! Congratulate me!' Tim gurgled back at him, but the sound was laboured.

Bridget stopped peeling potatoes and poked the kettle over the fire.

'Why, that sounds splendid! But two jobs?'

He pulled a face. 'Not as splendid as it sounds. They're only part-time but it's a start. Three mornings a week tutoring two unwilling schoolboys in Latin, and two afternoons teaching an extremely untalented young lady the piano. There are two more advertisements but they're box numbers. I'll write and catch the morning post.'

She set the mugs on the table and sighed. 'Indeed, 'tis wonderful to have an education.' She felt pride at Anthony's achievements, but also a sadness for her other children that over the past year had gathered in her chest, blocking it like a drain.

He threw himself into a fireside chair and rested his feet on the fender. 'I mean to see that the others will have an education too. Before the autumn term I intend to find full-time work at a school.'

He seemed to read her thoughts! She dried her hands on her apron and sat opposite him. 'Now why would you be doing that when you can be a tutor to rich people? 'Tis easier than teaching a class full of bairns that don't want to learn.'

'But not as rewarding. Poor children need the help more. And maybe some will thank me for it when they're grown up.'

She nodded. 'Aye, mine couldn't wait to get away from lessons and go to work. But now they admit they'd rather be back at school.'

Anthony leaned forward, in his excitement his face winding up like a spring. 'They're still children, Bridget. I mean it! I'm going to earn enough to enable them to go back to school.'

For a second hope kindled in her eyes, till reality, like cold water, doused it. He was young and eager and headstrong. He didn't understand the enormity of his promise – keeping eight children, and her. She shook her head. 'Sure, that's a kind thought, Anthony. But you're trying to take on too much. I'm grateful for your help, but I can't let you take care of us completely. The bairns'll have to do their bit as well.' She changed the subject and started to rise. 'And now I bet you're starving. The kettle's just boiling.' But he raised his hand to restrain her.

'No, thank you, I'm not hungry. I bought some fish and chips and ate them on the tram. Quite an experience.' He smiled as Bridget's eyebrows rose.

'Fish and chips on the tram! My, but you're coming down in the world. I'd never've thought—'

'Neither would I.' He grinned at her like a schoolboy trying to charm his way out of a scolding. 'And I meant what I said about the boys. But now come on. You promised to walk out with me this afternoon.'

'Oh, dear, I know, and I'd dearly love to but I can't.' She took refuge in poking the fire.

'Why not?' His disappointment was evident.

'I've got a sack of nails due in the morning and I'm but halfway through yet. Meg's taken the bairns off me hands for the afternoon so I can get on.'

'A sack of nails! Due in the morning?' His voice was incredulous. 'But you don't need to do that now. I've told you, I've got work. And what about the money I gave you?'

She poked the fire more furiously. 'I bought some boots for Tommy. Mick's are too small so Tommy's can go down to him. And I got a bacon joint for tea.' She sat again and glanced at the mantelpiece. 'The rest's up there. I promise I'll use it for emergencies but I can't just go on spending your money.'

He rebuked her with his eyes, his voice as firm as a stone wall. 'Put Tim in his pram and we're going out as planned. But first we'll drop off the nails and tell them you're not doing them any more. And that money's there to be used, not to decorate the mantelpiece.'

She bit her lip. He was so determined. Well, she knew where he got that from. But Tom wouldn't have let her do nails either if he'd had any say in it. Her shoulders dropped with gratitude and relief. 'All right. I can see there's no arguing with you.' Then she smiled. 'Now that's the first time I've seen a hint of the Irish in you.'

After dropping off the nails Bridget took Anthony to the pleasant part of Byker. Tim slept in his pram all the way. They reached the top of a steep hill and Anthony drew in his breath in surprise as the narrow streets suddenly gave way to an impressive sight. Large, luxurious houses stood alone and aloof from one another, lording it over acres of undulating farmland in a wide valley. An imposing church stood half secluded behind tall beeches and oaks. 'This is Byker Village,' she said with pride. 'Still like it used to be. There's six farms left, and that's St Michael's Church over there, and those fine houses mostly belong to the factory owners.' She pointed to a particularly ornate miniature brick castle. 'The Lawson family lives there. They own most of Byker.'

Anthony's eyes raked in the scenery. It was a delight to behold, a world differing absolutely from the one they'd passed through. The same sun that seemed merely to flicker on the wasteland of terraced flats and belching factories blazed down on large fields, giving an unenclosed quality to the landscape. From the top of the hill the hedgerows below formed a network of shining green cords separating the multicoloured crops. The church steeple blinked in the sun, keeping a watchful eye over the rural scene. He drew in a breath. 'It's strange to be in the country yet so close to . . .'

She knew what he couldn't say. 'I know, the factories and flats. When I first came here I couldn't believe it either.' For a moment she felt overwhelmed by nostalgia. Her past years had washed away so swiftly, like sand castles at high tide. She went on, 'Tom took me for a walk here on our wedding day. He said he was going to save up and some day we'd live on one of those farms or in one of those houses. It sounded wonderful.'

Anthony gave her a compassionate look. 'How sad that he died and it never happened.'

She managed a chuckle. 'Sure, Tom had no idea how to farm, and no idea how to save either. I knew it would never be, but it was nice to dream about. When you're brought up on a farm you never quite get used to the city.' She inhaled deeply. 'Sure, I love the smell up here.'

Anthony's eyes roved over the fields again, pausing at the grey-stone farmhouses and barns, the cows and sheep grazing with no thought of where their next meal would come from. 'Would you still like to live on a farm?' he asked.

She laughed. 'Oh, aye! And I'd like to live in Buckingham Palace and all.'

He indicated the red-brick castle she'd pointed out earlier and smiled. 'Would that smaller palace do?'

She laughed again, louder. 'Now I think I could lower me standards and make do with that. But then again, a farmhouse is cosier, and the boys would have healthy work.' Her eyes twinkled up at him. 'I'll think on it and make up me mind later. But in the meantime I've got to get this little lad home and fed.'

On the way home Tim still slept, breathing noisily. 'He's still asleep,' Anthony said in surprise.

Bridget stifled a sigh. 'Aye, he sleeps a lot – too much. He doesn't have the energy the others had. It's his chest. The doctor says he might grow out of it.'

'How long is it since he saw the doctor?'

She gripped the pram handle tighter. He was concerned about his baby brother. Already he'd settled into the family like a cushion on a

372

couch. 'I take him whenever he gets a bad bout,' she said in a voice choked with emotion. 'And I put warm poultices on him every night and get some linctus down him. But it doesn't seem to do much.'

'Why don't we take him tomorrow? Another examination wouldn't hurt, and perhaps a tonic?'

They were back in the terraced streets, but suddenly they didn't look so bleak. She smiled up at him. 'Yes, tomorrow. I'm that grateful to you, Anthony.'

While Bridget fed Tim and cooked the evening meal Anthony wrote applications for the two box-number jobs. Then he wrote to Arlette and Michelle. He chewed on his pen. What to tell them? The truth was out of the question. Though not personally acquainted with his parents, they were neighbours. He decided to introduce Bridget and his new family to the girls as very dear friends, like Megan and Ally and the other islanders. He wrote that he was lodging with a most wonderful family near Newcastle and would stay there and teach for a while. Then he wrote to his parents, telling them that he'd found pleasant lodgings and two tutoring jobs so far. He gave Meg's address. He couldn't risk his father paying a visit while on one of his trips to Newcastle.

The entire family and the lodgers were home when he returned from the post box. The bacon joint was a great success and after the meal Anthony entertained everyone with anecdotes of his time on the Isle of Skye. Even Mabel, the surly sister, smiled now and then at this accounts of Megan's and Wee Morag's antics. But he didn't mention the reason for his stay – *that* he would tell Bridget when they were alone. For the first time, he wanted to talk about Adelle. Bridget's gentleness was drawing him out, just as Adelle's had done. And he knew that Bridget wouldn't be shocked.

Tim lay in his cot, Sean in bed, and the other children hunched on the floor around Anthony's feet, fascinated by their strange and interesting new brother. 'Go on,' Joseph said, 'I bet you're just making it up. Da used to make up stories and all.'

'I'll prove it to you. Wait a moment.' Anthony stepped over the children and crossed the road to Meg's, where he retrieved Ally's flask and the sea shells from his bag. The children's eyes widened when he returned and arranged the items on the floor beside them. He grinned. 'Now do you believe me? I brought these back as souvenirs.'

'Aw, can we touch them?' Mick asked.

Anthony nodded. 'But remember the shells break easily.'

373

They each picked up a treasure to feel the evidence. Dan unscrewed the empty flask and sniffed it. 'Pooh!' His eyes watered as he turned to Anthony in disbelief. 'It smells like paraffin.'

'And it tastes like it at first,' Anthony said. 'But you grow to like it.'

'Are you ever going back there?' Dan stroked the crab shell and gave Anthony a searching look.

'I'd like to, one day.'

Tommy looked up at him, his eyes filled with longing. 'Aw, can I come?'

'Now that's enough,' Bridget scolded. ''Tis rude you are, always asking for things. You can have one more caramel and then bed, and let Anthony have some peace.'

Fanny, the younger lodger, rose. 'I'm for bed and all. Are you coming, Mabel?'

Mabel grimaced. 'Aye, me back's breaking. I must've ironed two hundred shirts the day.'

As the women left, Mick tugged at Bridget's skirt. 'Aw, Ma! We don't all have to go, do we? Can we stay up with Anthony?' Bridget smiled as she scooped Tim from his cot. 'If Anthony doesn't mind, half an hour and not a minute more.' She propped Tim over her shoulder and pulled Sean up from the floor. 'But you're coming with me, me lad, and Kate and Eileen and all.'

Eileen opened her mouth and let out a howl like a factory siren. 'I want to stay up with Anthony.'

'Me and all.' For once Kate pulled a sulky face.

'Now didn't I say bed?' Bridget gave Anthony an apologetic smile.

Without taking her eyes off Anthony, Kate backed out of the room, dragging Eileen with her. 'I want more stories,' Eileen said, before hooting again.

Anthony tried to keep his face stern, but it cracked into a smile. 'I'll tell you more tomorrow if you do what your mother says tonight.'

When everyone was in bed Bridget sat by the fire with Anthony, contentment seeping over her like a warm bath. 'They all loved your tales, and me and all. But why in heaven's name did you want to go off to a deserted island?'

He looked at her for a long time before he spoke. 'I'd like to tell you.'

Bridget's face mirrored every emotion in his voice as he told her about Adelle. She struggled to hold back her tears. 'Oh, my poor

374

Anthony,' she said at last. She knew too well what it was like to love and to lose. But she tried to console him. 'Sure, I can feel for you. She must have been a wonderful lady. But you're young. You'll love again.'

He shook his head. 'Never like that. I could never love another woman. But I've learned a different kind of love. And I'm still learning.'

Chapter Thirty-Five

Anthony moved into the lodgers' room when they'd gone. Bridget had been near to tears when he'd insisted that two of the boys share his bed. She hadn't expected him to give up his comfort and the only solitude he could get in the flat. But he'd been adamant. And the boys had fought for the honour of sleeping with him, forcing her to settle the argument by tossing a coin. Now, instead of four to a bed, she and the two girls shared one, Dan, Joseph and Sean the other. The comfort of the extra space was like taking off a pair of tight boots.

In such a short time Anthony had made life worth living again. He'd even accompanied them to church on several occasions, 'out of curiosity', he'd said. Though Bridget had been careful not to encourage him to convert as she had Tom. No. If Anthony wanted to turn to the faith he should do so because *he* wanted to, not to make her happy. And he did so much to make her happy, and the children.

Though he'd only managed to find one more tutoring job, the extra money had made the difference between bare existence and comfort. The children had forgotten they'd ever suffered the pangs of an empty belly and didn't even complain much about the evening tutoring sessions Anthony gave them. He was determined the boys should catch up on the year's schooling they'd lost while working, and Kate joined in as an eager participant. Bridget had never dreamt she could be as happy as this again with Tom gone. The only thought that nagged her was that Anthony would leave one day.

Towards the end of the summer holidays he received the letter he'd been hoping for. He read it on his way down the hall and shouted to Bridget through the kitchen door, 'I've got the job at Fowley Road School!'

Bridget dropped her scrubbing brush into the bucket and sat on her haunches. 'Holy saints! That's grand news indeed.'

He tiptoed over the wet floor and sat on the table, putting his feet on a chair out of her way. 'I can't believe it. They didn't even interview me.'

'Sure, now why would they be needing to do that? Your education speaks for itself.'

Anthony read the last paragraph of the letter. 'They say to report an hour early for classes and they will apprise me of my duties.'

'Well then, that will be a sort of interview. But it's grand to know beforehand you've already got the job.'

'Indeed it is. The boys can hand in their notice tomorrow. They're going back to school in a fortnight.'

Bridget brushed her hair from her forehead with the back of her hand, her smile fading. 'Oh, Anthony, it sounds so wonderful, but I'm worried about letting you take on so much responsibility. I'll only agree if I do nails at home again to help out. And maybe the boys can do some after school.'

Anthony shook his head. 'You've got more than enough to do, and the boys will also be too busy for nails. I'm going to continue tutoring them.'

Her worry deepened to dismay. Already she imposed on him too much. 'Dear Lord, Anthony! You know I'm grateful to you for helping them catch up but how can you give them extra tutoring with a full-time job?'

'Why not?' His voice gave away his surprise at her reaction. 'You know there's nothing I'd rather do with my free time. I'm going to keep on my Latin students on Saturdays as well. All together I'll be earning nearly ten pounds a week.' He gave her a triumphant look.

'Ten pounds!' She slid off her haunches and sat on the floor as if for more solid support, her eyes staring up at him.

Anthony gave her a victorious smile. 'So you see, there's no need for anyone to do nails.'

She abandoned her bucket and sat beside him on the table, her legs dangling. 'Sure, that's a lot of money. But I can't let you do it.'

'Bridget!' His tone turned serious. 'I mean it. There's nothing else I want to do with my time and money.'

She wondered when exactly this determined young man had emerged from the soft bundle of new life she'd borne. But then she'd always known he would assert himself one day. 'I know I can't stop you,' she said, 'but I just want you to know that it scares me that you're so good to us. The bairns love you that much already.' She bit her lip and forced herself to say what had been on her mind since the day he'd arrived. 'And . . . and we shouldn't get used to you spoiling us so. 'Tis going to be hard enough anyway for all of us when you go.'

Anthony threw back his head and laughed, his deep, pleasing laugh. 'Is *that* all that's worrying you?' Then his laughter died and his voice was filled with compassion. 'Poor Bridget, you've become so used to loss, even when good fortune comes your way you look ahead to losing it. If anything you'll be better off when I go. I'm almost embarrassed to tell you that my allowance is more than my salary. And what do I need it for? An occasional tailor's bill?' At Bridget's distressed expression, he took her hand. 'And already you're thinking about my leaving when I've barely arrived?'

Her face crinkled and she burst into tears. 'I can't help meself. It's always at the back of me mind that your real home's up there and that this is only a . . . a visit.'

'Come on,' he coaxed, chucking her chin. 'This is my home, too, and when I do go back you'll still be my family. You know I'll come to see you as often as I can.'

She sniffed and dried her eyes on her apron. 'Sure, I know that. I'm just being selfish and spoiling your wonderful news. I can't wait to see the lads' faces when you tell them.'

When everyone was home for the evening meal Anthony made his announcement.

Tommy stared at him in disbelief. 'You're kidding! Hand in our notice the morrow? And we won't have to go back there, ever?'

'Never,' Anthony assured him. 'Not if you work hard at your lessons *and* do the homework I give you.'

Tommy's face cracked into a grin, but Mick's delighted expression faded. 'Homework?' he said, looking stunned. 'You mean you're still going to give us lessons at home and all?'

Bridget laughed. 'Now then, would you rather do a couple of extra hours learning after school or spend your whole day at the factory? And you'll have the long school holidays again,' she added as further enticement.

Mick's face brightened. 'Aye, I never thought of that.'

Bridget was changing Tim's nappy and he gurgled up at her. 'And just listen to your little brother – hardly a trace of a wheeze since he's been on that medicine. Now there's an example of what money can do.

Doesn't that make you want to get an education and find a good job?'

Anthony added his own encouragement. 'And I'll show you another example tomorrow. We'll have a ceilidh to celebrate.'

Kate gazed at him in wonder. 'One of them parties you had on that island?'

'That's right,' Anthony said. 'We can afford a little party now whenever we want.'

The next day Bridget shopped and cooked. The table was laden with sandwiches, pastries, and lemonade. Towards evening she got out the paper hats and set one at each plate. They were now faded and torn but still looked festive. She sighed as she recalled all the happy occasions those hats had seen when Tom was alive. Well, she comforted herself, he'd be delighted to look down and see Anthony wearing his hat at the table.

The children were washed, groomed and dressed in their Sunday clothes when Anthony arrived home. Bridget looked smart in her best blue frock. Even Tim in his cot wore a fresh nightgown. 'Well, you all look splendid,' Anthony said, then frowned and shook his head. 'But you don't dress up for a ceilidh. Here, this is what you do.' Much to the children's delight he ruffled each head in turn, then he withdrew some of the pins from Bridget's hair. It flopped about her face in Megan's fashion and everyone laughed.

'Now put the hat on, Ma,' Dan begged, with a grin that stretched his face in all directions.

'And all of you, and Anthony,' Bridget said. 'Sure, I'm not going to be the only one to make a fool of meself.'

They all pulled on their hats and more laughter followed as Anthony ruffled his own hair and put on his red crêpe paper crown. Then he took a small bottle of whisky from his pocket. 'And this is for Bridget and me.'

'Whisky!' Bridget smiled and shuddered. 'Sure, not for me.'

'It's delicious in tea, with sugar.' Anthony took Ally's flask from the mantelpiece, where it had sat since he'd moved in as physical proof of his adventures on Skye. 'And it tastes even better from Ally's flask.'

'I want whisky,' Sean said, jumping from his chair and tugging at Anthony's jacket.

Bridget wagged her finger at him. 'Not till you're as big as Anthony, me lad. Now go and sit yourself down.' She grinned at Anthony. 'Well, I suppose if that's what you drink at a ceilidh, then that's what I'll be having, but *in tea*, mind you.'

Eileen climbed on to her chair at the table and looked with longing at the array of treats. 'Can we start now, Ma?'

'I'll pour the lemonade.' Kate opened a bottle without waiting for Bridget's answer. Anthony took control.

'One moment! You can pour, but you must wait until the tea's ready before you drink. We make a toast first.'

The tea made and everyone with a mug in hand, he toasted: 'To our first of many more ceilidhs.'

Bridget sipped her spiced tea and her eyes filled. But not because of the whisky. 'Sure, it brings the tears to your eyes, this stuff,' she said. 'All right, you can eat now. But we must say grace first.' She was glad to bend her head while she uttered the short prayer, 'For what we're about to receive, may the Lord make us truly thankful.' No sooner were her words out than a jumble of arms attacked the food.

After the meal, the table suitably littered with dirty plates, ceilidh fashion, Anthony rose to make an announcement: 'Now it's time for a song, and as *I'm* the host I make the first request. Bridget starts. I'd like her to sing "The Irish Girl".'

Bridget bowed her head and swallowed hard. She hadn't sung that song to him since he was four years old. And it was Tom's favourite. She took the floor and the catch in her voice when she began disappeared after the first line. She was back in the nursery singing to Anthony and, at the same time, in her own home singing to Tom as she had on their wedding day. Her audience was hushed and Anthony never once took his eyes off her. When she'd finished, she sat, head bowed. Anthony clapped and the others joined in. There was a catch in his voice, too, as he thanked her. 'That was wonderful, thank you,' was all he said, but he gave her a look that told her much more.

Kate banged a spoon on the table for attention. 'Now it's Anthony's turn, and then me and Eileen, and then Dan, and—'

Bridget smiled. 'Now contain yourself, Kate. One at a time and, yes, Anthony first.'

Anthony stood. 'I think you'll all know this one, and it's my next favourite after "The Irish Girl".' He sang "The Nursemaid", and this time Bridget wept openly. His voice was so deep, yet with the same purity of his childhood soprano.

The girls sang in turn, but afterwards the boys' combined version of a clog dance was interrupted by a loud thumping from above. Bridget looked up at the ceiling with a smile. 'Well, I thought Mrs Gray would've thumped her broom before now.' She explained to Anthony,

380

'She used to do it every time we had a party when Tom was alive.'

'Aye,' Tommy said, 'the old crow can't stand people having a good time.'

'Miserable old spoilsport!' Joseph yelled to the ceiling.

Bridget gave him a stern look. 'That's quite enough. Haven't I told you not to be rude to people? Just take your boots off now and finish your dance quietly.'

Dan pulled a face. 'Aw, Ma, it's not the same without boots. Let's make the old goat mad.'

'Stop that nonsense, Dan, and do as I say.' Bridget gave Anthony a hopeless smile.

In bed that night she lay awake for hours, reliving every event of the evening. Anthony's words the previous day were true. She must stop this fear of losing him again, and stop this selfishness of wanting to have him all the time. Even if he didn't have to go back to the house, like all the children he would get married and leave her some day. God only allowed parents to rent children, not own them.

Chapter Thirty-Six

Anthony's first day at Fowley Road Elementary School came as an unexpected shock. Though he knew the public education system to be inadequate, he wasn't prepared for what he found.

He arrived one hour before class time and made his way through the deserted corridors, the brown paint peeling off the walls, the wooden floors filthy. His heart sank. He found the office and hesitated outside the open door. A slight, elderly man sat behind a large ink-stained desk and indicated the chair opposite. 'Ah, Mr Hayward, I'm Mr Simms, the headmaster. Sit down, sit down.'

Anthony bowed and sat. The bare office was little more cheerful than the corridors. Mr Simms leaned back in his chair and knotted his bony knuckles. 'I was impressed by your education and background and you have had some experience. I can't think why you want to work in a place like this, but it's *my* gain. Qualified teachers are hard to find.'

'I'm, er, delighted you chose me for the job, sir.'

Mr Simms' narrow face widened slightly as he attempted a smile. 'I hope you're still delighted after your first day. It's not a bed of roses here, you know. You can expect at least two hundred brats in your class, probably more.'

'Two hundred?' Anthony's eyebrows rose, and Mr Simms made a throaty sound that passed for a chuckle.

'Yes, it sounds a lot. But it's a great improvement over the old days. There used to be more than twice that number and the classes were mixed.' He shook his head in disapproval. 'Can you imagine? Boys and girls in the same playground. Quite indecent! We've come a long way.'

'But it seems we still have a long way to go,' Anthony countered.

Mr Simms' balding head wagged again. 'No, young man. They get as good an education as they need. Remember, we're teaching the

382

working masses the basics they need to carry on working in a society that's becoming more industrialized and complex daily. They need to read in order to learn to fear the word of God, otherwise their social behaviour would disrupt our modern society. And, of course, they should be able to read such things as danger signs and simple instructions for operating machinery in the factories. We're not preparing them for Oxford or Cambridge, you know.'

'I understand that, sir. But the classes do seem to be rather large for one teacher to cope with, even using the monitor system.'

'You may be right, my man, but teachers cost money, monitors don't. You'll soon get the hang of it.' He stood. 'Glad to have you join my staff, Mr Hayward. Your classroom is down the corridor and to the right. The books and slates are kept in the cupboard. You might want to glance through them before the mob gets here. You'll soon get the hang of it,' he repeated with absolute confidence.

'Thank you, sir.' Though he wondered if he would ever 'get the hang of it' Anthony rose and shook the man's proffered hand.

His doubts doubled as he entered the classroom. It was little more than twice the size of the schoolroom on the island yet had to accommodate four or five times the number of children. The desks were crammed so closely together he had to inch sideways down the aisle to his desk. The windows were small and high, giving barely enough light for him to look at the books for the day's lessons. The books in the cupboard were already sorted into subjects and he glanced through them in despair. They covered all levels, from beginners to school-leavers. He'd gained experience at teaching such a mixed class on the island – but two hundred or more pupils? He took out his pocket watch. Twenty minutes before classes started. He would go out for a breath of fresh air to calm himself.

When he returned and made his way down the corridor, poorly dressed boys, some barefoot, milled almost shoulder-to-shoulder around him. His spirits plummeted even further. But he braced himself and entered his classroom.

Already at least two hundred boys, ranging in age from six to thirteen, had crammed themselves into the available desks. The later arrivals filing in found space on the floor. The noise was deafening.

He took his place in front of the class and rapped his ruler on his desk for silence. Nothing happened. In desperation he took the 'punishment' stick from its hook by the blackboard where it hung as a visible reminder of its existence. He banged the stick on the desk. It worked. A sea of blank faces turned silently towards him. 'Good morning, pupils,' he said.

'Good morning, sir,' came the reply as if in one voice.

'I'm your new teacher, Mr Hayward, and I'd like to start by getting to know you.' Such a task, he thought. How to begin? He composed himself. 'First, I'd like the monitors to stand and each tell me your name and which subjects you teach the younger ones.'

About a dozen boys ranging in age from ten to thirteen stood. He nodded to the first on the right. The boy, about twelve, gave him a resentful look. 'I'm Jimmy Biggs and I give the little 'uns writing, sir.'

Anthony wrote the boy's name and subject in his register and went on to the next. By mid-morning he'd organized them into groups, a monitor in charge of each, while he made his rounds to supervise the activities. It was like the Tower of Babel – so many different lessons being conducted in one room.

One of the monitors raised his arm for attention but Anthony was engrossed in another group. 'Sir, sir!' the boy shouted.

Anthony turned. 'Yes?'

'It's Willy Smith, sir. He's filled his britches, sir.'

A snicker travelled around the room.

Willy, about seven years old, let out a wail. 'He's a liar, I haven't done nothing.'

As Anthony approached the group he realized the older boy had told the truth. 'It's all right, Willy,' he said. 'It's nothing to get upset about. But why didn't you ask your monitor if you could leave the room?'

'I . . . I put me hand up but he took no notice, sir.'

Anthony turned to the monitor. 'What's your name?'

The boy stood with blatant reluctance and glowered at Anthony. 'Jack Billings, sir.'

'And why did you ignore Willy's request to leave the room, Jack?'

'Aw, he's always wanting to go to the bloody privy, sir. And once he starts everybody puts their hands up. He's a flaming nuisance.'

'Well, it's a nuisance for you that you ignored his request, Jack. Take him out now and see that he gets cleaned up.'

'Me, sir?'

'Yes, *you*. And never ignore such a request again.'

Holding his nose and pulling a face, Jack yanked Willy up by his shoulder with an unnecessary jerk and marched him from the room. The class tittered.

'Enough,' Anthony said. 'Back to your lessons.'

384

The day passed somehow and he went home with a feeling of achievement that at least he'd managed that much.

Bridget glanced up from her ironing and smiled at him. 'My! You look as if you've been pulled through a hedge backwards. Was it that bad?'

'Worse.' Anthony slumped into a chair and poured out the events of the day.

Bridget sighed. 'Aye, I know it's hard on the bairns, but at least it's better than no schooling – and it's free.'

'Free or not, it's inhuman. A disgrace!' His face flamed with anger.

'Calm yourself, now. You're doing your best to make a difference to some of them. I'll make you a nice cup of tea and you'll feel better.' Bridget left her ironing and poked the kettle over the fire.

Anthony managed a smile. 'Your cure for all ills.'

On the last day of term Anthony arrived home tired but happy. Be brushed chalk dust from his jacket sleeve, threw himself into a fireside chair and grinned at Bridget. 'Well, I made it to the end of term. Though there were times when I wondered.'

She laid Tim back in his cot. He chortled up at her with only a tiny rasp of mucus still in his chest. Smiling, she took down Ally's flask from the mantelpiece and poured whisky into a mug. 'I filled up the flask for you to celebrate.'

He took the mug with a sigh. 'Ah, thank you. I've earned it.'

She sat opposite and appraised him as if for the first time. Each day when he came home she had to mentally pinch herself. He was actually here, sitting in her kitchen. 'I suppose the children were worse than usual today with the holidays starting,' she said.

'How did you guess?' Though his voice was tired, there was a smile in it. 'Jimmy Black put a rat in my desk drawer. Matt Blake turned his inkwell upside down over Davey Buchanan. Mike Jaimeson threw a stone at Bill Simmons and cut his forehead.' He sipped the whisky and put his feet on the fender. 'I can't blame the children for being delighted to get out of that place for a while. Ah, for a few peaceful weeks.'

She leaned forward in her chair. 'I'm that excited about your first Christmas. And I'm making two cakes – a special birthday cake for your real birthday and a fruit cake for Christmas Day.'

He looked into his glass. 'I appreciate the thought, but I should go home for Christmas. I've been wondering what to do, but today it's been decided for me. I had a letter from Mother.'

Bridget felt a chill of premonition and shivered. She'd known he would have to visit them soon but had prayed it would be after Christmas. 'Is something wrong at the house?' she asked, always careful not to call it 'home'.

'My father's been in bed for four days. The doctor says it's either an ulcer or simply severe indigestion. But Mother sounds worried. I really should go while I'm on holiday from school. And I haven't seen them for six months. I'll leave tomorrow.' His eyes studied her as he spoke, but she was determined not to show her disappointment too much. It was hard on him being pulled in two directions.

'We'll miss you,' she said, standing to check the potatoes on the stove. The steadiness and brightness of her tone surprised her.

'I shall miss you all too. But you can expect me back for New Year, or rather the new century. We must bring nineteen hundred in with a ceilidh.'

'Aye, we'll have a grand party then. I hope 'tis nothing serious with your father.' She busied herself setting the table. 'The bairns are in the back lane. Would you mind giving them a shout?'

He stood and put his empty mug on the table. 'Thank you for the whisky. We'll save the rest for the New Year.'

She watched his back through the window as he disappeared down the yard and prayed silently that his father would get well soon.

Mildred was reclining on the *chaise-longue* by the drawing room fire digesting her lunch when Harold, the butler, announced Anthony's arrival. She jerked up. 'Send him in immediately.'

Anthony strode across the room with a smile on his face, but it faded when he saw his mother's expression. He bent to kiss her cheek. 'Mother, it's nice to see you. How's Father?'

She waved a hand for him to sit and he took the winged chair opposite. 'Not well, Anthony. I'm glad you've come at last. I wish you'd been here earlier.'

Concerned by her tone, he scrutinized her face. Her eyes were red. 'I received your letter only yesterday, Mother. Is he worse?'

She nodded. 'The doctor now thinks it's either an ulcer or . . .' She shuddered. 'Some sort of growth. He's got to have one of those new X-rays. They took him to the hospital this morning. I'm waiting for the results now. Indigestion, indeed! I've called in a specialist and a surgeon from London, just in case.'

Anthony sat beside her and took her hands. He was surprised to find

386

they trembled. 'I'm sorry, Mother. But with modern science and the best of doctors, he's in good care.'

'I should have called in the physician earlier, but your father's such a stubborn man. He insisted it was only a stomach upset.' She withdrew her hands from his and covered her face with her handkerchief.

He was used to her tears and mild, constant worries, but now she was obviously distressed. The only emotion he'd ever witnessed between her and his father had been anger, or at least irritation. He felt moved by her concern. Though she'd never shown it until now, she must still feel love for his father. Did he return it? Were they a loving couple in the privacy of the boudoir? It was hard to imagine. But how could any outsider know about the personal feelings between a man and a woman? He kissed her cheek and rose. 'I'll go to the hospital and find out what's happening. Why not come with me? It's better than sitting here worrying.'

She shook her head and spoke in a voice distorted by pain, 'He said I'm not to bother him there, that he can do without my hysterics.' She gave Anthony a pathetic look before wailing into the handkerchief.

'Oh, Mother!' Anthony put his arm round her shoulder and there was genuine concern in his voice. 'Don't upset yourself so. Illness does nothing to improve anyone's humour, and we both know that Father is, well, uncertain at the best of times.' He forced a smile.

She sniffed and rose, bracing her shoulders. 'I'll come with you and stay in the waiting room, until and *if* he wishes to see me. He'll be happy to see *you*, of course.' She rang the bell and Harold stepped soundlessly into the room. 'Please order the car immediately,' she said.

'Yes, madam.' He bowed and slid back out through the door.

Anthony put his arm under Mildred's elbow. She leaned heavily on him as he led her from the room. 'Is Margery coming?' he asked on the way downstairs. He hoped not, for that would mean it was serious indeed.

Mildred sniffed again. 'She's still incarcerated in India, *and* the children have measles. I wish she'd never married an army man. She's never here when I need her. On top of everything, she's in an interesting condition again – five children in eleven years. It's not decent.'

Anthony smiled, thinking of the eight vice-like hugs he'd received from the children when he'd left Byker. He hadn't even seen Margery's two youngest. He must make more of an effort to keep in touch with her. 'I'm sure she finds her family rewarding, Mother,' he said. 'I shall write tomorrow and congratulate her.'

In the hall, the ubiquitous Harold already awaited them with their outdoor clothes. Mildred shivered and wept all the way to the hospital in Morpeth.

'Visitor for you, sir,' the moon-faced nurse boomed as she ushered Anthony into the hospital room. He could taste the smell of carbolic, a painful reminder of Adelle.

Richard lay back on his pillows on an iron cot in the green-painted room. It was furnished with two leather guest chairs by the bed, a bedside locker laden with flowers, and white curtains at the window – sparse by Richard's standards but undoubtedly the most expensive room in the hospital. Richard's half-closed eyes opened in pleasure at the sight of Anthony, but sickness had fallen like a fog over his face. His ruddy complexion was grey, his eyes dull, his cheeks and jowls slack. 'Anthony, me boy!' he said, easing himself up with difficulty. 'I'm glad to see you've come to visit your old father on his deathbed.'

Anthony sat on the bed. 'Nonsense, Father. The nurse said you'll be home for Christmas.' Somehow he couldn't bring himself to address his father as 'sir' on his sickbed.

'Christmas? Bah! That nurse would consider a corpse as fit as a lop. I can't stand all this false cheerfulness.'

'And how do you feel?'

'As if I'd swallowed a gallon of sulphuric acid.' Richard's face twisted in pain for a second, then relaxed.

'The nurse said your X-ray results should be ready in an hour. At least we'll know what's wrong, and you've got the best physicians in the country at your service.'

'Yes, yes, yes! I'm tired of hearing all that. I just want to get out of this place.' There was a hint of the old tetchiness in Richard's voice and Anthony felt relieved.

'Mother's outside,' he ventured. 'She dearly wants to see you.'

Richard waved away the idea. 'Heaven forbid! I'm sick of her blubbering all over me. I want some peace and quiet.'

'She's concerned about you,' Anthony persisted. 'You'd care more if she weren't. And she misses you.'

'Misses me? God knows, she can't be lonely! She's got enough friends to entertain her and keep her company.'

'That's hardly the same as having her husband at home and healthy. Please see her, if only for a few minutes. She's come all this way in the cold.' It felt strange, pleading his mother's cause to his father.

388

Richard contemplated the green wall for a moment. 'Aye, I know she's worried about me. She's spending enough on those private physicians to finance this hospital for a year. All right, if it'll keep her satisfied, and if she'll promise not to blubber. But not yet. I want a word with you alone.'

Anthony knew what was coming and felt a deep sadness. He'd have to stay, at least until his father was well. He hated to disappoint Bridget and the children over New Year, and he'd miss them. 'Don't worry, Father,' he said, 'I plan to stay and look after things until you're on your feet again.'

Richard laced his hands on the blankets above the mound of his belly. 'Until I'm on my feet? You mean you still want to go back and live in a hovel and teach a horde of ruffians? I'd hoped you'd have got that teaching nonsense out of your system by now.' The growl was back in Richard's voice and Anthony forced himself to speak calmly. He didn't wish to upset his father in his present condition.

'I still enjoy it, Father. But we'll discuss my return later, when you're well.' He stood to end the dispute. 'Now I should get Mother. She'll be freezing to death in that waiting room.' He left before Richard could argue.

Mildred sat on a wooden bench in the bare room, her hands stuffed in her muff, her eyes fixed on the door. She jumped up and ran to meet him. It was the first time he'd seen her run.

'How is he?' Her eyes searched his for reassurance and he smiled encouragement.

'Cantankerous as ever – an excellent sign. He'd like to see you.'

She flushed with pleasure like a débutante being asked for her first dance. 'He said that?' There was a half-note of disbelief in her voice.

He nodded and took her arm. 'Only one thing, Mother. It upsets him to see you weeping. Could you try to be cheerful and not show too much concern?' He felt pleased with himself. He'd dealt with that one nicely. He'd never envisaged playing the role of peacemaker between his parents.

Mildred took his advice with the gratitude of a dog given a bone. 'Yes, yes, of course,' she said, and quickened her steps. She surged into the room and bent to kiss Richard's brow. 'I hear you're feeling better, my dear. Such good news!'

Anthony cringed. She was overdoing it. But Richard suffered the kiss and waved her to the bedside chair. 'I'll feel better when I'm out of this place,' he muttered.

Mildred sat and studied Richard's face, her flush of pleasure fading. 'You still look pale. Are they feeding you well?'

'Food? What's that? Don't talk rot, woman. Do you call bread and milk food?'

Remembering his first taste of boily, Anthony smothered a smile. 'While you have Mother for company, I'm going to see if the X-ray results are ready,' he said, glad of an excuse to escape for a while.

Richard snorted. 'Photographs! Can you believe it? They take photographs of your innards now instead of giving you medicine.'

As Anthony left he saw Mildred give a surreptitious dab at her eyes with her gloved hand. At least the handkerchief remained out of sight.

The moon-faced nurse showed him to a small office at the end of the hall. She knocked timidly, her boisterous manner now deferent. 'Mr Hayward to see you, sirs.'

Two elderly men were holding up to the light a large transparent photograph. They placed it on the desk and nodded permission. The shorter man held out a pale, slim hand and inclined his greying head. 'Ah, Mr Hayward. I'm Mr Fitzgerald and this is Dr Kimberley.' Dr Kimberley also held out his hand and shook Anthony's heartily, then he pulled at his bushy-white beard. It stuck to his face like cotton-wool swabs.

'We were just going over your father's X-rays,' he said.

'How are they?' Anthony didn't like the sombre tone of the man's voice.

Mr Fitzgerald, who from his title Anthony took to be the surgeon, indicated the visitor's chair in front of the desk. 'Please sit down.' Both men sat on leather swivel chairs and studied him across the desk. Mr Fitzgerald went on. 'It doesn't look good. Though it seems not to be an ulcer, there's some sort of foreign tissue on the stomach lining. Only an operation will determine the problem.'

Dr Kimberley rested his elbows on the chair-arms and pressed his fingertips together as if about to play church and steeple. 'Of course we can't say what it is at this stage, but Mr Fitzgerald will conduct an operation tomorrow. At least your dear mother summoned us in good time.'

At Anthony's dismayed expression, Mr Fitzgerald cut in, 'It may be nothing serious, but we can't take the risk, you understand. Better safe than sorry.'

It came to Anthony with sudden clarity that his father might indeed

390

be on his deathbed as he'd said. He'd always thought him invincible, despite his moans and groans of late. 'You can't tell from the X-ray what the problem is?' he asked, surprised by the urgency in his voice.

Mr Fitzgerald shook his head. 'No, but the photograph indicates the location, which eliminates exploratory surgery. We can go straight to the trouble spot in one operation.'

'When?'

'Tomorrow morning,' Mr Fitzgerald said. 'He should be over the worst by late afternoon.'

Dr Kimberley rose. 'We were just about to inform your father.'

'No.' Anthony jumped up. 'My mother's with him. I fear she'd take it badly in his presence. I'll send her home and stay with my father. I shall tell her later. Would you mind giving me a few minutes?'

'As you say.' Dr Kimberley sat again, seeming relieved.

Anthony guessed they weren't looking forward to delivering the news any more than he. He trailed back to his father's room in a daze. It was so sudden. What if the worst happened? Operations of any kind were dangerous. Of course he'd known that one day . . . But the day had seemed so far off. And how would he break the news to his mother? His fingers curled into his palms. He hated himself for his next thought but he couldn't banish it. Even if all went well, his new-found freedom was at least interrupted for a time. And if it didn't go well? He shook his head to rid himself of his guilty musings like a puppy shaking itself dry after a bath. But out of the confusion of his thoughts came one certainty. Whatever happened, he could not relinquish his new family, though he would do his duty by his parents. He would take over his father's estate responsibilities, but not his life. He could never renounce his new independence.

He stepped into Richard's room with an imitation smile.

'The results aren't ready yet.'

Mildred put her hand to her mouth. 'Oh, dear!'

'By God!' Richard barked. 'I could die in the meantime.'

'I think not, Father.' Anthony kept the smile on his face and turned to Mildred. 'Why don't you go home before it gets dark, Mother? I have an errand in Morpeth, then I shall call for the car. The doctors will telephone when they know.'

'I suppose you're right,' Mildred said, a note of relief in her voice. However much she wanted to see Richard, the strain of being with him in his present state showed in her tight face. She allowed Anthony to help her up from her chair and bent to kiss Richard's forehead again.

'We don't wish to weary you too much, dear. I'll come back later with Anthony.'

Richard waved his hands in impatience. 'No, no. I'm tired. Let me rest.'

Anthony noted that his father's voice was tired, or resigned; the growl had gone out of it.

After escorting Mildred to the waiting Daimler, Anthony turned as if to walk into town. But as soon as the car was out of sight he retraced his steps to the hospital and returned to the office. Mr Fitzgerald and Dr Kimberley accompanied him to his father's room. Like Anthony, they smiled as they entered.

'Begod! You're back already, boy,' Richard said, then noticed the two doctors behind Anthony. They all assembled at the foot of the bed. Richard's face paled even further as his gaze returned to Anthony. 'Ah, I see! Wanted to get rid of your mother before delivering the news? That means it's bad.'

'Not at all, sir,' Mr Fitzgerald said. 'We've located the problem and will operate tomorrow.'

'The problem? What the devil is it?' Richard gave the doctors a frightened look. He listened silently to the news, then closed his eyes. 'All right! Cut me up. Do your worst. I can't go on like this anyway.' His voice was controlled, but his hands gripped the sheets.

'You won't feel a thing during the operation, the chloroform will knock you out,' Mr Fitzgerald soothed.

Dr Kimberley smiled encouragement. 'It's rather like getting drunk. You won't remember anything afterwards either.'

'Aye, and what about the hangover? How long does that last?'

'A bit of nausea at first, that's all. You should be on your feet again in a couple of weeks.' Dr Kimberley's voice was too loud and cheerful.

Richard let out a long breath. 'I want to go home after the operation. I'm not staying here a minute longer than I have to.'

'Naturally, and we shall be on hand to attend you twenty-four hours a day,' Mr Kimberley reminded him. 'We shall stay as long as is necessary.' Then he turned to Anthony. 'If you wouldn't mind leaving for a while? In view of the X-rays we need to conduct a further examination. And would you please tell your dear mother that we shall be in good time for dinner.'

Of course, Anthony realized, they would be staying at the house. His mother had spared no effort. 'I'd like a few minutes with my father before

392

I leave,' he said, and the men nodded and disappeared into the corridor.

Richard grimaced. 'So, you want to give me your last blessing?'

Anthony sat on the bed. 'No, Father, I simply want to tell you not to worry about estate matters. I'll take care of everything until you're well again.'

'And if I'm not?'

'If you insist on looking on the black side – of course, you know I will.'

Richard sighed, 'Aye, well, in any event it'll be yours to do with as you like soon enough.' His eyes travelled to the blank green wall and stayed there. 'If . . . anything happens, you'll take good care of your mother, won't you? You've forgotten about that . . . silly business?'

'Yes, I have, Father. And you know I'll take good care of Mother.'

Richard's gaze returned, but a blanket of silence fell over him. Then he patted Anthony's hand. 'You'd better go now and tell her the news.' He made a sound resembling a chuckle. 'I don't envy you the task.' Anthony felt his father's hand still over his and realized it was the first time since he'd been a child that their hands had touched, other than in a man-to-man handshake. He grasped the hand for a moment before standing. Richard screwed up his eyes.

'Goodnight, Father,' he whispered. 'I'll be back first thing in the morning.'

Richard nodded and his dull eyes opened, gleaming wet, before he closed them in dismissal. Anthony wondered, were they tears of self-pity? Or had that touch meant something to his father as well? But whatever the reason for the tears, the touch had not stemmed from self-pity. Old age and illness were certainly mellowing him.

On Anthony's return, Mildred took the news as expected. But a strong dose of smelling salts followed by a large brandy helped to restore her composure. And when the surgeon and physician arrived, they further comforted her with their light-hearted assurance that Richard would be on his feet within a couple of weeks.

But the following morning, when the butler followed Anthony's instructions and put the telephone call through to the study, Mr Fitzgerald's voice was no longer jocular: 'I'm sorry to have to tell you, your father failed to come out of the chloroform,' he said.

'He's dead?' Anthony's hands tightened on the telephone. Like his mother, the doctors' confidence had relieved his anxiety and he'd refused to anticipate the worst.

The formless voice went on, 'But it was a blessing for your father. He wouldn't have lasted more than six months or a year, and it would have been an excruciating time. The damage was much more extensive than the pictures showed. X-rays aren't an exact science, you understand.'

Anthony replaced the receiver as Mildred entered. 'I heard you talking. Was it the doctor?' He nodded and she bustled towards him, her hands to her cheeks. 'How is he? Is it over?'

He stood and put his arms round her shoulders. 'He's gone, Mother,' he said softly.

A little sound, like a mouse's squeak, came out of Mildred's mouth before she slid from Anthony's grasp.

Chapter Thirty-Seven

Mildred took to her bed and left Anthony to arrange the funeral. He was surprised by the extent of her distress; she'd taken nothing but broth and brandy since receiving the news. Accustomed now to funeral formalities, he organized everything and sent black-edged invitation cards to everyone on Mildred's endless social list. Although too ill to take part in the preparations she'd insisted it be a grand affair.

On the funeral morning Anthony sat by the drawing room fire, waiting for Mildred. He was dressed in the grey suit and black armband he'd worn to Adelle's funeral and felt a double sadness. Losing his father had touched him more than he could have imagined and had evoked painful memories of Adelle. Memories. He was building unhappy ones so quickly! Though he felt only loss for Adelle, the loss he felt for his father was mingled with regret. He'd grown to understand love too late. Now he knew that had he tried, he could have felt and shown more love for his father despite their differences. And, as Adelle had said, his father had loved him, in his way. He'd expressed it in that single moment in the hospital when they'd clasped hands, and Anthony had returned the emotion in that grip. He was thankful for that.

His thoughts were interrupted when Mildred entered on the arm of her personal maid. He was struck by the change in her appearance. In bed she'd looked ill, but today her severe black bombazine gown emphasized her pallor and weight loss. Her chins hung in limp folds over her high neckline. Here eyes, glazed and lifeless, peered through red rims. And her face, featureless without its make-up, was crushed in the grip of her grief. He jumped up and kissed her cheek. 'Are you sure you feel well enough to attend, Mother?'

'Indeed, I must see him off. But promise you'll stay by my side. Oh, if only Margery could have been here!' Her voice, too, was crushed.

She pressed her black lace handkerchief to her eyes and the maid lowered her on to a chair.

Anthony placed his hand on her shoulder. 'Of course I'll stay by you, Mother, and Daisy will be at your other side.'

Daisy, standing at a respectful distance behind Mildred, nodded her grey head. Instead of her usual starched white linen, she wore a black lace cap and apron over her black dress, and her long, thin face was almost as melancholy as Mildred's.

He took out his pocket watch. 'It's nearly ten o'clock. Would you like a brandy before we leave, Mother?'

She shook her head. 'No, please order the car now. I want a few minutes with Richard before the guests arrive.'

The Hayward family chapel and crypt were laden with wreaths and hothouse flowers. Flanked by Anthony and Daisy, Mildred sat in the front pew, taking refuge behind her veil. Her gaze never left the wreath-covered coffin and her breath came in muffled sobs. Anthony held her gloved hand. Since his father's death he'd held her hand more than he'd done throughout his life. She seemed glad of the comfort and he enjoyed giving it. In their shared sorrow a tenuous bond was developing between them. He was sad only that it had taken his father's death for his mother to turn to him. With Margery away he was all she had left, and he was glad to have found a purpose in their relationship.

Mildred recovered sufficiently to sit in state and accept the mourners' condolences. But after the luncheon she retired to her chamber.

Relieved that the ordeal was over, Anthony also took refuge in his room. This was the first moment he'd had to do his personal correspondence. He must write to Bridget, and to Arlette and Michelle.

Bridget heard the letter box rattle and ran down the passage. It *must* be a letter from Anthony! He'd been gone a week and not a word. Surely he wouldn't simply forget about them once he got up there?

She ripped open the envelope and began reading on her way back to the kitchen.

Dear Bridget,

I hope you and the children are well. I miss you all.

I am sorry not to have written earlier, but my father died the day after I arrived. My time has been taken up attending to Mother and the interminable funeral arrangements.

Father had an operation and failed to come out of the chloroform. It was blessedly peaceful and swift, though a shock to everyone, especially Mother. She is taking it badly. I have been so blind. I had no idea she felt such affection for him. And I, too, feel sad at his loss.

I must, of course, stay on here. But I intend to visit you as soon as I can, and as often as I can. In the meantime, I enclose twenty pounds. There will be plenty more coming. Do not be sad that I have had to change my plans. I have other plans in mind that I'm sure will please you.

Tomorrow I will go to town to buy the children's Christmas presents. You should receive them in time. I will also visit your friend Nellie with some gifts to show my gratitude. But for her, I should never have found you all.

Please tell the children I shall be checking on their school work when I return. I know you will continue to encourage them.

Kiss them all for me, and have a wonderful Christmas.

Your loving son,

Anthony

Bridget put the letter in her pocket and sat at the table with her head in her hands. Sorrow tightened about her like an iron corset and tears started. He could never come back to live with them now. His life was up there, with Mildred. She was sorry to hear of Richard's death. He was the only father Anthony had known, and it must be painful for him. But she was ashamed that her tears were for her own loss, hers and the children's. All the wonderful times they'd had with Anthony! And all the wonderful plans for next term!

She sat up and wiped her eyes on her apron. She was being completely selfish. He'd said he would still visit, and he'd sent money. The children wouldn't have to return to work. For that she was grateful. She rose and splashed her face at the bucket. She'd call the children in to tell them the news. But she'd mention the Christmas presents first.

Chapter Thirty-Eight

The fire blazed in the stove, the kettle puffed on the hob, a joint of pork spattered in the oven, and despite the lashing February rain Bridget fluttered about the kitchen like a butterfly in a flower garden. He was coming today! She set the pan of potatoes and sprouts on the hearth in readiness and laid the table for tea.

Her eyes stole to the clock every few minutes – Tom's clock. She'd retrieved it from the pawn shop with the Christmas money from Anthony. It stood in its old place on the mantel, flanked by Anthony's souvenirs of Skye. She'd lost her fear of the minutes ticking away. Now the monotonous sound soothed her. Three o'clock! He'd said about three! Excitement strummed like wires through her body. She took a deep breath to calm herself and sat by the fire. Since his father's death Anthony had written regularly, but the thought of seeing him, chatting with him across the fire, making his tea, filled her with the same joy as on the day of his first visit.

His footsteps echoed down the passage. She smoothed her hair at the mirror and composed herself like a young girl going to her first ball. He stopped halfway down the passage and dropped his bags. In an instant her eyes had searched his face. He looked somehow different, with an inner glow she hadn't seen before. She ran to meet him and he lifted her and laughed with delight. 'Now, put me down won't you and let me have another look at you. I swear you're more handsome than ever.'

Chuckling, he lowered her to the floor and dislodged her hair from its pins. 'And you look prettier than ever. But you'll need your party hairstyle. We're celebrating with a ceilidh tonight.'

Bridget smiled. 'Sure, just seeing you's celebration enough for me.' She took his hand and led him to the kitchen.

Tim blabbered a welcome and attempted to climb over his cot rails. 'Wait one minute, young man.' Anthony wagged a finger at him. He

398

hung his raincoat on the door before lifting Tim and throwing him in the air. 'My, how you've grown!'

Hands clasped, Bridget stood watching the scene, her face expanding and glowing with pride like a lamp being lit. She nodded. 'Aye, going on fifteen months and just as big a handful as the rest at his age. His chest's almost cleared up. The doctor says he'll grow out of it now.' Her eyes welled with tears as she watched her youngest son chortling with delight in the arms of her eldest. 'Tim's health is only one of the things I have to thank you for.' She averted her head to hide her tears.

Anthony sat in Tom's fireside chair and bounced Tim on his lap. 'I don't want your thanks, Bridget, only your happiness – and a cup of tea, please.'

With her back to him, she wiped her eyes, then smiled as she took the tea caddy from the mantelpiece.

Still bouncing Tim, Anthony glanced around the quiet kitchen. 'Where are Eileen and Sean?'

She gave him a guilty look. 'They were that impossible because you were coming, I sent them to Meg's for a couple of hours. I fibbed and told them you wouldn't be here till after four. Now I'll have to go to confession on Saturday.' She lowered her eyes in mock penitence and spooned tea into the pot.

Anthony rocked Tim to quiet him. 'I would have got here earlier,' he said to Bridget, 'but I had some business to attend to in Newcastle. I'm glad to tell you my news alone.'

'News?' She glanced at his face. It was smiling. Her shoulders dropped with relief. 'Sure, it's hard to break the habit. I always expect news to be bad.'

'Not any more, Bridget.'

'Aye, I'll have to learn.' She smiled and took Tim from him. 'You go and get your tea while it's hot. It's time for his nap.'

Anthony sat at his usual place at the table and looked around. 'It feels so homely sitting here again.'

'It *is* your home, Anthony.' She laid Tim in his cot and he wailed. She stuffed his teething ring into his mouth. 'That'll shut him up till he drops off. Now we can enjoy a bit of peace.' She sat opposite Anthony, pouring his tea, and suddenly it seemed as if he'd never left. 'I made your favourite – granny loaf.' She handed him a plate of buttered currant bread, and his grin of delight was the same as that four-year-old boy's in the nursery all those years ago.

He swallowed a mouthful, then set aside his plate. 'It's delicious.

But I can't eat till I tell you my news.' In his eagerness, he strained across the table like a greyhound waiting for the start.

She smiled. 'It must be quite some news if it stops you polishing off me granny loaf.'

'It is.' His voice was serious but his eyes smiled into hers. 'I didn't mention it in my letters, but just before my father died he told me that when he went, the money would be mine to do what I like with. I remember his exact words and have no guilt that I'm using it in a way he wouldn't have understood.'

She raised her eyebrows. 'How, then? You mean keeping me and me family? But you did that before he died.'

He shook his head. 'More than that. I hardly know where to start.'

She felt his excitement bubbling up in her like water from a spring. 'Well, now, isn't it always best to start at the beginning?'

He reached for her hands across the table. 'Do you remember that day we went for a walk to Byker Village?'

She breathed a deep sigh. 'Sure, I'll never be forgetting that day.'

'And do you remember what you said about the miniature brick castle and farms?'

'Holy saints! You haven't—'

He chuckled at her expression. 'Not exactly. The castle wasn't for sale. But another house just as nice was.' His grip on her hands tightened. 'And one of the farm owners was glad to take my offer. Farming isn't a booming business nowadays. But there's always the future.'

Her mouth gagged open as if she'd choked on his words. 'You've ... you've bought a posh house for us! At Byker Village!' She withdrew her hands from his and pressed them to her cheeks. Though immeasurably grateful for his help in feeding and clothing the children, she couldn't accept such a lavish gift.

He seemed to take her gesture as surprise and pleasure, and went on, his words leaping over one another. 'You'll love it, Bridget. It overlooks the meadow and has a big garden back and front. And there's indoor plumbing. And five bedrooms. Lots of room for all of you, and for me when I visit. It'll be my home too.'

She savoured his last words – *his* home too. 'Indeed, I can't believe me ears,' she said, trying to collect herself. 'I mean, I knew you'd take care of us, but I never expected anything like this. 'Tis too much money you're spending on us.'

He waved his hands to dismiss her doubts. 'I'm a rich man now.

Buying you a house is no more to me than buying you a dress. It's a beautiful house, Bridget. But it's large to keep clean. You may need help with the housework and gardening.'

'Never!' Her initial reservations had given way to joy and gratitude. 'It'll be my pleasure to keep it nice. And the girls'll help. And the lads'll enjoy the gardening, especially Dan. I've given up praying that he'll ever be any good with books but he loves to work outside – even swilling the yard here's a pleasure to him.'

Anthony gave her a sly, pleased look and leaned back in his chair, his arms folded across his chest as if to restrain his enthusiasm. But his voice gave it away. 'And that brings me to the farm. I've bought it in your name, as well as the house. In the meantime I'm employing a manager. But I thought that one day, should any of the boys want to take it over . . .'

Bridget burst into tears. 'Oh, Anthony, you're doing too much for us. I feel that guilty. There's so little I can do in return.'

He reached for her hands again, his voice soft. 'You'll never know what you've done for me, Bridget. But enough of that for the moment. I haven't finished yet.'

'Glory be! There's more?'

He smiled and his voice rose again in excitement. 'I'm having a school built at Byker Village, close enough for the town children to attend. I'm thrilled at the prospect. All my disjointed dreams suddenly came together. I intend to run it as a trust school – not charity, mind you. I dislike the word. I want to make it possible for children of all creeds to enjoy a good education.'

'All creeds? Surely to goodness, how can you be doing that?' She stared at him with such disbelief that he threw back his head and laughed, that deep laugh she knew and loved so well.

'I'm not proposing to abolish religion, Bridget. I plan to have the first hour of the day taken up with religious instruction and, of course, have Sunday school. There will be separate classes for all ages of each denomination. And the children will not only be taught their own faith, but also tolerance for and acceptance of others.'

She smiled at his excited voice. But she had to say what she felt. 'My, but that's a hard task you're taking on. And how are you going to stop the bairns from calling each other cattywags and proddydogs and dirty Jews – and fighting?'

A glint of amusement remained in his eyes but his tone turned sober. 'I admit it will be difficult at first, especially with the older ones. But children don't learn to hate one another unless they're taught, and in my schools they won't be. After the religious instruction of their choice, they will share the same classrooms, teachers and lessons. And I intend to employ only the best teachers and have no more than seventy pupils per class – fewer if possible.'

Bridget shook her head and the locks Anthony had unpinned fell over her face. She pushed them back slowly, thinking. Much as she wanted him to achieve his dreams, this notion seemed unrealistic, and she couldn't bear the thought of his failing. She must try to say what she felt without dampening his enthusiasm. 'It sounds a grand idea but I don't see how it could work. Surely the government – and the parents – would never allow it?' Her eyes implored him to abandon his plan. But he returned her gaze with such earnestness she knew he would never change his mind.

'Tell me, Bridget.' He leaned back and studied her like a schoolteacher waiting for the right answer from a pupil. 'If you were still poor would *you* object to your children going to a free mixed school with hot midday meals provided, lessons in their own religion and excellent general tuition, the only stipulation being that they mix with children of other faiths?'

She looked down and rubbed an imaginary spot off the table, remembering the agony of sending the children to school with only a cup of weak tea in their stomachs. 'Aye, you're right,' she finally admitted, raising her head. 'Indeed, I would've sent them for the free meal alone.'

'There, you see! And you a staunch Catholic!' He gave her a triumphant look. 'You've answered the parent problem, and the government problem is little different. My private school will save them money. I'm sure they'll agree for financial reasons at least. My solicitor is already negotiating the legal obstacles and applying for a licence. What do you think, Bridget?'

She rested her elbows on the table and rubbed her temples to clear her mind. 'Sure, I hardly know what to think. Such a determined man you are. I always knew you'd get what you wanted out of life one day. I never dreamt it would be anything like this, but I'm beginning to think you could be right.'

'I know I'm right,' he said with a satisfied smile.

But she was still cautious. 'And isn't it going to cost an awful lot? You can't be spending the entire family fortune.'

'I shan't need to. Though I don't intend to call them charity schools,

402

I do intend to get donations. I shall put it to the factory owners that in return they will get workers better prepared for apprenticeships and supervisory jobs. In the long run it will save them training time and money. And I also mean to get endowments from the rich. I certainly know plenty of those. As far as they will be aware I am simply an interested participant. With enough of my own and donated money and careful investment of funds, the school could perhaps even generate money. But I hope not to stop at one. If the scheme works I want to build as many as I can in poor neighbourhoods. It's the only thing I want to do with my life.' He gave her a look of such supreme confidence that she was almost reassured. But suddenly a new thought troubled her.

'And why would the government and rich people be wanting poor children to be so educated? 'Twould be a queer thing if there was nobody left to do the hard work. Have you thought of that?'

He nodded. 'That's the sad part. But it's a reality I must accept. Obviously, I can't make it a grammar school. But the pupils will get a basic education at a higher level than they do now. And of course they will learn skills such as woodwork and cookery. There will always be those children who can't make the grade and will end up doing unskilled work. And I must stress that fact in my licence application. But the brightest children will at least have a chance of a better start in life.'

She gave in with a smile. 'You've got the gift of the blarney all right – an answer for everything.'

'Thanks to you,' he reminded her, returning her smile. 'I can make it work, I know I can.'

'I pray you do, and I'm that happy for you. Have you told your mother about this?' At the mention of his mother, Bridget bit her lip and gave him a guilty look. 'And, dear me, I haven't even asked how she is.'

'She's improving slowly – eating again and having her lady friends to tea occasionally. I think she'll pick up her life normally after her mourning period.' His voice grew solemn and he made circles on the table with his mug. 'I still find it hard to believe how much Father's death distressed her. I thought I knew her, yet I had no idea she felt such fondness for him. It's taught me not to judge people by their public behaviour.'

Bridget sighed. 'Aye, I did the same. I'm glad at least there's a bit more to her than I thought.'

But he went on as if she hadn't spoken, 'If only I could have known

403

then that she was jealous of my father's affection, I should have understood her coolness towards me.' He stopped playing with his mug and looked up with a smile. 'But she's glad of my company now. We're getting along amicably.'

'Indeed, that's a blessing!' Though happy that his and Mildred's relationship was improved, Bridget was worried about Mildred's reaction to his intentions with the family money. 'And does she know about your idea?' She tried to keep her voice airy.

He shrugged, then gave her a wicked grin. 'I thought it better not to tell her. She's never been interested in business affairs anyway. So long as I'm around to look after the estate she won't care if I have to take short trips for . . . my other businesses. And she won't ask.'

Bridget hated herself for her next question but she had to know. 'Are the bairns and me one of your "businesses"?'

He shifted in his chair. 'Bridget, you know I could never tell her about you and the children, but believe me I do not consider you part of my business affairs. You should know by now you're my family.'

She nodded. 'I do indeed, and I only meant . . . well, is there any chance she could ever find out about us?'

'None, I assure you. She doesn't know one end of a ledger from another, and besides, all those affairs are in my solicitor's hands.'

It was Bridget's turn to look uncomfortable. 'I most certainly know that if by chance she did find out it would make no difference to *you*. But it would to her. And she must've been an unhappy woman all these years, loving a man who didn't love her back. I was so lucky with Tom. She's missed such a lot.'

Anthony gave her a look of admiration and affection. 'It wouldn't be you if you weren't sorry for her. But don't be. She finds entertainment in her own activities. And I find it easy to be pleasant with her now, though I never *have* and I never *could* feel like a true son to her.'

Bridget's heart soared with joy like a kite in the wind. She wrapped her hands around the teapot as if to anchor herself. The pot was cool. 'Just look you now!' she said. 'With all this talk we've let the tea get cold. And you've hardly touched your granny loaf. I'll make a fresh pot and you eat that up.' She took the teapot to the stove, but before Anthony attacked the granny loaf, he went on:

'There's one more piece of news but I'm saving it until the children come home.'

No sooner had he uttered the words than there came a sound like an army of foot soldiers stomping down the yard. 'Speak of the devil,'

Bridget said, adding more water to the kettle.

The door exploded inwards and an avalanche of bodies tumbled in. Without bothering to take off their wet coats, they hurled themselves at Anthony, shrieking a jumble of greetings and strangling him with hugs. Anthony did his best to hug them all at once. 'All right! All right! I'm happy to see you too. But let me breathe, eh?' He unravelled the network of arms from his neck and Kate climbed on to his lap. The boys hovered over him with eager faces.

'What you got for us, Anthony?' Dan asked with his usual candour.

Tim shrieked and Bridget sighed in despair. 'Look you now, you've woken Tim. And Dan, haven't I told you not to ask for things?' She gave him a pat on the bottom and picked up Tim from his cot. 'Here, Kate, you hold him while I get on.' He stopped crying, but for once Kate was unwilling to look after her little brother. Her face puckered.

'Aw, Ma, do I have to?'

'Yes.'

'Can I have him here on Anthony's lap then?'

'Of course you can,' Anthony said, spreading his knees to make room for the extra load. Then he smiled and chucked Dan's chin. 'You must do what your mother says in future and don't ask for things, but it's all right this time. This is a special occasion and I *have* got things for you. And some surprises.'

'What things? What surprises?' Dan ignored his mother's warning.

'You'll see later,' Anthony said, 'when Eileen and Sean get home. And we're going to have a ceilidh to celebrate.'

There was a stunned silence. Tommy was the first to find his voice. 'Tonight? And paper hats and lemonade and everything?'

The rest wound their arms round him in another stranglehold and whooped with joy.

Bridget put a fresh mug of tea before Anthony and shot him a helpless look. 'Dear me! I've got a special feast ready but no whisky or lemonade.' She wagged her finger at the children and assumed the sternest tone she could muster. 'Now, you lot, take off your wet things and let Anthony have a sup of his tea.'

With reluctance Kate shuffled off Anthony's knee with Tim in her arms. 'I'll go to the shops now, Ma, afore they shut. We can't have a ceilidh without lemonade.'

'And I'll help her carry it,' Joseph volunteered out of character, but added, 'If I can get some sweets and all.'

Bridget laughed. 'Aye, I thought there'd be something in it for you,

you little monkey. But Anthony'll have to go for the whisky. You can both go with him. Maybe then I can feed and clean this little lad in peace.' She took Tim from Kate and put him over her shoulder.

'We'll all go to the shops,' Dan said, speaking for everyone and glancing around the room as if taking a vote.

'Aye!' Mick shouted. The decision was unanimous. They'd reached the kitchen door before Bridget had got the money tin from the mantel.

Freed of his circle of disciples, Anthony rose like a drowning man gasping for air. He grinned at Bridget as he put on his raincoat. 'I don't need money,' he reminded her, glancing at the tin in her hand.

Of course he didn't need money! 'I'm that daft,' she said with a smile. ''Tis going to be hard getting used to being well off. But I'll try.'

'You can start this minute.'

She nodded and smiled again. 'Thank you for taking the bairns. And would you mind picking up Sean and Eileen from Meg's? They'd never forgive me if they missed an outing with you, especially for lemonade and sweets.'

Tommy twisted his face. 'Aw, can't we pick them up on the way back? They walk so slow.'

'No, I'm sure they'd like to come with us,' Anthony said, 'and they walk *slowly*, not slow.' He buttoned his raincoat and ushered the children out.

Bridget heaved a sigh at the sudden quiet. After seeing to Tim, she could get the potatoes and vegetables on and put the apples in the oven to bake. The pork would be almost done and would keep hot on the hearth till she could pop it back in again. In the meantime she could make the custard.

The table was set, the paper hats on the plates, the meal just about ready, and Bridget wondered what to do next. Automatically she went to tidy her hair at the mirror and smiled at the untidy mess. She'd forgotten. And the children had been too preoccupied with Anthony to notice her ceilidh hairstyle.

The unmistakable clatter down the passage announced their return. Anthony led, holding Sean and Eileen by the hands. Bridget looked at him and their eyes locked in silent communication. She knew he was as happy to be with the children as she was at the sight. 'Now come on, all of you, and get your wet things off,' she said. 'Everything's ready.'

Dan dumped the shopping basket on the floor. 'Look, Ma, four bottles of lemonade and *half a pound* of mixed caramels.'

'And Anthony let us have one each on the way home,' Eileen said, her jaws still chomping.

Bridget shook her head in despair. 'Spoiling your appetites he is! And where's the whisky then?'

Anthony patted his raincoat pocket. 'I didn't trust them to carry that.' He took Ally's flask from the mantelpiece and filled it ceremoniously. 'We have a special reason to toast Ally and Megan tonight.'

When all were seated at the table, hair ruffled and paper hats in place, Anthony chatted to the children about school, saving the big news until the meal was over. After the baked apples and custard he told them about the house.

Tommy plunked down his glass so hard his lemonade splashed over the rim. 'A posh house! In Byker Village!'

'You're kidding!' Joseph said. The others simply gaped at him.

Anthony's eyes gleamed with excitement. 'That's right. We can go to see it tomorrow. You can't move in for a month but we can start buying furniture.'

Kate jumped off her chair and climbed on to his knee. 'Can I help choose?'

'And me?' Eileen squeezed herself on to his other knee. 'It'll be like playing big doll's house.'

Bridget rocked Tim in her lap. He was nodding off despite the chatter. 'Of course you can help,' she said. 'And Anthony's got something else to tell you.' She looked expectantly at him.

'Soon you'll be going to a new school,' he said, scanning their faces.

The reception to this news was less enthusiastic. They listened in silence until Anthony mentioned the free meal and the five-minute walk to school.

'Aw, a free hot dinner!' Dan couldn't believe his ears.

'And only five minutes' walk from the new house!' Tommy was jubilant. 'We can have an extra half-hour in bed.'

'Trust you to think of that, lazybones,' Kate said. '*I'll* get up at the same time and help Ma with the breakfast.'

Bridget straightened from laying Tim in his cot. 'That's a nice thought, luv. And now Anthony's got something else to tell you.'

They greeted the farm news with shouts of glee, especially Dan. 'You mean I can be a farmer when I grow up?'

'Of course, and anyone else who wants to.' Anthony gave Dan a particularly pleased look. 'But some of you may change your minds before you're grown up and want to do something different – perhaps be businessmen. Time will tell.'

'Never!' Dan said. 'I'll never change *my* mind.'

'Can we milk the cows?' Eileen wanted to know.

'And ride the horses?' Sean straddled his chair and shouted, 'Gee up, horsy!'

Bridget held up her hands for silence. 'You can all learn to do anything you like and find out what you're best at.' She sipped her spiced tea and absorbed the happy scene through her pores. How could such good fortune happen to her?

'And there's something else even your ma doesn't know.' Anthony surveyed them with a sly glint in his eyes. 'I've bought Jock's cottage on Skye.'

'Glory be! You've bought that and all?' Bridget clapped her hand to her mouth.

But Tommy looked downcast. 'Are you going back to live there again, Anthony?'

'No, not to live. It's for all of us to use for holidays.'

'Holidays?' Kate's eyes opened wide. 'We're going on holidays to Skye – and see Meg and Ally and all them?'

Anthony sipped his whisky and surveyed the array of bright faces. 'Absolutely! But not until summer. I'm having the cottage extended and, er, making some improvements to the "wee hoosie". I also hope that my two, well, sort of adopted nieces will be able to join us sometimes. It was their mother who introduced me to Skye.'

Bridget gave Anthony a quick glance, but his eyes gave away no sorrow at the mention of his dead lover. Suddenly Bridget became as excited as the children. A holiday! The family had never been away except for day trips to Tynemouth or Cullercoats when Tom was alive. She tried to swallow the lump in her throat as she thought how Tom – and Annie – would have loved a real holiday.

A whoop of delight from Joseph brought her back to the present. 'Can we go fishing in the sea, Anthony?'

'And make sand castles?' Eileen wriggled in such excitement she slipped off Anthony's knee. But she climbed up again and gave him a baked-apple kiss on the cheek.

He suffered the sticky mess on his face and nodded. 'If your mother says so, you can do all those things and more.'

'And sing and dance with Megan and Ally and have a *real* ceilidh?' Dan asked.

Anthony pretended to look disapproving. 'What do you mean? This *is* a real ceilidh. We just haven't got to the singing and dancing yet. It's time we did.'

They all clamoured to be first and Anthony settled the dispute by tossing a coin. All went well until it was Kate and Eileen's turn to dance the Irish jig and the boys insisted on accompanying them. Tommy played the spoons, Dan beat time on the table with the rolling pin, and Joseph tooted like a reed pipe through his clenched fists. The inevitable broom from upstairs thumped on the ceiling.

Bridget looked up and shouted above the din, 'It's all right, Mrs Gray. You can thump all you like. We'll be leaving in a month, and then you'll be that sorry that you've got nothing to thump about.'

Joseph giggled and yelled to Bridget, 'Do you think she heard, Ma?'

Bridget grinned. 'What if she did and what if she didn't? I'll take her up some cold pork tomorrow, that'll straighten her face.' She looked sad for a moment. 'Sure, I hope another big family moves in after us. Poor old Mrs Gray'll be that bored and lonely if she's got nothing to complain about and nobody to knock down on.'

'Just think, Ma,' Tommy said. 'In our new house we won't have anybody whacking on our ceiling.' He cupped his hands and yelled up, 'When we move we can make as much racket as we like, Stick Face.'

Bridget tried to give him a stern look. 'Now didn't I just say that's enough? And haven't I told you never to call her that?'

'Stick Face,' Dan whispered to the ceiling, cupping his hands in imitation of Tommy.

Bridget rose. 'That's it! Both of you. It's bedtime anyway. You've still got school tomorrow.'

'Aw, Ma!' they wailed.

'And don't "Aw, Ma" me. Off with you. And you, Eileen, come here till I clean you up. Sure, you were supposed to eat that baked apple, not paint your face with it.'

At last the children were in bed, though still chattering noisily. Bridget flopped into the fireside chair opposite Anthony and shook her head in happy despair. 'I don't know if they'll sleep at all, they're that excited. But at least we can have some peace for a bit.'

Anthony gave her a weary smile. 'They thoroughly enjoyed themselves.'

'Thank you, Anthony,' she said softly. 'For everything – not just the big things, but for the wonderful party and all. You don't know what it means to me – and them – to have you here.'

She looked down and knotted her hands in her lap. Despite the happy occasion, one thought had weighed on her mind all day.

''Tis certain I couldn't be happier for the bairns and me. And for you. Except one thing.'

'And what's that?'

'Well,' she began, knotting her hands tighter, 'I mean, I love the plans you're making for your life. It's a fine thing to do good works for others – and rewarding. But there's more to life than just helping other people. You need a life of your own and all.'

Anthony leaned his head against the chair-back and looked at the ceiling. 'I know what you're trying to say. But not yet.'

She looked pained. 'You still haven't got over Adelle, have you?'

He gave her a wan smile. 'I shall never get over Adelle any more than you will get over Tom. She will always be a precious part of my life and she's rarely out of my thoughts. But she taught me so much about love between a man and a woman that I know now it's too wonderful to live without. When the right woman comes along I shall be ready to love that way again.' He chuckled. 'But in the meantime I've got more than enough love here to keep me going.'

Bridget felt a warm glow all over. 'Aye, me and all,' she said, thinking how Tom would be looking down on them with that contented grin of his. 'I swear, if God Himself had told me I'd ever be this happy again, I'd have said straight to His face He was full of the Blarney.'